THROUGH
THE
MIST

THROUGH
THE
MIST

a novel

LINDSAY JAYNE
ASHFORD

LAKE UNION
PUBLISHING

Published by Lake Union Publishing, Seattle

www.apub.com

Amazon, the Amazon logo, and Lake Union Publishing are trademarks of Amazon.com, Inc., or its affiliates.

ISBN-13: 9781662514630 (paperback)
ISBN-13: 9781662514647 (digital)

Cover design by Faceout Studio, Molly von Borstel
Cover images: © detchana wangkheeree / Shutterstock; © Didik12 / Shutterstock; © Media Guru / Shutterstock; © Nadya Dobrynina / Shutterstock; © vexturo / Shutterstock; © VJ Tar / Shutterstock; © WHISKHEELS/ Shutterstock

Printed in the United States of America

In memory of my father, Graham Molton
November 7, 1931–November 29, 2023

PROLOGUE

Cornwall, England 1938

The way to Pendour Cove is treacherous in the veil of white that comes in off the sea. It's a steep climb downhill to the village, past the old church that looks fragile and unreal, as if it could disappear. The outline of The Tinners Arms pub is hazy, too, like a charcoal sketch smudged by a careless finger. Beyond it, where the cliffs drop away to the ocean, lies a field of spectral sheep.

The mist begins to clear as I scramble down the path to the cove. After a while I find what I'm searching for: the body of a crow, its bones washed clean by the tide. There's a whiff of rotting seaweed as I pull it free from the tangle of flotsam on the strand. I take the skull only. My fingers feel slimy, so I wash them in a rock pool before wiping them on my coat.

When I get back to the cottage, I lay the skull out next to the other things I have collected: five strips of white linen, tufts of moss from the rocks on Zennor Carn. And—the hardest thing to come by—long strands of auburn hair.

A mommet. That's what the Cornish people call it. The crow's head gives it such a malevolence, with its great hollow eyes and its cruel beak. It's the strangest thing I have ever created. I wind the hair and the moss around the spindly arms and legs I have stitched and stuffed. Then I stick it with pins. For the blood, I use drops of beetroot juice.

I place it in a cigar box and hide it on a ledge inside the chimney. Would it survive a fire? I doubt it. So, its work must be done before winter comes.

---

28 Tasker Road, Hampstead, London.
12th April 1938
Dear Tony,
    Just to let you know that I got back from Cornwall last night.
    It really was the most delightful house party—if a little cramped! The cottage is quite small—a sort of cowshed on the side had to serve as extra accommodation. Luckily, we were all too tipsy most of the time to notice the smell!
    I'd been told that Zennor was beautiful, but the reality took my breath away. You would love it—it's an artist's dream. Wild moorland, the sea crashing against the cliffs, and, on the hill above the cottage, huge granite boulders that glint like diamonds where the sun catches them. When the mist comes down, all the shapes and colours blur, as if everything in the landscape belonged to a different world.
    It's the perfect place for the kind of party Leo likes to throw. Warm enough to be outdoors most of the time and far away from prying eyes. One of the St Ives chaps had a shock when he arrived: two of the girls stripped naked and ran out to meet him. They pranced around him as he stood rooted to the spot. Poor thing didn't know quite what he'd stumbled into!
    Anyway, there's to be another gathering at the end of the month. We're going to light a bonfire on the hilltop

and dance around the stones like witches—what fun! You must promise to come this time.

Yours next Tuesday,

Nina x

⊰⊱

The Cornish Times, 24th May 1938

Obituaries

Mrs. Stella Winifred Bird, of Rowan Tree House, near St Ives, has died at the age of thirty-four. Her death came with complete suddenness in the most unfortunate circumstances.

Except for a slight cold during the last few days, she appeared to be perfectly well, and on Saturday evening was visiting a neighbour at a cottage on the moor near her house when she was taken with a seizure while walking home.

She was found the following morning and taken to hospital, but she never regained consciousness and died on Sunday evening.

One of the most tragic features of the situation is that her husband, Mr. Lionel Bird, is at present bound for Canada on a business trip, his arrival there being due on Thursday.

CHAPTER 1

Cornwall: Christmas Eve 1947

It came out of nowhere, shrouding the leafless hedgerows and obscuring the road ahead. Ellen's left hand darted from the steering wheel to her throat, tugging the blue woolen scarf up over her mouth—a reflex honed by years of enduring dirty London smog. The sulfurous clouds that sometimes blanketed the city in winter were something she had learned to dread. But this was different. The West Country mist had an ethereal beauty that made her feel as though she were entering a magical realm.

Ellen slowed to a crawl as she took a bend. She could just make out Tony, a ghost-rider on his motorbike. He glanced back over his shoulder. She wondered if he thought she might hit him. She couldn't blame him for being nervous. It was only the second time she had driven the jeep.

Her mother had handed her the keys the week before the wedding. An unconventional present—but no gift had ever thrilled Ellen more. Sturdy and practical, it said everything that her mother couldn't bring herself to put into words: that she wanted Ellen to succeed in this new life that she had chosen, even if it wasn't what she had envisaged for her only daughter.

The light was beginning to fade even before the mist had come down. Tony had warned her that the journey would take all day—that unless they set out at dawn, they'd be lucky to make it to the cottage before dark. Not the most romantic start to married life, traveling for hundreds of miles across the country by separate vehicles—but there was no other way of doing it.

An image floated into her head: of the royal couple, showered with rose petals as they left Buckingham Palace in an open-topped Rolls-Royce for a honeymoon at Balmoral Castle. The contrast made Ellen smile. As new brides, the only thing she and Princess Elizabeth had in common was the color of their going-away outfits—although her duffle coat and corduroy slacks hardly merited such a lofty description.

There had been little else but wedding fever in the papers these past few weeks. From the number of seed pearls sewn onto the bridal gown (ten thousand) to the quantity of sugar used to make the nine-foot-high cake (three hundred and twenty-two pounds, provided by the Girl Guides of Australia). Ellen's mother had been swept up by it, begging her to wait until spring to get married so she could save up her clothing coupons for a version of the ivory duchesse satin gown the princess had worn (minus the pearls and the thirteen-foot train). But Ellen hadn't cared about having a new dress to walk down the aisle. Nor had she minded about the sugar ration not being sufficient for a proper wedding cake. How could she think about waiting to get married when Tony had been promised the keys to the cottage by Christmas?

The weather began to clear as the jeep climbed uphill. When it reached the top, Ellen caught her first glimpse of the sea. The sun was sinking into it, just half of a scarlet orb visible above the waves. The sky was a bonfire of colors. Charcoal wisps of cloud and streaks of red and gold. They must be nearly there. Now she could see a cluster of houses and a harbor. Was that St Ives?

Tony pulled up a few yards ahead of her and dismounted. "It's up there." He jerked his head as she opened the door. "Just follow me up the track—and try to avoid the rocks."

Ellen glanced up at the hillside to her left. The landscape was rough grass and heather; bare, stunted trees and huge white boulders protruding from the earth like the bones of buried giants. There were no houses. No people. Just a few sheep scattered across the moorland.

"Don't worry—you'll be fine." Tony wasn't smiling. He looked impatient, as if he wished he could speed off up the hill instead of taking it at a snail's pace for her sake. He was excited—of course he was. She couldn't blame him for that. She was excited, too. It was just that he knew the place and she didn't. She couldn't wait to see what the cottage looked like.

Ellen had never driven off-road before. Sometimes she'd had to dodge bomb debris in the ambulances she'd taken across London during the war. She told herself that a rocky moorland track couldn't be any worse than that. Raindrops spattered the windshield as she urged the jeep forward. The sky had lost all its color. She turned on the headlights. Tony was almost out of sight.

The last part of the journey took only ten minutes, but it felt like an eternity. Every bump made her tense up. It wasn't that she was afraid of a few scratches—the jeep was ex-army and came with a few battle scars—but she was terrified of hitting a sheep. In the gathering gloom, it was hard to tell rocks from animals.

Suddenly there it was: a long, low building, black against the gray silhouette of a hilltop. The motorbike lay abandoned on the grass by the gate. Ellen could see the beam of a flashlight. She scrambled out of the jeep. A gust of wind sent her scarf flying out behind her. She could smell wet grass and sheep dung and the faint salt tang of the sea. The gate groaned as she pushed it. It swung back as she passed through, snagging the hem of her coat.

"Come on!" Tony turned the flashlight her way, dazzling her before he angled it to shine at the ground.

She unhooked herself and stumbled toward him, almost tripping on the clumps of weeds that had colonized the path to the front door. When she reached him, he grabbed her and lifted her off the ground. "Welcome to Carreg Cottage, Mrs. Wylde."

His hair smelled of tobacco. It had been strange and thrilling, waking up this morning, breathing in that smoky, bittersweet scent. But there hadn't been time to linger. They had scrambled out of bed, pulled on their clothes, and crept out of the house as dawn broke over London.

Their wedding night had been spent in her old bedroom, her mother and stepfather on the other side of the wall. Tony had been kissing her neck, murmuring words she couldn't make out. She could hear her mother's voice next door; the creak of the floorboards and her stepfather striking a match to smoke one last cigarette before he settled down for the night. Tony had stopped kissing her. When she'd turned to him, she realized he was fast asleep.

But now everything would be different. In their own home, they could do exactly what they wanted without having to worry about anyone else. She felt something brush her forehead as he carried her across the threshold. As he set her down, something crawled across her left cheek. "Ugh!" She swiped at it, shaking herself.

"What is it? What's the matter?" Tony was still clutching the flashlight. In its beam she saw a big black spider running down the front of her coat. Tony laughed. "Is that all it was? I thought you'd been bitten by a rat or something."

"A rat? There are rats?"

"No, silly! Well, there could be some in the cowshed—I don't know. We'll find out in the morning. Anyway, I'm starving—what have we got?"

"I . . . er . . . brought tins of soup to heat up—and there's bread and cheese. It's in a box in the passenger footwell."

He left her standing in the dark while he went out to fetch the food. This wasn't what she had imagined. But he was right—they should eat after such a long journey. She took a breath. The cottage had a damp, stale, neglected smell. They needed to get a fire going.

"Are the candles in here, too?" Tony's silhouette filled the doorway. He'd warned her that the electricity had been disconnected, that it would be a few days before they could get someone out to fix that.

Ellen had thought it would be quite romantic to live by candlelight over Christmas.

The inside of the cottage slowly came to life. The flickering flames revealed one large room with a kitchen at one end and a living area at the other. There was a lumpy-looking sofa in front of the fireplace and a chair with the stuffing protruding from one of its arms. Tony was pulling logs from a basket festooned in cobwebs. He'd already set fire to the tapers of newspaper and sticks of wood she'd tucked around the food she'd brought for their supper.

Ellen went out to the jeep to get the bundle of sheets, blankets, and pillows her mother had given them. She'd pictured their bedroom hundreds of times in the past few weeks: the two of them, limbs entwined, lying beneath a sloping roof with the moon shining in through a tiny window. When he'd scooped her up and carried her over the threshold, she'd thought—*hoped*—that they might go straight upstairs.

She stumbled back along the path, almost unable to see over the pile of bedding. When she pushed the door open, Tony was coughing. Smoke billowed out of the fireplace. He waved his hand in front of his face. "The wood must be damp—can't get the damned thing going."

Ellen dropped her bundle onto the sofa and tried to fan the choking clouds toward the door. "We don't have to have a fire tonight, do we? We could just heat up the soup and . . . well . . ."

He didn't return her shy smile. "We can't." He huffed out a breath. "No fire, no soup."

Ellen felt foolish for not remembering. It wasn't just the lights that didn't work. The cooker was electric, too.

He turned to her. "Let's go to the pub. They're bound to have something to eat—and it'll be warm."

"Oh. Okay." She tried to smile. "Is it far?"

"Just down the hill. We can take the bike."

"I . . . I'd better make the bed up first, hadn't I?"

Tony glanced toward the stairs. "Er . . . yes, I suppose so. You'd better take the torch." He sounded as though the thought of them going to bed hadn't crossed his mind.

Ellen leaned across to retrieve the bundle on the sofa and lifted it high so that he couldn't see her face.

CHAPTER 2

London—the same day

The train on platform four at Paddington Station shot out a plume of smoke and began to roll forward. A young woman in a gray felt hat trimmed with a scarlet band of grosgrain ribbon watched it disappear. She glanced over her shoulder. She'd felt safer huddled among the passengers waiting for the Bristol train, but now that it was gone, she felt exposed. She looked at her watch. Only fifteen minutes until the Cornwall train was due. She took a breath of the tainted air through lips painted the same shade as her hatband. The lipstick had been applied half an hour earlier in the ladies' cloakroom. She hoped it made her look older.

Stepping back from the platform into the shadow of a doorway, she dug her hand into her purse, checking that the precious ticket was still there. Her fingers found the receipt the jeweler had given her. She pulled it out along with the ticket and read the neat copperplate handwriting that was her passport to freedom: *Twenty-two carat gold ring in the form of a serpent, with two emerald eyes—twelve guineas paid.*

She murmured a silent thank-you to the old man who had once owned the ring. Mr. Crowley. She hadn't known him. An old family friend, her father had said when he came back from the funeral. She didn't know if the ring had been left to her in the man's will, or whether her father, as executor, had simply helped himself to it. When he'd shown it to her, she'd thought it a big ugly thing. He'd tucked it away in the desk drawer, telling her he would have it made into something she would like better: a brooch, perhaps. It wasn't until she was lying in bed last night that the idea had come to her.

She told herself it wasn't really stealing. It was hers, after all. But still she felt like a criminal. She'd left a note on her dressing table, but it contained no hint of where she was headed. Her father wouldn't find out until he came home from work—and her stepmother would be so caught up in the preparations for the Christmas Eve party that she probably wouldn't notice anything was wrong until the train was well on its way.

A policeman was walking along the platform. She shrank back, trying to make herself invisible. He stopped a few yards from her, looking toward the end of the platform. Was he looking for her? They couldn't know, could they? Even if the note had been found, they couldn't possibly have guessed that she was running away to Cornwall. She clung to this thought as she watched the policeman make his way slowly back along the platform. He disappeared just as her train chugged into view.

She fought the urge to run to the edge of the platform; made herself wait until the train came to a stop and the guard was going along, opening the doors. Then she walked as slowly as she could, trying to look as though she didn't have a care in the world, until she reached the third-class carriage at the back of the train.

—◆—

It was getting dark by the time they crossed the Tamar Bridge. She remembered this part of the journey from when she was a child. Her mother would always hoist her up to look out of the window and tell her that the bridge was the gateway to Cornwall.

She felt a bubble of excitement, seeing the metal framework flash by. But she remembered what a distance she still had to go. As a little girl, she had thought that once they were over the bridge, they were there. But St Ives was a long way down: on the knuckle of the finger of land that pointed across the Atlantic Ocean. It would be another two hours before she reached her destination.

Rain began to spatter the windows. It grew heavier as the sky turned from gray to black. She had to change trains at a place called St Erth. The wind whipped at her skirt as she stepped onto the platform. She grabbed her hat, afraid of losing it. It would be half an hour before she could get the connecting train to St Ives.

In the waiting room she watched the rain streaming down the windows. She hoped it would stop before her journey ended. She didn't know what it was going to be like, trying to find a hotel room on Christmas Eve. Getting soaked to the skin certainly wouldn't make it any easier.

There were hardly any passengers on the next train. She was glad about that; had dreaded someone coming to sit next to her, asking questions. It was pitch dark now, but she knew it was only three stops to St Ives. No one was on the platform at Lelant Saltings. It looked bleak and windswept, rain dripping off the tin roof. It seemed like an age before the train juddered forward again. At the next station the only person to get on was a uniformed guard. Her heart thudded as he came toward her.

"You'll have to get off, here, miss."

Panic surged in her stomach. "B . . . but I'm going to St Ives."

"Not tonight, miss. There's a problem with the engine. Can't go any further. There's a telephone in the stationmaster's office if you need to let people know."

"I . . . er . . ." She swallowed hard. "It's all right—I don't need to phone. How far is it to St Ives from here?"

The corners of the guard's mouth turned down. "About four miles. But you're not thinking of walking it, are you, miss? Not in this weather?"

"I thought I might get a taxi."

"Not from here—not on Christmas Eve."

"Well, I . . . ," she faltered, tears prickling the back of her eyes.

"There's a place just up the road—The Lelant Arms. I'd get a bed there for the night if there's no one coming to collect you." The expression on his face was not unkind. She sensed that he had weighed her up, decided that something about her didn't quite add up. She had to get away before he asked any more questions.

There was another man on the platform—a porter who offered to carry her suitcase. As she shook her head, he smiled and said, "Terrible weather, ain't it, miss? The stars were too close to the moon last night."

In other circumstances she would have smiled back; the accent and the quaint manner of his speech were pure Cornwall—the place she had missed so much. But her childhood memories were of sun-filled, carefree days—far removed from the cold, wet, dark place the train had dumped her in.

It took only a matter of minutes to find The Lelant Arms. The way in was through the public bar. She stood by the door, dripping wet, listening to the rise and fall of the voices inside. *The only women who go into pubs on their own are prostitutes.*

Her stepmother's voice echoed through her head. What would happen if she went through that door? Water trickled down the back of her neck, making her shiver. She had no choice—staying out in the rain all night was not an option.

The room was packed. A fug of smoke hung over the drinkers. As she made her way toward the bar, the chatter and laughter subsided. They were all looking at her. All men. The only woman in the room was behind the bar, pulling a pint of beer.

"Excuse me . . ."

The woman glanced up with a look of undisguised curiosity. She swept a lock of gray hair back across her forehead, tucking it behind her ear.

"I . . . I was wondering if you might have a room for the night."

The eyebrows slid upward. This was a face that had seen people at their worst and would not stand for any nonsense.

"It's just that I . . . I'm on my way to St Ives, but the train's broken down. The guard said I might be able to stay here."

The expression softened a little. "You'd better come through to the back." The woman cocked her head at a door beside the bar.

"Thank you." It felt as if the eyes of all the drinkers were boring into her back as she left the room.

"Just for tonight, is it? Only we close for Christmas—you'd have to be out of the room by nine sharp—and we can't do a proper breakfast. A bit of toast, that's all."

"That's quite all right. I plan to set off early—as soon as it's light."

"I'll need payment up front: it's seven shillings."

"Yes, of course."

"And I'll need to see your identity card."

"Er . . . yes . . . I have it here." Her hand trembled as she dug into her coat pocket. The folded piece of cardboard felt soggy round the edges. She hadn't anticipated this. Perhaps she could pretend she'd lost it on the train.

"We have to register guests, see." The woman's hands went to her hips. She looked impatient. "Can't get the rations to feed folk, otherwise."

But I'm only having toast. She didn't dare to say the words out loud. With panic rising in her stomach, she handed the card over. The woman opened it up. "Miss Winifred Iris . . . what's this say?" She held it out.

The rain had smudged the last letter of the surname. "Er . . . it's Birch. Iris Birch—I don't use Winifred." Thank God for the rainstorm. Birch. That would be her new surname.

<hr>

Ellen heard the rain against the bedroom window as she laid an army-issue blanket over the mattress. Coarse and slightly ragged at the edges, it would feel itchy against bare skin. She hadn't really wanted it—nor the half dozen others her mother had bundled into the jeep with the sheets and pillowcases. They had lain untouched in the airing cupboard since the end of the war, when the Red Cross depot had closed its doors. *Waste not, want not,* her mother had said when she brought them home. *Cut them up for dusters,* Ellen had thought. But now she was glad of them because the mattress felt cold and damp. A double layer of blankets under the bottom sheet would do until Christmas was over and they could buy a new bed.

She paused, angling the flashlight toward the window. The rain was streaming down the glass. Surely, they couldn't go to the pub in this weather. She pointed the flashlight higher, checking the walls for damp patches. They looked sound enough, although the paint was flaking in a couple of places. She saw that the ceiling had exposed wooden beams. Very characterful, but a haven for spiders. As she moved the flashlight, something caught her eye. Between the beams above the bed was a strange-looking figure, almost life size. It reminded her of something she'd seen on a school visit to the British Museum: paintings found on the walls of ancient Egyptian tombs. She climbed on the bed to get a closer look. It was a human body dressed in the short tunic and headdress of a pharaoh—but with the head of a bird, its slim, curved beak pointing toward the window. Staring up at it she almost lost her balance. The wavering light made the creature look as if it were moving—as if it might swoop down from the ceiling and peck out her eyes.

She scrambled off the bed, wincing as she caught her shin on the metal frame. Why would anyone want such a sinister thing in a bedroom? It would give you nightmares. She wondered if Tony had noticed it when he viewed the place. They would have to paint over it. Redecorate the room along with the rest of the cottage.

"Are you coming?" Tony was calling her. "I think we'd better take the jeep—it's hammering it down out there."

He was standing by the door when she came down. "We'll have to make a run for it." He turned up the collar of his leather jacket. "Ready?"

The rain was horizontal and the sky pitch black. Not a night for going anywhere. How she wished they could have got the fire going.

"Sorry you've got to drive," he said, as he slammed the passenger door shut. Tony only had a motorbike license. He didn't seem interested in driving anything else. She started up the engine, hoping they wouldn't encounter any sheep on the way down the hill. Did sheep stop grazing at night? Did they shelter somewhere when it rained? Two more questions in the ever-growing list of unknowns about this far-flung corner of England; this new home that had sounded so idyllic in Tony's descriptions, but was dirty, damp, and crawling with spiders. She told herself that everything would look different in the morning. They would sweep away the cobwebs, get a fire going and . . .

"Watch out!"

She swerved hard to avoid hitting a lump of granite that gleamed silver as the headlights glanced off it. She must concentrate. The track down to the road was like an obstacle course. Not only rocks but sheep—still grazing, despite the dark, foul night, their eyes burning yellow as they turned startled heads toward the jeep.

"It's not far now—left here, then the road to the village is off to the right." Tony patted her knee as the wheels rolled onto tarmac.

"What did you say the pub's called?"

"The Tinners Arms. Zennor used to be a big tin mining area. Not much left of it now. Mainly farming and fishing in this part of Cornwall nowadays." Tony grabbed the wheel. "Sorry—nearly missed the turning."

Ellen narrowly avoided scraping the side of the jeep on a stone wall as they swerved right. She slowed to a crawl as they passed a string of cottages. She glimpsed a Christmas tree draped in tinsel through one of the windows, flickering firelight through another. Then she caught sight of the looming stone tower of a church. The pub was right next to it. The painted sign—of a man holding a pickax—was slick with rain. It gave the face a strange look, as if the skin was melting.

A smell of stale beer and tobacco greeted them as they pushed the door open. But at least it was warm, Ellen thought, as she followed Tony to the bar. The place was packed. Men mostly, but one or two women among them. The noise level dropped as people caught sight of Ellen and Tony. It was a momentary hush, like the lull between waves breaking on a beach. The conversations and the laughter picked up again, but the sense of being watched was palpable.

The man behind the bar was tall and hollow eyed. Ellen thought he looked as if he could do with a good meal. Tony ordered a pint of beer and turned to ask Ellen what she would like. She didn't think alcohol was a good idea on an empty stomach—especially with the drive back to the cottage, so she asked for lemonade.

"Are you doing food tonight?" Tony pushed a half-crown coin across the bar.

The barman shrugged. "Packets of nuts and pork scratchings. That's all we got." He had several teeth missing, and those that remained were chipped and stained.

Ellen glanced at Tony. She had no idea what pork scratchings were. They didn't sound appetizing.

"I'll have two of each, then." Tony sat down on a barstool. Ellen looked over her shoulder. There was nowhere else to sit—all the tables were taken. She caught the eye of an older woman, ruddy faced, with a mop of curly hair. The woman stared with undisguised curiosity. Ellen turned away and climbed onto the stool beside Tony's.

The smell when she prized open the packet of pork scratchings made her stomach rumble. It was the meaty, fatty essence of pre-war Sunday dinners. In London, roast pork was still a rare treat. Although the war had ended more than eighteen months ago, there were still food shortages. Ellen's mouth watered as she dug her fingers into the packet.

"Not bad, eh?" There was a loud crunch as Tony bit into a chunk of the fried, salted skin.

Ellen couldn't reply. The initial taste was delicious, but once the outer fatty layer had melted away, a hard lump of gristle was left in her mouth. Try as she might, she couldn't break it as Tony had done. She was afraid of swallowing in case she choked.

Tony grinned at her helpless expression. "Want to spit it out? Here." He dug in his jacket pocket and pulled out a grimy handkerchief. The one he used to wipe his goggles. Ellen dropped her head, hoping no one would see what she was doing. But as the pork scratching slid out of her mouth, she caught sight of someone coming to perch on the vacant barstool next to hers.

"Evening." The man looked about the same age as her stepfather. A pipe stuck out of the left side of his mouth, and he carried a pint glass with an inch of liquid in it. "Visitin', are yer?" He managed to speak without removing the pipe. "Where yer stayin'? Up there, are yer?" He pointed to the ceiling. "We don't get many people comin' this time of year. You got folks round 'ere?"

Ellen shook her head. She glanced at Tony, but he was talking to the barman. "We've just moved into a cottage near the village."

"Oh? Whereabout?"

"It's up on the hill."

"On the carn, you mean?" The man sucked on his pipe.

"The carn, yes." Tony had explained about this Cornish word. It meant more than just a hill. It was a high place with huge, bare rocks at the summit. And the word for the rocks was the name of their cottage.

A curl of smoke snaked toward Ellen's face. "Not the Crowley 'ouse?"

Ellen stifled the urge to cough as she breathed in the woody, acrid scent of his tobacco. "No," she said. "It's called Carreg Cottage."

He nodded, then glanced across to the woman who had stared at Ellen earlier. Ellen saw the look that passed between them. As if something they suspected had been confirmed. She wondered if someone had spotted the jeep and the motorbike going up the track and put two and two together. In such a small village, news was bound to travel fast. She wanted to know about the other place he'd mentioned. Was there another cottage on the hillside? She hadn't seen one. But then again, it had been almost dark when they'd arrived. She was about to ask when she felt Tony's elbow nudge her ribs.

"There's a table free over by the fire, now," he said. She saw that he'd ordered a second pint of beer. There was a smaller glass next to it. "Thought I'd have a whisky chaser." He smiled as he climbed off the barstool. "It's nearly Christmas! You sure you won't have one?"

"I'd better not. We'll open that bottle of bubbly Mum gave us when we get . . . ," she faltered, unable to say the word *home*. Was it because the place was so cold and dark and unkempt? Was it because they hadn't had the chance to cook a meal or unpack properly? Or was it something else? She thought of the spider that had dropped onto her face as Tony had carried her over the threshold. Stupid to let something like that put her off. Spiders, she could deal with. But that weird image above the bed . . . She couldn't help wondering who had painted it, what sort of people had lived there before. And why had the cottage been left in such a state? From the look of things, it had stood empty for a long time.

As they made their way over to the table by the fire, Ellen felt something catch the sleeve of her coat. She turned to see the woman looking up at her. Blue eyes set above cheeks crisscrossed with broken veins.

"It's true, then?" The soft Cornish lilt was at odds with the penetrating gaze.

"I beg your pardon?" Ellen took a step back.

"You've bought the Crowley 'ouse."

Ellen shook her head. She glanced at the man with the pipe, who was now deep in conversation with the barman. Apparently, his message had been misunderstood.

"Yes, we have." Tony was suddenly beside her. "It's going to need some work, but we'll have it shipshape in no time."

Ellen turned to him, bewildered.

"Well, good luck to you." The woman raised a half-pint glass and swigged the dregs of the beer left in it. She muttered something else as she put the glass down. Ellen couldn't hear it above the noise in the room.

Tony's arm slipped around her back, pulling her away. "Come on," he said. "Let's get by that fire."

"Why did she call it that?" Ellen said as they sat down. "Did it have a different name—before you bought it?"

"No, it's always been Carreg Cottage." Tony shrugged. "It was rented out before the war. Crowley was the name of the tenant."

"Oh—that explains it." Ellen took a sip of lemonade. Over the rim of her glass, she spotted the man with the pipe carrying drinks across the room. The woman said something as he set them down. Whatever it was made him shake his head in the way a person might if they'd just received dreadful news.

CHAPTER 3

When Iris woke up it was still dark outside. It took a few seconds to work out where she was. She'd been dreaming about Christmas—about the party she would have been at last night if she hadn't run away. In the dream she had been dancing with a man who had the face of the policeman she'd seen at Paddington Station. He was holding her very tight—too tight—and then he tried to kiss her. As she struggled to break free, she caught sight of her stepmother standing on the edge of the dance floor, smiling.

Iris felt for the bedside lamp and pressed the switch. What a relief to find that she was in this strange little bedroom above a Cornish pub instead of her father's house in London. Her stepmother had made it abundantly clear that the purpose of the party was to find a husband for Iris. There was to be no more art school—her father had refused to fund a second term at The Westminster on the grounds that he disapproved of the company Iris kept there. Instead, her stepmother had enrolled her at a school of domestic science: a suitable preparation for an early marriage.

You just want me out of the way. It hadn't taken long to realize what was afoot. For years she *had* been out of the way: at boarding school for the duration of the war—and unable to return home for the holidays because of the bombing in London. Leaving school had been like a second bereavement. Her father was a stranger to her. The woman he had married was something worse than that: an imposter who pretended she only had Iris's best interests at heart.

Her watch was on the bedside table. She reached for it, peering at the hands in the lamplight. Seven fifteen. She climbed out from under the covers and went to the window. Pulling the curtains aside, she could see the blurred silhouette of what looked like a tower in the distance. Suddenly there was a yellow flash. It revealed a glittering expanse of water beneath the tower. The lighthouse! Her throat constricted as memories flooded back. She and her mother had picnicked on the beach, within sight of it. Godrevy. That was its name.

She lifted the latch and pushed on the pane of glass, opening it just wide enough to get her hand through. She held it there for a moment, breathing in the sharp tang of the sea. No rain, thank goodness. The four-mile walk to St Ives would be easier than she had feared.

She was about to pull her hand back inside when she felt a sudden rush of air. She yelped as something stabbed the soft flesh of her palm. She jumped back. There was a flurry of wings against the glass. A gull alighted on the window ledge, fixing her with its hard yellow eyes.

"Shoo! Go away!" She waved her arms at it. A trickle of blood ran down her left wrist. She grabbed her handkerchief from the bedside table, catching the blood before it reached the sleeve of her nightgown. When she turned back to the window, the bird had gone.

She folded the handkerchief into a strip and, with some difficulty, managed to tie it around the wound. Then she got dressed as quickly as she could. She glanced at her reflection in the square of mirror above the dressing table. She'd gone to bed looking like a bedraggled fox, and now her hair was all frizzy. It would be hard to fashion it into a bun with her hand bandaged up. She would have to tuck it inside her hat when she was ready to leave.

The smell of the public bar rose to greet her as she made her way down the stairs. She grasped the banister. Something about that mingled essence of beer and sweat and smoke made her wary. It was as if the ghosts of all the drinkers who had locked eyes on her last night were still there, watching, waiting.

Her instinct was to run back to her room. But she could see that the door to the bar was ajar. She made herself go and look inside. The room was abandoned and forlorn. On the tables were ashtrays overflowing with cigarette ends, along with unwashed glasses, some half-full of cloudy brown liquid. A broken paper chain hung from the ceiling—its ragged end stuck to the carpet. No wonder the landlady wanted her out so early: there was a lot of work to do before she could sit back and enjoy Christmas.

A different scent drifted along the hallway. Toast. It smelled as if whoever was making it had left it cooking a little too long. It wouldn't matter—she quite liked burnt toast. Her mother always used to tell her that it would give her a lovely singing voice because charcoal was good for the throat.

Her breakfast was brought by a boy who looked no more than nine or ten years old. He pointed to a door opposite the bar, which opened onto a small dining room. There was just one place set on the bare wooden table.

Iris's attempts to strike up a conversation with the boy failed dismally. When she wished him a merry Christmas, he muttered something inaudible and shuffled out of the room. He reappeared with a tray that held a teapot, a jug of milk, and a saucer containing a dollop of marmalade and a single cube of sugar.

He had forgotten the butter—something Iris didn't notice until he'd gone. Perhaps they didn't have any. Maybe that was why the landlady had been so keen to see her identity card. Iris wondered what she was worth in terms of extra rations. And whether anyone would realize that Birch was a fake surname. There must be someone in Great Britain with that name. She had to hope and pray that the lie would never come to light.

She left The Lelant Arms half an hour before the appointed time. There was no one around downstairs, so she put the key to the room on the hall table and let herself out. The air tasted cool and fresh after the fuggy atmosphere of the pub. The street was deserted. The only sign of life was a couple of seagulls pecking at a crust of bread lying in the gutter a few yards away. Iris wondered if one of them was the bird that had attacked her. Perhaps they were used to people feeding them scraps. She clenched her left fist inside her coat pocket. It felt sore. She was going to have to use her other hand to carry her suitcase the whole way to St Ives.

The pub stood on the main road through the village. There were no signposts. All over Britain, they'd been removed during the war to thwart the expected invasion by German troops. With so much else in disarray, restoring signposts was not top of the list. But the sea was the only guide she needed. From the road she could see the whole sweep of the bay. To reach St Ives, she just had to keep the sea on her right as she followed the coast.

Although the rain had stopped, there was no sign of the sun. A biting wind tugged at her hat as she walked. The sea was the dirty gray of dishwater. Not at all how she remembered it. Impossible to think of swimming in those angry-looking waves. But in the faraway summers with her mother, most days had been spent at one of the many beaches along this bay.

Soon she left the village behind. The grass bordering the cliffs looked too muddy to walk on, so she had to go along the edge of the road. There wasn't a car in sight. But she felt exposed, vulnerable, trudging along with her suitcase. What would she say if someone *did* come along and stopped to offer her a lift? They'd be bound to ask questions.

She thought she'd better work out a story, just in case. She could tell the truth about the train breaking down. But where would she say she was going? How would she explain the fact that she was alone, with no one waiting for her in St Ives?

She decided to invent an aunt who was already in residence at The Porthminster hotel. Iris would say she was on her way to join this relative for Christmas. The Porthminster was a place her mother had sometimes taken her to for afternoon tea, and Iris planned to stay there for a couple of nights. She had no idea what it would cost—probably at least double the price of the room at The Lelant Arms—but once Christmas was over, she could look for cheaper lodgings elsewhere in the town.

She'd been walking for about half an hour when a car came up behind her. But it didn't stop. There was a loud toot of the horn as it passed her. She dodged sideways onto the grass verge. When she looked up, the driver was leaning out of the window, waving as he receded into the distance.

"Merry Christmas to you, too!" she muttered. Looking down, she saw that her shoes were now caked in mud. There was nothing to wipe them with, other than the handkerchief wrapped around her injured hand. Gingerly she pulled it back. The bleeding had stopped. After untying the handkerchief, she spat on it and cleaned her shoes as best she could.

By the time she reached the outskirts of St Ives, her cheeks were numb with cold, and her right arm ached from the weight of her suitcase. Rounding a bend in the road, she caught sight of fishing boats moored in the harbor, and beyond them, the rocky promontory called The Island. Nearly there. She smiled and blew out a breath. As the road took her downhill, she spotted the station where the train should have brought her last night. Just above it, to the left, was The Porthminster hotel.

It looked even more grand than she remembered. An imposing four-story mansion with gables and a glass-fronted terrace running its entire length. The sight of it triggered memories of smoked salmon sandwiches and scones with clotted cream and raspberry jam. She recalled being rather afraid of the waiters, who wore black tailcoats and bow ties and looked as if they might lock up any child who made too much noise. She felt afraid now, walking toward the place.

Stepping into the lobby, she breathed in the scent of pine. An enormous Christmas tree stood by the fireplace, its topmost branch almost touching the ceiling. It was strung with fairy lights and baubles. Parcels wrapped in shiny paper were arranged around the base of the tree. Iris didn't know if it was the sight of it or the smell that brought a lump to her throat. Christmases in London had been magical when her mother was alive.

She walked toward the desk, rehearsing what she was going to say. There was a man in the same uniform she remembered from those summer afternoons before the war. He was looking down, writing something in a book.

"Excuse me."

He looked up. Smiled. A polite, practiced smile that involved his lips but not his eyes.

"I'd like to book a room. A single, please. For two nights."

The smile disappeared. "I'm sorry, miss, we're fully booked over Christmas."

"Oh . . ." This hadn't occurred to her. A surge of panic rose from her stomach. "Er . . . do you know of anywhere else that might have a vacancy?"

"I'm afraid not, miss. There's the Tregenna Castle up the hill, but they called us yesterday asking if we could take any extra guests. I'd suggest trying the boardinghouses—but nearly all of them close in winter." His eyes flicked sideways as he spoke. The words had come out too quickly, as if he was impatient to get rid of her. She could hear other voices now. The excited chatter of a group of guests coming from the terrace to the lobby. Iris backed away as they approached the desk. Something hard stabbed the soft flesh at the back of her neck, knocking her hat over her eyes. The Christmas tree. She had walked right into it.

She stumbled down the steps of The Porthminster, hot humiliation stinging her eyes. She headed downhill, with no idea where she was going. She passed shops with their shutters down; guest houses with "No Vacancies" signs hanging in the windows. Not a single person passed her on the street. St Ives felt like a ghost town.

She turned a corner and found herself right next to the sea. A narrow walkway led toward the harbor. The wind carried the stink of rotting fish from the lobster pots stacked on the stone pier. Boats lay idle, swaying with the white-tipped waves. There were wooden dinghies tethered to iron hoops on the harbor wall. It occurred to her that if she were to take one of those little boats and somehow paddle out to a bigger one, she could stay hidden there overnight. Would anyone notice? On Christmas Day?

As she drew closer to the harbor the sound of singing rose above the noise of the wind and the sea. "O Come, All Ye Faithful." It was coming from a building she recognized: an ancient stone church she used to go to with her mother. She remembered the name: a strange one that she'd had to ask how to spell. Saint Ia's. It rhymed with *wires*. Her mother had told her it was named after a young woman who had sailed across from Ireland in a boat made from a leaf in the sixth century. It was a nice story, even if it wasn't true.

As she turned toward the church, the wind took her hat, sending it flying over a low wall that ran along the edge of the graveyard. She scrambled after it, darting between the tombstones, trying to catch it. But a fresh gust of wind bowled it along until it disappeared around a corner of the church.

It had come to rest in the bare branches of a shrub in a sheltered spot between the walls. She bent to retrieve it, pushing back the wisps of hair the wind had disarranged.

"Merry Christmas!" A man's voice made her jump. "You're a little late for the service—but if you're quick, you can take a pew before they finish the carol."

He was sitting beneath a lichen-spotted stone obelisk that stood beside the entrance to the church. He looked a little older than her, but not much. His black hair and light-brown skin reminded her of the French fishermen she used to see on trips to the harbor to buy crab. But his voice had sounded English. He smiled at her as he took a drag on the cigarette in his hand.

"Just popped outside for a smoke. Dad doesn't approve, so I need to pick my moment." He cocked his head toward the entrance. "When they're in full throttle is the best time to escape." He glanced at her suitcase. "Did you come on the train? I didn't think they ran on Christmas Day."

"They don't." She hesitated, aware that whatever she said, she must be careful not to give herself away. "I got stuck in Lelant last night—the train broke down. I walked the rest of the way this morning." She heard the singing inside the church reach a crescendo. Then came a faint rumble as the congregation sat down. "Actually, I wasn't planning to go to the service," she said. "I was supposed to meet my aunt at The Porthminster hotel—but when I got there, they said she hadn't arrived. She doesn't have a telephone, so I can't call her. I didn't know what to do, so I went for a walk—then my hat blew off and . . ." She broke off, aware that she was talking too fast.

"Sounds like you've had rotten luck." He took another drag on the cigarette. "Was she coming by car? I heard some of the roads were flooded after all that rain yesterday."

Iris shook her head. "She was supposed to be here two days ago. The man at the hotel said that when she didn't turn up, they gave the room to someone else." She wondered if he could tell that she was making it all up. The expression in his dark eyes was sympathetic, concerned. She felt a rush of guilt. What would her mother think of her, standing outside the church where they'd knelt in prayer, telling lies to a member of the congregation?

"So, you've got nowhere to stay?"

She shook her head, the threat of tears bringing that treacherous lump to her throat once again. Sternly she swallowed it down.

"We can't have that." He stood up, dropped his cigarette, and stubbed it out with the toe of his shoe. "I live just over there." He gestured to what looked like a small park, enclosed by metal railings. Beyond it she could see an old stone building with lettering mounted on its wall. "The Golden Sheaf."

"The pub?"

He laughed. "No—although that would be fun, wouldn't it? I live next door. The vicarage. Perk of Dad's job."

"Your father's the vicar?" Iris felt her mouth go dry. Was this the same vicar her mother had liked so much? The one who had invited Iris to attend the Confirmation class he had been running during that last summer in St Ives? It couldn't be. Because she was certain she would have remembered this son of his.

"The thing is," he went on, "there's a place next door—the other side from the pub. The Parish Rooms. We had evacuees staying there during the war. It's not exactly luxurious, I'm afraid—but you'd be welcome to stay tonight."

"Oh . . . that's . . . that's . . . ," she faltered, her tongue sticking to the roof of her mouth. "B . . . but your father. Won't he . . ."

"He'll be fine. Honestly." He held out his hand. "I'm Dan, by the way. Dan Thomas."

"Iris." She bit her lip, unable to say the new, fake surname. His kindness shamed her.

Inside the church, the organ started up again. The opening bars of "Hark the Herald Angels Sing." Dan glanced at his watch. "We'd better go in if that's all right. He'll be wondering where I've got to."

"Of course." Iris went to pick up her suitcase.

"Please, let me take that. You must be worn out, walking all that way."

"Thank you." She followed him through the weathered oak door with its curlicued metal hinges, breathing in the mingled scents of old, polished wood and smoking incense. It was a smell she remembered. It made her feel safe.

CHAPTER 4

Ellen was the first to wake on Christmas morning. Through the gap in the curtains, she could see a glimmer of red. She lay there for a moment, listening to the sound of Tony breathing. She could smell cigarette smoke in his hair. And something else: a sweet, ripe scent that intensified as he exhaled. Whisky. He'd fallen asleep in the jeep on the way back from The Tinners Arms. She'd had to shake him awake when they reached the cottage. He would have collapsed on the sofa and spent the night there if she hadn't guided him up the stairs.

She slid off the bed and felt around on the floor for her socks, trying to stifle the surge of disappointment at what hadn't happened last night. Her clothes were draped over the iron bedstead. She reached for her sweater and pulled it on over her nightdress. She tiptoed across the floorboards and drew back the curtain. For a moment she couldn't make sense of what she was looking at. The hillside rose in front of her, crowned with huge stones that glowed scarlet, as if the earth had erupted. She gazed, mesmerized, as the colors changed. Fiery red gave way to coral, then the palest pink. Slowly the sky above turned blue. Now the stones were white, glinting with a diamond sheen where the sunlight glanced off them. They had the look of something constructed by ancient human hands. A tumble-down version of Stonehenge. But Tony had said they were just chance formations of nature.

She looked back toward the bed. He was still fast asleep. She headed for the door. Now it was light, she might as well take stock of the place; tidy up and try to get a fire going.

The bathroom was across the landing. Last night it hadn't looked too terrible. Tony had said that for a house of this age, it was unusual to have any kind of bathroom. A tin bath and an outside toilet were still common in this part of Cornwall. Now Ellen could see that, apart from the dust and a few dead flies, there wasn't much wrong with this room.

She feared that the ground floor of the cottage would need a lot more work. But as she descended the stairs, it didn't look too bad. The furniture was a bit shabby but could probably be smartened up with a few cushions. The curtains were faded and frayed at the edges, but she could make some new ones. She looked around for a broom to tackle the cobwebs and the dust. Perhaps she'd find one in the outhouse Tony had mentioned. The cowshed—that's what he'd called it. She stuck her feet into her boots, not bothering to do up the laces, and stepped outside.

The first thing Ellen noticed was a twisted tree with a tangle of bare branches growing up against the wall of the cottage. Thorns studded the whip-thin twigs. It was lucky they hadn't got scratched by those on the way in last night. But the tree had a stark beauty. Raindrops clung to the thorns, sparkling in the morning light.

She stood for a moment, listening to the clear, wistful call of a bird. It was somewhere close, hidden in the ivy that cloaked the garden wall. There was no other sound but the distant bleating of sheep. No cars. No people. It felt strange, a little unnerving, after the relentless clamor of London.

She headed around the corner of the cottage, almost tripping on a rusty bucket that lay on its side in the tussocky grass. Kicking it aside, she went on until she came to the cowshed. This was the place Tony was planning to turn into an art studio. It was a low building, tacked onto the back of the cottage, with a sloping roof of rusty corrugated metal. There were patches of peeling red paint on the wooden door.

She pushed against it. At first it wouldn't budge, but when she shoved it with her shoulder it gave way. A shaft of sunshine lit up dancing dust motes. There was a definite whiff of animals. She wondered how long it had been since the cows had gone.

Opening the door wider, she saw a shelf stacked with tins and bottles. Beneath it was a row of what looked like camp beds. Had people *slept* in here? It seemed unlikely, given the smell. But it was hard to imagine how all those beds could have fitted in the cottage. One of them had toppled onto its side, the canvas ripped and frayed. Tony had said there might be rats in here. By the look of things, he was right.

Scanning the shadowy recesses of the place, Ellen noticed a spade lying on the floor. She stepped forward and nudged it with her foot. To her relief, there was nothing lurking underneath. Then she spotted a broom hanging from a hook on the wall. Beside it was a dustpan. She grabbed them and darted back outside.

When she got back into the cottage, there was no sign that Tony had been downstairs in her absence. She glanced at the cooker. An old tin kettle had been left on top of it. If only the electricity was working, and she could make a pot of tea to take up to bed. She had to find a way of heating up some water.

She went over to the fireplace and knelt on the floor, peering up the chimney. No wonder the room had filled with smoke last night. Something was blocking the flue. She poked the broom handle up as far as it would go, bringing down a shower of debris. Soot and twigs and fragments of broken brick. And something else. A wooden box. She picked it up and blew away the powdering of black on the lid. *Manikin Cigars*. As she tilted the box to the light, she felt something shift inside it. Why would anyone hide cigars up a chimney?

There was a tiny brass catch on the front of the box. It was speckled with rust, and as she prized it open the lid came away in her hand, revealing not cigars, but the skull of a bird. The empty eye sockets and the great curved beak gave it a truly evil look. She picked it out of its wooden coffin, staring in horrified fascination. There were arms and legs: a crudely fashioned body of stuffed linen had been glued onto the base of the skull. It was stuck with pins and stained with what looked like drops of blood. And there was something twisted around the spindly limbs. Dry brown fragments, like miniature fronds of seaweed, held in place by . . . She lifted one of the arms away from the body. It was hair. Long strands of reddish-brown hair.

A groaning, creaking sound made her jump. As if the thing in her hand had come to life. Ellen dropped it on the hearth.

"Hey, you're up already! Why didn't you wake me?" Tony was coming down the stairs, clutching the rickety banister, which looked as if it could give way at any moment.

"I . . . I was going to try and get the fire going." She walked toward him, gesturing with her hands. "I stuck a broom up the chimney to unblock it, and something . . . *horrible* fell out."

He raked his fingers through his hair, looking at her with a bemused expression.

"It's over there." She glanced over her shoulder, half afraid the doll had come to life and followed her. "I don't know what it is. It was in a cigar box."

Tony went over to the fireplace and dropped to his knees. "Oh." It was a small sound. Like a damp firework that goes out before the flame reaches the gunpowder.

"What do you think it could be?" She hovered over him.

He got to his feet. "I don't know." He rubbed the dark stubble on his chin. The sight of it had not affected him the way it had affected her. He didn't look in the least perturbed. "The cottage is hundreds of years old. There are some odd customs in this part of the world . . . but you say it was in a cigar box?"

"Yes. Manikin Cigars. That's what was written on it. It's down there, by the log basket."

Tony reached for the broken lid of the box and examined it. "So, not all that old, then—probably this century." He turned to her. "The guy who lived here before the war was friendly with the arts crowd in St Ives.

This could be one of their offerings. A would-be Dalí?" Tony kicked the gruesome doll into the log basket. "Not quite *Lobster Telephone*, though, is it? Maybe that's why it got stuffed up the chimney."

Ellen stared at the crumpled form. Why would anyone want to create something so ugly, so repellent? She and Tony had met at an exhibition in London by artists from the St Ives School—it had been mostly seascapes in oils and watercolor. Nothing unusual or outlandish. And yet . . . an image flashed into her mind: the Egyptian figure she'd caught sight of last night. Turning to him, she said: "Did one of those artists paint the thing on the ceiling above the bed?"

"Oh—you saw that." He gave her a wry smile.

"It has a bird's head—just like this thing. I can't think why anyone would want to look at something so weird when they're about to go to sleep."

"Don't worry—we can paint it out."

"Well, I *am* worried." She searched his face. "That couple in the pub last night . . . did you see the way they looked at us when they heard we'd bought this place? It made me wonder what went on here. And why the cottage has stood empty for so long. What if something awful happened, and it's left some kind of . . . I don't know . . . bad atmosphere, or something?"

"Listen, a house that's lain empty for years is bound to develop a spooky reputation."

"But . . ."

"Hey, Ellie, lighten up—it's Christmas Day!" He took her hand and held it in both of his. With his mouth, he pulled back the sleeve of her sweater. Then he ran his tongue slowly and gently along the bare flesh, from the inside of her elbow to her wrist. It was an exquisite, almost painful sensation, as if hot needles were prickling her skin. It pierced the very core of her. She heard a long, low sound like an animal might make. It was coming from her.

"Is that nice?" He was smiling up at her, his gray eyes glinting through dark lashes.

Her mouth wouldn't open. She was incapable of speech.

"Come on, then." He tugged her toward the stairs.

The sheet shifted sideways as they fell onto the bed. She could feel the scratchy fibers of the army blanket against her skin as he yanked up her nightdress. Then his fingers were on her body, so gentle, almost teasing, tracing a path of fire that made her feel as if her belly were melting.

"Won't be a second." She heard him curse under his breath as he reached across the bed. "Where did I put the bloody things?"

When he came back to her, she closed her eyes, letting out a breath as he slid inside. In that moment all the negative thoughts about the place he had brought her to vanished. This was what she had longed for: to be together, like this—just the two of them.

Later, when it was getting dark, Tony brought his wind-up gramophone in from the jeep. They might not have electricity, but they could still dance. He put on a Dizzy Gillespie record, and they did a rumba in front of the fire that now blazed brightly in the hearth. Then, when they collapsed on the sofa, he buried his face in her long brown hair and nuzzled her neck, the way he had on their first date.

Ellen lay back, eyes closed, remembering that night. He'd taken her to the Feldman Club on Oxford Street. She'd never heard of Latin jazz before—and the only dancing she'd ever done was sedate waltzes and foxtrots. Tony had taught her how to bebop and to jive. It was the most fun she'd ever had in her life. And now, just five months later, they were married. He was going to be a brilliant artist—and, in the meantime, she was going to earn enough money to keep them both. As soon as Christmas was over, she would start looking for a shop to rent in St Ives.

She opened her eyes and gazed at the flickering tongues of fire. The cottage felt very different now: warm and cozy. Tony must have disposed of the spooky doll she had found up the chimney, because it was no longer lying in the log basket. And he had promised to paint the bedroom ceiling. She smiled as he nestled into the crook of her arm. He was right: there was nothing to worry about. This new life was going to be blissful.

⊶

Iris hadn't expected the church to be so full. On summer visits as a child, half the pews had been empty. But it was Christmas Day. And she supposed that for most people, Christmases must feel even more special than they had before the war. There was a tangible sense of excitement; of delight at being able to celebrate after so many years of uncertainty and separation. You could hear it in the way they sang the carols; see it in the smiles that passed between parents and children. It was a bittersweet thing to witness the joy of these families. During the prayers, when her eyes were closed, she allowed herself to imagine, just for a moment, that her mother was sitting beside her.

When the sermon started, she watched the vicar climb up to the pulpit. She had a better view of him now, elevated above the congregation. Was this the same man who had been here a decade ago? She couldn't be sure. In her memory, his hair had been black, not white. She had never known his name: her mother had only ever called him the vicar.

She glanced at Dan, who was sitting at the end of the pew, a polite distance away from her. He wasn't looking at his father. His face was tilted upward. He seemed to be studying the wooden figures mounted around the edges of the arched ceiling. These miniature people had fascinated her as a child. They were Cornish saints, carved by fishermen from broken oars. She had asked her mother how they could know how to do that, when they spent their lives catching fish. And she was told that the fisherman grandfathers practiced by making dolls for their granddaughters. After that, Iris had looked longingly at the old men mending nets on the harbor wall, wishing that she had a fisherman for a grandfather instead of the stern-looking oil painting that hung in the dining room at Rowan Tree House.

She tried to concentrate on the sermon. It would be good manners to make an appreciative comment to this man whose home she would soon be invading. But her mind kept going off at a tangent. She wondered where Dan's mother was sitting. Near the front of the church, presumably, close to her husband. Dan hadn't mentioned her when he'd invited Iris to stay with them. He must be very sure of his parents' generosity, she thought, to make such an offer without consulting them first.

The sound of people getting to their feet brought her back to the here and now. The organ struck up the notes of the final carol. Dan flashed her a conspiratorial smile. *Not much longer now.* That's what it seemed to convey. She wondered if he was here under sufferance; whether he believed in any of it—or was in church only because his parents expected it. Whatever the explanation, she was grateful. If he hadn't been smoking that cigarette outside the door, she would probably be well on the way to committing her second misdemeanor in as many days: and stealing a boat was sure to be a far worse crime than taking that ring.

<hr />

If the Reverend Idris Thomas was surprised that his son had invited a stranger to their home on Christmas Day, he didn't show it. Up close, Iris could see that this *was* the vicar she remembered. She crossed her fingers behind her back when Dan introduced them, praying that he wouldn't recognize her. He tilted his head and looked at her for a long moment. But he didn't say anything. Just shook her hand.

He had aged considerably since she'd last seen him, but she was older, too. No longer the little girl with a sun-freckled face and her hair in plaits, but a grown woman. In those days, she had been Winnie, not Iris. She'd only started using her second name when she went to art school, thinking it sounded more sophisticated. She told herself that there was no reason for the vicar to associate Iris Birch with the child he'd once known.

It felt awful, hoodwinking people who were offering such kindness— but she had to stick with the false name and the story about the aunt. Because a vicar, of all people, wouldn't be able to lie if the police came looking for her.

There were only two places laid at the lunch table and Dan hastily arranged more cutlery. After saying the grace, the vicar raised his glass to a painting that hung above the fireplace. It was of a beautiful dark-skinned woman wearing a vivid flowered dress. She was looking at something cradled in her lap: some sort of ornamental tree with birds in its branches.

"To Mama." Dan echoed his father's gesture. Turning to Iris, he said, "We lost her just before the war. And Christmas is never the same without her, is it, Pa?"

"I'm sorry," Iris said. *I lost my mother, too.* She stopped herself before the words were spoken. Her silence felt like a betrayal. But such an admission would have invited questions. Her mother had died here, in Cornwall. The vicar would surely have heard about it. Aware that she was welling up, she turned back to the painting. "It's a lovely portrait. What is she holding in her lap?"

"A Tree of Life," Dan replied. "My mother was a Mexican folk artist. She made religious statuary—clay models."

"She took her inspiration from the natural world," his father added. "The Mexican Catholics have an unusual approach to sacred art—it's very much influenced by the old ways of the indigenous people."

"Really? How fascinating." Iris gazed in awe at the painting. This woman had done what she dreamed of doing—spent her days creating truly original works of art. "How did you meet—if you don't mind me asking?" She felt herself blush as the question came out. She hoped it didn't sound impertinent.

41

"Not at all." The vicar gave a wistful smile. "Florencia came over here after the Great War. Her grandfather was a Cornishman—a tin miner who had immigrated to Mexico when the industry collapsed around here. They needed skilled men to develop the mines out there. He married a local lady—a potter. The tradition was passed down the female line. So, when things became difficult in Mexico, Florencia brought her skills back to Cornwall."

Iris wondered how she could have missed Florencia Thomas in those pre-war visits to St Ia's. Such a person would certainly have stood out among the local congregation. And Dan, who bore a much closer resemblance to his mother than to his father—where had he been?

She wondered who had cooked the roast chicken she tucked into with such relish. And who had laid the table so artistically, with a centerpiece of candles embellished with fronds of ivy and clusters of holly berries? Perhaps the vicarage had a housekeeper who had prepared all this before returning to her own family for Christmas dinner.

When the meal was over, Iris helped Dan to clear the table. His father excused himself and disappeared off upstairs. "Poor old chap's worn out," Dan said, as he picked up the silver platter containing the remains of the chicken. "There was midnight Mass last night and an early Communion service before the main one this morning. He'll probably spend the rest of the day in bed."

"And what about you?" Iris was carrying the empty wineglasses in one hand and a bowl of leftover sprouts in the other. "If you have plans, you mustn't worry about me: I'll be quite happy to go to my room and read a book."

"No, I don't have any plans—not really. I thought about going for a walk along the beach, once this lot's gone down." He patted his stomach. "Would you like to come?"

Iris nodded. She was longing to change out of the twinset and skirt she'd been wearing since yesterday morning. She always felt more comfortable in trousers and a baggy sweater—and they would be much more suitable for a walk on the beach. "If you could show me where I'll be staying, I'll go and sort out my things," she said.

He took her outside the front door and through a tall iron gate. The Parish Rooms were a few yards up the road. The building was of old stone, like the church. The roof was uneven and covered in moss. Inside, the whole of the ground floor was a large hall with a stage at one end. Wooden chairs were stacked against the walls, which were adorned with black-and-white photographs. As Dan led her through the hall, she saw that the photos were of church events going back to before the Great War. Harvest festivals and summer garden parties, concerts and children's picnics.

A staircase led to the bedrooms. There were three dormitory-style rooms, each containing six bunk beds. "As I said, it's a bit basic." Dan set down her suitcase. "There are sheets and towels in the cupboard on the landing. And the bathroom is at the far end. The plumbing's a bit dodgy—there's a hot water boiler, but you'll need to give it a while to heat up if you want a bath." He gave an apologetic shrug. "I hope you'll be okay in here."

"I'll be absolutely fine." She smiled. "Honestly, I can't tell you how grateful I am. I really don't know what I'd have done otherwise."

"Well, I'll let you settle in. Shall we meet outside in about half an hour?"

When he'd gone, Iris sank onto one of the lower bunks near the window. She could see the tower of St Ia's beyond the little public garden that separated it from the vicarage. She ran her fingers over the knitted blanket that covered the bed. It was a riot of color: squares of red and pink and yellow, probably made by some kind old lady to keep an evacuee child warm through the winter. Sleeping in this room would be a bit like being back at boarding school, minus the other girls.

It didn't take long for her to unpack and change her clothes. After a quick trip to the bathroom, she made her way downstairs. It was another five minutes before Dan was due back. She spent the time studying the photographs on the hall wall, curious to know if any of them featured him as a boy. She found one snap of a group of Scouts lined up in their uniforms, dated 1937. Reverend Thomas was sitting in the middle of the group. But she couldn't see anyone who resembled Dan.

The photograph next to it was captioned *Women's Institute 1936*. Beside a table laden with cakes stood a group of smiling women of varying ages. As Iris took in the faces, her heart missed a beat. It couldn't be, could it? She moved in closer. Yes, it *was*. That was her mother, peeping out from behind two older ladies.

Iris didn't see Dan looking in through the window. Nor did she hear the click of the latch as he came in.

"Looking at the rogues' gallery?" He grinned as she spun round.

"I was looking for you, actually." She smiled back as she moved away from the photo of her mother. "I was curious to see if you'd been a Boy Scout."

"Well, I was—but not with the St Ia's pack. It would've been a bit awkward with Dad in charge. I was up the road, at Sacred Heart."

"The Catholic church?"

He nodded. "Mum and I used to go there. People thought it was a bit strange, with Dad being the vicar here. But Mum was very devout. She wanted me brought up a Catholic—and Dad, bless him, didn't mind where I went as long as it had a cross on it."

That explained why she hadn't ever seen Dan or his mother in church. She followed him outside and waited while he lit a cigarette. "Sorry," he said, "I should have offered you one." He pulled the pack from his coat pocket.

"It's okay—I don't smoke." She had tried it once, at the urging of a boy at art school she used to fancy. She'd kept it up for a while, just to impress him, even though the nicotine made her feel dizzy.

"I wish *I* didn't. I keep trying to give it up." He blew out a plume of smoke. "Maybe a New Year's resolution, eh?"

She walked beside him down the road to the quayside. They turned left toward the harbor wall, then went down a flight of steps to the beach. The sand was the palest yellow—almost white. As they walked, the sun came out from behind a cloud and turned the sea from gray to turquoise. This was how Iris remembered it—the jewel-like color of the water and the soft, sugary sand that seemed to absorb the sunlight and give off a glow of its own. How wonderful it would be to paint it.

Dan darted sideways, bending down to pick up something from among the trail of seaweed on the strandline.

"What is it?"

He came back to her, stretching out his cupped hand. "A Christmas present." He smiled as he opened his fingers. In his palm was a chunk of opaque glass, the palest aquamarine, its edges worn smooth by the ocean. As she went to take it from him, she could feel the warmth of his skin.

"It's beautiful." She held it up to the light, running her fingers along the edges.

"If you like, I can make it into a pendant."

"Really? How?"

"Just by twisting a bit of silver wire around it." His smile widened. The sunlight caught his eyes. They were liquid brown, like melted chocolate. She felt something in her stomach shift—and it was nothing to do with the Christmas lunch she'd just eaten.

"Can you really do that?" She fixed her eyes on the sea glass as she handed it back, unnerved by what she was feeling. He put it in his pocket, and they walked on.

"I've always loved the beach in winter." Dan shaded his eyes, scanning the broad expanse of sand. "It gets so crowded in summer. This year was the busiest I've ever seen it. I think people were desperate to get to the seaside again—and you can't blame them. I guess you've been here before, for holidays."

Iris hesitated. Whatever she said, she mustn't contradict the tale she'd spun about coming to stay with her aunt. Easier to pretend that she'd never been to St Ives before. She shook her head. But even as she did it, she realized she'd tripped herself up: she'd admitted to knowing the name of the Catholic church—how could she if she'd never visited the town?

There was no hint in Dan's face that he'd picked up the inconsistency. "I suppose you'll be going home tomorrow," he said. "Where is home?"

To avoid telling him another outright lie, she sidestepped the question. "Actually, I was planning to stay for a while. The idea was that I'd spend Christmas and New Year with my aunt, then look for digs. I . . . want to study art, you see."

"Really? Well, I can introduce you to a few people, if you like—most of my friends are artists." He tossed his cigarette onto the sand and stubbed it out. "And please don't think I was trying to get rid of you when I asked if you were going home tomorrow: you can stay as long as you like."

"Thank you—that's very generous. But I really would like to get my own place. I'll start looking as soon as Christmas is over." She hoped she didn't sound ungrateful. But studying art was not her only ambition: what she also longed for was independence. Iris had loved the teachers at her boarding school, but she'd grown to hate the regime imposed on her. You got up when you were told, went to bed when you were told, ate what you were told, wore what you were told. And at her father's house, things hadn't been much different. After years and years of living by other people's rules, she'd had enough. To live alone, to do exactly what she wanted when she wanted, was her idea of heaven.

Besides, she couldn't stay for long with Dan and his father, tempting as the offer was. She could barely keep track of the lies she was having to tell. And there was every chance the vicar might realize who she was. People had told her she was the image of her mother. One look at that photograph in the hall would give her away.

CHAPTER 5

Tony was awake early the morning after Christmas. Ellen was still asleep when he came upstairs with a breakfast tray.

"What a nice surprise!" She hoisted herself up on the pillows. "How did you manage to do toast?"

"The fire was still just about going from last night," he smiled. "So I banked it up and stuck the bread on a fork."

"Clever old you." There was a faint whiff of charcoal mixed with the orange tang of marmalade, but the fact that this was the first meal Tony had ever made for her made it taste wonderful. She thought how handsome he looked, sitting there on the edge of the bed, a beam of sunshine lighting up his face. She felt like pinching herself. How lucky she was to have him; to be *married* to him.

"There's somewhere I want to take you this morning," he said. "We'll have to go quite soon, otherwise we won't be able to see it."

"That sounds intriguing." She wiped a smear of marmalade from the corner of her mouth. "Where are we going?"

"It's a surprise." He tapped the side of his nose.

When she was dressed, she followed him outside. There was a soft dampness in the air. The sun was a milky glow, shrouded by an unbroken cloud. Dew soaked the edges of her boots as they walked down the path. They were going on the motorbike, he said, because it wasn't possible to go the way he wanted to take her by car.

Within minutes of setting off, she was clinging to him for dear life as they bumped across the moorland. He'd veered left, off the track, speeding across rough grass and clumps of heather. Sheep scattered at the roar of the engine. Ellen had to squeeze her legs in tight against the bike to avoid spikes of gorse clawing at her trousers.

They were circling Zennor Carn, heading to the other side of it. Suddenly she caught a glimpse of a square church tower far below, and beyond it, the sea. Seconds later, the bike plunged downhill. She let out a yelp of fear as they narrowly avoided a huge lump of granite.

"You all right?" Tony shouted.

She nodded, digging her face into the back of his neck. She couldn't look. It was too terrifying. She breathed in the salty, smoky scent of his skin, telling herself that they would be okay, that they were not going to die. Tony had done this before. He must know what he was doing.

When she opened her eyes, they were on a road. It wasn't until she saw the sign hanging outside the pub that she realized where they were. The Tinners Arms looked very different in daylight. And there was the church whose tower she'd spotted. Tony didn't stop in the village. He sped through it, driving across another field of sheep when the road petered out. With mounting horror, Ellen saw that they were heading toward a sheer drop.

"Tony!" she screamed.

He pulled up no more than a yard away from the edge of the cliff, laughing as he cut the engine. "We're almost there now. Come on!"

Her legs felt wobbly as she dismounted. But the view was heart-stopping. Below them, the sea was crashing against the rocks with a raw, elemental power. Even though the sky was overcast, the water had a vividness—a dark blue-green, frothing white where the waves broke.

Tony took her by the hand and led her to a rough, uneven path that wound down the cliff face.

"We're going down there?"

He nodded. "There's a beach. It's called Pendour Cove. You can't see it from this angle. The tide's going out, so there'll be sand."

She had to trust him. Every so often, their feet sent showers of small stones bouncing down onto the rocks below. If either of them lost their footing, they wouldn't stand a chance.

"There it is!"

Ellen's stomach lurched as she looked where he was pointing. She saw a curve of sand, as pale as the winter daylight, lapped by the receding waves. Minutes later they were down there. She sank onto a rock, not quite believing that they'd made it.

"What do you think?" Tony beamed at her.

"It's beautiful. Scarily beautiful." She ran her fingers over the surface of the rock. It was peppered with tiny barnacles, which gave it the rough feel of unworked wood. "What happens if the tide starts coming back in?"

"It won't." He glanced at his watch. "It's nearly full moon, which means the sea goes out farther than at other times. Low tide's not for another two hours. We're quite safe."

"You're very knowledgeable, for a city boy." She nudged him with her elbow. "How do you know these things?"

"I've been reading up on them. Ever since I knew there was a chance of buying the cottage." He bent over and untied his shoelaces. "I've been longing to do this."

"You're not going in?"

"Only for a paddle. Are you coming?"

"We'll freeze!"

"I know!" He grabbed her arm and pulled her up. "But how many people can say they've dipped their toes in the Atlantic Ocean in December? Imagine telling your mother!"

With whoops of delight, they chased each other to the water's edge.

Ellen only managed a couple of minutes. Her feet and ankles were cherry red when she came out. Tony lasted a good five minutes longer, kicking up the surf as he raced back and forth, his trousers rolled up to the knees.

While he was drying his feet, Ellen wandered to the boundary of the cove, where the rocks formed a wall at head height. Curious to see what lay beyond, she climbed up and over. There was another, much smaller, strip of sand. She could see a dark shape, like a solitary rock, in the middle of it. As her eyes focused on it, she saw that it was not a rock. It was a dead animal. Dark and sleek. A seal? She had never seen one, but she couldn't imagine what else it could be. It had fur, so it wasn't a dolphin or any kind of fish.

As she gazed at it, something else caught her eye. A couple of birds were hopping about on a rocky ledge over to her right. Suddenly they flew off together, their black wings spread wide as they swooped low over the waves. They circled around, and then landed on the carcass of the seal. Ellen's insides contracted as they stabbed their beaks into its flesh. The image of the doll in the chimney flashed through her mind. That malevolent skull with its cruel beak. Just like these crows.

"Ellie!" Tony was calling her. She scrambled back over the rocks and jumped down onto the sand. "I couldn't see you," he said, when she reached him.

"Sorry—I was curious to see what was on the other side. I wish I hadn't looked—there was a dead seal being pecked at by crows."

Tony grimaced. "Not nice. It's a shame—they're such beautiful creatures. But that's nature, I suppose."

She glanced back to where she'd been, unable to shake the image of the seal's body, invisible to her now, its flesh being torn from its bones by the greedy birds. It was strange how deeply it had affected her. She had seen lifeless bodies before. Dead people. Why was this so hard to stomach? Perhaps it was because, when the war ended, she'd shut those memories away in a dark corner of her mind, not expecting to confront death again anytime soon. And if she'd remained in London, she probably wouldn't have. In a city, you didn't see it. But here, in the countryside, it was going on all the time, all around her. It was something she was going to have to get used to.

Two days after Christmas the electricity was reconnected at Carreg Cottage. Ellen wasn't there when the power came on. She'd left Tony sorting out the cowshed while she drove into St Ives to buy food and look for premises for her business. She needed something with a shop window and a workroom at the back: large enough to accommodate a lathe and a band saw, with plenty of storage space for blocks of wood. And there had to be enough room for a table where the painting and finishing could be done.

Ellen had started making wooden toys when she was a child. There had been a factory next door to their house in Cheyne Walk—a place that made billiard tables. The men who worked there used to give her offcuts of wood to play with, and she had learned to fashion them into animals with a penknife from the age of ten. She still carried that penknife in her handbag, along with the first thing she had ever made: a tiny tiger made of rosewood. She had named her business after it.

The Toy Tiger had taken off in the eighteen months since the war ended. She'd expanded her range, making toy farms, Noah's Arks, and horse-drawn caravans. Big stores had started to take an interest in her work. The money from the Christmas order for Harrods would keep her and Tony afloat while they settled into life in Cornwall. And a further order from them had come in the day before the wedding.

Tony had made her see that she didn't need to base herself in London to run the business—she could make the toys anywhere with good rail links to the capital. And renting a workshop in St Ives would be much cheaper than her old base in Chelsea.

The little fishing port was just ten minutes' drive along the road at the foot of the hill—in the opposite direction from Zennor village. A low midwinter sun shone out of a cloudless sky as she headed down the track. The wild moorland was breathtakingly beautiful on such a bright, clear morning. She could understand why Tony called this place a corner of paradise.

Ellen passed a house soon after she reached the road. She wondered how she hadn't spotted it on the evening they'd arrived. Probably because it had been raining and almost dark. And from the cottage, you couldn't see this section of the road, so in daylight, it had looked as though there was no other human habitation for miles.

There was a wooden sign on the gate. Rowan Tree House. It was a large, elegant building perched on a rocky outcrop overlooking the sea. The occupants would be her nearest neighbors. There was no sign of life, though: no car in the drive or washing on the line.

Soon she was on the outskirts of St Ives. Heading down a steep hill, she passed a church, a school, and dozens of houses. After a tight bend she found herself in a narrow street lined with shops. There was nowhere to park, so she turned right, emerging on the quayside. What she saw through the window made her gasp. The sea glowed as if lit from beneath the surface—an almost unearthly shade of pale blue. Ellen had never seen water that color: it was like robin's egg blue—a shade of paint she'd chosen for embellishing the miniature horse-drawn caravans she'd turned out by the dozen in the weeks leading up to the wedding.

She pulled up by the harbor wall. As she opened the door of the jeep, her nose wrinkled at the smell of fish. There was a man in oilskins hosing down the cobbles, sending a mess of blood and guts onto the beach below. Other men were selling their catch—crates of flatfish and herring, live crabs and lobsters, their claws bound with rubber bands.

She attracted a few curious glances as she made her way back toward the main thoroughfare. The houses tumbled down the hill toward the harbor; stone-built, slate-roofed cottages with tiny windows, almost like a child's drawing of a town. There were scores of wooden boats lying on the sand, some brightly painted, others weather-beaten and in need of repair. Beyond them a square church tower rose above the huddle of houses, its honey-colored walls lit up by the morning sun.

She stopped outside a pub called The Sloop Inn, trying to work out which way to go. The agent she'd spoken to on the phone before Christmas had mentioned an empty property on Fore Street. He'd said it was just off the seafront, on a road that ran parallel with the quayside. She cut through an alley that ran along the left side of the pub and emerged into a street thronged with people. A sign on the wall above a butcher's shop told her that this was Fore Street.

She passed a line of women queuing outside a bakery. A sign in the window said customers could buy only one loaf per visit. The bread looked much more appealing than what was on offer in London. The aroma wafting into the street made her mouth water.

Ellen identified the empty shop she was looking for from the agent's sign in the window. It was opposite a pub called The Castle, sandwiched between a florist on one side and a funeral parlor on the other. She wasn't sure if she liked the idea of working next door to a place where dead bodies were taken. But the shop was in a very good location, right in the heart of the town. And the agent had said it was just a few minutes' walk from the railway station. He'd also said it was the only commercial property currently available in St Ives.

She glanced at her watch. Tony had warned her that the office would close at midday on a Saturday. She needed to get the keys and see what it looked like inside.

At the far end of the dormitory in the Parish Rooms there was a chest of drawers with a mirror on top of it. When she stood there doing her hair, Iris could see into the garden of the vicarage. On her second morning, she caught sight of Dan making his way along a path that led to some sort of shed nestled beneath a group of leafless trees.

He'd told her that he had to work on Saturday mornings, and when she'd asked what sort of work he did, he'd explained that he had two jobs. On three days a week, he worked for a St Ives–based sculptor who was gaining an international reputation in the art world. He was part of a small team of men who prepared the huge blocks of stone and wood she used in her work. The rest of the week he worked on his own, continuing his mother's ceramics business. He'd mentioned a studio and kiln that his father had had built at the end of the garden. That must be where he was heading now.

As she watched him disappear beneath the trees, Iris wondered if she would be allowed to see his work. She wouldn't dream of going and knocking on the door. Because if *she* had a place like that, she would absolutely hate the idea of anyone disturbing her. And besides, she had an important task of her own to get on with this morning. Christmas was over, and everything was back to normal. She could start looking for somewhere to rent—a home of her own, where she could live exactly as she liked.

Iris had only a vague idea of how much it was likely to cost. Some of her fellow students at The Westminster College of Art had lived in rented accommodation. She'd been appalled at what they were paying for cramped rooms with damp walls—and grimy bathrooms with dodgy plumbing, often shared by half a dozen people.

She hadn't liked to tell anyone where she lived. It had been embarrassing enough that her father insisted on sending his chauffeur to pick her up from college at the end of each day. The spoilt rich kid. She'd seen it in their eyes, even though no one ever said it to her face. *Well, not anymore.* Even though rents were sure to be much cheaper here than in London, her money wasn't going to last long. She was going to have to get some sort of job to fund this new life.

When Dan had told her about the sculptor he worked for, Iris had asked if there might be a chance of her joining the team of assistants. But he had said no: Barbara only employed men. When she'd asked why, he'd said that women weren't considered to have the physical strength to shift great blocks of marble and alabaster. Iris had puzzled over the logic of this. She thought it odd that a woman who was gaining such success in a man's world seemed not to want other women in her orbit.

She let herself out of the Parish Rooms and made her way past the church. A few yards up the road there was a newsagent's shop. She thought that the local paper would be the best place to start looking for accommodation. *The Cornish Times* was the only one she could find.

"Is there anything more . . . local?" Iris held up the newspaper, smiling at the girl behind the counter.

There was no reply. Just a shrug. She bought it anyway, and on the way out of the shop she spotted a noticeboard near the window. There were various handwritten advertisements—mainly items for sale—but there was one for a bedsitting room available to rent in Norway Square. Three guineas a month, including bills—much less than she'd expected. There was a date at the bottom of the notice. November 21—more than five weeks ago. Iris scribbled down the address. It had probably gone by now, but it was worth a try.

She turned back to the girl who had sold her the newspaper. "Excuse me—could you tell me how to get to Norway Square from here?"

Another shrug. "'Sdown by The Digey."

Iris had never heard of this place. "What's The Digey? A café?"

The girl gave her a pitiful look. "'Tain't a caff. 'Swhere the lugger boys live."

She might as well have been speaking a foreign language. Iris decided she was just going to have to wander around until she found Norway Square for herself. With a curt nod, she headed back out into the street.

She stood for a moment, wondering which way to go. Then she spotted Reverend Thomas coming out of the door of St Ia's. She ran to catch him as he crossed the road.

"Good morning."

He turned toward her, looking slightly flustered.

"Could I ask you something? I saw an advert for a room to rent—but I don't know how to find it. It's a place called Norway Square."

He nodded. "It's at the other end of the town. Not far. Just go along Fore Street—where the shops are—and turn left up a narrow lane called The Digey. Then it's a right turn onto Back Road West. Norway Square is halfway along there, on the right."

"Thank you. I'll jot that down." She smiled as she fished her notebook from her bag, thinking of the look the girl in the shop had given her.

As she turned to go, he caught her arm. "Iris, I wonder if you could assist me. There's a bird trapped inside the church. I was going to get Dan to help me shoo it out, but I'd rather not disturb him."

"Of course." She followed him through the arched oak door into the gloomy interior of St Ia's.

"It's a crow, I think." He pointed to the statue of Christ on the cross, suspended on a wooden frame between the nave and the altar. "I don't know how it got in—there must be a hole in the roof."

As Iris's eyes adjusted to the lack of light, she could make out a dark shape perched on the right arm of the cross. "Yes—I can see it. How can we get it down from there?"

"I've tried dislodging it with a feather duster—but it keeps flying back up there. If you could stand in front with the broom, you could shoo it up the aisle when it lands. Then, with a bit of luck, it'll fly out of the door."

It took three attempts before the crow was successfully evicted. Each time it flew down from the cross, Iris ducked, convinced it was going to attack her. She'd never been afraid of birds—but the incident with the seagull on Christmas morning had made her wary. And the crow had such a vicious-looking beak—bigger and more powerful than any gull's.

"Thank you, my dear." Reverend Thomas blew out a breath as he locked the church door. "Will you have a cup of tea before you go? I think we both deserve one."

"I'd better not, thanks." She smiled. "I'm not sure whether the room's still available—and if it's not, I'm going to have to look elsewhere in the town."

"Of course. But please don't think there's any pressure for you to move on. Stay with us for as long as you need to."

"Thank you. I'm so grateful to you for taking me in. I don't know what I'd have done without your kindness." As Iris walked away, she remembered that she was wearing her scarlet lipstick. She hadn't intended for Reverend Thomas to see her in her war paint. It seemed disrespectful, somehow. Like going to church without a hat.

She wondered what he made of her. At lunch on Christmas Day, she'd expected an interrogation. But he hadn't even asked her where she came from. Perhaps he'd grown so used to accommodating strangers during the war that he'd given up quizzing people who turned up at the vicarage. Or could it be that he suspected who she was but had decided to keep quiet about it?

Her mother was the kind of woman who had stood out from the crowd; even as a child Iris had noticed how people—men in particular—reacted to her. What if Reverend Thomas didn't need to have his memory jogged by the photo in the Parish Rooms? What if just seeing Iris's face was enough to make him guess that she was Stella Bird's daughter?

As she made her way past the shops on Fore Street, she asked herself what he might be thinking if he *did* know who she was. He would wonder why she was using a different name; why she hadn't acknowledged the fact that they had met before; why she had chosen to return to St Ives. He knew about her plan to study art. But would he realize that what had really drawn her back here was a longing for what she had lost?

He had lost someone, too—the pain of it was etched on his face. Just like her, his son had been left without a mother at a young age. So, was she wrong to worry about him recognizing her? Would he be on her side if the police came asking questions?

An image of her mother flashed into her mind's eye. Kneeling at the altar rail for Communion in a green silk dress and a wide-brimmed cloche. Iris remembered her mother laughing as she'd put on her hat that morning, saying she couldn't believe how warm the weather was for Easter—and that she hoped the chocolate eggs she'd hidden in the garden wouldn't have melted by the time they got back from church. That school holiday had been the last time she'd seen her mother.

After that, Iris hadn't wanted to go to church ever again. If there was a God, why had he taken her mother away? But she'd had no choice. At boarding school, church attendance was yet another rule that must not be broken. Now, she wasn't sure what she believed. But she would go to the service at St Ia's tomorrow. Not because it was what you were supposed to do on a Sunday morning, but because of what Dan and his father had done. They had made her feel that they really cared about her.

Finding Norway Square wasn't as straightforward as the vicar had made it sound. Iris realized that she must have taken a wrong turn at the end of Fore Street because she found herself on Wharf Road, facing the sea, outside The Sloop Inn. The wind had picked up. She'd been sheltered from it until now, but it gusted in from the water, tugging at her clothes, threatening to take her hat again.

With one hand on her head, she walked on, looking for The Digey. But the only left turn she could see was Fish Street. It was a narrow, cobbled lane that rose steeply from the quayside. Iris turned into it, thinking that the place she was looking for couldn't be far away.

The street was well named: the smell of fish was overpowering. Stone-built cottages, crammed together in higgledy-piggledy fashion, gave the place a dark, rather claustrophobic feel. There were lines of washing strung overhead. Fishing nets were strewn on steps that ran up the sides of the cottages to first-floor level. She caught a glimpse through a doorway of piles of silvery herring stacked in neat rows. From the look of it, the people who occupied these houses lived upstairs and used their basements for storing the daily catch.

Farther up the street she saw a group of small boys kneeling on the cobbles, playing marbles. Despite the cold wind, some of them were barefoot. They looked up, curious, as she dodged around them. Another thing she noticed was the number of cats. They seemed to be everywhere: curled up on steps, stalking along the cobbles, staring down from rooftops. She supposed it was the smell that attracted them.

At the top of Fish Street, she hesitated, unsure whether to turn left or right. She spotted an old man sitting on the steps of a house, smoking a pipe. A length of tangled net lay across his lap. "Excuse me," she said. "Could you tell me which way Norway Square is?"

He looked up, peering at her over the rim of his pipe. His eyes were a faded blue, almost translucent, as if the years he'd spent at sea had washed the color away. He jerked his thumb to the left. "'Sdown there, off Back Road West. Be you lookin' fer the lugger boys' church?"

That word again—the one the girl in the newsagent's shop had used. She wished she knew what it meant. "Er, no. I'm looking for Norway House."

The man nodded. "Opposite the pig-skinnin' place."

Iris didn't like the sound of this. The fishy smell was bad enough, but the thought of living within sight of a slaughterhouse was more than she could stomach. She told herself that she didn't have to take the room. If Norway House was horrible, she would just have to widen her search.

She thanked the old man and set off in the direction he'd indicated. The houses were much like the ones on Fish Street, although the road was a little wider, less canyon-like. Suddenly she caught sight of a sign that stopped her in her tracks: "The St Ives School of Painting." It hung from the top of a flight of wooden stairs belonging to a building on the left side of the road. This was the place she'd heard about at college: the one she planned to enroll at as soon as she could. Would it be open? She thought not, this soon after Christmas. But she climbed the stairs just to make certain.

It was no surprise to find that the door was locked. But she could see through the glass panes to a large room beyond. A surge of excitement welled in her stomach. There were easels grouped around a small central platform. Palettes and jars of brushes sat on a table on one side of the room. And beyond the easels was another window, through which she could see the sea.

She came back down the stairs, searching for anything that might tell her when the School of Painting would reopen. All she found was a flyer displayed in a ground-floor window, advertising a lecture to be held in the middle of January: "Dark Angel—A Feminine Perspective on Surrealism," by Nina Grey. Iris took out her notebook and scribbled down the date and the time.

A few yards farther along Back Road West she spotted Norway Square. It was a pleasant surprise to find that it was nothing like the nightmare vision the old man had conjured up. It was a quiet oasis, with a small public garden filled with palm trees and tamarisk at its center. Low-lying cottages surrounded the square. Norway House was a little taller than the others—a whitewashed house with a blue-painted front door in the center. A climbing rosebush curved leafless boughs around the slate-roofed porch. The windows on either side of the door had lace curtains, and the tiny front garden was bordered by a white picket fence atop a low stone wall. The overall impression was of a neat, clean, pretty house.

Iris looked across the square, wondering where the place the old man had mentioned could be. There was no evidence of any kind of industry. At the far end was a building that looked like a church. There was someone sitting on the steps. A man, getting to his feet, now, looking in her direction. Was it . . . ? It couldn't be . . . could it? She shaded her eyes with her hand. It *was* him.

"Hello." Dan came up to her, smiling. "What are you doing in this neck of the woods?"

"I might ask you the same question." She smiled back. "I thought you had to work this morning?"

"I did, but I got a call to help move a couple of Barbara's pieces. There's an exhibition." He cocked his head toward the church. "Quite a few of the local artists are involved."

"Oh?" Iris glanced at the tall stone building with its twin arched doors. The sign on the wall read "The Mariners' Church." "I didn't know that churches could hold art exhibitions."

"It's not a church anymore," he replied. "It was built for the lugger boys, but they preferred to come to St Ia's, so they could watch their boats through the windows. You can't see the sea from here."

"Ah." Her eyes widened. "So that word—*lugger*—it's a name for a fishing boat? I kept hearing it, and I had no idea what it meant."

Dan nodded. "Anyway, what brings you to Downalong?"

"Downalong?"

He smiled. "It's what they call this part of town."

"Oh?" Yet another thing she didn't know about St Ives. Well, at least her ignorance gave her fake backstory some credence. "I saw an advert for a room." She glanced back at Norway House. "It's in there. I haven't seen it yet. It looks like a nice place, but an old man who told me how to find it said they skin pigs across the road."

"Did he?" Dan chuckled. "They used to—but that was years ago." He pointed to the wall that encircled the public garden. "Over there— that's where pigs were brought to be slaughtered and skinned. People around here still remember it."

"Well, that's a relief. Anyway, the room's probably gone—the advert's been up a few weeks, judging by the date on it. But I thought it was worth a try."

"Want me to come with you?"

Was it her imagination, or was it just too much of a coincidence that Dan happened to be on the spot when she was about to inquire about the room? She wondered if what he'd said about the phone call from his boss was true—or whether his father had asked him to go to Norway Square to make sure the accommodation was up to scratch? If the latter were true, she was touched by their concern for her. But she didn't need help. She was quite capable of making her own decision.

"Thanks for offering," she said. "But . . ."

Before she could come out with a suitable excuse, Dan saved her the trouble. "You're right—it's probably best if you do this on your own. Wouldn't want the landlady getting the wrong idea."

Iris felt herself blush. She waited until Dan had disappeared back inside the Mariners' Church before ringing the bell.

The woman who answered the door was wearing an apron. She reminded Iris of the cook her father and stepmother employed.

"I've come about the room."

The woman looked her up and down, lingering on the gray felt hat with its red ribbon trim, and the matching slash of bright lipstick. Iris hoped she hadn't overdone the makeup.

"I . . . er . . . saw the advert in the newsagent's shop in town. I wasn't sure if it was still available."

The woman wiped her hands on her apron. "Yes, 'tis."

"Can I come in and take a look?"

"Oh, it ain't here, dearie—'sround at the back."

Iris followed her around the outside of the house. There was a courtyard at the back, with a wooden door in the far wall. When the woman opened it, Iris could see a row of cottages like the ones in Fish Street.

"This way." The woman indicated a set of stone steps that led up to the first floor of one of the houses. After unlocking a green-painted door, she showed Iris into a long, narrow room with one small window. There was a single bed in one corner, beside which sat a wooden stool and a chest of drawers. Wire coat hangers dangled from a row of hooks on the wall opposite. In the corner nearest the door there was a sink and a kitchen cupboard with a miniature gas hob set on top of it. The room had a slightly smoky scent to it—not cigarettes; more like a cooking smell. Iris wondered how long it was since the last occupant had left.

The woman pulled back a flowered curtain that screened off another corner of the room, revealing a lavatory and a washbasin. "If you want a bath, you can come to the 'ouse on a Friday mornin'. That's extra: sixpence a time."

It hadn't occurred to Iris that there would be no bathing facilities in the building. But the room had everything else she needed, and the sloping beamed roof gave it a certain charm.

"I'll be wantin' a month's rent in advance." The woman was looking at her again. Weighing her up, no doubt wondering if she had the money her smart London clothes suggested.

"Yes, of course." Iris drew three notes and two coins from her purse and handed them over. "Thank you, Mrs. . . ."

"Dixon."

"When can I move in?"

"'Safternoon, if you want. Just mind out for nets on the steps." She cocked her head toward the open door. "Down below's a smokin' cellar, see."

"A smoking cellar?" Iris had visions of men huddled over pints of beer, puffing on pipes.

Mrs. Dixon nodded. "Fer the 'errin'. 'Ope you like kippers—you'll be getting the smell of 'em reg'lar. Just keep the window closed when the smoker's goin', or you'll get it on your clothes."

Iris nodded, thinking what a fool she'd been to hand over the money so readily. No wonder the room was so cheap. Kippers were her father's favorite breakfast dish. It had seemed an odd thing to eat first thing in the morning. She'd never tried one. She didn't mind the aroma—but she didn't fancy the idea of going around St Ives stinking of smoked fish. She told herself that she didn't have to stay beyond the month she'd paid for. If it was really unbearable, she could look for somewhere else. In the meantime, she needed to find a job. With more money in her pocket, she'd have more options.

"You'll be needin' this." The woman dug in her apron for a key and handed it over. "'Ow long are you plannin' on stayin'?"

"I . . . er . . . I'm not sure." Iris felt cornered. She tried turning the question back on her new landlady. "How long is it available for?"

"Just till the end of May. I've got an artist from London booked in for the summer. A painter."

"Oh?" An artist. She wanted to tell her new landlady that she, too, would be painting in this room. But she didn't. Couldn't bring herself to say it. Was it because, as yet, she didn't have the wherewithal to support herself in this new life? Or was it something more fundamental? A fear that, deep down, she was never going to be good enough to call herself an artist.

CHAPTER 6

Ellen couldn't get off to sleep. She was thinking about the shop in Fore Street, working out the likely outgoings per month and how much she would need to spend on wood and transport costs, while also funding day-to-day living expenses at Carreg Cottage.

The roof of the cowshed needed repairing. Tony said he couldn't turn it into a studio until that was done. And they needed new furniture. The bed creaked with every movement, and the mattress had unpleasant-looking stains on it. Downstairs, the kitchen table had woodworm in three of its legs, and the mummified mice she had found under the armchair suggested it had served as a nest in the years the cottage had lain empty.

The dead mice had reminded her of the seal she'd seen on the beach, and the crows pecking it. Her mind had flipped once again to the strange doll she'd found up the chimney. She doubted she'd ever be able to erase that image: the evil-looking skull with its vicious beak, and the limp body wrapped with hair and stuck with pins. She tried to visualize the process of making such a thing. The hair was what really puzzled her. Where had those long copper-colored strands come from? A horse's mane or tail, possibly. But it had been so fine—not like horsehair, really. More like human hair.

Tony had dismissed the doll as an ineffectual attempt at surrealist art. That was a possibility, if the previous tenant had encouraged artists from St Ives to visit the cottage.

Ellen had a clear memory of visiting the International Surrealist Exhibition in Mayfair as a teenager. Salvador Dalí himself had been there, dressed in a diving suit. He'd caused a sensation, almost suffocating onstage as he gave a talk about his work—and having to be rescued by someone prizing off the helmet with a billiard cue. That show had featured some strange and intriguing pieces. But nothing as bizarre, as chilling, as the object in the cigar box. What had the person who made it been trying to say?

She slid out of bed, hoping the inevitable squeak of the springs wouldn't disturb Tony. She went over to the window and drew back the curtain. There was a full moon hanging above Zennor Carn. It gave the landscape an otherworldly look. As she turned away, she caught something on the edge of her field of vision: a flash of light on the hillside. She looked again. Was it the moon reflecting off the rocks the way the sun had done on Christmas morning? No—she could swear there were lights flickering on the summit: not bright, silvery moonlight, but pinpricks of glowing yellow, like candlelight. As she watched she thought she saw silhouettes moving between the giant rocks. She counted three, four, five of them. What were people doing on top of a hill in the middle of the night?

She thought about going to investigate. But something held her back, some nameless fear that stopped her heading for the stairs. Should she wake Tony? She stood at the window, the curtain clenched in her hand, listening to the sound of his breathing. He would be cross with her. Probably wouldn't believe her. Would say she was letting her imagination run away with her, just as she had with those people in The Tinners Arms. She would have to drag him out of bed and make him see what she had seen.

But when she looked again, there was nothing there. No lights, no dark human shapes. *Had* she imagined it? Was she getting so worked up about the cottage and the business that she was starting to hallucinate?

Her mother had warned her that getting married, moving to Cornwall, and relocating the business might be too much to cope with.

Ellen had brushed her fears aside. She was young and in love. And the war had made her grow up fast. Surely nothing could be harder to cope with than the sights she'd seen driving ambulances during the Blitz?

She crept back across the room and climbed into bed, snuggling against Tony, feeling the warmth of his body. She would go up onto the carn when it got light. If there had been anyone up there, there would surely be some evidence. No need to say anything to Tony. She would do this on her own.

One of the bedsprings in the lumpy mattress was pressing against her thigh. She shifted onto her back, trying to get comfortable. The moon was shining through the curtains now, playing on the grotesque figure painted on the ceiling. It seemed to hover there, exhaling a malign force, ready to swoop into her dreams and turn them into nightmares. Once again, a question echoed inside her head—the same as that triggered by the gruesome doll in the cigar box: What was the person who made it trying to say?

As she drifted into sleep, a whispered answer floated in. *This is a magical place—but the magic is black.*

———

The sun had been up awhile when Ellen climbed over the garden wall. Tony was in the cowshed, sorting out the tools and the tins on the shelves. She didn't tell him where she was going or why. After giving him a long, lingering kiss, she'd just said that she hadn't slept well and thought a walk would do her good.

The path was steeper than she'd anticipated. Halfway to the top of Zennor Carn, she paused for breath and turned to look back down at the cottage. It looked small—like one of her toy houses. She could see the place where the corrugated metal on the roof of the cowshed had rusted away to nothing, leaving it open to the elements. And she could see Tony throwing something onto a pile of rubbish in the garden.

Near the top of the hill, there were boulders everywhere. She had to scramble over them because the path had petered out. Some of the rocks were as tall as houses. Others were balanced precariously, one on top of another. She climbed onto a long, flat one that gave her a clear view of the coastline. Rugged and dramatic, it was so different from the tranquil turquoise bay at St Ives. Far below, hidden by the curve of the cliffs, was the tiny cove where she and Tony had paddled. The wind was stronger up here. She could feel it gusting in from the wide, open ocean. And she could taste the salt on her tongue.

As she turned away from the wind, Ellen caught sight of someone perched on a rock a few yards below her. A woman with dark, wind-blown hair, staring out to sea. She was leaning back, her arms behind her, like the figurehead of a ship.

Ellen threaded her way between the boulders that lay between them. As she drew nearer, she saw the woman toss her head, as if reveling in the power of the wind. She seemed to symbolize all that was wild and solitary in this place. Was she one of the shadowy figures Ellen had glimpsed last night? Could she and the others have camped out up here? There was no sign of a tent. And why on earth would anyone want to sleep on top of a windswept hill in the middle of winter?

"Good morning!" Ellen called out before she reached the woman, not wanting to startle her. But the face that whipped round was full of an angry intensity. Clearly she had not expected to be disturbed. "I'm sorry." Ellen didn't go any closer. "I didn't mean to frighten you."

The woman held her hand up, shading her eyes. The skin of her forehead furrowed into fine horizontal lines.

"Lovely view, isn't it?" Ellen smiled. The woman's lips contracted. She looked like a wary dog, weighing up whether to bark or bite. "It's the first time I've seen it," Ellen went on. "I . . . I've just moved into the cottage down there." She gestured with her arm, glancing back over her shoulder.

The woman's head tilted to one side. "Carreg Cottage?" She had a deep, throaty voice. A smoker's voice, Ellen's mother would have called it.

"That's right."

"But I thought Tony Wylde had bought that place."

Ellen stared at her. The way she'd said his name made it sound as if she knew him. "Er . . . yes. He has. I'm his wife."

"His *wife?*" The woman huffed out a breath. "He's a dark horse—he certainly kept that quiet." She patted the rock beside her. "Come and sit down. I'm Barbara, by the way."

"Ellen." It was a little awkward, scrambling up the vertical side of the granite slab. She shuffled along until she was a polite distance away. Tony hadn't mentioned anyone called Barbara. The only local person whose name had come up in conversation was the agent who had sold him the cottage.

"Well, I'm sure Tony will be in his element here." Barbara swept back a lock of hair that had blown across her face. "I often come up here for inspiration."

"Do you live nearby?" Ellen thought about the place on the main road that she'd passed yesterday: Rowan Tree House. Perhaps Barbara was their nearest neighbor. That would explain how she knew about Tony buying Carreg Cottage.

"No—well, not all that close. I live down there." She swept her hand toward St Ives. "But it gets a bit claustrophobic sometimes. Too many buildings and too many people. I need to escape." She ran her hand across the smooth surface of the granite. "This is a magical place. These rocks are the bones of the Earth Mother."

Ellen felt as if the cold stone had sent a chill right through her body. *This is a magical place.* Weren't those the very words she'd heard last night as she was falling asleep? She stared at the hand moving back and forth, inches away from her. The fingers were long, but the skin was coarse and red, the nails stubby. Hardworking hands. There were no rings on the fingers. Who was this woman? And how did she know

Tony? To ask would be humiliating, would reveal that there were things about his life he hadn't told her.

"I can't get over how beautiful Cornwall is." Ellen tried to sound light-hearted. "Tony's been wanting to move here for years." That was what he'd told her. She paused, glancing at Barbara.

"He used to come and stay with us during the war." There was a wistful note in the gravelly voice.

Us. Was she married, then, despite the ringless fingers?

"We moved down from London in August of '39. It was a good thing we did—my studio was bombed, and pretty much everything in it was destroyed."

So, she was an artist. Ellen wondered if she'd been one of Tony's tutors at the Slade.

"I knew from the first day we arrived that I'd never go back," Barbara went on. "It'd been Ben's idea to come here—but in the end I was the one who insisted on staying." She went on stroking the lichen-spotted rock as if it were a pet dog. "I love the sense of remoteness from the rest of the British Isles. There's a brooding, compelling quality in the landscape: almost like a magnetic force." Her fingers went to her hair, raking it back and twisting it around—as if her hands couldn't be still. "I quite envy you and Tony. I'd love to live so close to this place. But it's hard enough getting blocks delivered to St Ives: they'd never get them up here—not in a million years."

"Blocks?"

Barbara nodded. "I've scaled up my work since the London days. I'm mostly using marble and Nigerian hardwood. Tony hasn't—" She broke off, spotting something over Ellen's shoulder. "Oh, talk of the devil!"

Ellen twisted around. Tony was coming toward them, waving.

"Well, hello!" He scrambled past Ellen and kissed Barbara on both cheeks.

"I ought to slap you!" Barbara laughed as she pulled away. "Fancy not inviting us to your wedding!"

"Sorry. It was all a bit last-minute, wasn't it?" He glanced at Ellen.

"Oh? You're not . . ." Barbara's arch look made Ellen blush.

"You must be joking!" Tony grimaced. "I'm relying on Ellie to keep me in the style to which I'd like to be accustomed!"

"Well, aren't you the lucky one!" Barbara grunted a laugh. "Do you have a cigarette, darling? Stupid pack must have dropped out of my pocket on the way up here."

Tony fished inside his jacket. When the cigarette was in Barbara's mouth, he leaned in close to light it, cupping his hand around the match to shield it from the wind.

"What do you do, Ellen?" Barbara blew out a plume of smoke.

"She works with wood." Tony spoke before Ellen could reply.

"Really? You're a sculptor?"

Ellen shook her head. "I make toys. I carve some, but mostly I use a lathe."

Barbara nodded. The glimmer of interest had waned into an expression of barely concealed disdain. Ellen felt as if she were shrinking. She was not an artist, like these two. She was an artisan. And in this woman's eyes, that made her a second-class citizen.

As Barbara turned away, her hand went to the sleeve of Tony's jacket. "Listen, we're having a party on New Year's Eve. Everyone'll be there. Why don't you two come?"

"Oh . . . well, thank you. We'd love to, wouldn't we?" He glanced at Ellen. "It'll be a chance for you to get to know people."

"Yes. Thank you." Ellen smiled. A party. That ought to be fun. But the thought of it set off a frisson of . . . what? Not dread—that was too strong a word. But if Barbara's arty friends were going to be there, and they were all like her . . .

For heaven's sake, don't do yourself down! I'll bet most of them would give their eyeteeth to have their work on sale in Harrods!

Her mother's voice came through loud and clear. She was probably right. But somehow it didn't make the prospect of meeting the art crowd of St Ives any less intimidating.

CHAPTER 7

Dan helped Iris carry her things over to Norway Square after Sunday lunch. She'd been out the previous afternoon to buy a few basics: bread, milk, eggs, and cheese. She'd had to smudge her name on her ration book to match her identity card. To her relief, no one had queried it.

There had been nowhere to buy sheets and blankets—Truro was the nearest place for shops like that, which was more than twenty miles away. But Reverend Thomas had said she could help herself from the linen cupboard in the Parish Rooms.

"It's not as if we're going to need that stuff anytime soon," Dan smiled as they set off across the town. "Poor Dad—it was a real tonic for him when we had the evacuees staying. He used to sit in the garden, just watching them running around. He said there was nothing like the sound of children laughing. He knew how much my mum would have loved having them around."

"It must have been hard for both of you, losing her." She was looking at the cobblestones, not at him. She couldn't remain silent after such a heartfelt remark—but to look him in the face would have been to risk betraying the emotion his words had stirred up.

"Yes, it was. But I wasn't at home much. I joined the Merchant Navy at eighteen."

"Really?" If her estimate of his age was right, he must have joined up during the war. "Where did you go?"

"I was on the North Atlantic convoys. Back and forth to Russia, with food and ammunition."

"That sounds like pretty dangerous work."

He blew out a breath. "I guess it was. But other people had it far worse."

Something in the tone of his voice warned her not to probe further. She wondered what he'd seen, whether any of the ships he'd served on had been attacked by German U-boats. At school, they'd knitted socks for British servicemen. It had made her feel pathetic, useless, that she was too young to do anything of real value for the war effort. Dan might be only half a dozen years her senior, but he had seen and done things she could only guess at.

"Do you have any plans for this evening?" The sudden change of subject took her by surprise.

"Er . . . well, no. I thought I'd just settle in—maybe try and cook something. There's a funny little stove in the room—I might just about be able to boil an egg on it."

"Well, when you've done that, how about coming to the cinema? A few of us meet up there on Sunday nights. It's *Black Narcissus*. Have you seen it?"

"Oh—no, I haven't. Are you sure? I don't want to gate-crash your night out."

"You wouldn't be. It's just a casual thing. I don't know who'll turn up."

"Well . . ." She hesitated. Did he think she was going to be lonely, on her own in this new place? Was he just being kind? Or was there another reason for the invitation? *Don't be stupid,* she thought. His friends were going. It wasn't as if he'd asked her out on a date. "Thank you," she said. "I'd like that. I haven't seen a film in ages." It wasn't a lie. Going to the cinema had been forbidden at the same time as her forced withdrawal from art school. In the weeks before Christmas she had felt like a caged bird. They had said they just wanted to keep her safe. And yes, a bird in a cage *was* safe. But that was not where it was meant to be.

For a fleeting moment she tried to imagine what they would be thinking, her father and stepmother, what sort of Christmas they would have had without her. Perhaps she'd been foolish, thinking they would send the police looking for her. Because by running away, she had given them what they'd wanted all along. They were rid of her—well and truly. *And* she'd saved them the expense of a wedding—which would surely have been considerably more than the value of that serpent ring.

Thank you, Mr. Crowley. Those words had echoed through her head many times during the past few days. Not for the first time, she wondered what Dan and his father would think if they knew they'd been playing host to a thief and a runaway. She couldn't bear the thought of them ever finding out.

The casserole simmering in the oven sent a delicious aroma creeping up the stairs to the bedroom, where Ellen was standing at the window. She glanced at her watch, wondering how much longer Tony was going to be.

She hadn't really minded when he'd offered Barbara a lift back to St Ives on his motorbike. But Ellen had felt uneasy when she saw this friend of Tony's wrap her arms tightly around his waist as they bumped down the track. It shouldn't have taken him much more than half an hour to drop her off and drive back. A little longer, perhaps, if he'd been invited in for a cup of tea. But he'd been gone for nearly three hours. What could possibly be keeping him so long?

She told herself that he'd probably got chatting and simply lost track of time. The man Barbara lived with would have been sure to want to catch up on all the news. Ben—that was his name. Barbara had talked of him as if he was her husband. Maybe he was. Maybe the reason she didn't wear a ring was because it got in the way of hammering stone and chiseling wood.

Why is that so important? The question floated out of some dark recess of her mind. Was it the familiarity between Tony and Barbara that had made her feel so uncomfortable? Or the fact that he had never once mentioned this woman's name? If Barbara and Ben were old friends, why had he not talked about them?

A treacherous thought occurred to her: that the encounter this morning had been an act, that Barbara and Tony had planned to meet up there on the rocks and she had ruined things by getting up there before him.

You don't trust him. That voice again.

"I do!" She hissed the words, creating a tiny patch of condensation on the window. There was no escaping the irony. Those were the very words she'd said aloud just days ago, at the wedding. She lifted her hand to the glass, rubbing out the misty circle with the cuff of her sweater. Why would he have married her if he was in love with someone else?

She went downstairs and took the casserole from the oven, trying to suppress the wave of jealousy welling up inside. But as she stirred the pot, an image of Barbara filled her mind's eye—that wild, abandoned look as she had tipped her head back, her hair tossed by the wind. This was a woman of supreme confidence. A woman who feared nothing and no one. A woman who did exactly as she liked, when she liked. She was older than Tony—the fine lines on her forehead and at the corners of her eyes suggested that there was at least a decade between them. But the effect she'd had on him was undeniable. Ellen had never seen him so . . . She stood at the stove, the spoon frozen in midair, searching for a word to describe the change she'd seen in him.

A sound from outside distracted her. Was that him? She listened. No. It was a scratching, scraping sound—probably that tree by the path blowing against the front door. She put down the spoon and heaved the casserole back into the oven. She should light the fire. It was starting to get dark. But as she went across to the log basket, she stopped, listening again. This time there was no sound. It was something else: a strange sense of stillness, an obsessive quiet. As if something had seeped in through the windows from the twisted thorn tree outside to take over the cottage as night set in.

What are you doing here? You don't belong.

"Stop it!" She brought her hands up to her face, shaking her head. All worked up about Tony, she'd allowed her imagination to run away with her. She had to get a grip. She knelt at the fireplace, grabbed a sheet of newspaper, and scrunched it into a tight ball. Then another, and another. Stack the kindling; place the logs. Watch the flames.

With the fire blazing, she went back upstairs to draw the curtains. There was no moon tonight. The clouds made it impossible to tell where the hillside ended and the sky began. She stood for a moment, thinking about the lights she'd seen up there last night. Had she imagined them?

Suddenly she spotted a single light moving—not on the hill but off to the side. Then she heard the distant throb of an engine. Tony's motorbike.

⋙

Iris and Dan were waiting outside the Royal Cinema in Palace Yard. The light from the foyer cast a pool of yellow on the cobblestones.

"I forgot to give you this." Dan took something from his jacket pocket. It glinted in the light as he handed it to her.

"Oh!" It was the pendant he'd promised to make for her. She brought it closer to her face. An intricate tracery of silver wire encased the sea glass. "It's beautiful. Really beautiful. Thank you!" She went to put it on, fumbling with the clasp.

"Here, let me." He pulled her scarf away from her neck before fastening the necklace. She could feel his fingers on her bare skin and his breath as he leaned in. She shivered.

"Sorry—are my hands cold?"

"N . . . no." She couldn't tell him that the shiver was nothing to do with the temperature of his hands, that it was the sense of him touching her that had sent tingles down her spine.

"I think that might be Denis." Dan stepped away from her. He was looking down the street at a man coming toward them. "Yes, it is. Denis Mitchell. He's a painter."

Denis shook her hand when they were introduced. He looked older than Dan.

"Iris has come to study painting," Dan said, before his friend had time to ask her anything himself.

"Really?" Denis smiled at her from behind heavy black-rimmed glasses. "Well, there's no better place on earth as far as I'm concerned. Where are you from?"

"Hampshire." It came out easily. It wasn't really a lie: her school had been in Hampshire, and she'd lived there for years.

"You didn't fancy any of the London art schools, then?"

Iris shook her head. "I don't like cities much."

"Amen to that!" Denis grunted a laugh.

While Dan went to buy tickets, Iris and Denis carried on chatting in the street. He said that while St Ives was a fantastic place for an artist to live, he doubted he'd ever be able to support his wife and child on what he made from his paintings.

"Every day I say a prayer to Saint Barbara," he said, rolling his eyes.

"Saint Barbara?"

"Barbara Hepworth—the sculptor. Have you heard of her? She's doing rather well these days."

"Ah, yes." Iris nodded. "Dan told me he works for her part-time."

"Yes, we both do. She's a bit of a slave driver, but working for her is better than being a waiter, which was what I did before."

Iris told him that she needed to get a job but wasn't sure where to look.

"There's not much going at this time of year." Denis stroked his chin. "If I hear of anything I'll let Dan know."

Something in the way he said it made her wonder what Dan had told him about her, whether Denis thought that she was more than just a new arrival who needed a helping hand.

Dan appeared with the tickets then, and they all went inside. The place was full of people. Iris sat between the two men on a folding seat of threadbare purple velvet. They'd only just got settled when the curtains opened, and the title flashed onto the screen.

All Iris had heard was that it was a movie about British nuns trying to set up a school on a mountaintop in the Himalayas. It had sounded rather tame. But it soon became clear that it was anything but. The nuns lived in a palace that had once housed the harem of an Indian prince—and the walls were decorated with semi-naked women. The peculiar atmosphere of the place soon began to affect them in strange ways.

Iris glanced at Dan out of the corner of her eye, wondering what he made of the erotic images appearing on the screen.

Suddenly a latecomer squeezed past, blocking her view as he made for the vacant seat beside Denis. She pulled in her legs to make way for him, and as she did so, she felt Dan's arm brush against her knee. It was only for a split second, but, once again, the sensation was electrifying.

"Sorry." She heard Dan's whispered apology above the creak of the seat as the newcomer sat down.

Was *she* sorry? That he hadn't meant to touch her? Iris tried to focus on the action on the screen. It looked as if the Sister Superior was falling for the rugged estate manager. But so was one of the other nuns. The look in the younger one's eyes when she realized that she had a rival was chilling. The unfolding story grew more disturbing by the minute. There was a dramatic confrontation between the two women. One of them had taken off her nun's habit and put on a red dress. Challenged by her rival, she defiantly applied a slick of scarlet lipstick.

Iris felt her seat move as Dan shifted in his. The close-up of the nun's lips was uncomfortable to watch. The lipstick was the same shade that Iris used. And she had the same auburn hair and foxlike green eyes. When her chance came she slunk away to find the man she burned for. And when it all went wrong, she returned, terrifying in her rage, to take revenge on the Sister Superior.

"That was a bit heavy, wasn't it?" Denis glanced at her as the lights went up. "I think I need a pint after that!"

Dan nodded. "Would you like to come, Iris? We get a discount at The Castle—Denis's brother is the landlord."

"I . . . I'd better not." Iris didn't want to tell him how worried she was about making her money last. She'd insisted on paying for her own cinema ticket, but she had no idea how much she might end up spending at a pub, whatever the discount.

"Oh—okay." He turned to his friend. "Will you get me a pint in? I'll just see Iris home."

They set off along Fore Street, heading for the narrow, cobbled alleys of Downalong. "I guess you must be tired," he said, as they passed under a streetlamp. "It's been quite a day for you."

She wished he wasn't looking at her like that, with those dark, soulful eyes, wished she hadn't felt that frisson of longing when his arm had brushed her leg. She hadn't come to Cornwall to find a man. The idea of being tied to one was part of why she'd run away.

So why not tell him that you're only nineteen?

She couldn't answer that voice inside her head. All she knew was that something had changed. The tense, febrile atmosphere of the movie had infected her—and the image of the nun in scarlet lipstick was branded on her mind's eye. Did red lips signal sexual availability? She hadn't realized that, in trying to make herself look older, she was sending out the wrong signal.

⟢

Tony was in high spirits when he came home. After bursting through the door, he swept Ellen off her feet and danced her around the living room, singing some jazz number she didn't recognize.

"Hey—what's happened?"

He didn't reply. Instead, he kissed her, sliding his tongue inside her mouth. She'd wanted to yell at him, to ask him what on earth he'd been doing for the past four hours. But with that kiss all her pent-up anger melted away.

"Sorry I was so long." He whispered the words as he nuzzled her ear. "The bike broke down when I dropped Barbara off. One of the spark plugs was damp. I had to take it out and clean it."

She hugged him closer, ashamed of the disloyal thoughts that had filled her head as she'd waited for him to return.

"What's cooking? It smells fantastic!"

"Oh, just some stew," she murmured.

"Will it keep a little longer?" He slid his hand down her back, his fingers going under the waistband of her skirt.

They groped their way upstairs without bothering to switch the lights on. The thought of him wanting her so much made her ache for the feel of his body on hers. She heard him moan as he thrust inside her. It should have been as breathtakingly magical for her. But something robbed her of that moment of ecstasy. The feel of his hair. Her fingers were buried in it. And for some inexplicable reason, the image of the hideous doll, its spindly limbs wrapped in strands of copper-gold, flashed into her mind and killed the lovemaking stone dead.

Tony didn't sense that it hadn't happened for her, and she didn't like to tell him. After they'd lain there in silence for a while, he jumped out of bed and drew back the curtains.

"Look at that moon!"

Hoisting herself onto her elbows, she could see it through the window. Just past full, it was wreathed in a misty halo of pale yellow. "It's beautiful." She followed the beam of light it cast into the room. Her eyes went to the ceiling above the bed. The moonlight picked out the beak of the bird-headed pharaoh figure. She shivered. It felt as if the thing had been watching them.

"Tony . . ." She reached across the bed, stroking the curve of his back. "You know you said you'd paint the ceiling in here . . ." She hated the sound of her voice. Wheedling. As if she was trading on their lovemaking to get him to do what she wanted.

"Yes, of course. I promised, didn't I? I'll do it first thing tomorrow."
He didn't sound cross or irritated. To her amazement, he seemed happy,
almost eager, to get the job done.

His good mood continued as they ate their evening meal. He showered her with compliments about the stew, saying it was the best he'd
ever tasted. And as she cleared the plates away, he caught her by the
waist and told her he was the luckiest man alive to have found a girl like
her. Then he ushered her over to the sofa, telling her to put her feet up
while he washed the dishes.

When he came over to join her, he had a pipe in his hand. It gave
off a ripe, woody aroma. Not unpleasant. Quite different from the smell
of cigarettes.

"I didn't know you smoked a pipe." She smiled as he sat down
beside her.

"It's for my asthma. My chest felt a bit tight on the way home. I
think it's this damp weather."

"Oh, you should have said! We probably shouldn't have . . ."

"Shush." He put his hand across her mouth. "Yes, we should. It
doesn't affect me in *that* way." He took a long drag on his pipe and blew
a curl of smoke toward the fireplace.

He'd told her about his asthma. It was the reason he'd been declared
medically unfit for service in the war. While she'd been driving ambulances across London, he had been working as a laboratory assistant
in a research institute in Oxford. Testing the effects of bomb blasts on
monkeys. It had sounded horrible—as if he were being punished for
being unable to go and fight.

"What did you think of Barbara?" His question cut across her
thoughts.

"She's . . . very nice." Ellen tried to sound matter-of-fact. But
remembering that heart-shaped face framed by wild dark curls provoked
a stab of jealousy. "It was kind of her to invite us to her party."

"It'll be good for you to meet people."

"Do you have other friends in St Ives? You didn't tell me." She hadn't meant it to sound like an accusation—but that was how it came out.

"A few." He shrugged as he blew out another plume of smoke. "I used to come here quite often during the war. It was a bit of light relief from working in the lab. My boss, Solly Zuckerman, was a friend of Barbara and Ben. That's how I got to know them—and they introduced me to other people."

Ellen stared into the fire, picturing a younger Tony, angry and frustrated that the war had nipped his artistic ambitions in the bud, letting rip at parties in St Ives. There would have been other women, probably. But she didn't want to know about them. In her imagination, they were all versions of Barbara.

"Barbara's amazing." Tony walked across to the fireplace and tapped his pipe into the embers. "I don't know how she managed when the triplets were born."

"Triplets?"

"Didn't she tell you? They're teenagers now, but they were only about five when she and Ben moved to Cornwall. She has another son, too— from her first marriage. But somehow she managed to keep working right through the war. She used to tell me that she'd go crazy if she couldn't work. *If I can just find an hour a day,* she'd say, *that keeps me sane.*"

Ellen tried to imagine what that would be like. There were no babies in her family. One of her friends had given birth to a little girl a few months after the war ended and had found motherhood overwhelming. It had given Ellen the sense that starting a family while nurturing a business was a wholly unrealistic ambition. But Barbara had pulled it off. Amazing Barbara.

For heaven's sake, she's the first person you've met. Don't start hating her—make her your friend.

Her mother's voice, full of good sense, echoed through her head. But it was going to take a supreme effort to put on a smile at the New Year's party.

CHAPTER 8

A sharp slapping sound roused Iris from dreams of demon-eyed nuns on vertiginous mountaintops. She sat up in bed and peeled back the edge of the mildew-speckled lace curtain. Part of a fishing net flew past the window. She could hear men calling to each other across the street.

She reached for her watch, which lay on the stool that served as a bedside table. Twenty past nine. Amazing that she'd slept so late. Her hand went to her throat, fingering the pendant Dan had given her. She hadn't wanted to take it off last night. She thought about him getting out of bed at the vicarage. Imagining him putting on his clothes set her pulse racing.

To distract herself, she glanced around the room, making a mental checklist of what she still needed to do. Coat hangers. She needed to buy some sturdy wooden ones to replace the misshapen wire triangles dangling from the hooks on the wall. And a lamp, so she wouldn't have to get out of bed to switch off the light at night. Matches and kindling for the little pot-bellied stove in the corner of the room were other items to add to the list. At least she didn't have to worry about where to get logs: she'd been told she could help herself from the pile in the shed behind Norway House.

She'd never made a fire. Dan had had to show her how to do it. Lucky he'd had a cigarette lighter, as the shops were closed on Sundays. It had been nice, coming back to that warmth last night. She'd hesitated when they reached the bottom of the steps, wondering if she should invite him in. He'd come right across town to see her home: the cinema was at his end of St Ives, just a couple of minutes from the vicarage.

"See you around, then." He'd turned away before she'd had time to say anything. But when he was almost out of sight, he'd turned back and called across the street. "There's a party on New Year's Eve, if you fancy coming."

In the whirl of activity of the past few days she had completely forgotten about New Year. But she was glad of Dan's invitation. It might have felt lonely, knowing that everyone else in the town was out celebrating—although being on her own would have been preferable to last year, which had been spent playing cards with her stepmother while her father got quietly drunk in front of the fire. It had been the start of the coldest winter on record, when huge snowdrifts had trapped thousands of people in their homes. Things hadn't been quite so bad in London. But the icy roads and pavements had made it next to impossible to venture outside.

Iris smiled, imagining what she would have thought if she'd known that, a year on, she'd be celebrating New Year in St Ives. She wondered what sort of party it would be. Nothing like the one she'd escaped on Christmas Eve—she was certain of that. The dress she was supposed to wear that night had been left hanging in the wardrobe—far too fussy and flouncy to be crammed into her suitcase. But what should she wear to Dan's party? She hadn't brought anything special with her. Could she afford a new dress?

After a breakfast of tea and toast, she set off for the shops. Now that she knew the way, the maze of cobbled streets and alleyways was less confusing. Halfway along Fore Street she spotted an ironmonger, where she found coat hangers, matches, and kindling. They sold paraffin lamps, too. When she went to pay for everything, the man behind the counter asked if she already had some paraffin. He smiled at her bewildered face. It was yet another thing she'd had no idea about—that for a lamp like that to work, you had to pour the oil into it.

There was a dress shop across the road from the ironmonger. A large sign in the window announced a sale. Even from a distance she could tell that the clothes were upmarket. It was the sort of shop you'd expect to see in London. One dress caught her eye. There was a description of it on a card propped beneath the mannequin: "Charming day gown in fine corded emerald taffeta. Self-pleated on fitted bodice with full skirt. Usually three and a half guineas—reduced to forty-five shillings."

Forty-five shillings! That was two-thirds of her monthly rent. She was going to have to make do with what she had. Or maybe find a cheap length of fabric and make something herself. That was one thing school had equipped her for. It would take time, with no sewing machine, but until she found a job, time was something she had plenty of.

She wandered along Fore Street, looking in every window, hoping to spot an advertisement for a shop assistant. But she was disappointed. There was nothing going. Near the end of the street, she found a haberdasher with a basket of remnants on sale. Rummaging through the fabrics, she found a length of duchesse satin in peacock blue at only one-and-threepence. There wasn't enough for a dress, but Iris found a shorter piece of the same type of fabric in a deep mauve. The colors went well together. For less than half a crown, she could have a new outfit.

She took everything she'd bought back to her room, filling up the paraffin lamp and laying the fire ready for the evening. But before it got dark, there was something else she needed to do.

The bus station was across town, close to where the trains came in. Her mother had always gone by car to and from St Ives, but Iris knew there was a bus to Zennor, because the housekeeper had used it. She cast her eye over the timetable on the wall of the shelter. The bus to St Just stopped at Zennor. There was one every hour. She glanced at her watch. Twenty minutes to wait. Just enough time to go back to the florist she had passed in Fore Street.

Tony smiled as he watched the jeep disappear down the track. Ellen would be gone most of the day, signing the lease for the new workshop, organizing the delivery of her tools, and sourcing supplies of wood. It wouldn't take him more than an hour or so to paint the bedroom ceiling—and after that he could spend as long as he liked outdoors.

En plein air.

He loved that phrase—it sounded so much more alluring in French. It was why he'd come here: to paint the landscape *in* the landscape, to capture colors and changing light as he saw them, rather than from memory. And what he saw would transcend the power of the mortal eye. Because yesterday, in St Ives, he had managed to get hold of the magic ingredient—the key that would unlock his creativity.

He'd thought about telling Ellen, but he doubted she'd understand. There was a lot else he couldn't tell her. The painting on the ceiling had been easy to explain away—but it had been a shock when she'd found that thing up the chimney. The couple in the pub had spooked her, too. If she'd known what had gone on at the cottage, she would never have agreed to come here. But he'd done a good job of calming her down. Now he just had to keep her sweet.

He chuckled to himself as he carried a pot of white paint up the stairs. It wasn't exactly a chore, being married to Ellen. She was attractive, hardworking, and eager to please. Given the choice, he would've preferred to live alone. But to own this place, to be able to give up all the drudgery and do what he'd always dreamed of doing—it was well worth the sacrifice.

The bird's eye gleamed in the sunlight as he lifted the paintbrush. One stroke, two, and the whole head was obliterated. A shame, really. Frieda would be sad if she knew. The figure was the inspiration for the Tarot pack she'd designed for Crowley. Thoth. The Egyptian moon god. The god of magic.

When he'd finished painting the ceiling, he went downstairs and lit a pipe. The dried mushrooms had a strange, earthy smell. He filled his lungs with their smoke, then sat for a couple of minutes, waiting for the rush. He'd left everything ready by the door: paints, paper, brushes, easel. All he had to do was walk out onto the moor and let it happen.

⟨⟩

As the bus climbed the steep hill out of St Ives, a mist rolled in from the sea. The roofs of the houses on either side of the road disappeared first, then the bedroom windows, until the ghostly outlines of the front doors were all that could be seen.

As they left the town behind, the mist became patchy. Iris caught glimpses of the moor, where sheep grazed among great boulders of creamy white stone. Her heart did a strange thing, lifting and contracting, as if it were a rubber ball, tossed into the air and then caught and squeezed. She couldn't recall exactly how long it had taken, in the old days, to drive from St Ives to the house. Not long enough to suck and swallow one of the boiled sweets her mother always bought on a trip to town—she remembered that. All she knew for certain was that the bus stopped a few yards beyond the house. So long as the mist didn't obscure it, she would know where to get off.

The bus rounded a bend and suddenly, there it was. Rowan Tree House. It was exactly as she remembered it. The front door and the shutters on the windows were painted the same cornflower blue; the wooden sign was still there, nailed to the gate. The only difference from the picture stored in her memory was that the tree the house was named for was leafless, its branches stark against the white walls.

The image blurred as tears welled in her eyes. She swallowed them down. This was no time to cry—she had to ring the bell and get off, otherwise she'd end up miles down the road and have a long walk back. Clutching the bunch of flowers to her chest, she made her way to the front of the bus.

She was the only person to alight at the Zennor stop. She waited until the bus had gone, then crossed the road, passing the turning for the village and heading back in the direction of St Ives. The mist swirled in across the fields, making the road ahead disappear momentarily. There was no path to walk on. If a car came around the bend it wouldn't see her. But it was a quiet road and there wasn't far to go.

Soon she glimpsed the topmost branches of the winter-dead rowan tree. It looked ghostly, shrouded in a cloud of white. Reaching the gate, she traced the letters on the sign with her fingers. She hadn't noticed from the bus, but there was another sign attached to the stone pillar to the left of the gate. *"Chy an Kerdhinnen."* It was the name of the house in Cornish. She remembered Mrs. Richards, the housekeeper, telling her that. The new people must have decided they liked it.

The shutters were closed, and there was no car in the drive. It looked as though no one was home. Iris was tempted to open the gate and knock on the door, just in case. But what would she say if someone answered? To admit that she used to come here for holidays, that her parents had once owned this house, would be to give herself away. And to be invited inside, to glimpse those rooms again, would trigger such bittersweet memories.

She stepped away from the gate, reminding herself that this was not the real reason she had come. Turning around, she glanced across the road, to the place where a rough track led up the hillside. Somewhere up there was the place where her mother had died. She needed to walk that path, to see that place—even though she didn't know the exact spot it had happened. Because no one had thought to take her back there.

As a child, she had been told nothing but the bare facts: that her mother had collapsed while out walking; that she had died the next day in the hospital. The headmistress had relayed this news. Iris had been told that she was too young to attend the funeral. Tears stung her eyes as she remembered that day, how she was expected to go to her lessons, to carry on as if nothing had happened.

Lowering her head, she breathed in the scent of the narcissus and winter jasmine. She might not know what she was looking for, but she would find a place to lay her flowers.

The light began to change as Tony was painting the view of the sea. When he'd started, the water had been a bright triangle of cobalt blue framed by the greens and browns and yellows of the moorland. But as fingers of mist crept across the hillside, the distant waves turned dove gray, and the edges of the land dissolved. He studied the changing vista through half-closed eyes. The mist gave everything an interesting shimmer, a spectral look. He could work with that.

He wiped the brush clean and wet it in the jar of water he'd set on a slab of granite. Applying it to the paper, he dabbed away at what he'd painted, removing color, trying to capture the otherworldly look of the landscape. But it wasn't easy to concentrate. Every so often, something would distract him. It might be a tiny flower, leaping out from the sheep-bitten grass to blind him with yellow or violet, or a giant rock on the edge of his field of vision, suddenly morphing into a lion, crouching, watching, waiting for a chance to tear him limb from limb.

He had learned to accept these momentary visual disturbances. Not hallucinations—he wouldn't call them that. More like amplifications of what was there in the landscape. His job as an artist was to filter what his mind was allowing him to see, to interpret the shapes and the shades and capture them in watercolor.

He was dipping his brush into a smear of China white when he caught a movement on the track farther down the hillside. Was it an animal? Or a person? The mist was thicker down there. All he had seen was a flash of copper gold. It could have been a fox—although it was unusual for foxes to be on the prowl in broad daylight. He looked again. Perhaps he'd been mistaken. No—there it was again. Through a momentary gap in the billowing veil of white he glimpsed the unmistakable shape of a woman. A woman with long red hair. Coming toward him, holding flowers, like a bride on her way to church . . . Stella. She was coming for him. Not a bride. A ghost.

He shook himself, sending spatters of white across the painting. It must be the mushrooms. She wasn't real. She *couldn't* be there.

When he looked again, the mist had swallowed whatever he thought he had seen.

CHAPTER 9

"What do you mean, I can't sign it?" Ellen looked up from the paperwork spread out on the desk in front of her.

"I'm afraid it has to be your husband's signature on the lease, Mrs. Wylde." The agent sat back in his chair, rubbing his chin on his knuckles.

"But it's *my* business, Mr. Hardy. My husband has nothing to do with it."

"I appreciate that, Mrs. Wylde, but it's the law. A married woman has to have her husband's permission to take on a rented property."

"That's ridiculous!" Ellen stood up. "Worse than that—it's insulting!"

"I don't disagree, Mrs. Wylde, but my hands are tied. Would you like to call your husband? You're welcome to use our telephone."

"I can't." Ellen struggled to control her voice. "Because—as you know—the cottage doesn't have a telephone!"

"I'm sorry—I forgot." He didn't look sorry. Merely impatient, Ellen thought. He reinforced her suspicion by drumming his fingers on the desk.

"I'll have to go and fetch him. And let me tell you, he won't be happy about having his whole day disrupted by something so . . . ," she tailed off, struggling to find a word to describe her utter frustration. She took a deep breath. It was wrong to take it out on this man. It wasn't his fault that this stupid law existed. But knowing that didn't make Ellen feel any less angry.

"I'll be back shortly," she said. "*If* I can locate him. And in the meantime, don't you dare offer this property to anyone else."

The day after the lease was signed, Ellen's tools and machinery arrived by train from London. The lathe, with its various attachments, had been taken apart for transportation. To put it back together was going to be a two-person job.

"I didn't think it would come so soon." Tony huffed out a sigh as he climbed into the jeep.

"Neither did I." Ellen released the handbrake and started down the track. "But the sooner I get set up, the sooner I can start earning." She flashed him a smile as she rounded a bend.

He smiled back. "Don't get me wrong—I'm not moaning. I just wish it wasn't such a lovely day."

Ellen knew that he would rather be outside painting. It was the perfect weather for it: sunny, mild, and not a breath of wind. If it had been raining or blowing a gale it wouldn't have mattered that he was going to be stuck indoors all day.

"I've been thinking about that new order from Harrods," she said. "I might have to hire an assistant if I'm going to meet the deadline." She waited a moment, wondering how he would respond. They'd already discussed their working arrangements. Tony had made it clear that he couldn't help her while he was developing his own career. It would be too much of a distraction. But she hadn't expected to receive this big new order so soon.

"How much would you have to pay someone? Would you still turn a profit?"

"Well, I'd have to make sure I did. I'd probably only need part-time help. Someone to do the sanding and the painting."

There was an uncomfortable silence after that. She wished she hadn't used the word *painting*. It sounded as though she was having a dig at him. She could have said *the finishing* instead.

It occurred to Ellen that she shouldn't have to be tiptoeing around him like this. But as the thought crossed her mind, she batted it away. He was an artist. Sensitive and temperamental. She had known that when she married him. It was the quirky, wild, fun-loving flipside that she'd fallen in love with. Was it possible to have that personality without a darker shadow side? She very much doubted it.

When they arrived at the station, the conversation about getting an assistant was forgotten as they addressed the task of transporting the equipment to the new premises. The shop was less than half a mile away, but it took nearly two hours and three separate journeys to shift everything. Even though the lathe had been taken apart, the components were too heavy to take in one go without wrecking the suspension on the jeep. Then there was the workbench, the tools, and the display units to transport.

"Shall I go and get us a sandwich or something?" Tony wiped beads of perspiration from his forehead as he hefted the band saw out of the back of the jeep.

"Would you?" Ellen blew out a breath as she reached for the axe and the box of chisels. "I'll go and find somewhere to park, and then I'll get the kettle on."

Ellen walked around her new workshop as she waited for the kettle to boil, working out where everything would go. The lathe and drill press would go against the longest wall, with the plane in the corner to the right of the rear window. The workbench would go on the other side of the room, and the finishing table would sit in the middle. A long wooden ladder led to a small attic space. She'd been up there when the agent brought her to see the place. It would make a useful storage area for planks.

When she'd made a pot of tea, she took her cup outside, to the little walled courtyard at the back of the row of shops. This would be where she would chop the planks into workable lengths. As she stood there she caught a waft of the most heavenly scent. Glancing over her shoulder, she saw that the back door to the florist's shop was ajar. It would be nice to have that smell when she was working outside. Not so nice, though, to see the comings and goings at the business on the other side: there was no evidence, out here, that it was a funeral parlor, other than the extra-large door giving out onto the courtyard. That must be the way the bodies were brought in and the coffins taken out. She wasn't sure how she would feel, witnessing that.

But you saw much worse during the war.

"Yes, Mum, I did," she murmured. Sometimes those images came back to her, usually in her sleep. The people lying among the rubble in the bombed-out shells of houses. Some had died as she had tried to get them into the ambulance. Others were already dead. The worst thing was stumbling across the bodies of children. If she lived to be a hundred, the memory of those faces would never leave her.

Draining her cup, she went back inside. Where was Tony? She wondered what could be keeping him so long.

She was arranging different-sized drill bits on a shelf when he came in from the street.

"Couldn't find anywhere selling sandwiches." He sounded breathless. "But I got us these instead."

Ellen could smell the contents of the brown paper bag that he laid on the workbench. "Mmm! What is it?"

"Cornish pasties. If you haven't had one, you haven't lived!"

Ellen slid one out of the bag. It was a lumpy pillow of pastry, shaped like a half moon, with crimped edges. It was still warm from the oven.

"Careful," Tony said as she went to take a bite. "It might be quite hot inside."

It was. But not hot enough to burn her tongue. She smiled at him over the crust of pastry, savoring the peppery, meaty taste of the filling. "Is it lamb?" she asked when she'd swallowed it down. "And what else? Potato? Carrots?"

"Mutton," he replied. "And there's swede in there as well as spuds and carrot." He took a big bite of his pasty. Some of the gravy escaped and trickled down the side of his chin. He laughed as he wiped it away with the back of his hand.

Ellen thought how happy he looked in that moment: her tall, handsome husband, with his hat perched at a crazy angle on his mop of brown hair and his blue eyes crinkling at the edges. She felt a glow of pride that this business of hers would contribute to his newfound happiness.

"Tea in the pot?" Tony poured himself a cup then took his pipe from his jacket pocket. "I'll just nip out for a smoke—then we'll put that lathe together."

She watched him go outside. Was his asthma troubling him again? If he was suffering, he hadn't said. Perhaps that was his way of coping— to cover up how he was feeling. She didn't know what was in the pipe— but it certainly seemed to help. She wondered if it would be available via the new National Health Service. She hoped so. Otherwise, he'd have to go back to his doctor in London when he needed a fresh supply.

It was a good thing that Ellen knew how to assemble the various parts of the lathe because Tony didn't know one end from the other. He wasn't much help, other than holding things in place while she tightened nuts and fixed the attachments into position. But it didn't take long. Soon everything was how she wanted it.

"I'm going to a timber yard tomorrow," she said, as she locked the door. "There's one just outside Truro."

"Will you be able to find it okay?" Clearly he wasn't keen on wasting another day.

"I've got the map."

As they set off down the street, someone called out Tony's name. It was a man, standing in the doorway of The Castle pub.

"Denis!" Tony waved and strode back along the cobbles, clapping the man on the back as he reached him. Ellen followed behind.

"Ellie, this is Denis Mitchell."

"Pleased to meet you." She held out her hand.

"So, this is the new Mrs. Wylde." The man smiled at her from behind thick, dark-rimmed spectacles.

Tony grunted. "I'd forgotten how quickly news travels in these parts." He gave Ellen a wry glance. "You can't cough around here without someone knowing."

Denis chuckled. "Barbara told me. Although I have to say, she didn't do you justice."

Ellen felt the color rise to her face.

"How about a drink?" Denis cocked his head toward the dark interior of the pub. "It's a couple of hours until opening time, but Endell won't mind."

Tony arched his eyebrows as he turned to Ellen. "Denis's brother's the landlord."

"Oh, that would be lovely, but . . ." She hesitated, glancing at her watch. "What about that man who's coming to look at the roof of the cowshed?"

"Damn—I'd forgotten about that."

"Well, why don't you stay and have a drink? I can go and talk to the roofer."

"Are you sure?" Tony brightened. "I could get the bus back."

Ellen watched them disappear inside the pub. She didn't begrudge Tony an afternoon of drinking with his old friend after the work he'd put in for her. But, once again, she was left with the unsettling feeling that he had this whole other life that was a complete mystery to her.

———

There was a van parked outside the cottage when Ellen got back. As she climbed out of the jeep, she saw a shadow glide across the garden wall. It looked as if the roofer was already in the back garden, sizing up the repair job.

"Hello," she called as she walked around the side of the cottage. She saw that he had put a ladder up against the cowshed. Was he on the roof? She couldn't see him. Perhaps he'd gone into the shed to look at the damage from inside. The light was on in there—she could see the naked bulb through the window. Peering around the door, she saw that the man was crouching on the floor, looking at something. When she coughed to announce her presence, he jumped up, his hand flying to his chest.

He blew out a breath as she pushed the door open. "Yer scared me to death, missus."

"I didn't mean to startle you."

He was a big man, tall and sturdy. He didn't look the type to frighten easily. She could see a dark shape near his left foot. Had he found a dead rat? "I'm sorry for being late." She took a step forward. "I had to go into St Ives this morning."

"It's all right." He shook his head, like a dog shedding water. "It weren't your fault. 'Sthis thing 'ere put the wind up me." He nudged the lump on the floor with the toe of his boot, sending it skidding toward her. To Ellen's horror, she saw that it was the doll she'd found up the chimney.

"'Swhat they call a mommet, ain't it?"

"A mommet?" She searched his face. His eyes were full of suspicion. "I . . . I don't know. I found it up the chimney. I was trying to get the fire going, and it fell out. I thought my husband had got rid of it." Why had Tony kept it? She thought he'd thrown it on the fire.

The man nodded slowly. "Up the chimney. That'd be right. Ugly bugger, ain't it?"

"It's horrible," she said, nodding. "I think my husband must have been planning to burn it with the rubbish from in here." That would be it. Tony must have brought it in here to get it out of the way. He'd said he was going to build a bonfire in the garden once everything was cleared out.

"They made 'em to curse folk in the old days." The man rubbed his chin with the heel of his hand.

Ellen felt as if a breath of icy wind had blown against the back of her neck.

"I've come across one or two in my time," he went on. "In old 'ouses—up chimneys. Not like this, though. Ain't never seen 'un with a crow skull for an 'ead."

Ellen bit her lip. "My husband thought it was a weird piece of art. He said artists used to come here—before the war—and that maybe one of them had put it up the chimney. As a joke, I think he meant."

"Don't know 'bout that." The man folded his arms across his chest. "But I do know summat bad 'appened here round that time."

"Bad?" Fear surged from the pit of her stomach.

"A woman died after visitin' the cottage one night. They found 'er on the moor next day. Down there." He jerked his thumb in the direction of the track. "She weren't dead then, but she passed away in the 'ospital not long after."

"Wh . . . what happened?" Iris could hear the tremor in her voice. "Did she fall?" It wasn't hard to imagine someone having an accident, walking down the track at night.

"Nobody knows. But you know 'ow people talk. They said the folks as used to live 'ere were . . . well . . . a bit odd. They reckoned summat 'appened that scared this woman, and she ran off into the night." He hesitated, looking at her, weighing up the impact of what he'd said. "I'm sorry—I don't want to frighten yer, missus. It's just gossip. Nothin' in it, I don't s'pose."

Questions clamored inside her head. What had gone on in the cottage to make people say such things? Who was the woman, and when had she died? Was this tragic event the reason for the place lying empty all these years? She opened her mouth, but no words came out. The man was on the move now, pulling a chair across to where the sky showed through the roof, poking at the edges of the metal, sending down a shower of rust that glinted copper-gold as it fell to the ground.

You don't belong here.

She whipped her head around. The voice had been so clear she could have sworn someone was standing right behind her. But there was no one there. Just the door of the cowshed, moving gently in the breeze.

───◆───

It was beginning to get dark when the roofer left. Somehow Ellen had kept her business head on, discussing what it would take to make the shed sound, and agreeing on a price for the number of hours the work was likely to take. But it had felt as though she were outside her own body, listening to someone else speaking. Her mind had been swarming with what he'd told her—a picture of the dying woman, unconscious, helpless, slumped on the cold, damp ground, filling her mind's eye.

Inside the cottage she stood at the window, watching the van disappear into the twilight. Why hadn't she asked him more about what he'd heard? What had made her so incapable of putting her questions into words? She closed her eyes, remembering the voice that had sounded so clear, so real, in the cowshed. A man's voice. But nothing like the gentle Cornish lilt of the roofer. There had been a harsh, sibilant quality to it. And the accent was distinctly upper-class.

Ellen gripped the window ledge, afraid to open her eyes. Was it the ghost of someone who once lived here, hissing out a warning? Had she disturbed something when that box had come tumbling out of the chimney?

For heaven's sake, girl—get a grip!

It was a mercy to hear her mother's voice this time. Using that stern tone she always resorted to in times of crisis.

Ghosts! She could picture her mother rolling her eyes. *You're not going to let codswallop like that get to you, I hope!*

Ellen opened her eyes. Her face stared back at her, reflected in the windowpane. She reached for the curtains and yanked them shut. The force of the movement made the lining of one of them rip. She clicked her tongue against the roof of her mouth. Number five hundred and twenty on the list of things to do: make new curtains. But she wasn't going to think about that now. Because something had occurred to her. Tony had a box under the bed where he kept all the paperwork relating to the house. There might be something in there—some clue as to what had led to the cottage being abandoned.

Upstairs, she sat on the bed and spread the contents of the box across the eiderdown. The deeds to the cottage were there. Tony was supposed to have deposited them at the bank, but he hadn't done it yet. She cast her eyes over the first page, which was handwritten in elegant copperplate script with flourishes of red ink on each capital letter. It said that Carreg Cottage had been built in 1785 on land belonging to Rowan Tree Farm. That big place by the road was called Rowan Tree House. Had it once been a farmhouse? She turned over the page. The cottage had been owned by various members of a family called Trelithick until 1927, when it had been inherited by a married daughter by the name of Stella Winifred Bird. The final page of the deeds revealed that the transfer of the property to Tony had been signed by a Mr. Lionel Bird—presumably that woman's husband.

Tony hadn't mentioned Mr. and Mrs. Bird. But he seemed to know about the tenant who had lived in the cottage before the war. Mr. Crowley. Ellen rifled through the other papers on the bed. She soon found what she was looking for. There was a final demand for an unpaid electricity bill, dated June 3, 1938. The name on it was Mr. A. Crowley. The paper was yellowed and stained. She lifted it to her nose and grimaced. It smelt faintly of mice.

Laying it down again, she saw that the telephone number of the electricity company had been circled in pencil. Tony must have found it lying around and kept it so he could contact them to get the cottage reconnected. She stared at the date on the bill. It suggested that the cottage had been vacated by then. But why had Mr. and Mrs. Bird allowed the electricity to be cut off? Why had no new tenant been found for

Carreg Cottage? Was it because of the war? In June 1938, that had been more than a year away—so it seemed unlikely.

Ellen gathered up the papers and replaced them in the box. Tony should be on his way back by now, on the bus. He would have to walk up the track, in the dark. She should drive down there and pick him up. After shoving the box under the bed, she went downstairs and grabbed her keys from the hook on the wall. She wouldn't repeat what the roofer had told her. That would invite more irritated comments about her letting her imagination run away with her. But she was determined to find out what had happened here in that last year before the war—because she suspected that Tony knew more than he was letting on.

She told herself that he was probably just trying to protect her—as any good husband would. He knew what she'd sacrificed to come here with him, and he didn't want her getting upset by things she didn't need to know about. But she *did* need to know. Making this place a home wasn't just about sweeping away a few cobwebs and running up new curtains: it had to *feel* right. And until she could make sense of what had gone on at Carreg Cottage, she feared that it never would.

CHAPTER 10

Iris was stitching a hook-and-eye fastening onto the back of the dress she was making when she caught a whiff of smoke. At first, she thought it was coming from the stove in the corner of the room, but when she went to inspect it, she found no flicker of life in the embers of last night's fire. Opening the window, she realized the smell was coming from outside. There was a definite tinge of fish. The smoker must be going in the cellar downstairs.

Folding her dress carefully, she put it into the empty suitcase under the bed. Hopefully that would protect it. She didn't want to arrive at the party tonight stinking of kippers. Then she grabbed her coat and headed for the door.

Her morning routine was to walk through town, looking in all the shop windows, in the hope of finding an advertisement for a job. In the past few days she'd called at the cafés, too—the ones that were not closed up for winter—but there was nothing going in any of them.

As she crossed Norway Square, she spotted a couple of men putting a banner in place above the door of the Mariners' Church. She paused to read what it said. *The Crypt Art Exhibition: January 1–14.* That must be the event Dan had told her about. It would be something interesting to go to tomorrow.

The shops in Fore Street offered no glimmer of hope. She turned up the hill, into Tregenna Place, lingering in front of the window of Lake's Art and Literature. There was a set of watercolor paints on display that she coveted. They came in a little wooden case with a handle—perfect for carrying when painting outdoors. And next to the paints was a folding easel. The combined cost was fifteen shillings. She'd promised herself she'd buy it once she started earning. She let out a sigh as she turned away from the window. Right now, that seemed like a very distant prospect.

There weren't so many shops at this end of the town. There was a public library on the corner and a post office, but after that the buildings were mostly houses. The shop opposite Lake's had an unusual sign hanging above it. It was a picture of a hare looking up at a full moon. The name of the shop curved around the animal's feet: "The Botanic Store." Iris crossed the road and glanced in the window. It contained bottles and jars of all shapes and sizes. It seemed to be a place that sold herbal teas and remedies for various ailments. The only card on display was an advertisement for a mobile hairdressing service.

She crossed back over the road and went into the library—but the noticeboard in the foyer was devoted to news of local societies and sporting events. As she made her way back down the hill, she saw a woman emerge from the door of the herb shop with a bucket in her hand. Her gray hair was fastened into a bun above a turquoise scarf that was tied bandana-style around her head. There was something about her profile that stopped Iris in her tracks. It was Mrs. Richards. The housekeeper at Rowan Tree House. The woman who had made treacle sponge and lemon meringue pie and taught her how to boil an egg so that the yolk came out runny instead of hard.

Iris ducked into the entrance of Lake's. After a moment, she peered out. Mrs. Richards had her back to her now, cleaning the shop window. Thinking she was safe, Iris snuck out of her hiding place. But as she started walking, she heard the woman cry out.

"Missus Bird! Stella!"

Iris put her head down and didn't look up until she'd turned the corner into Fore Street. She didn't see the owner of The Botanic Store come out into the street as Mrs. Richards stood clutching her chest.

Nor did she hear the woman swear she'd seen a ghost reflected in the shop window.

Ellen studied her reflection in the bedroom mirror. It was the outfit she'd worn for their first date: a knee-length cocktail dress in midnight-blue crepe with a pleated skirt and a keyhole bow-tie neck. She thought that if it was all right for a London jazz club, it should be suitable for Barbara Hepworth's party.

"Will this do?" She stood at the foot of the stairs. Tony was standing at the sink, cleaning brushes. He'd spent all day outdoors while she'd been driving around Truro, trying to find the timber merchant. He'd been so preoccupied when he came back for tea, he seemed to have forgotten all about the party.

"Hmm?" He glanced over his shoulder. "Yes—lovely." He turned back to his brushes. "You'd better bring something warm to put on later, though. Barbara said we could crash in the attic—and it's like an icebox in winter."

"I didn't realise we were staying the night."

"It'll be better, won't it? You said you don't like driving when you've had a drink—and it'd be a shame not to let your hair down on New Year's Eve."

Ellen couldn't argue with that—although the thought of waking up in Barbara's house didn't exactly fill her with undiminished joy. She went back upstairs and put a nightdress, a sweater, slacks, and thick socks in a bag.

It was after eight o'clock when they set off. Tony said there was no point getting there too early. As she pulled off the track onto the road, she asked him if he knew who lived at Rowan Tree House.

"I don't," he replied. "I think it's probably a holiday place. There's no sign of life there."

"That's what I thought," she said. "Has it always been like that? When you used to visit before the war, I mean?"

For a moment, he was silent. "I think so. I didn't take much notice. I guess it's owned by some swanky London family—the type that has a mansion in Sloane Square and decamps to Cornwall for the summer." He gave her a sideways glance. "Why do you ask?"

"Oh—I just thought it would be nice to have some neighbours." She tried to make her voice light. "Not that I'm complaining," she added quickly. "It's wonderful to have that view, and no one around to see you. The garden's going to be glorious when the weather's a bit warmer."

"I knew you'd love it." He reached across the gear stick and squeezed her knee.

Ten minutes later they were descending the steep hill into St Ives. Barbara Hepworth and Ben Nicholson lived on the outskirts of the town, in a house overlooking Carbis Bay. To reach it, you had to drive through the center and head south.

"Oh, good—we're not the first here," Tony said, as Ellen pulled up behind a row of cars parked in the drive.

It was Barbara's husband who greeted them at the door. He was a small, wiry man of about fifty. He wore a navy-blue beret—at an angle that revealed a scalp as smooth and shiny as a billiard ball. Tony had explained that his surname was not Hepworth but Nicholson. Barbara had retained her maiden name in her professional life.

"Pleased to meet you." His hand felt cold and rather clammy as it closed over Ellen's. "Let me get you a drink."

They were ushered into a room full of people.

"Rum punch?" Ben was looking at Tony. "I warn you—it's pretty lethal. How about you, Ellen?"

"She'll have a rum punch, too, won't you?" Tony didn't give her time to reply. "Go on." He turned to her and winked. "Get into the party spirit!"

"Okay." Ellen nodded. "I've never tried rum—but I'll give it a go."

While they waited for their drinks, Tony spotted someone he knew on the other side of the room. "That's Clive," he said. "I'll just go and say hello. Won't be a minute."

Ellen felt like a spare part, standing on her own in a roomful of strangers. She looked at the walls, which were painted a daring shade of red. Paintings and drawings hung in carefully arranged groups. They were abstracts in vivid colors. Ben's work, presumably. Tony had told her that he was a painter well known on the British art scene—and that there was a certain amount of rivalry between husband and wife because Barbara was now becoming more famous than him.

"Drinks!" Ben appeared with two glasses. "Where's he gone? Not lost him already, have you?" He handed her drink over and went off to find Tony.

Ellen took a sip of the rum. It tasted like fruit juice—not at all what she'd been expecting. As she lowered the glass, she caught sight of a woman standing by the fireplace on her own. She was wearing the most unusual outfit—like a fancy-dress costume. Her long gown was of a sparkly silver fabric, low cut, with fluffy ball-shaped buttons down the front. On her head was a pork pie hat of the same silver material, adorned with a life-sized crab's claw—painted to match the hat and studded with glittering gemstones. Her hair was cut in an angular style and was dyed bright orange. In her hand was a long, silver-tipped cigarette holder.

Ellen looked at the floor, trying to avoid staring—but it was hard not to. Then she saw that the woman was coming over. Ellen took another gulp of rum. The woman had large pale green eyes, like opals, her lids outlined in smoky-gray pencil. The look on her face was challenging—almost insolent.

"Hello. You must be Tony's wife." She stretched out a hand heavy with rings. Her red-painted fingernails matched her lips. "I'm Nina. Old girlfriend—with the emphasis on the *old*." The crimson mouth curved up at the edges. "Did he tell you about me? No . . . don't suppose he did."

Ellen felt blood pulsing in her neck, surging to her cheeks. His *girl-friend?* She had never kidded herself that Tony had lived the life of a monk until he met her—but to meet one of his ex-lovers in the flesh . . . The features of the woman standing in front of her began to blur as lurid images flashed into Ellen's mind.

"I hear you've moved into the Crowley House." Nina sucked on the cigarette holder and let out a curl of smoke. "He always said he wanted to buy it—but I never thought he would."

Ellen's eyes snapped back into focus. If she had to talk to this woman, at least she could pump her for information. "I keep hearing people call it that. Who was this man, Crowley?"

Nina grunted. "I suppose you're too young to remember him. He was quite a celebrity twenty years ago—for all the wrong reasons. The papers had an absolute field day with him. They called him the Wickedest Man in the World. The Beast 666."

Ellen shook her head, bemused. "Why? What did he do?"

"What *didn't* he do, darling!" Nina rolled her eyes. "He was a disciple of the dark arts. Witchcraft—that sort of thing. He looked like a charming old gentleman—and he loved a good party—but you wouldn't want to get on the wrong side of him."

"You knew him?"

"Not very well. I went to some of the gatherings he had up at the cottage. They were great fun—but I wasn't really interested in the witchy stuff. He wanted to sleep with me—I mean, he wanted to sleep with *everyone*—but I didn't want to be one of his scarlet women." She took another drag on her cigarette and blew out a plume of smoke. "That's what *he* called them. If you hooked up with him, you were expected to assist with his magic rituals." She shrugged. "I didn't like that. I saw it as a form of control—which is something I've always resisted. It's why I've never married." She put a bejeweled hand on Ellen's arm. "Sorry, darling—that wasn't meant to be a dig. I'm sure you and Tony will be blissfully happy."

Ellen felt as if her tongue had glued itself to the roof of her mouth. What Nina had revealed was shocking. Explosive. It was too much to take in. She glanced toward the door. Where had Tony gone? She felt someone touch her shoulder.

"Sorry to butt in." It was Barbara Hepworth. "Can I introduce Dan to you, Ellen? He's one of my assistants, and he's also a potter. And this is . . ." Barbara turned to the girl standing beside him. "Sorry, dear, I've forgotten your name."

"Iris."

The girl looked awkward, as if she were embarrassed to be thrust into the company of people she didn't know. She was very pretty, with long red hair and eyes that were green, like Nina's, but a deeper shade. She was wearing a halter-neck dress in shimmering blue and mauve that hugged her slim body.

"Can I leave you youngsters to chat?" Barbara took Nina by the arm. "You know, I haven't had a drink yet? Ben's running around like a blue-arsed fly, looking after everyone else—but I haven't had so much as a sniff of that rum punch!"

"Can I get you a top-up?" Dan smiled at Ellen. He had very intense eyes—the color of ebony—and smooth bronze skin. "Barbara said you're new here—like Iris." He reached for Ellen's glass and disappeared into the crowd.

Ellen wanted to go looking for Tony. Nina's words burned inside her head. But politeness demanded that she make small talk with this girl—at least until her boyfriend returned with the drinks. "Where are you from, Iris?"

"Hampshire." Iris gave a nervous-looking smile. "How about you?"

"London." Despite her mounting impatience, Ellen felt a twinge of sympathy for her. She looked barely out of her teens. At that age, talking to strangers had always made Ellen break out into a sweat. "It's a bit different down here, isn't it?" She gave Iris a wry look. "I've only been here a week. I don't really know anybody." She paused. "What do you think of St Ives?"

"I love it here." The green eyes widened. "But I didn't realise how hard it would be to find a job—in winter, I mean."

"What do you do?"

"Well, I want to study art, but I need to get part-time work to keep me going."

Ellen nodded. She wondered what kind of home Iris had left behind in Hampshire. Were her parents still living? It sounded as though she wasn't getting any financial support from them. Perhaps the boyfriend was the reason for her moving so far away rather than going to art school in London.

Before she could frame another question, Dan reappeared with the drinks.

Afterward, Ellen couldn't remember how she got to the point of offering Iris a day's trial. She had a vague memory of scribbling down the address of the workshop on the back of a paper napkin. The next thing she recalled was linking arms with Dan and Iris to sing "Auld Lang Syne" and wondering why Tony wasn't there to let in the New Year. She didn't know how long after that he'd reappeared. She had the impression that not many of the guests were still there. She remembered that he'd brought her a glass of whisky—and she'd said she wanted punch, but he'd said there was none left.

He must have carried her up to the attic because she had no memory of climbing the stairs. And he must have undressed her, because she had woken sometime in the small hours, freezing cold, and discovered that she was naked under the blanket he'd pulled over them.

Ellen woke up with the morning sun shining directly into her eyes. The curtains were open. For a moment, she couldn't work out where she was. Her head throbbed, as if wild horses were stampeding inside her skull. She groaned and turned over.

Tony was unconscious beside her, his head on the pillow. As she lay there, images from the party came flooding back. That woman. Nina. With the brazen pale green eyes. She had been Tony's lover; had lain beside him, like this. When? Before the war? During the war? And how long had it lasted? Had Tony wanted to marry Nina? Had she turned him down?

Ellen forced herself to sit up. The movement made her feel sick. Water. She needed water. She reached for the crumpled frock lying on the floor beside the mattress. Then she realized she was already dressed. Somehow, when she'd woken up frozen in the middle of the night, she must have found the extra clothes she'd brought in the bag.

As she scrambled to her feet, another gaggle of images crowded her mind's eye. That man. Crowley. The things Nina had said about him. *He was a disciple of the dark arts.* Ellen shuddered as she thought of the gruesome doll—the mommet—made to curse people, according to the roofer. *You wouldn't want to get on the wrong side of him.* Nina's voice echoed inside her head.

Slowly, clutching the banister, Ellen made her way downstairs. Through the landing window she caught a glimpse of the sea. It shimmered, peacock blue, in the morning sun. The sight of it brought another snapshot of last night to mind: a girl in a dress that same color. What was her name? A flower. Rose? No—Iris.

Ellen remembered feeling pleased with herself when she'd written down the address of her new premises and handed it over to the girl. Without even having to advertise, she'd found an assistant. What on earth had she been thinking of? She knew nothing about Iris—other than that she'd come to St Ives to study art. Just because the girl wanted to be an artist didn't mean she'd be any good at painting toys. Ellen blew out a breath. She would have to go through with it now. If Iris proved to be hopeless, it was going to be awkward and embarrassing. The rum punch was to blame. If only she hadn't had that second glass.

Ellen found her way to the kitchen. Barbara was sitting at the table, smoking a cigarette.

"Morning." The voice sounded croaky. "There's coffee in the pot if you want some."

"Thank you. I think I'll just have water." Ellen rinsed out one of the dirty glasses standing next to the sink and filled it from the tap.

"Feeling a bit delicate?" Barbara grunted a laugh. "Have a cigarette." She pushed a pack of Senior Service across the table.

"It's okay, thanks—I don't smoke."

"Don't you? I couldn't face the day without a ciggy first thing. I come down here because Ben can't stand me puffing away in the bedroom."

"He doesn't smoke?"

"No. He suffers from asthma."

"Oh?" Ellen took a sip of water. "Tony does too. But he still likes a cigarette."

"He's a bit of a closed book, our Tony, isn't he?" Barbara flicked ash into her saucer. "All those times he came to stay during the war, he never mentioned having asthma."

Our Tony. Ellen bristled inside. But she mustn't react; mustn't be rude to her hostess. "It was why he couldn't serve in the armed forces," she said. Surely Barbara knew that? She paused, but there was no response. "He's started taking something recently," she went on. "Something herbal. He puts it in a pipe. It seems to help. Perhaps Ben should try it?"

Barbara released a curl of smoke that wafted across the table. Her eyes, small and birdlike, glinted with something like amusement. "Hmm. Perhaps he should."

⟞⟝

The daylight was fading when they left the house at Carbis Bay. Ben had insisted on them all going for a walk along the beach—to blow away the cobwebs, as he'd put it. It had turned into a five-mile round trip, with a stop for sketching the view of the Godrevy lighthouse.

There had been no chance to talk to Tony. She'd had to wait until they were inside the jeep. Ellen drew in a long breath as she released the handbrake. There were so many questions. She needed to be careful. He was tired and hungover. If she went in too hard, he might lose his temper.

"I had an interesting chat with Nina last night," she began.

"Oh? I didn't realise she was there."

Hardly surprising, as you disappeared for half the night. She didn't say what she was thinking. Could he really have failed to notice Nina, though? She must have arrived before they did. Had he said it to make her think that Nina meant nothing to him?

"She seemed to know quite a bit about the cottage," Ellen went on. "She said she went to parties there before the war." She paused, dangling the hook, waiting for him to take the bait. But he remained silent, his face angled away from her, looking out at the darkening landscape. "How did you get to know her? Was it in London?" It sounded innocent enough, not like an accusation.

"Yes. She was exhibiting at the big surrealists' show in '36. Everyone at the Slade went to see it. I liked her work, and we got talking."

How ironic, Ellen thought, that he and Nina had met at an art exhibition—just as she had met Tony more than a decade later. And even more ironic that Ellen had visited that same show herself, as a teenager. She must have seen Nina's work, unaware that her future husband had been looking at it, too—drawn not just to the art, but to the woman who had created it.

"How did she come to be living in St Ives?" Ellen was struggling to keep her voice matter-of-fact.

"I think it was because of the war. Like Ben and Barbara, you know? She was afraid of the bombs."

"And she decided to stay?"

"Well, who wouldn't?"

Were you there with her, at those parties, before the war? The question hammered inside her head. "Is that how you discovered the cottage? Did Nina tell you about it?" Ellen held her breath.

"We used to go for walks to Zennor Carn—Barbara and Ben and the whole gang. It was empty by then." He took a cigarette from his jacket pocket. "We sometimes peered in through the windows." It was an evasive answer—neither confirming nor denying what Ellen had asked.

"She said you'd always wanted to buy it," Ellen persisted. "But she never thought you would."

"Did she?" He struck a match. Ellen glanced sideways as the flare lit up his face. His expression was unreadable.

What does it matter if she was his girlfriend? Her mother's voice piped up, loud and insistent. *You're the one he married.* There was no question about that. But what she really wanted to know was whether there was still something between them. Was that why he'd been so keen to come to Cornwall? Had she been a complete fool?

Good heavens, my girl—first you suspect Barbara and now this Nina. And you've only been married a week!

Yes, she thought, *I'm putting two and two together and making five.* Tony would say she was letting her imagination run away with her— just as he had when she'd asked if he thought the cottage might be haunted. But what if he'd been there, with Nina, when what she'd called the witchy stuff was going on? And what if there was a connection between those gatherings and the death of the woman the roofer had told her about?

To press Tony about any of it would surely trigger an almighty row. The best course of action was to stick to her plan, to find things out for herself without him knowing what she was up to. It wasn't how married couples were supposed to behave. There were not meant to be any secrets between them. But there was no other choice if this marriage was going to work. And that was what she wanted more than anything.

CHAPTER 11

Iris unfolded the paper napkin and laid it out on the blanket. She sat for a moment, just looking at it, as she sipped the cup of tea she'd brought back to bed. She hadn't dreamt it. That woman at the party really had offered her a job. Ellen Wylde. The name was written above the address. And the date and time she wanted Iris to report for work was scribbled underneath. The second of January at nine thirty a.m. That was tomorrow morning.

Iris hugged the bedclothes to her body. What great good luck to have found something after almost a week of traipsing the streets of St Ives to no avail. And it wasn't just any job. Ellen had said it would involve painting and finishing wooden toys. She would be making things. She could hardly wait for tomorrow to come.

Dan had been almost as excited as she was. He didn't know Ellen Wylde, but his friend Denis had said that he knew her husband. Dan had whisked her off for a celebratory dance—and, when midnight came, he had kissed her. It meant nothing, of course: he had kissed all the women who had joined in the singing of "Auld Lang Syne." But he had kissed her on the lips and the others on the cheek. She hadn't been too tipsy to notice that.

His father had arrived soon afterward to drive them home. Iris had thought how good he was, turning out so late. Dan had said he had to be up late anyway, to take midnight Mass at St Ia's. Reverend Thomas took her all the way to Norway Square—even though she'd said she could walk home from the vicarage. Dan had given her a hopeless sort of look as she climbed out of the car. Had he planned on walking her home? She didn't know. He'd wound down the window and called after her. *See you on Sunday.* Was he just being polite—or was it his way of conveying that he wanted to see her, without giving anything away to his father?

After a late breakfast of soft-boiled eggs, Iris opened the door and sniffed the air. No hint of fish being smoked today. That was a relief. The air felt mild enough not to need a coat.

Half an hour later she made her way across the square to the Mariners' Church. The art exhibition was downstairs, in the crypt. An elegantly dressed woman with perfectly coifed gray hair was sitting at the entrance. She had a name badge pinned beneath the fur collar of her jacket. Lady Frieda Harris. Iris felt rather intimidated. She hadn't expected to be a greeted by a member of the aristocracy. But the woman was very welcoming. She told Iris that there was no admission charge, but visitors were asked to sign a book as a record of the interest the show generated.

Iris hesitated. She could hardly turn around and walk out. That would look suspicious. She took the pen and wrote *Birch* in the column for surname. There was a space marked "address" beside it. She filled it in, thinking that there was no point trying to avoid it. Ellen Wylde was sure to want all her details when she started work tomorrow. She was just going to have to get used to telling people some of the truth, if not all of it.

Iris handed the book back. But before she walked away, she remembered something. She'd meant to ask Dan last night, but it had slipped her mind. "Could I ask a question?"

The woman looked up. "Of course."

"I'm interested in attending classes at the School of Painting. Do you happen to know when it's due to reopen?"

"Yes—it's next Wednesday. The first session is a life class, in the evening. The principal will be there, so if you go along, you can register for other classes, too."

"Thank you." Iris walked away with a glow of anticipation.

The first thing in the room to catch her eye was a collection of sculptures by Dan's boss, Barbara Hepworth. Iris had met her only briefly last night. The look on her face when Dan had introduced them had made her feel as though she'd stepped in something unpleasant and brought it into the house.

The central sculpture was a baby, larger than life, sleek and dark, with the curved, flowing lines of something that might have come from the ocean—like a seal or an otter. Its chubby arms were raised, as if it longed to be picked up. The card beneath said that it was called *Infant*, and the material was Burmese wood. Iris gasped when she saw the price.

Next to it was an abstract piece entitled *Landscape*. To Iris, it looked like a large fruit bowl with a hole in it, and strings, like a harp's, stretched across its length. The card revealed that it was made of elm and was even more expensive than the wooden baby.

Farther away, on a table in the center of the room, a flash of gold caught her eye. At first sight, it looked like the head of a mannequin from a display in a shop window. As she drew closer, Iris saw that the head had been gilded and encrusted in hundreds of tiny pink shells, like a child's fingernails. It was called *Dreams of Aphrodite*, and the name of the artist was Nina Grey. Dan had pointed her out at the party. She'd been wearing the most incredible outfit, like a mermaid crossed with a clown. This was the woman whose name Iris had seen on the poster outside the School of Painting. Dan had offered to introduce them, but Barbara Hepworth had whisked Nina away before he'd had the chance.

Moving on, Iris spotted a group of paintings of boats. She smiled when she saw the name of the artist. Denis Mitchell. They were very good. And yet he had told her what a struggle it was to make a living from his work.

At the far end of the room was a group of three paintings, all the same size, arranged on easels. It was the colors that attracted Iris. The one in the center was a delicate composition of blues, greens, and creams, while the canvasses on either side were a riot of vivid reds and golden yellows. They were very different from Denis Mitchell's work. The middle one featured two Egyptian figures with the heads of dogs, each standing in front of a dark tower, like a lighthouse. They appeared to be guarding a beam of light dotted with strange symbols. Beneath their feet was a large beetle with a pale yellow disc held in its antennae. At the base of the painting was a white rectangle with the words *The Moon* inside it.

The image to the left of it was entitled *Lust*. Iris's eyes widened as she took it in. A naked woman with long red hair sat astride a creature like a lion. The woman was leaning back, one arm raised, in a way that could only be described as lascivious. At the tip of the lion's tail was the head of a snake, its fangs bared, hovering above the woman as if ready to bite. And the head of the lion was made up of many different faces, some human, some animal.

Iris stood, transfixed by the image. It seemed to exude a peculiar, hypnotic power. The composition and the use of color were exquisite— but there was something deeply unsettling about it.

She stepped back and turned her attention to the third painting in the group. This one was entitled *Princess of Wands*. A towering wave of yellow curved across a scarlet sky. Tumbling down the wave was a tiger, falling headfirst, and dragging with it a naked woman, posed like a leaping dancer. The tiger's tail was wrapped around the neck of the woman, who clutched a wand in one outstretched hand.

What did it mean? And what was the link between these three, very different, paintings? Iris glanced around, spotting something on a table nearby. It turned out to be a large explanatory notice, which had toppled over and now lay flat. "An Exhibition of Playing Cards: The Tarot (Book of Thoth)."

So, they were designs for Tarot cards. Iris's father had a pack—kept on a high shelf in his study. When she was about seven, she had climbed on a chair and reached for them, curious to know if they were like the set of Happy Families cards she'd received for Christmas. Her father had been furious when he'd found her. He'd said they were not to be touched—especially by children. He'd given the impression that there was something dangerous about them—like the bottles of pills locked up in the medicine cabinet in the bathroom.

There was another, smaller section of typescript farther down the exhibition notice: "Three of seventy-eight paintings by Lady Frieda Harris." Iris stared at the name. Wasn't that the woman at the door? She glanced back over her shoulder. But there was a man greeting the visitors now. Lady Frieda Harris had disappeared.

She turned back to the notice. There was an explanation of the meanings of the images, beginning with *The Princess of Wands*. This card, it said, symbolized a unique individual, a nonconformist, often something of a bohemian. "Independent by nature, and perhaps a mischief-maker, this person would rather go as a peasant among strangers than inherit a fortune." She couldn't help seeing herself in this description—although her father and stepmother probably had her down as something far worse than a mischief-maker.

The significance of *The Moon* was rather more sinister. "This card is a warning," the text read. "Not all is as it appears. It indicates that there is falseness, trickery, or double-dealing in your sphere of influence. This may be in relation to those around you, or internal, psychical."

Her eyes traveled down to the final paragraph, on the image called *Lust*: "Determination and ferocity of will. This card signals power from within. It heralds the act of discovery and indicates a primal strength."

Determination. Iris held on to that word as she made her way out. Was that why she had been so taken by that particular image, because it symbolized the quality she had most needed in order to embark upon this new life?

As she stepped out into the daylight, she couldn't help thinking that the artist had been trying to convey more than that—a message that couldn't be printed for fear of causing offense. *Unbridled passion. Sexual desire. Doomed love.* Those were the phrases that lodged themselves in her mind as she made her way back across the square.

⟶

Iris spent the afternoon sitting on a bench on the quayside. On this first day of a new year, it felt good to be out in the fresh air, on the brink of an unknown future. Like explorers of old, putting out to sea without knowing what lay beyond the horizon.

She sat for a long time, watching the ocean, noting the shapes of the waves and the way the light changed the color of the water. Although it was midwinter, the turquoise shimmer of the bay gave her the feeling that she had somehow slipped through the seasons into a summer's day. It wasn't just the sight of the sea, but the smell of it—that sharp, briny tang with the lemony hint of seaweed. And the sounds: the gentle swish of the waves as they lapped the sand and the mewing of the gulls as they swooped for what the fishermen tossed aside.

Her fingers traced the outline of the bench, feeling the grain of the wood. No wonder this place was a magnet for artists. It had an ethereal, bewitching quality that made you want to capture it and keep it forever. She could have gone back and collected her sketchbook, but she chose not to. Someone might walk by and peer over her shoulder. Could she ever handle that? Certainly not now, not yet.

Later she sat on the bed in her room, committing what she'd seen to paper. She only had pencils, but soon she would be able to buy that set of watercolors she'd seen in the shop in town. And hopefully, once she started taking classes at the School of Painting, she'd have the confidence to work outdoors.

As she recreated images of waves, a strange thing happened. The flowing shapes took on a life of their own. Animals and human figures started to appear on the page. A roaring lion, with a naked woman on its back. And a plummeting tiger, pulling the Princess of Wands to her doom.

She was so lost in what she was doing that she didn't hear the door at first. It was only when the knocking got louder that she realized someone was outside. She jumped off the bed and drew back the bolt.

"Dan!"

He was standing on the top step, holding her red scarf in his hand.

"Sorry to disturb you—but you left this in Dad's car last night. I thought you might need it."

She hadn't realized. The weather had been mild enough to go without the usual paraphernalia of coat, gloves, and scarf. As she took it from him, her fingers brushed his. A hot, tingling sensation shot up her arm and down into her belly. "Thank you." She opened the door wider. "Would you like a cup of tea?"

She gathered up her work before he had time to see it. As she put the kettle on, they talked about the party. He asked her what she'd thought of Barbara Hepworth.

"Well, she's very . . ." Iris hesitated, not wanting to say anything disrespectful about Dan's boss. "I got the impression that people are in awe of her. She's the queen bee, isn't she?"

"She certainly is!" He blew out a breath. "We're all terrified of her."

"I saw some of her work today. At the exhibition over at the church."

"What did you think?"

"I've never seen anything quite like it. I liked the piece called *Infant*. The way the wood was carved—the sleekness of it, and the curves—it looked so alive."

Dan grunted a laugh. "That baby weighs a ton! You wouldn't think so, to look at it."

Iris spooned tea into the pot. "I saw some of your friend Denis's paintings. He's very talented." She glanced at Dan over her shoulder. "I looked for your work, too—but there didn't seem to be any ceramics."

"Not in this show," Dan replied. "You're welcome to have a look at my stuff, though—if you really want to. Come on Sunday, after church."

"I'd love to."

As Iris poured boiling water onto the tea leaves, she told Dan that she was planning to go to the life class at the School of Painting in a few days' time. "The person on the door at the exhibition told me about it. Lady Frieda Harris. She was very helpful."

"Ah, yes," Dan said. "She's got paintings in the show. I haven't seen them yet—but Denis told me they're quite something. Did you see them?"

"Yes. They're beautiful—but quite strange. I was a bit mystified until I realised that they were designs for Tarot cards."

"Are they?" Dan's eyebrows arched. "I'd better not take Dad to the show, then—he can't abide them."

"I don't really know much about Tarot cards." Iris handed him a cup of tea.

"Me neither." He perched on a corner of the bed, leaving the one and only armchair free for her. "Dad says they're the work of the Devil. He had a bad experience with them, back in the mists of time, when he was at university."

"What happened?"

"He got in with an odd crowd. They were into black magic. One of the students died after they tried raising the spirit of some dead person in an old house in Cambridge. Dad said it was such a shock it turned him right round the other way, and he went into the church."

"I'm not surprised. It sounds terrifying." She sipped her tea, remembering the strange, hypnotic quality the paintings had seemed to exude.

"I saw a Tarot pack once," Dan said. "It was when I was in the Merchant Navy—at a bar in Murmansk. The images were quite crude—not what you'd call artistic. But you say the ones at the show are beautiful . . . ," he trailed off, looking at her over the rim of his cup.

Crude. Iris thought some people might use such a word to describe the card called *Lust.* But that would be unfair to the artist. The image had a sexual quality—that was undeniable. She wondered how to describe it to Dan without embarrassing herself. "It was the colours that drew me to them," she began. "When you're up close, the detail is incredible. It's as if each of them is telling a mysterious story—but you could gaze at them for ages and not work it out." She focused on the swirl of steam rising from the teacup, unable to meet his eye. "In one of them, there was a naked woman riding on a lion. Well, it looked like a lion at first, but then you saw that it had lots of different heads—some animal and some human. The whole image was done in reds and golds, as if the woman and the beast she was riding were enveloped in flames."

He grunted. "Sounds like something from Revelation."

"The Bible?" Her eyes widened.

He nodded. "'I saw a woman sit upon a scarlet-coloured beast with seven heads.'" He frowned. "I can't remember the exact words. Something like: 'The beast whose number is 666. And the name of the woman is Babylon the Great, the mother of harlots.'"

Iris's cup was halfway between her mouth and the saucer. It froze there as Dan's words sank in. If he was right, it gave a whole new layer of meaning to the painting. Now it seemed more like a warning, conjuring up the end of the world and the price to be paid for sins of the flesh.

"Do you know the artist?" Iris lowered her cup, misjudging the distance and making it chink against the saucer.

"I've heard of her, but I've never met her," Dan said. "I don't think she lives here. Probably visiting from London."

"She seemed to know all about the School of Painting," Iris said, shrugging. "I wish I'd had the chance to ask her about her work—but she'd gone by the time I saw it."

"Well, I'd better be going." Dan stood up. "Dad's expecting me back for supper. Thanks for the tea."

Iris followed him to the door. They stood together on the threshold, awkward, as if neither was sure how to say goodbye. She wanted him to kiss her, like he'd done last night. But that had been all about letting in the New Year. Nothing to do with romance. Or passion.

As he backed onto the step outside his head dipped down, like a bird swooping to drink on the wing. His lips brushed hers for a split second. And then he was gone.

Afterward, she lay on the bed, rubbing the bare sole of her foot on the place where he'd sat. Her whole body was aflame. She felt like the woman in the Tarot painting, riding the lion. Was that so wrong? Did it make her a harlot?

Another image filled her mind. The nun in *Black Narcissus*, with the red dress and the slash of lipstick. The movie had delivered a powerful message about repressed desire. Iris couldn't help imagining what might have happened if she'd reached out for Dan as he left her. Would he have wanted her? Or would he have been appalled at her forwardness and rejected her, like the lovesick nun?

She wondered what his life had been like in the Merchant Navy. There must have been women in all those places he'd visited—women who would have been drawn to him, as she was. It was all right for men. Society didn't judge them for sowing their wild oats. The gulf between his experience and hers was likely to be huge.

There had been an encounter a few months ago, with a boy from art school. He had invited her to tea at his parents' house, failing to mention that they were away on holiday. He'd grabbed her as soon as they were through the front door. It wasn't that she didn't like him—she'd been flattered when he'd asked her out—but he'd been rough, pulling up her skirt and thrusting his hand into her underwear. It had frightened her. When she broke away, he'd chased her around the house. In the end she'd escaped through the bathroom window.

It had put her off men for a long time. For good, she thought. So why was she lying here now, fantasizing about Dan? Was it because he hadn't tried anything? How could she know if his restraint was down to good manners or lack of interest?

She decided that a fantasy was fine. So long as she didn't allow it to consume her. Because embarking on this new life had taken every ounce of self-belief she possessed. To fall for Dan would make her vulnerable. He could break her. To have the future she'd promised herself, she was going to have to build a wall around her heart.

⋘

Ellen sat alone in front of the fire, eating a bowl of soup. There was no sound in the cottage, other than the hiss of the flames and the occasional crackle as the logs settled.

Tony had disappeared the moment they got back from Barbara and Ben's house—and in the time it had taken her to make a cup of tea and take it upstairs, he had fallen fast asleep.

She gazed into the flickering firelight, not really tasting the soup. Her mind was full of what Tony's old girlfriend had told her about Crowley.

He wanted to sleep with everyone . . . *I didn't want to be one of his scarlet women.*

Nina's words echoed in her head. They conjured up sordid images of what had almost certainly gone on in that bed upstairs. The thought of it made her feel sick. She wasn't sure she could bear the idea of sleeping in it now. There was a new mattress on order. It couldn't come soon enough.

Nina had implied that the sex had been part of something darker: that Crowley had used the women in his occult practices. Had the black magic taken place here, in the cottage, as well? Was the mommet part of some ritual he had carried out?

Ellen thought about the newspaper stories Nina had mentioned. The press had called him the Wickedest Man in the World. He must have done something abominable to merit that kind of attention. What was the other name she'd come out with? Something from the Bible . . .

The Beast 666. Ellen's knowledge of the scriptures was not great, but she knew it was something to do with the Devil.

They said the folks as used to live here were a bit odd.

The voice of the roofer floated into her mind. She wondered how much he and other local people had known about what had gone on at the cottage. And what about the woman who'd died? What on earth had she seen, to make her run off into the night?

It occurred to Ellen that her mother might remember the newspaper stories about Crowley. She could call her and ask. If only there was a phone here. It was so frustrating that the cables stopped a mile short of the cottage. She could telephone from the shop tomorrow, though. Ellen frowned, pushing the handle of the spoon around the empty soup bowl. No. That was a bad idea. She didn't want to worry her mother. Nor did she want to give any hint that Tony had concealed the cottage's past to sell her his dream of life in Cornwall.

The agent must have some idea of what had gone on here. Mr. Hardy had handled the sale of the cottage as well as the lease on the shop. She thought about how she might broach the subject with him. Would she go into the office on the pretext of some query about the lease? Perhaps it would be better to be upfront about it: tell him that she kept hearing gossip about the cottage and wanted to know the truth. It wasn't as if he'd have any reason to hide things from her, because the sale was a done deal.

She got up and took her bowl over to the sink. There wouldn't be time to call into the agent's first thing because the girl, Iris, was coming to the workshop. It would have to be later in the day.

Ellen went over to the window. The curtain with the rip in its lining wasn't closed properly. As she raised her arm to pull it, she jumped back. A terrifying face was staring in at her. She gasped. Shook her head. *Stupid* . . . It was just her reflection, distorted by the glass. She stared, transfixed by the luminous, catlike eyes and the sneering lips. Those were not *her* eyes; that was not *her* mouth . . .

She turned and ran to the door. Knowing that Tony was upstairs—albeit asleep—gave her courage she couldn't have mustered if she'd been alone. She threw the door open and ran outside. But there was no one there. Had she imagined that face? Were her eyes playing tricks on her?

She stood there in the dark for what seemed like ages, listening. There was no movement. No rustle of the bushes or creak of the gate. The only sound was the distant yelp of an animal—a dog or a fox.

Going back into the cottage, she felt the need for something to steady her nerves. The only thing they had was a bottle of Glenlivet her stepfather had slipped into the suitcase she'd brought from home. She'd never much liked whisky, but she poured herself a glass.

She shuddered as it went down. Her hand trembled as she angled the glass this way and that, watching the way the firelight caught the cut crystal, thinking about what she'd thought she'd seen in the window. A strange thing occurred to her. Could it be that she'd caught a glimpse of something from the past? Could she have seen what the woman saw? Was that evil face what had sent the poor thing running out into the night?

She'd heard it said that when people saw ghosts, what they were really seeing was some sequence of events imprinted on time, in a way that defied current scientific understanding. It was like hallucinating—but what they saw came from something outside themselves, *not* from their imagination. She couldn't help wondering what Tony would say to that.

It wasn't the first time she'd feared she was hallucinating. Those lights on the hillside on the night of the full moon—could that have been a replay of some ancient ritual? Something that had possibly happened hundreds of years ago, when people worshipped pagan gods?

The bones of the Earth Mother. That was how Barbara Hepworth had described the stones up there on Zennor Carn. As if they had a supernatural quality. Had the old man, Crowley, felt that same elemental sense of power? Was that why he had come to live here? To harness it for his black magic?

CHAPTER 12

Iris stood in front of the speckled square of mirror, brushing her hair. She decided she should plait it for her first day at work. It would be more secure than pinning it up in a bun. The last thing she needed was a stray lock of hair dangling into the paint. She wondered if she should go and buy a set of overalls to wear over her clothes. But that might make her look over-confident—as if she were expecting to be offered the job. It was only a day's trial. She had to create the best possible impression.

The place was easy to find, even though there was nothing in the window to give away the fact that it was a toy shop. It was next door to the florist's where she'd bought narcissus and winter jasmine to leave on the moorland, in memory of her mother. She stood outside for a moment, nervous about ringing the bell. She had never had a job; had never had to earn money. What if she blew it? What would become of her?

She took a deep breath and summoned up the words the headmistress had spoken on her last day at boarding school. *Nothing in life is to be feared—it is only to be understood.* According to the headmistress, it was a quote from Marie Curie, the first woman to have won the Nobel Prize. A day's trial in a toy shop was hardly comparable—but it was the right message, all the same.

Iris hardly recognized the woman who came to the door. In her memory, Ellen Wylde was a glamorous, willowy woman with long, shiny chestnut hair, who wore an elegant cocktail dress of dark blue velvet. In corduroy trousers and a chunky polo neck sweater, she looked quite different. Her hair was caught up in a ponytail, and her face bore no trace of makeup. The sprinkling of freckles on her nose and forehead gave her an almost childlike look. Iris thought she couldn't be more than midtwenties. Pretty impressive, for a woman running her own business.

"Good morning, Mrs. Wylde." Iris gave what she hoped was a polite smile. Not too wide. Not too familiar.

"Good morning." There was a clink of metal as Ellen turned toward the interior of the shop. Iris noticed that she was wearing a leather tool belt strapped around her waist. "Would you like to come through?"

Iris was taken through the small room at the front to a much larger one at the rear of the premises. It smelled of wood shavings. Looking around, she spotted a pile of sawdust on the floor, in front of a machine with a thin, jagged blade protruding from it.

"This is the workshop. I've brought a few items from my old place in London that need sanding and painting—so I'll get you started on those in a minute. But first I'm going to need a hand putting up the sign."

Iris followed her across the room to where a large rectangle of wood was propped against the wall. She helped to carry it through to the street, then went back into the workshop to take one end of a ladder that served as a staircase to the attic.

"I should've asked Tony to help me do this when we moved everything in, but we ran out of time. It's been nonstop since we moved here." Ellen propped the ladder against the front door of the shop. "If you could pass me the sign, once I'm up there, and then go across to the pub and tell me if I've got it straight."

Iris nodded. The sign was quite heavy. She wondered if she should offer to help hold it in place. But there was only one ladder. Perhaps if she went back and fetched a chair from the workshop . . .

"Okay—I'm ready." Ellen was already up the ladder.

Iris lifted the sign slowly and carefully. When Ellen took it from her, she glimpsed the name, scorched into the yellow-painted wood in flowing copperplate script: "The Toy Tiger." As she walked across the street to stand on the steps of The Castle, the image of one of the Tarot cards from the exhibition flashed through her mind. The Princess of Wands: a tiger tumbling down a golden flame, dragging a girl by the neck to her doom. She hoped it wasn't a bad omen.

———⟡———

Ellen telephoned her mother before locking up the shop that afternoon.

"You're in business already! I can't believe you've got it off the ground so quickly, especially . . ." The voice at the other end of the line tailed off.

"Especially in sleepy old Cornwall?" Ellen smiled.

"Well, I didn't expect things to move at the pace they would in London," her mother replied.

"The Harrods order made me shift up a gear. I've taken on an assistant. She came on a day's trial today, and I've offered her four mornings a week at a shilling an hour—do you think that's a fair wage?"

"How old is she?"

"Nineteen."

"I'd say that's more than generous. It must be much cheaper to live down there than it is here."

"It is—and there aren't many part-time jobs to be had, according to Iris, so if I'd advertised, I might have had people queuing up. That's her name, by the way. Iris Birch. She's an art student."

"And you think she'll be a good worker?"

"She's fast and she's meticulous. And she doesn't spend the whole time chatting—in fact, it was difficult to get her to say much at all."

"Sounds ideal." Ellen's mother chuckled. "And what about that husband of yours? He's helping, too, I hope."

"Of course, Mum." No point in telling her mother that Tony had no intention of coming to the shop anytime soon. He'd helped her with the heavy work, so it wasn't a lie. "I'd better go—I've got to call in at the letting agent's before they close."

"All right, my love. It's good to hear that everything's going so well for you."

Ellen let out a long breath as she replaced the receiver.

The agent's office was halfway up Tregenna Hill. Ellen thought about what she was going to say as she wound her way past the post office and the town library. She decided that a subtle approach was the best strategy. If she went in with all guns blazing, he was likely to be defensive.

"Mrs. Wylde. What a pleasure to see you." He didn't look pleased. No doubt he had her down as an awkward customer after the disagreeable business of the signing of the lease. "I hope that everything is to your liking at the new premises."

"It is, thank you, Mr. Hardy." She took a seat on the opposite side of his desk. "I haven't come about the shop. I wondered if you could tell me something about the history of Carreg Cottage?"

"Well . . ." He glanced at his watch. "I have a viewing in half an hour, I'm afraid."

"Of course—I know how busy you must be." She flashed him a smile. "But I was looking at the deeds the other day—quite fascinating, these old documents, aren't they?—and I saw that the cottage was originally part of Rowan Tree Farm. Am I right in thinking that's the property on the main road, where the track comes out?"

"Yes. It's no longer a farm, of course. It's a second home these days—owned by a London solicitor and his wife."

"Would that be Mr. and Mrs. Bird? Their names were on the deeds." If she could get him to talk about them, she could steer the conversation to questions about their tenant.

"What?" He shook his head. "No. Mr. Bird sold Rowan Tree House years ago, after his wife died."

"Oh?"

"It was terribly sad. The poor woman collapsed while she was out walking on the moor. She wasn't found until the next morning—and she died soon after. She was only thirty-four."

Ellen stared at him. This had to be the woman the roofer had told her about. It was Crowley's landlady, then, who had run, terrified, from the cottage. "That's awful. When did it happen?"

"It was the year before the war—May 1938. I'd only been here a couple of weeks. I was at the Falmouth office before that." He looked at his watch again. "I'm sorry, Mrs. Wylde—I really must be going."

"Please don't apologise." Ellen stood up. "Thank you for your time."

"Best of luck with the shop!"

Ellen closed the door behind her and set off down the hill. Now she had not just a name, but an approximate date. She stopped outside the library and read the opening times on the sign. She had just under an hour before it was due to close.

She found what she was looking for in a copy of *The Cornish Times*, dated May 24, 1938. It was a report in the obituaries column, which gave the name, address, and age of the deceased, along with a few lines about the circumstances.

It didn't tell Ellen much more than she already knew. Apparently, Stella Bird had been quite well until a few days prior to her death, apart from a slight cold. The report said that she was taken with a seizure on a Saturday evening while walking home after visiting a neighbor at a cottage on the moor. Discovered the following morning, she was taken to the hospital but never regained consciousness and died on the Sunday evening. The last paragraph stated that her husband was on his way to Canada on a business trip. It implied that he didn't yet know that his wife had died.

Ellen leafed through the pages a second time. There had to be something more than this scant outline of what had happened. But there was nothing—not even a photograph of Stella Bird. She thought about the likely sequence of events following the woman's death. There must have been some sort of investigation. When one of the carpenters at the factory next to her home in London had died suddenly at work, there had been an inquest. She remembered her mother reading an account of it aloud to her over breakfast.

She returned the newspaper to the rack on the wall and searched along the hangers until she found the editions for June of the same year. *The Cornish Times* was a weekly paper, so there were only four per month. She glanced at her watch. Just twenty minutes until closing time.

She skimmed through the first paper, looking at the headlines, thinking that the inquest was unlikely to have been held within a week of the death. Moving swiftly on to the second one, she spotted the story on the front page:

Woman Died After Visit to "Haunted" House

The inquest was opened yesterday in Truro into the death of Mrs. Stella Winifred Bird, aged 34, of Rowan Tree House, near St Ives.

Mrs. Bird was found unconscious on moorland near Zennor Carn on the morning of Sunday May 22 by Mr. Anthony Wylde, an art student from London, who was on a painting trip to the area. Mr. Wylde called an ambulance from the nearby Tinners Arms public house, and Mrs. Bird was taken to St Ives Cottage Hospital—but she never regained consciousness and died the same evening.

Ellen stared at the page, transfixed by the sight of Tony's name. He had *found* Stella Bird. A tide of emotion surged in her stomach. She knew only too well what that must have felt like. The shock of spotting the body. The panic of realizing that the woman was still alive and in desperate need of a doctor. And the lingering trauma of knowing that all he'd tried to do had been in vain. A lonely Cornish moor and a bombed-out London building—they were not so very different: to find a person dead or dying changed you forever.

Ellen's eyes traveled farther down the page.

According to the testimony of Mrs. Elizabeth Richards, housekeeper to the deceased, Mrs. Bird was in good health on the day preceding the seizure that ultimately resulted in her death. Mrs. Richards said that her employer had suffered a slight cold the previous week, but that it was not serious enough to keep her indoors. Asked why she thought Mrs. Bird might have been out on the moor on the evening of Saturday May 21, the housekeeper said that her employer owned Carreg Cottage, on the slopes of Zennor Carn, and one of the people living at the cottage—a young woman whose name Mrs. Richards did not know—had come to Rowan Tree House that day and had caused a disturbance. The young woman had claimed the cottage was haunted and had asked Mrs. Bird to keep her company as she was afraid to be there on her own that night.

The coroner asked the clerk of the court if this young woman had been called to give evidence at the inquest. He replied that she could not be summoned to appear, as she was currently under medical supervision at Bodmin Lunatic Asylum.

Ellen's eyes widened. From the sound of it, Carreg Cottage had been a deeply unhappy place at the time of Stella Bird's death. Could this unnamed person have been Crowley's lover? One of the scarlet women, as Nina had called them?

There was only one more paragraph in the newspaper report, stating that the coroner had recorded a verdict of death by natural causes.

There was no mention of Mr. Crowley, no suggestion that anything suspicious had happened at the cottage on the night Stella Bird had gone there.

Ellen heard a bell ringing at the far end of the room. The library was about to close. After replacing the newspaper in the rack, she made her way to the door. What she had read raised as many questions as it answered. She was no closer to finding out what had really happened at the cottage. And discovering that Tony had found Stella Bird meant that she must be extra-careful not to talk about it. It certainly explained why he had been so reticent to tell her about the history of the cottage. If he was troubled by the past, he was putting a brave face on it, not allowing the bad memories to stand in the way of the new life he longed for. And if he could banish those ghosts, then so must she.

<hr>

Tony glanced at his watch, then at the woman sitting across the table. "I'd better be getting you home—she'll be coming back soon."

"Now, wouldn't that be interesting?" Nina Grey's eyebrows disappeared under a henna-dyed curtain of hair. "You're not going to tell her, then?"

"There's nothing to tell." Tony stubbed out his cigarette in a saucer. "You wanted to see the cottage. That's fair enough. But Ellen has a vivid imagination. You should have heard her after the party. She tried to make out that you'd had a cosy little chat—but I could tell she was as jealous as hell."

Nina reached across the table, laying her bejeweled hand on his. "Well, darling, we could always give her something to be jealous about, couldn't we?"

He pulled his hand away. "No, Nina. That's all in the past. You can't just pick people up and cast them aside."

"Can't I? Spoilsport."

He huffed out a breath. "You know, you sometimes sound just like Crowley? I remember he and Dora having a conversation very much like that."

"Hmm. Poor Dora. Does anyone know what became of her?"

"Still in Bodmin Asylum, for all I know." Tony shrugged. "I told you: I wanted nothing to do with them after what happened. I didn't even know that he'd died. But you say it was in the papers?"

"Just a few lines, before Christmas. He was living somewhere obscure on the South Coast. Hastings, I think. Lionel Bird was mentioned. He gave the eulogy at the funeral. I was surprised they were still friends."

"Do you still see him?"

"Leo?" Nina shook her head. "Not since I moved down here. He writes to me occasionally—sends Christmas and birthday cards."

"Hmm." Tony frowned. "Well, I think he was very fortunate to have been en route to Canada when his wife died. If the police had known what went on here . . ."

"What? You think he put Crowley up to it?"

"It has occurred to me. The old man said Stella had to go because she was planning to evict him from the cottage. But you know what Leo was like. Not exactly the doting husband, was he?"

"Well, no—he wasn't. But he was always telling me how much he loved her. I never saw her, of course—but people said she was stunningly beautiful."

Tony grunted. "From what James Hardy told me, Leo didn't waste any time selling Rowan Tree House. He'd have got rid of this place, too, if he could've."

"But no one wanted the Crowley House." Nina rolled her eyes. "Until you came along. Tell me, darling, why were you so desperate to get your hands on it? Doesn't it bring back bad memories?"

Tony pursed his lips. "I couldn't let that stand in the way. I'd always loved it. From the first day you brought me here."

"Hmm." Nina glanced around, taking in the worn furniture, the threadbare curtains. "It's looking a bit down-at-heel since those days, isn't it? But I can understand how the place seduces you. Like a scruffy lover: could do with a haircut and some decent clothes, but you wouldn't kick them out of bed." She smiled. "I remember the look on your face when you came to that first party here. It was Frieda's initiation, wasn't it?"

Tony nodded.

"All that witchy stuff." Nina pulled a face. "I suppose you know that Crowley told her he couldn't work with her as an artist unless she became his disciple? Luckily for her, he didn't insist on the usual shenanigans. I think that was only because he thought she was a bit long in the tooth to be a scarlet woman. There was only a couple of years' difference in their ages. His usual victims were a good twenty years younger."

"I hear some of her Tarot cards are on display in St Ives."

"Yes—how did you know?"

"Denis Mitchell told me. I might go and have a peek." Tony stood up. "Anyway, we'd better get going."

"What a good little husband you are." Nina patted his shoulder as she followed him to the door. "I'm not sorry I made Ellen jealous. It's quite flattering. I can understand you wanting to be careful, though: you don't want to kill the goose that lays the golden eggs."

He turned to her as he opened the door. "Will you promise me something? If she comes asking questions about Crowley, don't tell her I was living here back then, will you?"

"Why not?"

"Because then she'd know I'd fed her a pack of lies. I had to. She'd never have agreed to come here otherwise."

"Hmm. I'll have to think about it." Tilting her head up, Nina kissed him on the nose. "A promise like that might come with conditions."

Nina's house wasn't far from the Mariners' Church. When he'd dropped her off, Tony decided to take a look at the exhibition in the crypt.

He didn't know the person at the door. A lot of new people had fetched up in St Ives during and after the war. Foreign artists fleeing persecution as well as Londoners like Nina, Barbara, and Ben. From the accent, the man who greeted him was one of the former.

After signing the visitors' book, Tony wound his way past the exhibits until he came to the set of Tarot cards. He took a long look at the image called *Lust*. Frieda had told him about this one. In a conventional pack, the card was called *Strength*. But Crowley had insisted on changing the name. Frieda had explained that the symbolism was the key to his perception of the universe and his place in it. He was the biblical creature in the painting: The Beast 666. Dora Montague, his Scarlet Woman, was riding on his back. Chilling to look at it, knowing that Dora had finished up in an asylum, and Crowley was dead.

You think you can just move in? Make a home in my centre of astral pestilence? You'd better be careful.

His heart missed a beat. The voice was horribly familiar. It had seemed to come from right behind him. He glanced over his shoulder. There was no one in the room except the man at the desk. Tony hurried out. He shouldn't have come. Stupid to open the door to those memories.

He emerged into twilight. Norway Square was deserted. Then he caught sight of someone: a woman, making her way past the little garden in the center. Something about her held his gaze. As he watched, she pulled off her hat. Her hair billowed out in the breeze. It shone red as she passed under a streetlamp. And then she turned, as if she'd sensed him watching her. Her eyes gleamed, like a fox's caught in headlights.

Stella.

His hands flew to his face. When he opened his fingers, she'd vanished.

He sped home, bumping his way up the track so fast it was a miracle the bike didn't strike a rock. No sign of the jeep, thank goodness.

He couldn't face Ellen—not yet. When he cut the engine, he heard the voice again.

You don't belong here. You're trespassing.

He fumbled for the door key and reached inside to turn on the kitchen light. Grabbing his pipe from the shelf above the fireplace, he went back outside, around the side of the cottage, to the cowshed. Once inside, he locked himself in. He had no idea when Ellen would get back. She mustn't see him.

With trembling fingers, he packed the bowl of the pipe with fragments of dried mushroom and set them alight. Filling his lungs, he sat for a moment, waiting, hoping. He might have called it praying if he'd believed in any sort of god. Gradually, the voice began to fade. But as the drug took effect, the images in his mind's eye grew ever more vivid. The red hair in the lamplight; those foxlike eyes. Stella. How was he going to exorcise *her* ghost?

An idea came to him. He grabbed a sheet of paper and clipped it to the easel. With a stick of charcoal, he made the fluid lines of the animal's body. A fox, with slim, delicate paws; a luxuriant tail, brushing the ground as it slunk toward its prey. But this was no ordinary fox. Its head would be human. He would paint the tumbling red hair the exact shade of the animal's coat. And the face would be Stella's.

CHAPTER 13

Iris took a gift for Reverend Thomas when she went to church on Sunday. It was a kneeler, made from remnants of red and purple velvet. In the central panel she'd embroidered the saint's name in golden thread.

"It's a thank-you present," she said as she handed it over. "I wanted to let you know how much I appreciate what you and Dan did."

"You made this?" The vicar fumbled in his pocket for his spectacles. "Look at this, Dan—there's the name, as well. Isn't it marvellous?"

Dan flashed her a wide smile as his father held the kneeler out for inspection. "It's first-rate. You'd better be careful, Iris—the Ladies' Sewing Circle will be after you."

Iris wondered what the Ladies' Sewing Circle would say if they knew what had been going on inside her head while she'd been making it; that she'd embarked on the project as a way of distracting herself from the lurid images that somehow appeared on the page every time she picked up a pencil.

As promised, Dan took her to see his studio after the service. There was an earthy smell as he opened the door: damp clay with a hint of tobacco. On a table in the center of the room was a tall shape wreathed in what looked like a large wet dishcloth.

"This is what I'm working on at the moment," he said. "I have to keep it covered up, otherwise the clay dries out." He lifted the cloth to reveal a tree, about three feet high. Tiny clay birds roosted in its sculpted branches, and at its base was the figure of a woman—a torso with an upturned head, smooth, with no features. Her arms were bent at the elbows, her hands cupping her breasts. Her head was encircled by what looked like hair—or possibly a halo. Even in its raw state—not yet fired or painted—there was an elemental beauty about it.

"It's about the Creation," Dan went on. "This is Mother Nature. I wanted to convey the way a woman nurtures life—through giving her milk. She'll be surrounded by fruits and flowers and animals, but I haven't made those yet."

Looking at the figure of the woman, Iris couldn't help imagining Dan's hands running over it, his fingers smoothing the clay as he shaped the breasts. She loosened her scarf, feeling uncomfortably warm.

"This is what they look like when they're finished." He opened a large cupboard at the back of the room. Inside was a tree covered in tiny angels. Two were carrying the body of the crucified Christ up to heaven, while others, around the edges of the tree, were weeping. At the base of the trunk was a nativity scene, complete with cows, donkeys, and shepherds. A bearded, white-haired man looked down from above the topmost branches of the tree, his hands outstretched.

"This one's going to a cathedral in Ireland," Dan said. "It's meant to show the circle of Christ's life—from birth to death."

"It's amazing." Iris stepped closer. The detail was astonishing. He'd even painted in the blood around the wounds in the doll-sized Christ's hands and feet.

"I want my trees to speak for themselves," he went on. "To be more than just religious imagery. When I made this, I was trying to convey the sadness you feel when someone has gone, knowing you'll never see that person again."

Iris nodded. "It's in the way you've done the angels," she said. "You can't see their faces—it's all in the angles of their heads and hands." She wondered if he'd been thinking about his mother when he made the piece. Looking at it, she couldn't help but think of hers.

"Would you like to have a go at making something?" He pulled out a bucket from beneath the table.

"I don't think I'd be any good at it."

He smiled. "Clay has a magic to it. You only need to touch it, and shapes start to form. I'll show you." He took a lump of clay and slapped it down beside the unfinished model of the Creation. "This is how I make a lily." He broke off a small piece and shaped it with his fingers. Then he rolled out a thin sausage, no thicker than a matchstick. He dipped his fingers in a bowl of water and wrapped the first piece around the second. And there it was: an arum lily.

"See?" He smiled. "It's easy!'" He pushed the remaining lump across the table. "Your turn."

"You make it *look* easy." She glanced up at him as she broke a piece off. The clay felt hard and unyielding at first, but it softened as she worked it with her fingers. She tried to replicate the thin, flat square he'd made for the sheath of the lily. Then she rolled out the piece that would be the stalk and stigma.

"Not bad!" Dan picked up what she'd made and examined it.

Iris laughed. "You're being kind—it looks more like a sausage roll than a flower!" She snatched it from his fingers and scrunched it up into a ball.

"I'm not letting you off that easily! Come on—have another try." He came around the table and stood beside her. When she started shaping the clay, he put his hands on hers, demonstrating how much pressure was required to get it thin enough to look like a petal. She could feel his breath on the skin of her neck. The touch of his fingers sent lightning streaking up her arms and down into her body. More than anything, she wanted to kiss him.

"See? You've got it." He took his hands away. "Now try the stalk. The trick is to keep it short. If you let it go too long, it'll bend when you attach this piece."

Her fingers trembled as she reached for a second lump of clay. Did he realize the effect he had on her? Was the invitation to try making something a deliberate ploy to get up close? Or was she sensing something that wasn't there? She mustn't think about what might not happen. She'd promised herself.

"Don't worry about messing up," he said, as she began rolling. "That's the great thing about clay—you don't have to be afraid of it."

She wanted to tell him then. That the reason her hands were shaking was nothing to do with the modeling. The thought of it made her press down too hard. The clay, as thin as a mouse's tail, broke in half.

"Dan . . . Can I come in?" The vicar's head appeared around the door. "I was just wondering if Iris would like to stay for lunch?"

⊰——

Ellen was pleased to see her new assistant waiting in the doorway of The Castle pub when she arrived to unlock the shop on Monday morning.

"Good morning, Mrs. Wylde."

"Please—call me Ellen. Mrs. Wylde makes me sound ancient." She opened the door and ushered the girl in. "You're nice and early."

"To be honest, I was glad to get outside," Iris said. "There's a fish cellar under my room, and they're smoking herring this morning. You wouldn't believe the smell." She sniffed her coat as she hung it on a peg. "I hope I haven't brought it with me."

"I can't smell anything." Ellen smiled. "I'm probably immune to it, with all the linseed oil and paint fumes I've breathed in." She went across the room and pulled a large box out from under the workbench, thinking that Iris seemed a lot brighter and more talkative than before. She'd probably just been nervous that first morning.

Ellen hefted the box up onto the table. "This is some of the old stock I brought from London. I wonder if you could give me a hand setting up the shop window before you get started on the painting?"

There wasn't much space for a display, but Ellen was keen to attract passing trade in addition to the orders from London.

"I remember playing with a farm set at school," Iris said, as she arranged a group of sheep beside a tiny wooden shepherd's hut. "But it wasn't half as nice as this. The animals were made of metal, I think, and the paint was all patchy."

"Was that in Hampshire?" Iris looked up. A frown creased her forehead. "You said you lived in Hampshire, before you came here."

"Oh, yes. That was when I was older. I went to boarding school there."

Not for the first time, Ellen wondered what had happened to Iris's parents. It seemed odd that she was having to support herself while studying art if they'd had the money to send her to a private school. Perhaps they were among the thousands who'd lost their lives when the bombs rained down on London. Best not to ask.

She took a Noah's Ark from the box and placed it in the center of the window. "I was thinking," she said, "once we've got the Harrods order out of the way, we should have a party. I don't know many people, but my husband does." She glanced at Iris. "You could invite your boyfriend."

Iris looked at her feet. "You mean Dan? He's not . . . We're not . . ."

"You're not courting?" Ellen hated that word. It sounded like something from the Middle Ages. "Sorry. I just assumed . . . because you were with him at the party . . ."

"He's just been helping me get to know people," Iris said. "I couldn't find anywhere to stay when I arrived here. I met him at the church down the road, and he offered me a room for a couple of nights. His father's the vicar."

"Is that the church with the big square tower?"

Iris nodded. "It's called St Ia's."

"That's a strange name."

"I know. The story goes that it's named after a woman who sailed from Ireland to Cornwall in a leaf for a boat. It's beautiful inside. There are painted figures all round the ceiling, carved by fishermen out of wooden oars."

"I must go and take a look." Ellen placed the figure of Noah at the head of a line of animals. It was a long time since she'd been inside a church. The one she and her mother used to attend had burned down after a bomb hit it. Services had been held in a school hall after that—and it hadn't felt the same. There was something about the beauty of old church buildings that always seemed to lift her spirits.

"I've been meaning to go to church since we moved here," Ellen went on. "There hasn't been time, with everything else I've needed to do. But . . . ," she trailed off. She shouldn't tell Iris how uncomfortable she felt at the cottage. She hardly knew her—and she was an employee. But she suddenly felt an overwhelming need to unburden herself, to confide her fears to someone who wouldn't be angry or worried by what she had to say.

"I think our cottage might be haunted." There. It was out. Her eyes were fixed on the pair of goats that brought up the rear of the procession of animals heading for the Ark.

"Really? Why?" There was interest in Iris's voice. No undertone of incredulity.

Ellen described what she'd found up the chimney on her first morning at the cottage. "A workman who came to fix the roof said it was something Cornish people call a mommet. They were used to curse people. And he told me that a woman died after visiting the cottage the year before the war. The rumour is that she was scared to death."

Iris gasped. "What? That's horrible. No wonder it feels creepy. Where do you live? Is it near Barbara Hepworth's house?"

"No. It's in the opposite direction, about four miles from here—near a village called Zennor. Have you heard of it?"

Iris nodded. She reached into the box and pulled out a miniature cow to add to the farmyard scene she was arranging. "I was there last week. I felt like a walk, and I saw there was a bus that goes that way. I was going to climb up the hill they call Zennor Carn—but a mist came down, so I didn't stay long."

"Well, if you'd gone up there, you'd have walked right past the cottage."

"Would I?" Iris was staring intently at the cow, as if it held the answer to some unfathomable puzzle.

"It's the only house up there," Ellen went on. "No one's lived there since before the war. Someone I met at the party on New Year's Eve told me the man who used to rent it was not very nice. She said he was keen on black magic. I started imagining all sorts of things after that . . . ," she trailed off, pushing back a wisp of hair that had slipped out of her ponytail. "I went to the library to see if I could find out any more about it. A report in *The Cornish Times* said that the woman who died was the owner of our cottage. She lived just down the hill. I keep wondering what could have happened the night she went up there: if she really was frightened to death."

There was no response from Iris. Ellen glanced at her. Had she said too much? Iris wasn't a child—but she'd probably led a sheltered existence at that girls' boarding school. It was easy to forget that not everyone had had to grow up fast during the war. "I'm sorry," she said. "I shouldn't go on about it. It's all in the past. And there's no such thing as ghosts. I need to remind myself of that and . . . well, just get on with life, I suppose."

Iris had shifted her gaze to the window, watching the people going past in the street. It was impossible to know what she was thinking.

⚜

A cold wind gusted up Tregenna Place when Iris came out of the library. She tried to put on her gloves, but her hands were shaking. It had been a shock, seeing her mother's name in black and white. The thought of her lying on the moor all night, cold and alone, was unbearable. And her father—on his way to Canada when it happened, and unable to be contacted. What a terrible shock it must have been, stepping off the boat to receive that news.

The report in the newspaper had said death by natural causes. So where had the rumor Ellen had heard come from? Apart from the claim that the cottage was haunted, there was nothing in the article to suggest that anything suspicious had taken place.

As she walked back through the town, questions filled her mind. The man who'd found her mother was called Anthony Wylde. It was an unusual spelling of the surname—and Ellen had said her husband's name was Tony. Surely it had to be him? Why hadn't Ellen mentioned it?

And what about the evidence given by Mrs. Richards, the housekeeper? What she'd said suggested there had been trouble between her mother and the woman who lived at Carreg Cottage. The report said that woman had been committed to a lunatic asylum. Could her mother have been attacked when she went to the cottage?

But Ellen had mentioned that there was a man living at the cottage, too. She'd said that he'd been renting the place before the war and that he wasn't very nice, that he'd been keen on black magic. Why hadn't *he* been questioned at the inquest?

Ellen's words rang in her head as she made her way along Fore Street: *I keep wondering what could have happened the night she went up there: if she really was frightened to death.*

Could that be true? And if so, what on earth had her mother seen?

As Iris turned up The Digey, a ginger cat slunk out of an alleyway and crossed the cobbles a few feet in front of her. It had a bird in its mouth. She stopped dead, suddenly remembering what Ellen had described finding up the chimney at the cottage. A blood-spattered doll with a bird's skull for a head.

A *bird*.

Why hadn't it occurred to her before? Had the man who'd rented the cottage made that hideous thing with her mother in mind? *Could it have killed her?*

CHAPTER 14

Tony wished it didn't get dark so early in winter. When he was outside, on the moor, he never seemed to hear the voice. But when the light began to fade and he returned to the cottage, it was as if the old man was there, waiting.

He went straight to the cowshed. His pipe was there. And the half-finished painting of the fox-woman. He selected the pigments to mix—vermilion, burnt sienna, and China white. Normally he would never paint in artificial light. But this was not something he would ever wish to exhibit. It was for his eyes only. A sort of talisman against the bad memories that threatened to unbalance him.

Then, as he loaded the brush, he heard Crowley hissing in his ear.

Did you really think you could live in peace here?

"Shut up! Leave me alone!" Tony reached for his pipe. The tin of dried mushrooms was under the bench, hidden behind an old watering can. Prizing off the lid, he saw that there were only a few fragments left. Just about enough.

There were no lights on in the cottage when Ellen arrived home. Tony's motorbike was there, so she guessed that he'd shut himself away in the cowshed. Now that the roof was sound, there was no danger of his work getting damaged.

She opened the front door, thinking how nice it would be to come home to the smell of something cooking. She doubted Tony would have given a passing thought to what they were going to have for dinner that evening. It wouldn't have surprised her if he'd had nothing to eat since the porridge she'd put in front of him this morning. When he was painting, he seemed to exist on fresh air.

She put her bag down on the table and went to fill the kettle. While she waited for it to boil, she raked out the ashes of last night's fire and laid the kindling and logs. She wondered whether to take a cup of tea out to Tony. But she decided he probably wouldn't want to be disturbed.

The fire took a while to get going. She sat at the kitchen table peeling potatoes and went over to prod it now and again. The second time she got up, she knocked some of the peel onto the floor by accident. As she scooped it up, she spotted something bright and shiny under the table. She reached for it, cradling it in her hand as she held it up to the light.

An earring.

Ellen felt her heart thud in her chest. It was made of two beads—a small black sphere and a larger red oval, with a silver wire linking them. Where had it come from? She had swept this floor several times since they'd moved into the cottage. How could she have missed it?

Hearing the click of the front door latch, she thrust the earring into her pocket.

"Oh, you're back." Tony looked confused. "I lost track of time." His eyes went to the potatoes. "What's for dinner?"

"Corned beef hash." She couldn't look at him. She sat down and carried on peeling, struggling to keep the knife steady. Had he had a woman here? Had he been unfaithful to her, right here, on this table? She swallowed hard, trying to shake the images that filled her head. She told herself that the earring could have belonged to someone long gone—to that woman she'd read about in the newspaper report: the one who ended up in an asylum. It could easily have lain undisturbed under a piece of furniture and rolled across the tiles when she started shifting things around.

Why don't you show it to him? Watch his face.

No. It wouldn't do any good. He'd just shrug and give her the same look as when she'd gone on about the couple in The Tinners Arms. The look that said *You're imagining things.* And afterward there would be an atmosphere between them. The evening would be ruined.

He went over to the sink to wash the paint off his hands, then he put a record on the gramophone. He came up behind her and massaged her shoulders. "I'll finish these. You go and sit by the fire."

"Tell me about the new assistant," he called across to her, as he sliced the potatoes. "What's she like?"

"Good so far," Ellen replied. "She's very willing and takes a lot of care over everything."

"Did you say she's an art student?"

"Yes. She's from Hampshire. I'm not sure why she chose St Ives rather than London. I thought she might have come here because of the boy she was with at the party—but she says he's just a friend."

"Who is he? Do I know him?"

"His name's Dan, and he's the son of the vicar at the church down by the harbour."

Tony shrugged. "Don't remember a Dan."

Ellen shifted her weight on the sofa, putting her feet up on the lumpy cushions. "Well, you'll probably get to meet them both before long. I'd like to have some kind of launch party at the shop once we've got the Harrods order out of the way. Cheese and wine—that sort of thing. Will you be able to round up a few people?"

"Should be no problem at all if there's free booze on offer." He grunted a laugh as he tipped the potatoes into a pan. "Just don't expect them to buy anything."

She wondered what he meant by the remark. He'd never commented on the quality of what she made—only on the amount of money people were willing to pay for it. She remembered Barbara Hepworth's reaction to what she did for a living—that barely concealed look of disdain. Did he think of her like that?

"Ben and Barbara's kids are too old for toys," he went on. "Most of my other friends don't have children. There's Denis, of course—but he's as poor as a church mouse."

"It's okay." She made space for him as he came to sit beside her, relieved to be wrong about what he'd said earlier. "I'm not doing it for that reason—it's just for a bit of publicity. I thought I might invite a photographer from the local paper."

"Great. Just let me know the date, and I'll put the word out." He slipped his arm around her shoulders and pulled her to him. As her hip met his, she felt something sharp. The earring. The wire had gone through her pocket and was jabbing her skin. She couldn't pull it out because he would see it. And she didn't want to spoil what he clearly wanted to do while the dinner was cooking.

As his fingers groped for the fastening on her bra, she closed her eyes. But the darkness was full of images. Of Tony and some other, faceless woman. So inflamed with passion that her earring came off in the encounter.

You're getting yourself all worked up over nothing.

It was an echo from the past—what her mother was always telling her. *Concentrate on the here and now.* In those days, she would reach for a piece of wood. Working with her hands was a sure way to drive away dark thoughts.

Ellen made herself concentrate on Tony's hands moving across her ribs; the contours of his body pressing against her; the feeling of his bare skin where their sweaters had ridden up. She found the waistband of his trousers, slid her hand beneath the corduroy fabric. His mouth was on her ear. His breathing intensified, a rushing sound that drowned out the whisper of doubt inside her head.

They fell asleep on the sofa after their meal, waking up to find that the fire had gone out. Ellen was unable to face going upstairs to the cold bed without first making a hot water bottle. And once they were up there, sleep eluded her.

She thought about the new mattress, which was due to arrive the next day. What a relief it would be to throw away the old one. It was the thing she most detested in the cottage, knowing what kind of person had once occupied it. Getting rid of it would be an act of banishment—a significant step in her bid to reclaim the place from the ghosts of the past.

The mommet had been consumed by the flames of the garden bonfire—and the bird-headed pharaoh on the ceiling had been painted over. It had been several days since she'd heard that horrible voice—or seen anything to frighten or unsettle her. Apart from the earring. But that was real, not ghostly. She mustn't allow it to prey on her mind.

After what seemed like hours, she fell into an uneasy sleep. It didn't last long. She sat bolt upright, her heart pounding, images from a nightmare filling her mind's eye. She had dreamed of Tony and Nina—together in this bed. She could see their bodies writhing as they made love. Nina was naked apart from her earrings—red and black, like the one Ellen had found on the kitchen floor.

In the dream she had tried to pull Nina away from Tony. But someone had come up behind her. Wheeling around, she'd seen an old man standing in the doorway. His head was bald except for a spiky tuft, like a horn, in the middle of his forehead. His eyes, great dark hollows in his face, were fixed on Tony and Nina. He gave a twisted smile as Ellen dodged past him. The last thing she remembered was losing her footing, flailing wildly for the banister as she fell down the stairs.

Ellen slid back down onto the pillow and took a few long breaths, trying to quell her racing heart. Why had she dreamed that? The earring that she'd found couldn't have been Nina's, could it? Why would Tony have brought her here? The worm of jealousy that had emerged at Barbara's party slithered out of its hole. She told herself that Nina was part of his past, that he was no longer close to her. He couldn't be, because he hadn't even told her he was getting married. If Nina had known about it, she'd have told her friend Barbara—and Barbara had clearly been taken by surprise at the news.

As she tortured herself over what Tony might or might not have done, something else struck her: that what she'd dreamed about could have happened years ago. The parties Nina had told her about—where nothing was off-limits: had Tony and Nina slunk away from one of those gatherings to make love in Crowley's bed?

Once again, Ellen was left with the horrible feeling that she had unwittingly tuned into something that had imprinted itself on the place. There was a sense of something truly evil in the room, something far too powerful to be exorcised by the simple act of replacing the mattress.

Ellen closed her eyes and did something she hadn't done since the war ended. Clasping her hands together, she whispered a prayer into the darkness:

Please, God—help me.

CHAPTER 15

Iris was horrified when she saw the blood.

"You've cut yourself!" She ran across the workshop and tore off a length of the paper towel she used to clean the brushes. "Here—wrap this round it."

"Thank you. It looks worse than it is." Ellen blew out a breath as she turned off the power to the band saw. "Stupid of me. I didn't sleep very well last night—it's made me clumsy."

"Well, it's not surprising you're having trouble sleeping—if you think the house is haunted." Iris had been waiting all morning for a chance to find out more about Carreg Cottage. She hadn't slept well herself after reading the report of her mother's death. But she'd found it impossible to think of a way of broaching the subject without giving herself away.

"It's probably the bed," Ellen said. "It's old and lumpy. We're having a new mattress delivered this afternoon. It's going to be a nightmare getting it up to the cottage, though. There's no road—just the track."

Iris couldn't imagine how something as big as that could be transported up the steep, uneven path she had walked along. She'd lain awake thinking of the final journey her mother had made, from the moor to the hospital. She'd thought about the ambulance arriving at the spot where the track began and wondered how it would have reached her. She'd pictured men carrying her down on a stretcher, struggling not to lose their footing as they dodged past giant rocks and vicious brambles.

"There's a first aid box up there on the shelf." Ellen's voice brought her back to the present. "Would you mind getting me some iodine and a bandage?"

"Of course." Iris found the green metal box and opened it. She shuddered when Ellen peeled back the paper towel to reveal a jagged wound on the outside of her left index finger. "Sorry—I'd never make a nurse," she said, as she passed the opened bottle of iodine across the table.

"Tony's the same," Ellen said. "He can't cope with the sight of blood."

Ellen's husband had been on Iris's mind ever since she'd read the report of the inquest. She didn't know what he looked like, but she had an image in her head of him finding her mother, kneeling on the grass, feeling for a pulse, then racing off on his motorbike to raise the alarm. She wondered if there had been any blood, whether her mother had been injured when she collapsed on the moor. If she had, Mr. Wylde was even more of a Good Samaritan than Iris had imagined. How she longed to speak to him. He was the last person, other than the hospital staff, to have seen her mother alive.

"He always says it's a good thing he wasn't allowed to fight in the war," Ellen went on. "Because he'd have fainted at the first sight of anyone getting injured."

Iris wondered fleetingly why Ellen's husband hadn't been permitted to serve in the military. Bad eyes or flat feet were the most common reasons. But there were far more important questions buzzing around in her head. There must be some way of getting Ellen to open up about the people who had lived at the cottage before the war. She just had to find the right words.

Something occurred to her as she shut the lid of the first aid box and replaced it on the shelf. Ellen had read the newspaper article in the library. She knew her mother's name. Had she made the same connection Iris had made?

"I was thinking about what you told me the other day," Iris began as she sat down at the table and picked up her paintbrush. "That doll-thing you found up the chimney—did you say it had a bird's skull for a head?"

Ellen nodded. "Why do you ask?"

"Oh, I just wondered—why a bird? If it was used to curse a person, you'd think it would have a human-looking head, wouldn't you?"

"I hadn't thought of that." Ellen frowned. "But now you mention it, there's a bit of a bird theme going on at the cottage." She told Iris about the painting on the ceiling above the bed.

Iris focused on the wooden figure of a pig whose eyes and snout she was picking out in black. She was willing the cogs to whirr in Ellen's mind.

"Oh! That's it, isn't it?" Ellen struck her forehead with the heel of her hand. "The name of the woman who died was Stella *Bird*."

Iris glanced up from her work, her face a mask of innocent surprise. "Really?"

"I don't know why I didn't think of it before. It's too much of a coincidence. I can't think of any other reason why it would have a bird's head."

"Do you think *he* made it—the man you were telling me about?"

"Him or one of his cronies," Ellen replied. "There was at least one woman living with him. He used them as assistants in his magic rituals, apparently."

What was his name? It was on the tip of Iris's tongue. And then the phone rang.

Tony parked the motorbike halfway up Tregenna Hill, well away from Fore Street. He didn't want to risk being spotted by Ellen. There was no need for her to know that he'd left the cottage. He'd be back well before the mattress was due to be delivered.

Clive Snow was waiting for him on a barstool in The Golden Sheaf pub. He wore a mustard-colored trench coat that had a smear of blue paint down the back and a green trilby hat adorned with the feather of a herring gull. Not exactly blending in with the surroundings, Tony thought, as he sat down beside him.

"What are you drinking?"

"I'll have a Bloody Mary." Clive hadn't lost his upper-class accent, despite having lived in Cornwall for more than a decade.

They took their drinks over to a table in a corner of the room. Tony could feel the soles of his boots sticking to the carpet with each step he took. The pub smelled as if someone had thrown up the previous night and whoever had cleaned it hadn't done a very thorough job. But it didn't matter. He wasn't going to linger, once he'd gotten what he came for.

"I couldn't get as much as last time," Clive said over the rim of his glass.

"Why not?" Tony glanced across the room, checking that the barman wasn't looking their way before he took the package Clive passed under the table.

"Dunno, old chap. You get shortages every so often, like everything since the war."

Tony raked his hair with his fingers. "They must grow around here," he whispered. "I bet we could pick our own, if we knew where to look."

Clive shrugged. "I daresay you're right. But there's the rub: we don't know, do we?"

"What about that place on Tregenna Hill—the shop that sells herbal tea and dandelion wine?"

"The Botanic Store?"

"That's the one. I bet they'd know."

The ice in Clive's glass chinked as he downed the dregs of the Bloody Mary. "They probably would. But I hardly think they'd tell you. I went in there once, thinking they might do a sideline in that sort of thing. The woman who owns it gave me my marching orders. Denis reckons she's a white witch."

"She's not one of Crowley's old flames?"

"I don't think so. I didn't know her face—she wasn't at any of the parties."

"Hmm." Tony stared at the froth on his beer. "I heard that he died. Just before Christmas."

"Did he?" Clive shook his head. "Poor old sod. He must have been getting on a bit, though?"

"Early seventies, according to Nina."

"Well, I'm surprised he lasted that long. The stuff he took . . ." Clive glanced at the pocket where Tony had hidden the illicit package. "That would merely have been the hors d'oeuvre. Dora once told me his daily dose of opium was enough to kill a horse."

"He offered me some of that, but I wouldn't touch it. It used to knock him out for hours." Tony patted his pocket. "Did he ever show you his version of this stuff?"

"No. What was it?"

"Some sort of cactus. He said he discovered it in Mexico. He called it peyote."

"Never heard of it."

"I tried to get hold of some in London. There's a pharmacy in Stafford Street, near Piccadilly, where you used to be able to get things under the counter. But they got busted—and then the war came." Tony took a mouthful of beer and wiped the froth off his lips with the back of his hand. "So, I'm making up for lost time."

"Things going well?"

Tony nodded. "When I was stuck in that bloody laboratory in Oxford, I used to go to sleep dreaming about Zennor Carn. I don't know what it is about it: the wildness, the lack of people . . . I feel free when I'm up there."

"Well, you've got some guts. Don't think I'd fancy living in Carreg Cottage after what happened to Dora and that other poor woman."

"You don't believe all that mumbo jumbo, do you?"

"What? About giant lizard-headed aliens invading the place?" Clive chuckled. "No, I've never believed that—despite what the locals say. I imagine it was the drugs that sent Dora off her rocker. As for the other one . . . well, you found her, didn't you? What do you reckon happened?"

Tony shrugged. "She was unconscious. Never said a word."

"I don't suppose we'll ever know, then." Clive leaned forward and clapped Tony on the back. "Congratulations, old chap. I suppose you got the place for a song?"

"You could say that." Tony drained his glass and stood up. "Better be getting back. Don't want to push my luck."

"Cheerio," Clive called after him as he walked away. "You'll have to let me in on your secret one of these days!"

"What?" Tony glanced back over his shoulder, alarm creasing his forehead.

"I want to know how you did it."

"Did what?"

"How you managed to bag a girl who's not only beautiful but rich enough to fund your . . . extramural pursuits." Clive winked.

Out of the corner of his eye, Tony could see the barman looking at him. He huffed out a breath as he made for the door. Clearly Clive had him down as a parasite. Was that how other people saw him? The thought gave him a salutary jolt. Ellen didn't deserve that. She was working so hard to give him what he craved. He had to show her—and everyone else—that he was worth it.

⊸━⊷

Iris woke with a start when her sketchbook clattered to the floor. She'd dozed off in the armchair, which she'd positioned in front of the mirror, intending to work on a self-portrait as a practice piece for the life class.

No one could possibly have seen her through the lace curtains, but she'd felt strangely vulnerable, sitting there naked, holding out the pencil to gauge the proportions of her body. In the end she'd draped a blanket over one shoulder and arranged it, toga-style, over her breasts and thighs.

"Why am I so tired?" She asked the question aloud to the empty room. She knew why. The pages of the sketchbook bore the evidence. She'd sat up drawing into the early hours after getting into bed last night. There were four pages of skulls. Every sort of bird she could imagine—from a sparrow to a seagull. As she'd sketched them, she'd agonized over what her mother could possibly have done to provoke the occupants of Carreg Cottage. If they'd been causing trouble, why hadn't her father gone to sort them out? How could he have sailed off to Canada, leaving her to deal with the situation on her own?

Glancing at the clock, she scrambled to her feet. The class was due to start in under an hour. She needed to get dressed, have a bite to eat, and get over there.

It was dark when she headed across the square. As she turned into Back Road West she saw a group of men standing at the bottom of the steps that led up to the School of Painting. She hung back, hiding in the shadow of one of the doorways, suddenly nervous about what she was about to do. What if she was the only female in the class? And the youngest? Those men all looked older than she was. How could she sit alongside them and attempt to draw? They'd see how inexperienced she was. It would be utterly humiliating.

"Evening, Iris." She jumped at the sound of a familiar voice. It was Denis Mitchell. She hadn't heard him coming around the corner.

"I thought I was late," he said, "but I can see a few stragglers." He nodded toward the men at the foot of the steps. "Are you waiting for someone?"

"Er, no . . . I . . ." She hesitated. There was something very reassuring about Denis. She'd sensed it within minutes of their first meeting, outside the cinema. He made you feel that whatever you said, he wouldn't be judgmental. "I . . . was just a bit nervous of going in on my own."

"No need to be," he said. "They're a real mixture at the life class. You get retired people who're doing it as a hobby, working artists who need the practice, and, sad to say, some blokes who just want to ogle a woman with no clothes on."

"Really?" Iris clicked her tongue against the roof of her mouth.

"They don't usually come more than once. Mr. Fuller gives them short shrift."

"Is he the principal?"

Denis nodded. "He's a veteran of the Great War, and he doesn't suffer fools. But don't be put off. He's a brilliant teacher."

The studio at the top of the building was brightly lit and bustling with activity. People were grabbing easels from the side of the room and arranging them in a circle around a dais in the center. As Iris found a spot, she caught the glitter of the sea through a window that ran the whole length of the far wall.

There were only two other women. Several decades older than Iris, they stood side by side, deep in conversation. Denis was chatting with a man on the other side of the room. By the time he grabbed an easel, there were only a few gaps left in the circle. Iris was glad he wasn't next to her. Much as she liked him, it would have been horribly intimidating.

Mr. Fuller, the principal, was a tall, thin man with a balding head and round tortoiseshell glasses. He was immaculately dressed in a tailored three-piece suit with a paisley-patterned tie. He climbed onto the dais to address the class:

"Welcome back to Studio Eleven, ladies and gentlemen. I trust you're all feeling rejuvenated after the Christmas break. I'm afraid the person booked to sit for us tonight has taken to her bed with a bad case of flu. But Miss Nina Grey has very kindly agreed to step in . . ." He turned to the side of the room that was curtained by blackout sheets nailed to a wooden rafter. A hand appeared, pushing the fabric aside. Iris recognized the woman from the party—the one whose outfit had outshone every other. Now she was wearing a green silk kimono, and her head was uncovered. Her hair blazed like a vivid sunset as she passed under one of the lights hanging from the ceiling.

Without a word, she stepped onto the dais and nodded at Mr. Fuller, who withdrew to a vacant easel. Then she dropped her kimono to the floor. Iris blinked. Nudity had been nothing remarkable at boarding school. She had seen female bodies of all shapes and sizes. But never had she seen a woman whose pubic hair was dyed to match the hair on her head.

Nina Grey positioned herself astride a rather uncomfortable-looking chair, sitting the wrong way around, so that she was gazing out over the back of the headrest. Her torso was bisected in three places by the wooden crossbars, her nipples framed by the topmost section. The look in her eyes reminded Iris of the gulls on the quayside, scavenging fish from the boats. There was the same brazen defiance about it. Clearly this woman had no qualms about what anyone thought of her. And that, Iris decided, was something to be admired.

There was a rustle of movement as people took up their pencils and began to draw. Iris felt self-conscious at first. But she soon realized that the men on either side of her were far too preoccupied to notice what she was doing. As she made the first strokes on the paper, she lost the sense of being surrounded by people. And the initial embarrassment at staring at the woman's body wore away. Sketching the lines and curves felt no different from capturing the contours of a landscape.

When a bell rang to signal the end of the session, Iris couldn't have said how long she'd been standing at the easel. The awareness of time passing had been eclipsed by her total absorption in translating what she was looking at into a two-dimensional image.

Her nerves returned when she realized that Mr. Fuller was coming around to look at everyone's work. When he reached her, he stood for a moment, studying her drawing without passing comment. He asked her if she'd had any previous instruction, and she mumbled something about art classes at school. To mention her term at The Westminster would be too risky. He might know people there.

"Your sketch is very fluid," he said. "And you've captured the expression in the eyes exceptionally well."

Iris felt a glow of pride. It was the first compliment she'd ever received about her work. Before leaving the studio, she picked up a list of the other classes available in the coming weeks. As she made her way back down to the street, Denis asked her if she'd like to join him and some of the others for a drink at The Castle.

She hesitated. There was no reason to worry about buying a drink or two now that she had a job.

The pub looked even more ancient inside than it did from the street. A sign on the dark wood paneling above the fireplace said that it dated back to 1840. She ordered a lemonade, then followed the others through the smoky public bar into a narrow corridor that led to the back room. To Iris's surprise, Dan was there. The sight of him triggered a very different tension from the nervousness about entering the pub. Her breath felt hot against the roof of her mouth.

Dan shuffled along the bench seat to make room for her and the others. Iris tried not to sit too close to him, but there wasn't much choice. The small room wasn't quite big enough for the dozen or so people in the group. She took a big gulp of lemonade, trying to subdue the heat in her face.

"How was the class?" he asked.

"I loved it." She rummaged in her pocket for the pamphlet she'd taken from the studio and laid it on the table, studying the list of classes to avoid his eyes. "I can't wait for the other sessions to start. There's seascapes next Monday—which is held outdoors—and a class on portraiture on Thursday afternoons. And then there's use of oils and perspective on Saturdays."

"Goodness!" Dan chuckled. "How are you going to fit them all in—with your job, I mean?"

"Ellen says I can be flexible." Iris wrapped her hands around her glass. The ice cubes were starting to melt. "She's paying me for four mornings a week, but she says that as long as I do the hours, it doesn't matter which days I come in."

"She sounds like the ideal boss." Dan took a swallow of his beer. "I wish Barbara was as understanding. There's no flexibility with her."

Iris felt the heat in her face receding a little. She could look at him now. "Ellen does seem very nice. She treats me more like a friend than an employee, really."

"Well, she didn't look much older than me, so I suppose that's not surprising."

Iris nodded. "I think she's finding it a bit of a struggle, setting up a business in a place she doesn't know. And I get the impression she's not exactly happy in the cottage she's moved into."

"What's wrong with it?"

As Iris repeated what Ellen had said, it occurred to her that Dan might have heard the rumors about Ellen's cottage.

"I remember people talking about it at school," he said. "There were all kinds of stories. Some said the man who lived there used to conjure up the Devil." He shook his head. "Another theory was that reptilian aliens had landed a spaceship on Zennor Carn."

"Really?"

He shrugged. "I've no idea where that came from. I had a friend, Pete Crocker, whose dad was a policeman. He had to go to the cottage after the woman died. He told Pete they found another woman there— and she was like a wild animal. She bit him when he tried to arrest her. He said the sight of her was enough to scare anyone to death."

Iris lifted her glass to her mouth. She didn't want Dan to see her welling up.

"My dad knew the woman who died," he went on. "She used to come to church. I remember him and Mum talking about how sad it was that she had a little girl who was going to grow up without her mother." He let out a long sigh. "Of course, I didn't know then that my own mum wouldn't be around for much longer."

Iris stared at what remained of her lemonade, watching the slivers of ice sink to the bottom. She had so many questions. But it would be utterly insensitive to ask any of them now.

CHAPTER 16

The new mattress smelled very different from the one that now lay outside in the garden, waiting to be burned. It reminded Ellen of the day she and her mother had moved into the house on Cheyne Walk. She had been seven years old and very excited to be having a room of her own after sharing a bed with her mother for as long as she could remember.

But this new mattress hadn't induced the deep, dreamless slumber she had been hoping for. Tony had been talking in his sleep—something she'd never heard him do before. And his voice had had a guttural, almost menacing quality. It didn't sound like him at all. At one point he had reached out for her, grasping her arm as he spoke. She had recoiled at his touch. It had felt as though a stranger were lying beside her.

He's your husband.

Why had she pulled away from him? She should have held him close, offered comfort from whatever was tormenting him. But something about the sound of that voice had repelled her.

It had taken a long time for her to get off to sleep after that, and when it did come, the horrible, leering man from the nightmare about Tony and Nina came back into her dreams. This time he was not standing in the doorway but climbing into the bed, his hands clawing at her naked body.

She woke in a sweat. It was still dark outside. Tony was facing away from her, his breathing slow and steady. She ran her hands over his hair, just to be sure it was him and not the bald-headed monster from her dream.

She peered at the luminous hands of the clock on the bedside table. Five thirty-five. It was too early to get up. She must try to get back to sleep. But as she closed her eyes, Tony's night-time ranting played back inside her head. Only a few of the words had been audible. She'd caught the name of his friend, Clive—and something about mushrooms. It hadn't made much sense. But one mumbled sentence had really frightened her: *He's dead, but he keeps talking to me.*

Had Tony been hearing the same voice she had heard?

She heard him blow out a breath as he shifted his head on the pillow.

"Are you awake, Tony?"

There was no response. She started to rehearse what she might say to him, how to broach the subject without triggering that impatient, irritable brush-off. She could begin by saying he'd been talking in his sleep. She would wait for him to ask her what he'd said. And then she'd repeat that one sentence. Watch his face.

She must have fallen asleep again thinking about it. When she opened her eyes, he wasn't there. The hands on the clock had moved to eight fifteen. Ellen leapt out of bed. She needed to get to the shop. She was expecting a delivery of wood at nine o'clock.

Tony parked his bike in the same spot as last time and headed down Tregenna Hill. He could see the sign for The Botanic Store. In the sea breeze coming up the hill, it swayed slightly, making the white hare look as if it were about to leap down onto the head of some unwary passer-by.

He stopped outside the shop and scanned the window display. Peppermint tea at fivepence an ounce was the cheapest thing. That would do.

A bell tinkled as he opened the door. The place had an unusual smell. Not unpleasant. Wildflower meadows with a hint of something musky. It transported him back to the days with Nina, when he'd watch her mix henna powder into a paste and then help her to apply it to the trickier patches of hair.

A woman in a striped apron appeared from behind a curtain.

"Good morning. Four ounces of the peppermint tea, please." He watched her as she weighed it out. Shortish, with ample curves and curly light-brown hair. Pretty pale blue eyes that crinkled at the edges as she peered at the scales. She looked midforties. Maybe a little younger. Certainly nothing like the stereotypical image of a witch.

"I do like this shop," he said, as she handed the package across the counter. "Such an amazing range—and so attractively displayed. Are you the owner?"

"Thank you. Yes, I am." There was only a trace of a Cornish lilt, as if she'd been away for a while.

"I wonder if I could ask your advice. I'm a vegetarian, and I'm keen on mushrooms. I've heard that this part of Cornwall is a good place to find them growing wild—but I'm not sure where to look."

"There's not many to be had at this time of year." She screwed the lid back on the jar of tea and replaced it on the shelf before turning back to him. "You might find oysters on the dead trees in Steeple Woods."

"Oh?" He smiled. "What do they look like?"

She smiled back. "The clue's in the name. The tops are creamy white and oyster-shaped. They're good to eat. Especially in a casserole."

"That sounds promising."

The woman nodded. "If you do go looking, you'd better watch out for wavy caps. They're about the only other mushroom you're likely to find in January. They're not poisonous, but they'd make you feel a bit peculiar."

"Ill, you mean?"

"Well, no—light-headed. A bit dizzy. They're hallucinogenic."

"How would I know if I found one?"

"They're small—much smaller than the oysters. They've got wavy tops and they're yellowy brown—like caramel."

"Thank you, I'll make sure to avoid them." He put the packet of tea in his pocket. "You've been very helpful."

As Tony stepped out into the street, another woman emerged from behind the curtain. "You know who that was, don't you, Mary?"

"No, Ma, I don't. What's his name?"

"Well, I can't remember *that*—but 'e was one of them as lived up at Carreg Cottage. If I remember rightly, it was 'im as raised the alarm when poor Mrs. Bird came to grief on the moor."

"*He* found Stella?"

"That's what Fred Vigar at The Tinners said. I used to see 'im go by on his motorbike. Fred was standing chatting to me one time, and 'e told me 'ow the feller 'ad come to the pub and asked them to call for the ambulance."

Mary went across to the window, watching Tony as he strode up the hill.

"It's a bit odd, that, don't you think, Mary?"

"What is, Ma?" Mary glanced back over her shoulder.

"That 'e comes in the shop within days of me seein'—"

"Oh, Ma! Don't upset yourself!" Mary crossed the room and wrapped her arms around her mother's shoulders.

"I can't help it. She looked so . . . *real*. Like she'd never gone away."

"*He* went away, though, didn't he? They all did. You said the place has been empty for years."

The older woman nodded. She pulled a handkerchief from her pocket and wiped her eyes. "Somethin's brought him back 'ere. I wonder what? It's got to be . . . nine years now, is it?"

"Ten years on May the twenty-second," Mary said. "I was in the hospital—remember?"

"'Course you were."

"I've always felt guilty about that, you know; wondered if things might have turned out differently if I'd been there to go with her to the cottage."

"But how could you? Even if you 'adn't gone into labour that day, you'd never 'ave made it up that track."

"I know." Mary stared at the row of jars on the counter. "But it's never left me, Ma: the feeling that I wasn't there for her when she needed me."

CHAPTER 17

The workshop was full of the smell of lime wood. The man who had delivered the logs had helped her to get them up the ladder into the storage area, which had saved her a good deal of time. Nevertheless, it was midafternoon before she turned off the band saw. She'd been trying to get ahead with production while she was alone in the workshop. On the bench beside her was a stack of the parts required for the farmhouse sets. Iris would have plenty of sanding and painting to do on her next shift. But now Ellen's arms ached. She needed a break. She took off her tool belt and reached for her coat.

As she walked down Fore Street, she realized that she wasn't hungry, despite having had nothing for breakfast. She wondered if she was coming down with something. But she didn't feel ill. Just tired. And unsettled. She couldn't get Tony's words out of her mind.

He's dead, but he keeps talking to me.

Was Crowley dead? Or had Tony dreamed it? How would he know?

As if she'd summoned him out of thin air, Tony suddenly appeared on his motorbike. He was coming around the corner of Tregenna Place. Was it really him? As the bike headed off up Gabriel Street, the registration plate on the back was clearly visible. The sequence of letters and numbers was imprinted on her brain after following him all the way from London.

Why was he in St Ives? He hadn't said anything about coming into town. He'd probably run out of something. There was an art supplies shop on Tregenna Hill. She'd been there herself to buy paint. More than likely that's what he'd done. But why hadn't he popped in to see her? The question nagged at her as she carried on walking. To be fair, she had told him what a busy morning she was going to have.

To be fair? Why are you always giving him the benefit of the doubt?

Her mother's voice interrupted the chatter inside her head. It was true—she did make allowances for Tony. But wasn't that how marriage was supposed to work? There must be things that he found both irritating and inexplicable about her—but the only time he ever criticized was when she said something negative about the cottage. And that was his baby. His dream. If only she could feel the same, find a way to vanquish whatever it was that wouldn't let go of the place.

A shadow fell across her path as she neared the sea. Glancing to the left, Ellen saw that she was passing the church Iris had mentioned. Its square tower rose high above the surrounding buildings, the stone glinting where the sunlight caught it. The door was open. Remembering what Iris had said about how beautiful it was, she decided to take a look.

The air inside was still and musty, with traces of something smoky and aromatic. Incense or candle wax. Maybe both, mingled with furniture polish. The smell transported her back to London, to those predictable Sundays before the war, when going to church was something she took for granted. It wasn't something she'd looked forward to particularly—it was just part of the weekly routine. It was only when the Germans dropped a bomb on the place that she realized what she and her mother had lost. Part of the fabric of their lives had been blown away. And after that, things had never felt as safe again.

Ellen wandered up the nave, looking up at the carved, painted figures that jutted out where the stone walls met the barrel-vaulted ceiling. They were like something from before the dawn of Christianity, the kind of thing she could imagine people making when pagan gods still held sway. Amazing to think that they had once been oars wielded by Cornish fishermen. She wished she could fly up to take a closer look at the workmanship.

"They're beautiful, aren't they?"

Ellen hadn't realized there was anyone else in the church. The man was standing near the pulpit. White-haired and bespectacled, he wore a priest's collar that was just visible above the crew neck of his sweater. "I wish I could get up there and clean them," he said, as he closed the distance between them. "We've had a problem with birds getting into the church. But the ladder we have isn't long enough." He paused, resting a hand on the end of a pew. "Are you visiting St Ives?"

"No—I've just moved here," Ellen replied. "I've opened a shop in Fore Street. I make wooden toys." She gestured at the figures overhead. "That's what brought me in here—to see the carvings. I have an assistant—Iris. She told me about them."

"Ah! Our young Christmas angel."

"Is she?" Ellen smiled. "Why?"

"She appeared, as if by magic, on Christmas morning. She'd had a problem with her hotel booking, and Dan, my son, offered her a bed for a couple of nights. She really brightened up our day." He took off his spectacles and polished them on the hem of his sweater. "Christmases have been rather sad affairs since my wife passed away."

"I'm sorry to hear that." She wondered how long ago he'd been widowed. He was clearly struggling to keep his grief in check. "I met your son—at a party on New Year's Eve," she said. "That was how I got to know Iris, actually."

"Oh, the Hepworth-Nicholsons," he said, nodding. "Barbara has been very good to Dan. He was a bit lost when he came back from the war. She's helped him a good deal. Not just financially—she's given him the confidence to start making things." He shifted his weight, as if standing in one position for too long was uncomfortable for him. "She's a friend of yours, is she?"

"Well, I've only just met her. My husband used to visit Barbara and her husband during the war. He's an artist."

"And now you've moved here. Splendid! Where are you living?"

"Over at Zennor. We've bought a place on the slopes of the carn."

His face was partly shadowed by the winter sunlight filtering through the stained-glass windows, but Ellen caught a change in it, a slight movement of the lips and the eyebrows that gave away his reaction. It was a look of surprise mixed with concern. The same expression that had crossed her mother's face when Ellen had announced that she was marrying Tony.

"Do you know Carreg Cottage?" she asked. In the silence of the church, she could hear her blood surge.

"I haven't seen it, but I know where it is," he said. "One of my parishioners used to own it before the war. It's very beautiful up there, I believe." His smile erased the traces of worry. She got the sense that he was being very careful; he was a priest, after all—the last person to want to say anything negative or upsetting about someone's new home.

"It is." She nodded. "And the cottage is full of character—but I don't think anyone's lived there for a good many years." The parishioner he'd mentioned had to be Stella Bird—or one of her parents. So, he knew the family. He must know something about the circumstances of Stella's death.

"It was rented out, I believe, and one of the tenants fell ill and had to leave," he said. "And then the war came, of course."

He was telling her a version of the truth—one that wouldn't be difficult to hear. But she couldn't allow that: she had to know the whole of it. How could she get him to reveal what he knew?

"I'm afraid that the place might be haunted." The shock tactic. She watched his face.

"Oh?" It was a single syllable—enunciated in a way that conveyed a great deal. Ellen sensed that what she'd said wasn't a surprise to him; it was almost as if he'd been expecting it. He lowered his head, rubbing his chin. "What makes you think that?"

"I . . ." Now that the ball was in her court, she faltered. "I don't know how to describe it—and you probably don't believe in that sort of thing, anyway . . ."

"Ghosts, you mean?" His directness took her by surprise. "I do, as a matter of fact."

"Really?"

He nodded. "As a Christian, I believe in life after death—that we move on, to a better place. But it seems that there are earthbound spirits abroad, and some manifest themselves from time to time." He drew in a long breath and let it out. "I'm convinced that I saw something supernatural once—whether it was ghostly or something equally inexplicable, I can't say. I was a chaplain in the Great War. The fighting had ended, and we were in the trenches, just marking time until we were all sent home. Suddenly, in broad daylight, I saw a cavalry skirmish between soldiers wearing uniforms from a century earlier. It was at a spot on the Franco-Belgian border where, I found out later, fighting had occurred during the Napoleonic wars."

"You really saw that?" Ellen's eyes were locked on his. "You don't think you imagined it?"

"I wasn't alone. A companion saw them, too." He shook his head. "I've puzzled over it down the years—and the conclusion I've come to is that I witnessed a recording of something that somehow imprinted itself on the place where it happened. We don't have the scientific knowledge to understand how that could be—but one day we might."

Ellen nodded slowly. "That's exactly how I feel about the cottage. At first, I thought it was my imagination. But I've seen things that seemed so real. I can't shake the feeling that it's like what you've just described: scenes from the past playing back like a record—only you see it as well as hear it."

"What have you seen?"

She told him about the grotesque face at the window and the strange lights on the hillside. "And a couple of nights ago I had a vivid nightmare. There was an evil-looking man with a twisted smile standing in the bedroom doorway." She left out the description of what the man had been looking at: no point in embarrassing herself and the vicar with that. "I sometimes hear a voice as well," she said. "A man's voice. Telling me that I don't belong at the cottage."

"Do you have any idea why the cottage might be haunted?"

"I've heard rumours. I know there was a man called Crowley living there before the war, who . . . held black magic ceremonies." She lowered her voice at the end of the sentence because, in a place like this, the words sounded blasphemous. "And I know that a woman had a seizure and died after visiting the cottage. Was that the parishioner you mentioned?"

"Yes. Mrs. Bird. I wondered if you knew. I wouldn't have said anything . . ." He pressed his lips together.

"I've put you on the spot. I'm sorry. I didn't come here with that in mind. But I need to know what happened. What *really* happened." She took a breath, closed her eyes for a second. "I've been to the library and read a newspaper report of the inquest—but there's no mention of Crowley. I feel as if there's something . . . *malevolent* in the cottage. That's the only way I can describe it." She glanced up at the huge crucifix that hung between the nave and the altar. "I probably shouldn't say that in a church."

"Why ever not?" He followed her gaze. "Jesus himself struggled against the Devil when he was out in the wilderness—and Saint Paul wrote about man fighting against principalities and powers of darkness. Those powers are not to be sneered at—nor should they be tampered with. We need to be constantly on our guard against their influence." She heard him catch his breath. "Forgive me, my dear—the old legs aren't what they used to be." He stepped sideways into the pew and sat down. "You believe it's Crowley's ghost that's haunting your cottage?"

"I . . . it's just a feeling, really. I don't even know that he's dead."

"Well, he is dead. His obituary was in the *Times* a couple of weeks before Christmas."

Ellen stared at him. "Do you think he's what you were describing? An earthbound spirit?"

"It's quite possible. The things he did when he was alive certainly didn't mark him out for a swift passage to heaven. Quite the reverse." He shook his head. "People like Crowley—dabblers in black magic—are murderers of the soul. I can say that with some conviction because I used to know the man who rented your cottage. We were friends for a time, at university. He devoted himself to becoming an active disciple of the Devil—and he very nearly succeeded in taking me with him. Suffice to say I went the other way. Then, some thirty years later, he fetched up here. I caught him once, doing something to the old Celtic cross that stands outside the porch."

"What was he doing?"

"Heaven knows. He had a paintbrush in his hand, as if he was planning to deface it. I threw holy water over him, and he came out with the most horrible language. Damned me and my family to hell and cursed us all to die from slow and agonising diseases."

Ellen's eyes widened. He'd said his wife had died. Had Crowley's curse caused that?

"He went quiet after that," the vicar went on. "I didn't know he was renting Carreg Cottage until I started hearing gossip about the place. I thought then that it was only right to tell Mrs. Bird what I knew about her tenant. You can imagine how I felt when I heard what had happened to her."

"Do you know what she saw there—what brought on that seizure?"

"Like you, I can only imagine." He steepled his fingers on his lap and contemplated them for a moment before looking up. "We haven't properly introduced ourselves, have we? I'm Idris Thomas. What's your name, my dear?"

"Ellen. Ellen Wylde."

"Well, Ellen, I'm at your disposal. I don't know how well acquainted you are with the ways and means of the Anglican Church, but there are certain services we vicars can offer in circumstances like these."

"Are there?"

"Yes. In a case of suspected haunting, an exorcism can be carried out. I'm afraid I'm not up to climbing that hill of yours—and I'm not sure my old car would make it, either—but if you could arrange transport, I'd be more than happy to oblige."

"Th . . . that's very good of you." She was thinking about Tony, of his reaction if she brought this man to the cottage. She could imagine the vicar, no doubt dressed in full clerical regalia for such a ritual, stepping out of the jeep, his robes flying in the breeze. She had no idea what an exorcism involved. She imagined that crosses and holy water would be required, readings from the Bible. What would Tony—an avowed atheist—make of that? She knew the answer: he'd be furious. He'd probably throw the vicar out.

"No need to make a decision now." He gave her a wry look, as if he'd read her thoughts. "But the offer's there, should you choose to take it. And in the meantime, if you ever feel the need to talk, I live over the way, at the vicarage. I'm always on call, so please don't worry about arriving unannounced. Day or night."

"Thank you." As Ellen headed for the door, she was in turmoil. She could hear her mother's voice, urging her to take up the vicar's offer. But Tony would never stand for it. The only way to do it would be to take the vicar to the cottage when he wasn't there. But he was *always* there. Apart from brief forays into St Ives, there was no reason for him to be away. Even if he was out painting on the moor, there was always the risk that he might return unexpectedly.

As she stepped outside, she passed by the ancient, lichen-spotted cross that cast its shadow across the porch. The face of the man from her dream filled her mind's eye. She could picture him standing there, wielding his paintbrush like a magic wand. If Crowley had felt *that* powerful, *that* untouchable—to stand within the precincts of a church invoking curses on a priest—what chance did *she* stand against his ghost?

Tony groaned as he stood up. His legs were stiff from squatting beside a dead tree. The rank smell of fox filled his nostrils, and the leaf mold around his feet was littered with rabbit droppings. It had taken a good while to find what he was looking for, but now the pockets of his jacket bulged with illicit bounty. He would need to find a place to dry out the strange-smelling wavy-capped fungi—a place where Ellen wouldn't discover them.

He smiled as he wound his way back through the woods, dodging moss-covered rocks, to the clearing where he'd parked the bike. He must have ridden past Steeple Woods dozens of times, never realizing what treasure lay within. It felt good, knowing that he wouldn't have to rely on Clive's supply chain anymore. If he liked, he could turn the tables and sell to Clive. That would be a trick worth keeping up his sleeve if money ever ran short.

Emerging from the trees, he could see the full sweep of Carbis Bay. There was a swathe of cloud on the horizon—gunmetal tinged with purple. Would he make it back to Zennor before the heavens opened? Deciding that the answer was probably no, he took a right turn, heading for Barbara and Ben's house.

He left the motorbike under the shelter of the overhanging roof and made his way around the side of the house to Barbara's studio. Through the window he could see two men chiseling away at a towering block of stone. One of them was Denis Mitchell. He didn't recognize the other—a younger man with olive skin who was head and shoulders taller than Denis.

Tony tapped on the window. Looking around, Denis waved and came to unlock the door.

"Is Barbara at home?" Tony asked. "I was passing and thought I'd stop by."

"She's just got back," Denis replied. "One of the triplets has come down with a chest infection, and she's had to take him to the doctor."

"Oh—I'd probably better not bother her, in that case." Tony glanced outside. The dark clouds seemed to have dissipated. Perhaps he wouldn't get soaked, after all. But as he turned to leave, he heard Barbara's voice.

"Tony! Come through to the kitchen!" She had opened a window in the wall that divided the house from the studio.

"Are you sure?" he called back.

She nodded. "I'm gasping for a cup of tea and a ciggy after the morning I've had."

Half an hour later, Tony was on to his second cup of tea, and the ashtray on the kitchen table was on the verge of overflowing.

"How are you getting on at the cottage?" Barbara asked, as she reached for her lighter. "Or should I say, how's Ellen getting on?"

Tony shrugged. "All right. She's not there much—she's taken on a shop in town, and she's got a big order to fulfil. From Harrods, actually."

Barbara's eyebrows lifted. "Impressive. She must be tougher than she looks. I should have realised that—let's face it, there can't be many women who'd be prepared to live in a place with a reputation like Carreg Cottage's."

"She doesn't know about all that." Tony sucked on his cigarette. "Nina put the wind up her a bit at your party, but I've asked her to keep a lid on it in future."

"Seriously?" Barbara shook her head. "You think Ellen won't find out? I heard rumours about the place when I was still living in London."

"What did you hear?"

"That something very nasty happened there—that one woman died, and another went raving mad." Barbara tapped her cigarette against the rim of the ashtray. "Nina filled me in on some of it. I already knew about the parties the pair of you went to at the cottage. Ben went once. Were you there that time? He was a bit wet behind the ears in those days—he told me he hadn't even made it up the path when two girls came running out, stark naked, and started cavorting around him."

Tony rolled his eyes. "That must have been before I went there. I didn't know Ben was friends with Crowley."

"He wasn't. Nina invited him. He thought they were going to spend the weekend painting outdoors. That's what he told me, anyway. He never went again. But *you* liked Crowley, didn't you? Nina said you practically moved in after she took you there."

"I didn't *like* him. I suppose I found him interesting, at first. He wanted me to be his assistant—with the stuff he wanted to do up on the carn. I didn't believe in any of it—I only went along with it because of what he gave me in lieu of wages."

"Well, you don't have to be a genius to guess what *that* was," Barbara grunted. "Did Ellen tell you she suggested Ben should try what you smoked to help his asthma?"

"What?"

"She was sitting in here with me—the morning after the party—and I was saying that Ben didn't like me smoking in the bedroom because of his asthma. She said you had it, too, and that you took something herbal in a pipe to ease it. I nearly burst out laughing when she said it might help Ben." She tipped the pack of Senior Service, shaking out the last cigarette. "You don't have asthma, do you? That's another lie you've told her, I suppose."

"I haven't *lied* to her. I did have a bad chest, as a kid, but I grew out of it."

"So, that wasn't the reason you didn't join up?"

"I was a conscientious objector. I didn't want to tell Ellen that in case she . . . ," he trailed off with a shrug.

"In case she thought less of you?"

"She drove ambulances through the Blitz, Barbara. She was only seventeen when she started."

"My goodness. *What a tangled web we weave when first we practise to deceive.* You're going to have to be careful not to lose track of all these stories you've told her." She glanced at the clock on the wall. "I'm afraid I'm going to have to kick you out now, sweetie—I've got to get on. Did I tell you I've been invited to enter a competition to design a sculpture for Westminster Bridge? I have to submit sketches by the end of next week."

"Congratulations," Tony said, stubbing out his cigarette. "How nice to be in such demand." He hadn't meant it to sound peevish. But he couldn't help feeling deflated as he kissed her goodbye. Barbara was well on the way to achieving what he could only dream of. Her reputation was spreading far beyond the galleries of St Ives. And Ben wasn't far behind her. Articles were being written about them in the newspapers: they were the golden couple of the art world.

As he climbed onto his motorbike, the old, familiar doubts flooded in. That he would never achieve that kind of recognition, that he would never be regarded as anything more than mediocre. But as he settled into the saddle, he could feel the bulk of the woodland harvest in his jacket pocket. The mushrooms would open the door to what he craved. All he needed to excel as an artist was that extra dimension. He opened the throttle, revving the engine as he pulled out onto the road.

Don't forget who showed you to that door. A servant can never be greater than his master.

The voice in his head drowned out the roar of the motorbike. He swerved so hard he almost hit a lamppost.

CHAPTER 18

Word had spread about The Toy Tiger. Without any of the publicity Ellen had planned, people started to drop in. Some were merely curious, but others were genuinely interested in buying what was on display in the window. Ellen made the decision to move the finishing table into the front of the building, so that Iris could deal with the customers when she was there. Iris was under strict instructions only to call Ellen away from the workbench if a sale was in the offing.

Iris didn't mind this arrangement—but she missed the chance to talk to Ellen. It had been good to have female company—and there was so much she burned to know about what had gone on in Carreg Cottage. But she soon realized that even if they'd continued to work in the same room, there was unlikely to have been much opportunity to ask questions. Ellen seemed to have a lot on her mind. She was clearly racing against time to get the order completed—and the band saw made such a racket that conversation was difficult. Whether her self-absorption had anything to do with her fears about her home being haunted, it was impossible to know.

Iris spent very little time in her room above the fish cellar over the next few days. If she wasn't at the shop, she was attending a class. Monday afternoon was seascapes, which took place, as planned, out on the harbor wall. The weather had turned very mild, with almost no wind, which was perfect for painting outdoors.

They set up easels on the cobblestones. Mr. Fuller encouraged them to sit for a while before attempting to get anything down on paper, just taking in the mood of the sea and the sky. She found herself mesmerized by the gentle lap of the waves. The look and the sound of it was like a soothing balm—so different from the angry gray surge that had chilled her bones as the wind whipped across it on Christmas Day.

A tiny shoal of clouds drifted across the sun. With Mr. Fuller's guidance, she learned how to mix pigments to quickly capture the patterns of light and shadow on the water.

When the class ended, the principal announced a lecture that was to be held that evening at Studio Eleven. Nina Grey was giving a talk entitled "Dark Angel—A Feminine Perspective on Surrealism." Iris had almost forgotten. She'd jotted down the details in the back of her notebook the day she'd been trying to find Norway Square.

As she packed away her paints and brushes, she thought about Dan. She would have asked him if he wanted to go to the lecture, but he probably wouldn't be well enough. He hadn't been in church yesterday, and the vicar had told her he was in bed with a chest infection. This morning she'd taken grapes and a copy of *Moving Picture World*, hoping to see him. But Reverend Thomas had said he was sleeping.

Despite the busyness of the past few days, Iris really missed Dan. She wondered if he thought about her at all. She hated the idea of him lying there, feeling ill, his father too preoccupied with the responsibilities of his job to be able to spend much time looking after him. She couldn't help picturing herself sitting at his bedside, watching him as he slept; feeding him grapes when he woke up hot and thirsty; maybe reading to him if he wanted her to.

She'd missed that so much, as a child, her mother reading to her—especially when she'd been ill. At school, if you came down with something, you were packed off to the sanatorium—a stark, comfortless room with beds divided off by curtains. You could hear other girls coughing and sneezing, sometimes crying out in pain, but you weren't allowed to talk to them. On nights like those, she had longed for her mother.

As Iris picked up her easel and followed the others to the studio in Back Road West, her mother's face filled her mind's eye. She couldn't bear the thought of her being frightened and alone on that bleak hillside. Would she ever know what had really happened to her?

The platform in Studio Eleven where Nina Grey had posed naked for the life class had been turned into an exhibition space for the talk she was about to give. The centerpiece was a head, like the one Iris had seen at the Mariners' Church—but adorned with layers of silver-painted dried seaweed for hair. A headband of mussel shells encircled it, the mother-of-pearl glinting where the light caught it. Two lengths of stiff black fishing net were attached to the band, swept back like wings. Beneath the chin, the neck was covered in strips of white fur, stitched together like flesh mended by a surgeon. And across the eyes was a blindfold made of pale blue silk embroidered with yellow fish.

Iris stood for a moment, trying to decipher the language of the piece. Behind it was a series of collages, blending objects from the sea with human faces. The largest was one that, at first glance, looked like a ship in full sail but, on closer inspection, revealed the profile of a woman whose face was constructed from swirls of tiny feathers.

She moved aside to allow the other people gathering around the exhibits to get a better look. Some were picking up objects that had been scattered around the front of the platform: pieces of driftwood, the claws of lobsters and crabs, the skeletons of fish, and a bowl containing jewel-like fragments of glass, like the one Dan had made into a necklace for her.

The room was filling up. Iris spotted Barbara Hepworth and her husband chatting with Mr. Fuller. After a moment he turned away from them to ring the bell he'd used to signal the end of the life class. "Could you all please take a seat, ladies and gentlemen?"

When everyone was sitting down, a woman came to the front to introduce the speaker. Iris recognized her. She was Lady Frieda Harris—the painter of the Tarot card images.

"Good evening to you all." The cut-glass accent, the upswept gray hair, and the tailored clothes were so at odds with the disturbing images this woman had created. Iris stared in fascination as she talked about the accolades Nina had received. "And I think I am correct in saying that no other artist invited to speak in this studio has ever done so *wearing* his or her own creation . . . Ladies and gentlemen, please welcome Miss Nina Grey, modelling *Stargazy Pie!*"

There were whoops of delight as Nina stepped from behind the curtain, resplendent in a sequined evening gown that flashed iridescent colors as she walked across to the platform. On her head was a wide, disc-shaped hat whose silver brim held what looked like an undulating layer of golden-brown pastry. Peeking out from around the edges, as if tucked under a blanket, where what appeared to be the heads of a half a dozen dead fish. Emerging from the middle of the hat was a ballerina doll, holding a glittering starfish above her head.

"Thank you." Nina Grey gave a theatrical curtsey. "In case you're wondering, the mackerel are not real—they're painted kidskin—and the pastry is calico soaked in plaster of Paris. The hat is an *homage* to the women of Cornwall—the bakers of this most traditional of fish pies, in which the heads are arranged outside the pastry, as if gazing up at the stars." The red lips slid into a smile. "I found myself wondering what the women might be thinking as they made these pies, of their hopes and dreams—possibly of escaping the domestic drudgery and living a life more exciting, more glamorous, than that of housewife." She raised her hand, touching the brim. "The hat might look comical, but it carries a message for those who choose to delve deeper. Can the creation of a pie unlock the inner world of the woman who made it?"

Her wide green eyes ranged over the audience. The expression was challenging, defiant—the same look she'd given Iris and the other students when she'd posed for the life class. "To me, this is the essence of surrealism. It aims to subvert reality."

She gestured toward the centerpiece of the artwork on the platform. "This is called *Dark Angel: Our Lady of the Sea*. Its starting point was a cast of my own face. It's embellished with found objects from the seashore." She reached out to touch the blindfold. "The embroidered silk fabric is the only exception." Her fingers traveled down to the fur strips covering the neck. "This is the skin of a baby seal I found washed up at Pendour Cove. Some of you might think it distasteful to take a dead animal and use it in this way, but I prefer to see it as a sort of resurrection—a way of giving the creature another life."

Iris found it hard to imagine the glamorous Nina kneeling in the sand, stripping fur from flesh.

"In making this piece," Nina went on, "I sought to portray the sea as a force of ancient, anarchic power. *Feminine* power. It encircles the lonely moors and ancient burial places. It is never at peace. Even on a calm day, there is a sense of inward, seething strength, of dangerous, hidden currents."

Iris listened, spellbound, as Nina drew out the central theme of her lecture: the idea that women were more closely connected with nature, with the earth, than men—and that their ability to give birth gave them a unique artistic insight not granted to the male sex.

Iris wasn't sure whether she agreed with this last point. She thought of what she'd seen in Dan's studio: the Tree of Life piece that told the story of Creation and the woman, the giver of life, cupping her breasts. Just because Dan had never and would never give birth to a baby didn't mean he was incapable of imagining what that might feel like.

Iris was suddenly aware of people clapping all around her. The talk was over. Lady Frieda Harris thanked Nina and invited everyone in the audience to continue the evening with drinks at Number Five, Bellair Terrace.

Iris didn't think she would go. It would be awkward, going to someone's house on her own, not really knowing anybody. But as she put on her coat, Ben Nicholson came over to her.

"Hello. You're Dan's friend, aren't you? Is he feeling any better?"

"I'm not sure." Iris felt embarrassed that everyone seemed to think she and Dan were an item. "I called to see him, but he wasn't well enough to get out of bed."

"Poor chap. If it's the same bug our kids have had, he'll be out of the picture for at least a week." He glanced over his shoulder toward the platform, where his wife was chatting with Nina Grey. "Are you coming to the drinks do?"

"I . . . er . . . ," Iris faltered. "I wasn't going to."

"Oh, you must! If you're a fan of surrealism, you'll see a good deal more of it at Frieda's place." He smiled. "You can hop in the car with us, if you like—as long as you don't mind stopping off at Nina's first."

Iris felt a stab of panic at traveling in such august company. But it would only be for a short time—and the prospect of seeing Lady Frieda's art collection was too tempting to refuse.

She helped Ben to pack away the exhibits—including Nina's fishy hat. Close up, she could see the exquisite workmanship that had gone into creating the mackerel. Had they been laid on a fishmonger's slab, they would have fooled any passing shopper. Iris wondered what kind of paint Nina had used to achieve that glistening, lifelike effect on the kidskin. Did she ever teach at the School of Painting? If she did, there had been no mention of it in the list of upcoming classes.

They took the boxes out to where Ben's car was parked under a streetlamp. It was the same make and model as Dan's father's—a Morris Ten—but it looked a lot newer and shinier. As Iris handed Ben the last box, Nina came down the steps, arm in arm with Barbara.

"Oh, hello," she said to Iris. "I don't think I had any clothes on last time I saw you!"

"Er . . . no . . ." Iris felt herself blushing. "I . . . I'm surprised you remember me."

"Well, it's not the most scintillating way to spend a couple of hours," Nina said. "I tend to watch the students watching me. You stuck out like a sore thumb. Probably brought down the average age by about fifteen years."

She slid into the back of the car, tapping the seat beside her. Iris climbed in. She could smell Nina's perfume. It reminded her of the night-scented tobacco flowers that used to grow in the garden at Rowan Tree House.

Nina's house was in Rose Lane—a street so narrow that Ben had to slow to a crawl to avoid scraping the car. While Nina let him in, Barbara and Iris waited in the car.

"It's very *bijou* in there." Barbara twisted her head round. "Small but perfectly formed—like Nina." She put a cigarette in her mouth, lit it, and blew smoke the other way before turning back to Iris. "You'll love Frieda's place. Bellair Terrace is very la-di-dah for St Ives." She took another drag on the cigarette, tipping her head back this time to send the smoke toward the roof of the car. "Her husband's a baronet. She only uses it for holidays."

Iris glanced out of the window as Ben and Nina reappeared. She saw Nina tap Ben's bottom as he stepped across the cobbles. Had Barbara noticed? If she had, she didn't say anything when they got back into the car. Perhaps this was considered normal behavior among the arty crowd of St Ives.

Lady Frieda Harris's summer residence was a far cry from the fishermen's cottages of Downalong. Number Five was in a terrace of elegant Regency houses with ocean views. Inside, there was art everywhere. With a glass of champagne in her hand, Iris wandered around, taking in the paintings on the walls.

A group of four to the left of the fireplace was instantly recognizable as the hostess's own work. The images had names, like the ones Iris had seen in the crypt at the Mariners' Church. There was *The Tower, The Hierophant, The Queen of Wands,* and *The Fool.*

The Queen of Wands exuded the same hypnotic quality Iris had experienced while looking at the image of the card called *Lust*. It was striking and threatening at the same time. A gigantic woman with long red hair falling ramrod straight over her shoulders sat stroking the head of a leopard sitting at her feet. Shards of gold radiated, starlike, from behind her warrior's helmet. In her left hand she held an enormous rod tipped with a golden pinecone. Jagged shapes, outlined in red, flared up like flames around her legs.

"What are your impressions?" She hadn't spotted Lady Frieda coming toward her. "I love to hear what people think when they look at them."

Caught off guard, Iris felt out of her depth. For a moment she felt unable to speak at all.

"Don't be shy. You can be totally honest—I'm used to it."

"Th . . . they're very powerful," Iris began. "I saw some of the others—at the exhibition."

"Yes—I remember you." Lady Frieda smiled. "You asked me about the School of Painting."

Iris nodded. "I wanted to ask you about your work—but by the time I realised you were the artist, you'd gone."

"Well, I'm here now. Tell me what you were thinking."

Iris's initial panic at being put on the spot began to subside. Lady Frieda reminded her of Miss Tucker—her history teacher at school. She had a kind face. "I found it hard to tear myself away from them," she said. "What attracted me at first were the colours. Then, when I got closer, I was fascinated by the imagery. The animals: the lion and the tiger—and now I see a leopard in this one." She gestured to *The Queen of Wands*.

"Yes, I used the big cats to convey raw, instinctive energy. As symbols, they have great resonance—in the same way that Nina harnesses the power of images from the sea. But I also drew on the world of magic, astrology, and alchemy." She pointed to the upper section of *The Queen of Wands*. "You see that her helmet is topped with a winged sun, which represents the potency of creative power—and there are flames around her legs, which symbolize the fire of enlightenment. The paintings were commissioned by a man with a great interest in world religions. His particular focus was the mythology of ancient Egypt." She placed her empty champagne flute on the mantel shelf over the fireplace. "Unfortunately, they have yet to be published. And as the gentleman in question died recently, they probably never will be."

"Frieda—there you are! Someone's just arrived who's longing to meet you." Mr. Fuller gave Iris a nod as he took their hostess by the arm and guided her across the room.

Iris stayed where she was, examining the Tarot card pictures with renewed interest. She couldn't imagine how long it must have taken to create seventy-eight such detailed paintings. How frustrating for Lady Frieda that they were not going to be published.

A uniformed waiter came to top up her glass. She wasn't used to drinking alcohol, and she felt a little unsteady as she continued her tour of the art on display in the house. In the dining room she spotted a collection of photographs. There was a wedding portrait of Lady Frieda, several decades younger, standing next to a man in top hat and tails. Another photo showed her standing at an easel, paintbrush in hand, in a room that looked very much like Studio Eleven.

Iris's gaze shifted to the image below it. It was a shot of a strange-looking man. He was sitting in a garden, holding a silver-topped cane in one hand, and staring into the camera with a rather menacing expression. His head was bald apart from a tuft of dark hair at the top of his forehead that stuck out like a horn. Her eyes widened as they traveled over the image again. On the index finger of the hand holding the cane was a ring in the shape of a serpent.

"Ugly old sod, isn't he?" Nina's voice made Iris jump.

"Who is he?"

"Frieda's friend, Aleister Crowley—otherwise known as the Beast 666. She worked with him on the Tarot card paintings."

Crowley. It couldn't be, could it? And yet . . . Iris looked at the photo again. Lady Frieda had said that the man who commissioned the paintings had died recently—just like the Mr. Crowley her father had known.

"He lived here for a while," Nina went on. "Well, not *here*, in this house—he rented a cottage at Zennor. That photo was taken in the garden there."

Without really knowing what she was doing, Iris lifted her glass to her lips and drained what remained of the champagne. She was already woozy, and her head began to spin. She thought of her father, returning from the funeral with the ring. Had he taken it from the dead finger of this nasty-looking man? A man who had once lived at Zennor?

"Are you all right?" Nina's hand was on her shoulder.

"I'm fine . . . thank you . . . I just need some air." Iris made her way unsteadily toward the door. It *had* to be him: the man Ellen had told her about. The man her mother had gone to confront on what would be her last night on this earth.

And Lady Frieda had been his *friend.* No doubt she knew Iris's father. They had probably been there together, at the funeral. But how, why, would her father have kept company with a man who, according to Dan, was rumored to have conjured up the Devil? What kind of husband would leave his wife at the mercy of such a monster?

CHAPTER 19

Ellen sat in front of the fire with a cup of tea, glad that tonight's meal wouldn't take much preparation. All she had to do was grate some cheese and beat the eggs for the omelet. If Tony was still hungry after that, he could make himself a sandwich.

Outside, the wind was picking up. She could hear the thorn tree tapping against the window. If she'd been here on her own, she might have been spooked by the sound. But she wasn't on her own. Tony was in the cowshed. He'd taken to working away in there long after it got dark—which flew in the face of what he'd always said about needing to paint in natural light. It wasn't good for him. It was making him irritable—as if whatever he was working on wasn't turning out the way he'd hoped, and all the extra hours he was putting in were just making things worse.

The click of the latch broke into her thoughts.

"You could have brought me a cup of tea." His voice had that whiny edge she was coming to dread.

"I didn't want to disturb you. I could see the light was on in the cowshed."

"I wish you'd stop calling it that. It's *not* a cowshed—it's my studio." He stamped his boots on the doormat.

Ellen said nothing. With Tony in this mood, it was better not to rise to the bait.

"What are we having to eat?"

"Cheese omelette."

"Great." He clicked his tongue against the roof of his mouth. "Couldn't you get any meat?"

"I would have, but I was too late. The butcher was closed by the time I locked up."

He grunted. "I suppose an omelette will have to do, then. What time are we having it? I'm ravenous."

Ellen got up and walked past him, grabbing the grater from the shelf. The cheese was on a slab in the little larder off the kitchen. She brought it out and dropped it with a thud onto the wooden chopping board. Then she started grating, fast and furious, clenching her teeth as her hand worked away.

"There's no tea left in the pot."

"No." She didn't turn around. "I had a second cup."

"I'd better make myself one, then, hadn't I?" The kettle clattered against the hob as he yanked it off the stove and took it over to the sink to fill.

Yes, you better had. She didn't say it aloud, but she attacked the cheese with even more force, wincing as she caught her knuckle on the grater. She brought her finger up to her mouth, sucking the blood away.

"What's the matter? Cut yourself? Hope you haven't bled all over the cheese."

"Oh, heaven forbid!" As the words came out, she realized she sounded exactly like her mother. "I suppose it wouldn't occur to you to get me something to put on it?"

"Temperamental bitch." He said it under his breath, but she heard, all right.

"What did you call me?"

"You really want to know?" His lip curled, insolent, as if he was daring her to start a fight.

"Why are you being so horrible?"

"*Me?* You've hardly said a word since I came through that door. I've been slaving away out there all day, and you couldn't even be bothered to bring me a cup of tea!"

"Oh, because I've been lazing around all day, haven't I? Do you really expect me to wait on you hand and foot?"

He grabbed his leather jacket from the hook on the wall.

"Where are you going?"

"Out."

"Out where?"

"I don't know." He pushed the door open, letting in a gust of cold air, and strode out into the night. "Don't wait up!" he yelled over his shoulder.

Ellen slammed the door and slid the bolt across. If he thought she was going to run after him, he could forget it. She slumped onto the sofa, pulling her knees up to her chest. She heard him revving up the engine of the motorbike. Would he go to The Tinners? Have a few drinks and come back all elated, expecting her to behave as if nothing had happened?

As she sat there, listening to the sound of the bike die away, a different, darker thought occurred to her. What if he was going to see Nina?

She buried her face in the soft woolen sleeves of her sweater, trying to shut out the images from the nightmare. The two of them, making love in this house. Had that really happened? Would it happen again tonight, in a different bed, in a different house?

You'll have me for company when you go upstairs. Won't that be cosy?

She leapt off the sofa. That voice. That spine-chilling, sinister whisper. Was it in her head? Was he a ghost? Was he waiting for her, up there in the bedroom?

She stood there, paralyzed, terrified. All she could hear now was the crackle of the fire and the moan of the wind in the chimney. She felt as if she were sliding out of her own body, as if her inner self had taken leave of its physical shell and was hovering somewhere near the ceiling. She was looking down at the pathetic, cowering creature she had turned into. And what she felt at that moment was not fear but anger. White-hot, incandescent fury. This was Tony's fault. He had brought her here. And now he had left her to face this eerie, malevolent thing on her own.

Well, two could play that game. She was back in her body, heading for the door, grabbing her coat and the keys to the jeep. Better to spend the night at the shop than alone in this creepy cottage. When Tony came back, *he* could wonder where the hell *she* was.

She drove down the track faster than she had ever done, swerving past the rocks and scattering the startled sheep.

When she got to St Ives, the streets were deserted. She parked the jeep outside the back entrance to the shop and switched off the engine. As she went to open the door, she was blinded by the headlights of another vehicle. It stopped right in front of her, and the driver got out to open the gate to the yard shared by her shop and the two on either side. There was no name on the van, but she recognized it as the one that brought dead bodies to the Chapel of Rest.

Ellen stayed in the jeep until the driver had had a chance to unload the corpse and get it inside. It seemed disrespectful, somehow, to wander past a recently deceased person that no one was supposed to see until he or she had been properly prepared for the mourners. Besides, she didn't particularly want to have to explain why she was going back into her shop at this time of night.

When she thought the coast was clear, she got out, carrying an armful of the blankets still left in the back of the jeep. There was a pile of sacks in the attic that would do for a bed. As she made her way past the undertaker's van, it occurred to her that Stella Bird would almost certainly have been brought to this place from the hospital where she died. She pictured the husband, Lionel, going to see her body after rushing back from Canada. How awful for him, to live with the knowledge that if he'd been there with her at Rowan Tree House, she wouldn't have gone to the cottage alone on that fateful night.

Ellen unlocked the back door of the workshop, flicked on the light, and went straight over to the kettle. As she waited for it to boil, she climbed up the ladder to retrieve the sacks and arranged them on the floor, next to the lathe. In her rush to leave the cottage, she'd forgotten to bring anything to eat. But there was a packet of biscuits in the cupboard. She wouldn't starve.

Half an hour later she switched off the light and tried to make herself comfortable on the improvised bed. But it was no good. She was so wound up that sleep eluded her. She couldn't stop thinking about where Tony had gone, what he was doing—and who he was with. Why had they fallen out over something as stupid as her not making him a cup of tea? They'd been married for less than a month. It shouldn't be like this. Ellen could imagine her mother shaking her head, saying that this was what she'd feared all along: that Tony was not the steady type she had hoped her daughter would fall for, that they should have waited longer, found out more about each other, before plunging into marriage.

She told herself that Tony was just tired, that his irritability was down to nothing more than frustration that his painting wasn't going as well as he'd hoped. And that, right now, all he was doing was sinking a few pints at The Tinners Arms. She tried to shut him out of her mind by thinking about work. About the next batch of toys, the practicalities of transporting them to London, and the list of jobs she'd have ready for Iris when she came in tomorrow.

As she tossed and turned, her mind wandered to what she'd seen when she'd pulled up outside the shop. The van returning to the silent heart of the town, delivering a corpse to the funeral parlor. She wondered how many more bodies there were on the other side of the wall. Lying there, as she was, but no longer breathing.

As she teetered on the brink of sleep, she imagined the souls rising from the lifeless shells of the people they had been. She opened her eyes, rigid with fear, as she pictured them drifting through the plywood partition in the attic, descending the ladder to hover over her. In the deep quiet, the air seemed full of the gathering dead. Had *he* followed her here? Was Crowley martialing an army of ghosts to send her screaming into the night, like Stella Bird?

If you ever feel the need to talk, I live over the way, at the vicarage. I'm always on call . . .

Reverend Thomas's voice emerged from some distant place inside her head. He was just a couple of streets away. But as the thought crossed her mind, she dismissed it. It wouldn't be fair to go banging on his door when he was probably tucked up in bed. She told herself that she was stronger than that. She shouldn't need to go running for help when the only *real* problem was her inability to get off to sleep. God knows she'd had enough sleepless nights after what she'd witnessed during the Blitz. She'd coped then, and she would cope now.

Throwing off the blankets, she stood up and felt along the wall until she located the light switch. Then she fetched planks from the attic and set the band saw in motion.

Iris took a wrong turn on the way home from Bellair Terrace. The road took her uphill instead of down. She stopped beside a low wall. There was no moon, but the sky was clear. The starlight revealed row upon row of tombstones.

She recognized this place. Barnoon Cemetery. It was where the ashes of her grandparents were buried, brought from India after they died of cholera within weeks of each other. Her mother had told her the story, had described the way she'd heard the news, via a telegram from the British Embassy in Delhi. At the age of twenty-three, she was suddenly an orphan.

Iris had been brought here once, to see the grave. But her mother was not there with them. Her body had been taken back to London. Iris didn't even know which cemetery she was in. Her father had never taken her to the burial place.

As Iris turned away from the graveyard, she felt a stab of panic. It wasn't ghosts she was afraid of—more the thought of being lost at night in a part of town she didn't really know. She told herself to keep calm and get her bearings. She could see the sea, far below, a dark mass fringed with breaking waves that caught the intermittent flash from the lighthouse. The strip of pale sand exposed by the receding tide was Porthmeor Beach—and the finger of land that reached beyond it was The Island. All she had to do was keep going down, into the jumble of streets with their pinpricks of light. Sooner or later, she would find her way home.

Following Barnoon Hill took her too far east. She found herself at the wrong end of Fore Street, near to St Ia's church. But at least she knew the way back from there. As she passed The Toy Tiger, she saw that there was a light on. It wasn't the one in the window, which lit up the display—it looked as if it was coming from farther back, in the workshop. Surely Ellen wasn't working at this time of night? Iris wondered if she should ring the bell. Offer to keep Ellen company. But no. If she'd given up her evening to work, she probably wouldn't want to be disturbed.

Iris made herself a cup of cocoa when she got back and sat in bed drinking it, her mind full of everything she had seen and heard at the house in Bellair Terrace. When she turned off the lamp, she couldn't get the face in the photograph out of her mind—those dark, staring eyes, the bald head with the strange tuft of hair sticking out of it, and the serpent ring on the index finger of the left hand.

As she lay there in the darkness, she thought about her father, bringing the ring home after Crowley's funeral. She'd puzzled over why it had been left to her when she'd never known the man. Was it down to a guilty conscience? Was he trying to make up for whatever it was he'd done to her mother? And if that was the reason for the gift, why on earth had her father colluded in it?

When, at last, she fell asleep, Crowley's face was still there. In her nightmare, he was Ellen's husband, sitting at an easel in the garden of the cottage, his silver-topped cane exchanged for a paintbrush. He was waiting for Ellen to come home, and when he heard her coming, he hid behind a wall of the cottage, jumped out, and grabbed her by the throat.

Iris woke up with her heart thumping at her ribs. A sliver of pale morning light showed through the gap in the curtains. She scrambled out of bed and pulled on her clothes. She had to go there. See the cottage. Be sure that the dream wasn't real.

He's dead, stupid—it can't be real.

The voice inside her head was her own. But she couldn't shake the feeling that Ellen was in danger, that something terrible had happened to her after she'd gone home last night. What if Ellen was right about the place being haunted? What if Crowley was the ghost? Could he frighten her to death, as he'd done in life to Iris's mother?

⟞⟝

The whoosh of water on metal woke Ellen. She sat up, blinking in the sunlight filtering through the window. It took several seconds to work out where she was, that the noise outside was the sound of buckets being filled at the outside tap for the flowers being delivered to the shop next door.

She slumped back onto the makeshift sacking pillow, memories of last night's row with Tony hitting her like a punch to the gut. Stretching out her arm, she groped for her watch. She groaned when she saw the time. Ten to nine.

Raising herself on one elbow, she spotted the pile of half-formed farm animals lying in a basket next to the workbench. It had been close to midnight when she'd started working. She'd gone on into the small hours of the morning, glad of the noise of the machinery and the concentration the work required. Finally, she had lain back down, exhausted, onto the pile of sacks. But she hadn't meant to sleep for so long. Tony would be wondering where on earth she was. What if he thought she'd driven back to London? He might go and telephone her mother . . .

She had to get back there. Talk to him. Make up with him. Her arms and legs felt stiff as she heaved herself up off the floor. She gathered up the sacks and inched her way up the ladder to toss them back into the attic. Iris wasn't due in until half past ten. She had time to get back to the cottage and return to the shop if she was quick.

⟞⟐⟝

The bus to St Just was more crowded than last time. Iris climbed the stairs and took a seat next to an old lady who took out a clay pipe as soon as they pulled away. Iris had never seen a woman smoke a pipe. The smell was not unpleasant—a woody scent with a hint of something fruity, like cherries—and better than the sharp tang of the cigarettes being lit by most of the other passengers on the top deck. Breathing it in, Iris felt the pounding in her chest begin to ease.

She had run all the way to the bus stop. Now, as the sky turned pink in the early morning light, she felt featherheaded. She had allowed the irrational frenzy of a nightmare to send her on what would no doubt turn out to be a fool's errand. What on earth was she going to say to Ellen when she knocked on the door of the cottage?

She rehearsed a speech as the bus climbed the steep hill on the western outskirts of St Ives. She would say that she'd come out to Zennor for a walk and thought she'd stop by to say hello. That sounded reasonable, didn't it?

The thought of going to Carreg Cottage, of possibly being invited in, triggered a frisson of dread. She would be doing just what her mother had done: calling, uninvited, to find out what was going on there. And in her mother's case, it had ended in tragedy. As she turned it over in her mind, it dawned on her that the urge to see the place was as much about retracing her mother's last journey as it was about her concern for Ellen. On her last visit, she'd wandered up and down the track with her bunch of flowers, not knowing what had happened. The real cause of her mother's death remained a mystery—but the cottage was the one solid link. She *had* to go there.

The moorland looked very different in the sunshine. Last time, the landscape had been swathed in mist. Now she could see the rough edges of the granite boulders protruding from the sheep-bitten grass, the tufts of rust-colored bracken, and the bent black fingers of wind-blasted thorn trees. And there was Rowan Tree House, no longer shrouded in a veil of white, but standing proud against a blue sky.

This was how she remembered it, on that final holiday. Running around the garden in the sunshine, hunting for miniature Easter eggs. The smell of chocolate, almost melting as she peeled off the shiny paper. And her mother, sitting beneath the rowan tree in her green silk dress, watching her, laughing as Iris scrabbled around in the flower beds for the hidden treasure. Unbelievable that just five weeks later she was dead.

Iris searched the dark corners of her memory for something, anything, about that time that could cast a light on what had happened. Her father was not there that Easter—of that she was certain. But that was not unusual. He'd often stayed behind in London when she and her mother went to Cornwall for holidays—or he'd come down for a few days before leaving them to return to work. She wondered how he had become friends with Crowley. It seemed unlikely that the association was made on her father's brief visits to Rowan Tree House. Had they been friends before Crowley rented Carreg Cottage? In London, perhaps? Had Crowley been offered the tenancy by her father?

With so many questions whirling inside her head she almost missed the stop. The bus jerked to a halt when she rang the bell, almost throwing her down the steps. She jumped down onto the grass verge and made her way back along the road to the place where the track began. The air smelled different in the sunshine. The mist had brought a salt tang from the sea, but there was no hint of that today—no clue that the Atlantic Ocean lay just beyond Zennor Carn. As she climbed higher, she caught the honey scent of gorse flowers mingled with the earthy aroma of sheep dung.

She passed the place where she'd laid the bouquet of narcissus and winter jasmine for her mother. She'd chosen a broad, flat-topped rock a few yards from the path, out of reach of the sheep. Held down by a stone, the bouquet had defied the wind. The flower heads were withered, and the ribbon frayed, but it was still there.

She glanced back down the track. From here, you couldn't see Rowan Tree House. The contours of the land hid it from view. She thought of her mother, living down there, less than half an hour's walk from the summit of Zennor Carn, but with no way of knowing what was going on at the cottage nestled beneath it.

It was another ten minutes until she caught sight of Carreg Cottage. She paused on the pathway, wary now that she was almost there. There was no sign of Ellen's jeep, but she could see a motorbike parked outside the gate. Did that belong to Tony, the husband? Was he there alone? Ellen glanced at her watch. It was only half past eight. Had Ellen left already?

She walked on, toward the summit of the hill, thinking that she'd get a different view from up there. Perhaps the jeep was parked out of sight, around the back of the building. She reached a place where she could see the whole of the cottage and the walled garden, spread out below her like one of Ellen's toy farms. No. The jeep was not there. Her fears for Ellen had been misplaced. She was not here. But as Iris walked back down the path, she felt an overwhelming urge to go through the gate and knock on the door. Was this how her mother had felt? As if a magnetic force was pulling her to the place, even though she feared what she might discover inside?

Iris stopped a few yards short of the gate. She told herself it was ridiculous to be afraid of Ellen's husband just because she'd had a nightmare about him. She could give Tony Wylde the same story she had planned to tell Ellen: that she was out for a walk and had called by to say hello. Perhaps he would invite her in for a cup of tea. Perhaps he would talk about the day he found a woman lying unconscious, just down the track . . .

No. Don't go there.

It was her mother's voice she heard—as clear as if she'd been standing right beside her.

※

Ellen ground to a halt a few yards short of the turnoff for Carreg Cottage. A man was standing in the road, holding up his hand to oncoming vehicles. Before she had time to open the window to find out what was going on, a herd of sheep emerged from a gate at the side of the road.

She could hear their bleating as they scrambled past, inches from the front bumper. She drummed her fingers on the steering wheel, wondering how long she would have to wait until the herd was penned up in the field on the other side of the road. As she sat there, she scanned the road ahead. There was nothing coming the other way. She had been unlucky—the only motorist to be held up. But then she caught sight of a bus coming around the bend. It came to a stop a good distance away from the crossing sheep. There was a flash of movement—someone must have been waiting at the bus stop. Ellen craned her neck. From this distance, it looked just like Iris. The same long auburn hair, the same gray coat. But it couldn't be her. What on earth would she be doing catching a bus from Zennor to St Ives at twenty past nine in the morning?

She heard a shout from the man standing in the road. He was waving her on. She put the jeep into gear and edged forward, through a trail of droppings that glistened like black olives in the sunshine. The bus passed her as she was about to swing left up the track. There was a face looking out of the window, a hand raised. It *was* Iris.

As Ellen bumped up the track, she puzzled over what she'd seen. Iris had said she'd once caught the bus out to Zennor to go for a walk. But to have gone out so early—when it would only just be getting light . . . That seemed an odd thing to do. But then Iris was single. She lived on her own. She could do exactly what she liked when she liked.

Just like Tony—except he's married.

Her mother's voice taunted her as she dodged the biggest rock along the path.

"Stop it!" Ellen said the words aloud, shaking her head. It was true, though. Tony could be very . . . She searched for the right word. Not selfish, exactly. It was more that he was a law unto himself. When he was painting, he went into his own parallel universe. She had to try to understand that; try not to mind when he behaved in a way that her mother would call unreasonable. She'd made a promise. *For better or worse.* Last night had been worse—far worse than she could ever have imagined when she'd made those vows. Now she must try to make things better.

A surge of relief rose from her belly at the sight of Tony's motorbike parked by the gate. As she jumped out of the jeep, she hoped that he would come to the door, run out to meet her, just as eager to make up as she was. But the front door remained shut as she walked up the path. There was no sound as she stepped over the threshold. She ran up the stairs. No sign of him up there, either.

Thinking that he must be working, Ellen went back outside and made her way around the rear of the cottage. She knocked on the door of the cowshed, not wanting to startle him. But there was no response. Was he still sulking? Or had he gone out onto the moor to paint? The window was too high up in the wall for her to peer in and see if he was there. She shouldn't go in. This was his inner sanctum. He'd be furious. But she had to know if he was hiding from her. With a deep breath, she lifted the latch and pushed the door open.

What she saw stopped her in her tracks. A huge canvas, propped on an easel, with a creature from a nightmare painted on it: a fox, with a gleaming, rust-colored coat and a bristling white-tipped tail. But it had a human face—a woman's face. And as she stepped closer, there was no mistaking whose face it was.

Iris.

Ellen's mouth went dry. She felt her heart shift in her chest, as if it were about to break through her ribs. *How, why had Tony painted Iris?* As far as she knew, he'd never even met her. He'd disappeared with his friend Clive by the time Iris had arrived at the New Year's party—and he'd never once visited the shop since Iris had started working there.

But she had sat for him. How else could he have captured her face so perfectly? She must have been coming out here while Ellen was working.

The bus. She was on the bus. The memory of what she'd just witnessed brought bile to Ellen's throat. Had Tony gone to Iris after the row last night? Had he brought her back here?

Ellen ran back to the jeep, her throat burning and her breath ragged. She drove down the track as if the gates of hell had opened and a gang of devils were chasing after her. She entered the shop moments before Iris rang the bell. With trembling fingers, she pulled back the bolt on the door.

"Good morning!"

How could she do that? Come waltzing in as though nothing had happened? The brazen little bitch had waved to her from the window of the bus, for God's sake.

"Are you all right?" Iris took off her coat and hung it up. "You look a bit pale."

Ellen opened her mouth, but only silence came out. She tried to swallow. "I saw you—on the bus." She sounded a hundred years old.

"Yes. I didn't realise it was you until we'd almost gone past."

"What were you doing in Zennor so early in the morning?"

Iris huffed out a breath. "You're probably going to think I'm off my rocker, but I had a nightmare last night. I woke up in a terrible state, thinking you were in danger. I couldn't get it out of my head—so I jumped on the first bus. I walked up to your cottage, but you weren't there. I felt so stupid when I spotted you on the road."

"You expect me to believe a cock-and-bull story like that?"

Iris stared at her. The expression was exactly what Tony had captured on canvas. The green eyes narrow, wary. A fox caught in the henhouse. "I . . . don't know what you mean."

"You've been seeing my husband, haven't you? I saw the painting. And you have the nerve to come in here, all sweetness and light, pretending you were worried about me."

"Ellen, please! I don't know what you're talking about—I've never even met your husband!"

There were tears in the girl's eyes. She was a good actress, the little slut. "Never met him? Then how do you explain the fact that he has a painting of you in his studio?"

"I . . . I don't know." Iris reached for Ellen's arm. "You have to believe me!"

Ellen elbowed her away. Iris sank onto the stool next to the finishing table, tears streaming down her face.

"It's you, Iris. To the life. Why are you even *trying* to deny it?"

"B . . . because it's n . . . not . . . true." The words were punctuated by sobs. "I . . . d . . . don't know him. I w . . . wanted to . . . but I . . ." She bent over, her head on her arms, her words muffled by the sleeves of her sweater.

"You *wanted* to?" Ellen grabbed her by the shoulders, pulling her head up.

"O . . . only to . . ." Iris wiped the back of her hand across her face.

"Only to *what?*"

"T . . . to ask . . . h . . . him about my m . . . mother."

⚬⚬⚬

Iris took the cup of tea that Ellen handed her. They were sitting in the back now. Ellen had locked the street door and put the "Closed" sign in the window.

"People have told me I look just like her." Iris gazed at the curl of steam rising from her cup. "She's the reason I came here. I had no idea that there was anything suspicious about the way she died—I just wanted to be back in a place that held such happy memories. But ever since I saw that photograph on the wall of the vicarage, I've been afraid someone would realise who I was."

"Why didn't you tell me all this before?"

"Because I was scared that my father would have the police looking for me. I couldn't give anyone my real name." She glanced up, her eyes red-rimmed from crying. "You won't tell people, will you?"

"Not if you don't want me to." Ellen spooned sugar into her tea. She didn't usually take it, but she felt the need for something sweet. "I don't know how you managed not to let on, though—when I was talking about what happened to your mother."

"There was so much I wanted to ask you." Iris let out a long breath. "I went straight to the library when you told me what you'd read in the newspaper. I put two and two together when I saw the name of the man who'd found my mother. I wondered why you hadn't mentioned that."

"I didn't even mention it to Tony," Ellen said. "I thought he must have a good reason for not telling me about what had happened. He's very sensitive—and I was afraid of upsetting him, just as he was starting to build a new life."

Iris nodded. "I don't suppose he would have been able to tell me much more than I got from the newspaper. It's just that he was one of the last people to see my mother alive . . ."

"Perhaps he will be able to talk to you about it, in time." Ellen took a sip of tea. It was too hot. It burned her lips. She couldn't imagine Tony wanting to see Iris—let alone speak to her—if the memory of finding her mother had triggered that bizarre painting. If the cottage really was haunted, was Stella's ghost there, too? Had he seen her as well as hearing Crowley's voice? Poor Tony—no wonder he'd been so wound up these past few days.

"I found out something else last night," Iris said. "I went to a talk at the School of Painting, and there were drinks afterward at the home of one of the artists. There was a photograph on the wall of the man who used to live at your cottage."

"A photograph?"

"Taken in your garden. And when I heard his name, I realised he was a friend of my father's."

Ellen's cup stopped midway between the saucer and her mouth. She sat, transfixed, as Iris told the story of her father coming home from Crowley's funeral with the serpent ring.

"I couldn't sleep last night, thinking about it," Iris went on. "I mean, even if they'd been friends before, how could my father have carried on seeing him after what happened?" She shook her head. "I was scared, too. I realised that the woman whose house I was in was close to Crowley. She worked with him on designs for a pack of Tarot cards. So, there's a good chance she knows my father. If she were to find out . . ."

"You think she'd tell him where you were? Who is she?"

"Lady Frieda Harris. She wasn't in the room when I spotted the photograph, though. It was one of the other artists who told me his name: Nina Grey—she was at the party on New Year's Eve. The one in the mermaid dress and the crab's claw hat."

Ellen nodded. "It was Nina who told me what had gone on at the cottage. She said she used to go to the parties Crowley held, and that he was into black magic." She didn't want to tell Iris the rest. She hated the thought of people knowing that Nina and Tony had been lovers. "I'd felt uncomfortable in the place even before she told me, though," Ellen went on. "The first night we arrived, we went to the pub at Zennor, and the look on people's faces when they found out we'd bought the Crowley House, as they called it . . . And then, the next morning, when that hideous doll came tumbling out of the chimney . . ."

"Do you still think the cottage is haunted?"

Ellen hesitated. Took a breath. "I keep hearing this voice. A man's voice. I think Tony's heard it, too. He woke up the other night, talking in his sleep, saying, 'He's dead, but he keeps talking to me.' And I had a dream about Crowley—a nightmare, I should say. He was standing in the doorway of the bedroom, and when I tried to get past him, I fell down the stairs."

"What did he look like?"

"Horrible. He had dark, brooding eyes. And this weird tuft of hair sticking out of his forehead like a horn."

"Oh, Ellen," Iris whispered, "that's exactly like the photograph I saw."

CHAPTER 20

It was nearly one o'clock by the time Ellen got back to the cottage. She'd left Iris minding the shop. Wherever Tony had gone, she had to find him. She'd tramp the moor all afternoon if she had to.

His bike was still there—parked in the same place. As she walked up the path, the door opened. He was standing there, his arms folded across his chest. She ran to him, went to hug him, but he backed away.

"You finally decided to come back, then?" His eyes narrowed as he looked her up and down.

"I came back this morning—but I couldn't find you."

"Well, I couldn't find *you*." He grunted. "I went up on the carn to paint. Where on earth were you all night?"

The tone of his voice cut her like a knife. He made it sound as if she was the one in the wrong. But *he* had left *her* last night. "I could ask you the same question," she said.

He huffed out a breath. "I only went to The Tinners. I was back before midnight."

"And I went to the shop. I couldn't sleep after we argued. I thought I might as well get some work done."

"And you didn't think I'd be worried? Bloody hell, Ellie . . ."

"I'm sorry. I should have left a note or something. But I was upset—and I was . . ." She hesitated. She needed to get things out in the open. Give him a chance to talk about how this place was affecting him. "I was frightened of being here on my own at night. After you left, I heard this voice in my head. I've heard it a few times. A horrible, scary man's voice. You've heard it, too, haven't you?"

"What?"

"The other night, you were saying things in your sleep. You said, 'He's dead, but he keeps talking to me.' It's Crowley, isn't it? He doesn't like us being here."

"Oh, no, not this again." The look Tony gave her was one of pure disgust. "It's *you* that doesn't want to be here, isn't it? Come on—admit it. You don't like the cottage—you never have. And now you're using this nonsense as an excuse to ship out and leave me high and dry."

"No!" She closed the space between them, wrapping her arms around him. "I just want things to be like they were." She mumbled the words into his sweater. "I love you, Tony."

She felt his hands slide up under her clothes. She hugged him tighter as his fingers stroked the bare flesh of her back. Somehow, they stumbled up the stairs, still entwined.

Their lovemaking was fast and frenzied. She wanted him so much, ached to make things right. But he was hurting her. Thrusting so hard her head was hitting the metal bedstead. She couldn't cry out because his mouth was clamped against hers.

You fool. He doesn't love you.

In her anguished state, she couldn't tell if it was Crowley's voice or her own.

Afterward, as they lay there in silence, she thought about what she'd tried and failed to do. Clearly Crowley was out of bounds. She couldn't risk bringing up the subject of the voice again. But what about the painting? Could she mention that she'd glimpsed it while searching for him this morning? Ask who the beautiful face belonged to? Perhaps talking about Stella would help him to let things out.

As she stared at the patch of ceiling where the bird-headed pharaoh had been covered up, she searched for the right words. How could she frame the question without making it sound like an accusation? She could just imagine his reaction if he'd witnessed the chain of events her discovery of the painting had triggered. Thank goodness he would never know about the confrontation with Iris. She couldn't bear the thought of ruining this reconciliation, of saying anything to bring back that look of loathing. Any hint that she'd suspected him of being unfaithful almost certainly would.

Her eyes traveled across the ceiling to the window. The sun was shining through the lace curtain that screened the lower pane, dappling the wall with light. Outside, she could hear the trilling of a bird. In daylight, this room looked lovely. You wouldn't think that anything sinister or sordid could ever happen in such a place. If only it could always look like this. Perhaps the voice would stop, the nightmares go away, if only it didn't get dark.

⸺

Iris put down her paintbrush and went across the room to the street door. Ellen had asked her to put up the "Closed" sign at three o'clock. As she hung it on its metal hook, she spotted a familiar figure coming along the cobbles. Dan. He looked a little paler than usual. And thinner in the face. But he was well enough to be out of bed. She felt the familiar surge of longing as she pulled back the bolt and opened the door.

"Hello!" He grinned. "I thought I might find you here."

"You haven't been all the way to Norway Square?"

He nodded, turning away to cough into a handkerchief.

"Come in. Sit down. I'll make us a cup of tea."

"I don't know whether I should. I don't want to spread my germs. I only wanted to thank you for the grapes and the magazine. Dad told me you'd come by."

"I don't think it'd hurt if you came in for a few minutes."

"Are you sure?"

She nodded. She wanted to say that she didn't care about his germs, to give him a big hug and tell him that she'd missed him more than she could possibly have imagined these past few days. But that would probably send him running back to the vicarage. She led him into the back room and pulled a stool out from beneath the workbench.

"One good thing about being ill," he said, as she filled the kettle. "I've given up smoking. I haven't had a cigarette for nearly a week."

"That's good." She turned to him and smiled. "Do you think you'll be able to keep it up—when you're better, I mean?"

"I hope so. I think the smoking made me more ill than I should have been. It's bound to weaken your lungs, I suppose, breathing in tobacco all the time. I was on forty a day." He grunted a laugh that threatened to turn into another coughing fit. "Sorry," he mumbled into his handkerchief. "I blame the Merchant Navy. For the smoking, I mean. I'd never touched a cigarette before I joined up." He glanced around the workshop. "So, this is where the toys are made . . . Has the boss left you in charge?"

"Yes. Ellen had to go out." Iris wondered what Dan would say if he knew that Ellen had accused her of having an affair with her husband. That would remain their secret—hers and Ellen's. But what about the fact that Ellen now knew her real name? She'd asked Ellen not to tell anyone. But now it was out, she felt somehow lighter. Was it right to go on pulling the wool over Dan's eyes? She'd hated lying to him. From that first meeting outside the church, she'd longed to tell him the truth. He was her friend. Surely, he wouldn't give her away.

"Something happened this morning." She hesitated, feeling as though she were about to jump off a rock into the sea with no idea of what lay beneath the surface. "There was a misunderstanding that . . . well, it turned into a row. I got upset—and I . . ."

"What?" His face was full of concern.

Iris tried to swallow. Her throat was tight with emotion. "I told Ellen something that I've been hiding ever since I arrived in St Ives: something I've lied about to everyone—including you. My name isn't Birch—and I didn't come here to spend Christmas with my aunt. I ran away from home—and I couldn't give my real name in case the police came looking for me."

She held her breath.

For a long moment he was silent. Then he said, "Well, things must have been pretty bad at home for you to run away on Christmas Eve." A pause. "Why do you think the police would be looking for you?"

She looked at the wood shavings littering the floor, unable to meet his gaze. "I took something—a ring—and I sold it to keep me going until I could earn some money. Technically, it was mine—it was left to me in a will—but my father was keeping it for me, and I stole it from his desk."

"That doesn't sound like such a terrible crime."

"That's what I kept telling myself. But it didn't make me any less afraid."

"How long have you been here now? It must be nearly a month."

She nodded. "But I'm still not safe. I keep thinking someone's going to recognise me—because I look like my mother."

"Your mother?" She could hear the confusion in his voice. She'd been so cagey about her past. He didn't even know that her mother was dead.

"We had a house here when I was a child. She loved Cornwall, and so did I. It was such a happy place. But then she died, and I . . ." She gulped in air, trying to still the rush of emotion. "That's why I came here when I ran away from London. And last night I nearly got caught. That woman—the one who painted the Tarot cards—I think she knows my father. She had a photo of this horrible man, and I think he . . ." Her words were swallowed by the sob that rose from her chest.

"Hey, it's okay . . ." In one movement Dan got off the stool and gathered her up in his arms.

⟞✦⟝

It was almost dark outside. In the tower, the bell of St Ia's rang the hour. Five peals that echoed across the empty square.

"You were the little girl? The one I overheard my mum and dad talking about?"

Iris nodded. She was sitting on the sofa in the front parlor of the vicarage with a glass of brandy in her hand. Dan had insisted. His father was out doing house calls, so there was no chance of them being disturbed. "I was away at school when it happened," she said. "I was told that my mother had died after an accident when she was out walking. That was all I ever knew. It wasn't until Ellen started telling me about the cottage that I began to wonder what had really happened."

"I remember you asking me about it in the pub. If only I'd known . . ."

"Like I said, I was terrified of being found out. The very first day I was here I spotted a photo of my mother on the wall in the Parish Rooms. It must have been taken at a church event before the war. I was on tenterhooks the whole time after that, thinking your dad might realise who I was."

"I don't think you have anything to worry about there—he'd be on your side, absolutely." Dan walked across the room to draw the curtains. "I don't know if Dad would have known your father. Did he come to church?"

"No. He's always said he's an atheist—although he has books on every religion under the sun. I came across a Tarot pack in his study when I was little—he was furious when he found me looking at it. I don't know if he was always interested in that kind of thing, or whether it was Crowley who drew him into it."

Dan shook his head. "I think I told you about Dad's views on the occult. He caught Crowley outside the church once, trying to deface the big stone cross. Dad threw holy water over him, and Crowley put a curse on us." He let out a long breath. "Mum died six months later."

"Oh, Dan." Iris put down the brandy. It was the lightest touch, her hand on his back, but she could feel his ribs contracting.

"I'm sorry." He fumbled for his handkerchief, stifling a sound that turned into a cough.

"Shall I get you some water? Or would you like some of this?" She proffered the brandy.

"No, I'm okay, thanks. I'll be fine in a minute." He coughed again. "What I could really do with is a smoke—but that would be stupid." He rubbed his chest and settled back against the cushions. "Remember me telling you about the father of my school friend—the policeman involved in your mother's case?"

"Yes. Why?"

"Well, he's retired now, but he still lives in St Ives. I could call him. Ask if he'd see you. He probably knows a lot more than was reported in the paper."

She hesitated. "I'd be really worried about going to a policeman—even a retired one."

"Hmm. I didn't think of that." He raked his hair with his fingers. "I wonder if I could ask him about it . . . What could I say?"

"Ellen might want to talk to him," Iris said suddenly. "She's desperate to know what went on at the cottage. I told you she thinks the place might be haunted?"

"Poor woman—I'm not surprised," he said. "Okay. That sounds like a plan. And in the meantime, do you think it would help to talk to Dad? He should be back soon."

"If you're sure he won't be cross with me for telling lies."

Dan gave her a wry look. "He doesn't judge people, Iris—he's a vicar: it's in the job description."

⟞⟝

Iris helped Dan prepare a meal while they waited for his father to come home.

"We used to have a housekeeper," he said with a smile as he opened the oven door and glanced inside. "But we lost her when the war came—she went to work in the dockyard at Plymouth, and she never came back to St Ives. Dad managed on his own for a while—goodness knows how, with the evacuees to look after—and then, when I came back, I started doing the cooking."

Iris reached for a potato and started peeling off the skin. "From the smell of that chicken pie, you're a better cook than me."

He grunted. "You haven't tasted it! I did learn the basics in the Merchant Navy, though. I didn't have much of a clue before that."

The sound of the front door opening made them both look up.

"I'll go and put him in the picture, shall I?" Dan put down the knife. "Could you put the kettle on? He'll probably want a cup of tea. I won't be a minute."

Iris was pouring hot water into the teapot when he came back.

"He's in his study," Dan said. "It's the room on the left at the end of the hall. Don't be nervous—he's really pleased you want to talk to him."

The teacup rattled in the saucer as Iris carried it down the hallway. Despite Dan's reassurances, she couldn't help feeling apprehensive. She knocked on the door and waited.

"Come in, my dear." His voice boomed from inside the room.

He was sitting by a small electric fire, warming his hands in front of the single glowing bar.

"I want to say how sorry I am," she said.

He waved away the apology. "No need for that." He thanked her for the cup of tea and motioned to a chair on the other side of the fireplace. "I had a feeling I'd seen someone like you before, but I couldn't put my finger on it. I quite understand why you felt the need to conceal your identity. My only concern is that your father will be worried about you." He blew onto the surface of the tea before taking a sip. "I wonder if it would be possible to write to him—not revealing where you are but letting him know that you are safe."

"I did think about that," she replied. "But the postmark would give me away."

"Dan has to go to London at the end of the week—did he tell you?" Iris shook her head.

"He could post a letter while he's there."

London. That would be perfect: it would really throw them off the trail. She wondered if Dan was going there to hand over one of his Tree of Life sculptures. Something so fragile would probably need to be delivered in person. "Thank you," she said. "That's a good idea."

"I think you were extremely brave, coming all the way to Cornwall on your own," he said. "I'm so sorry about your mother. She was a lovely person. It must have been an awful shock for you, finding out about the business with Crowley."

Iris felt the prickle of tears behind her eyes. "It was." She stared at the glowing red bar of the fire. "Did Dan explain how I came to know?"

"I gather that your employer told you—and that she's living at Carreg Cottage."

Iris nodded. "Her name's Ellen—Ellen Wylde."

"Yes—I've met her." He took another sip of tea. "She came into the church one day to look at our carved oars."

Iris wondered if Ellen had talked to him about the cottage, whether she'd told him she thought the place was haunted. If she had, he wouldn't want to betray that confidence.

"It must have been torture, listening to her and not being able to admit that it was your mother she was talking about," the vicar went on. "Dan said you were told very little, as a child, about the circumstances."

Her tongue stuck to the roof of her mouth as she opened it. She wished she'd poured a cup of tea for herself. "M . . . my father left it to the school to tell me. All I got were the bare facts." She swallowed hard. "I wasn't allowed to go to the funeral, and I have no idea where my mother is buried. At the time, I thought the reason my father never talked about her was because he was grieving. But knowing what I know now—that he was Crowley's friend . . . ," she trailed off, unable to voice the treacherous thoughts that had surfaced on the walk home from Lady Frieda Harris's house.

"I never met your father." Reverend Thomas pushed his spectacles farther up his nose. "Your mother used to spend whole summers in Cornwall, but she told me that he only visited when work allowed, and that anyway, he was not a churchgoer." He pursed his lips. "I wasn't aware that a friendship existed between your father and Crowley. If I'd known, I wouldn't have repeated what I'd heard about the mischief-making at Carreg Cottage to your mother."

"Is that why she went up there?" Iris hadn't meant it to sound like an accusation—but that was how it sounded. "I'm sorry—I didn't mean . . ."

"It's something I bitterly regret." He stared into his cup. "I thought your father would take charge of the situation. It didn't occur to me that your mother would go there alone."

"That's what I can't understand," she said. "How could he have left her to deal with a situation like that? How could he even have been friends with someone so . . . so *evil*?"

"Perhaps you shouldn't judge your father too harshly, Iris." The vicar leaned forward in his seat. "I've never told Dan this—but *I* used to be friends with Crowley."

She stared at him, incredulous.

"We were students together, at Cambridge. When I first knew him, he was an utterly delightful person—an extrovert, a champion chess player, and keen on sport. He was very good company—until I began to see that he had a dark side."

"What did he do?"

"He became obsessed with the possibility of there being a technique by which man could force the powers of nature into submission— to harness them to do his bidding. He embarked on a reading program of every mystical work he could find; made himself an expert on everything from alchemy to occult symbolism." The vicar was looking beyond her, his eyes focused on the wall above her head. "He invited me to accompany him on trips to London, to visit the establishment of a purveyor of narcotics near Piccadilly—believing that mind-altering substances would open the door to the power he craved. When I turned down the chance to experience drugs, he invited me to attend a black mass at an abandoned house on the outskirts of town, with the idea of raising a demonic spirit."

"Dan told me about that," Iris said. "Didn't someone die?"

He nodded. "One of our friends. He was so terrified that he had a nervous breakdown and committed suicide."

Iris shook her head. "That's awful. I didn't know Crowley was the person behind it."

"Neither did Dan. I didn't tell him about my history with Crowley because I thought it would upset him." He tilted his head as he looked at her. "I suppose he's told you about the confrontation outside the church?"

"He did." She hesitated, not wanting to repeat what Dan had implied about the curse on his family. The silence hung heavy in the air.

The vicar rubbed the gilded handle of the teacup between his finger and thumb. "Crowley could have done so much good in this world. He had a first-class brain—and he inherited a fortune when he was still a young man. But he chose the wrong path." He clicked his tongue against the roof of his mouth. "The trouble was, he had an overpowering charisma. It often destroyed those around him, although he never saw his part in their downfall. He drove people to despair."

"Why did he come here?"

"From what I heard it was because of the stones."

"The stones?"

"On Zennor Carn. People in this part of the world call it a thin place—a place where this world and the next are very close. The stones up there are granite, which contains quartz. I think Crowley believed they could act as a channel—a sort of portal to the universe. His aim was to use them to draw down demonic power."

Iris felt the hairs stand up on the back of her neck. "Is that what he was doing? On the night my mother went up to the cottage?"

"I don't know. Nobody knows. The only witness was the poor woman the police found when they went up there—and she had lost her mind."

"So, Crowley wasn't there?"

"He'd gone to London. Apparently, he'd bought a train ticket on the very evening your mother went to see him."

"I don't understand." Iris searched his face. "Was it the woman, then? Did *she* do it?"

The vicar shook his head. "I'm sorry, Iris—I don't think we'll ever know what really happened."

CHAPTER 21

When Ellen woke up next morning, Tony wasn't there. She found a note, propped against the salt and pepper pots on the kitchen table: *Gone to buy paint. Don't worry about food for tonight—I'll pick something up in town.*

Gone to buy paint? At eight o'clock in the morning? She read the note again, wondering if it was a dig at her—a reminder that she had failed to leave one for him when she'd gone to spend the night in the shop. But the two kisses beneath the scrawled words gave the lie to that. And the fact that he'd offered to save her the trouble of going food shopping suggested he was trying hard to please her.

Don't be fooled. He'll act the willing servant when it suits him—but there's always an ulterior motive.

She jerked her head toward the front door. The voice was so real she thought he must be standing there, watching her as he had watched Tony and Nina in bed in her nightmare. But what she saw was nothing but the shadow of her coat hanging from the hook.

"Why can't you leave us alone?" Her words rang out in the silence. She could feel anger pulsing in her chest. In the daylight, she didn't feel so afraid. "This is *our* house now."

Stupid girl. You think that love conquers all. But sometimes it carries you into the abyss.

Ellen tasted bile in the back of her throat. Her fingers trembled as she made a grab for the keys to the jeep. Without a backward glance, she darted out of the cottage and ran down the path.

—✦—

Iris didn't usually work at the shop on Wednesdays, but she came in anyway. Ellen hugged her as she came through the door.

"Thank you for holding the fort yesterday. I meant to come back, but . . ." She shrugged as she took Iris's coat. There was no need to go into detail, no point in embarrassing the girl by revealing what had happened when she and Tony had made up.

"I don't want to hold you up," Iris said. "I just wanted to tell you what I found out last night at the vicarage." She sat down on the stool by the workbench. "I decided to tell Dan and his father the truth—I've hated lying to them all this time—and Reverend Thomas told me everything he knew about Crowley. He said he wasn't there the night my mother died."

"Wasn't there?"

"He caught a train to London that evening—before she went there."

"So . . ." Ellen searched Iris's face.

"So, that just leaves the Scarlet Woman."

"The one who couldn't appear at the inquest because she was locked up in Bodmin Asylum?"

Iris nodded. "Dan thinks his friend's father could tell us more about what happened: he was the policeman who went to the cottage to investigate. He's retired now—but I'm scared of spilling the beans to anyone like that."

"That's understandable. Do you think he'd talk to me?"

"I suggested that to Dan. He's willing to set up a meeting."

"What's this man's name?"

"Ray Crocker. His son was in school with Dan."

"Okay." Ellen blew out a breath. "It's worth a try, isn't it?"

———⋘———

Iris spent the whole afternoon trying to write a letter to her father. She couldn't even decide on how to address him. When she was at school, letters home had always begun with "Dear Papa"—but to call him *dear* sounded hypocritical. He was not dear to her. The last vestige of familial attachment had been blown away by the discovery of his disregard for her mother's safety.

In the end, she simply wrote his name and address at the top of the page, with her message beneath:

I am writing to let you know that I am in good health and settled in my own rented apartment.

That made the room over the fish cellar sound very grand. Lest he should suspect her of being a kept woman, she added:

I have a part-time job as a painter and finisher of wooden ornaments (suitably vague, she thought), *which allows me to study art, pay the rent, and feed myself.*

I am sorry for taking the serpent ring—but you said that it was mine, and I needed to sell it to fund the first few weeks of my new life.

I am happy, and I want for nothing. Please understand that I choose not to divulge my whereabouts.

She signed it *Your daughter, Iris.* The name itself was a declaration of independence: he had always insisted on calling her Winnie, even though he knew she hated it.

The letter was sitting on the stool by the bed, sealed up in an envelope with a second-class stamp on it, when Dan came knocking at the door.

"Hello." She thought he looked better than he had yesterday. The color had come back to his face. But he was standing at the top of the steps, with his hands behind his back, as if he was hiding something.

"Dad wanted you to have this." He produced a potted plant—a delicate orchid, creamy white, with spots of magenta on the petals. "He grows them in the greenhouse."

"Oh, it's lovely!" Iris took it from him, angling it to the light to inspect the cluster of perfect blooms.

"And this is from me." He pulled a tissue-wrapped shape from his pocket as he followed her inside.

"What is it?" She set down the plant and peeled back the layers of paper. Inside was a ceramic figure of a woman, the size of her hand. It was identical to the one he'd shown her in his studio. She was emerging from the earth, surrounded by vines and lilies, cupping her breasts as she gazed at the sky.

"This is so beautiful." She ran her fingers over the smooth surface of the glaze, touching the place where the cinnamon flesh of the woman's shoulder met the glossy black of her hair. "I don't know what I've done to deserve this—or the orchid."

He smiled. "We just wanted you to know that we're on your side. You've been through hell and high water to make this new life for yourself."

"Well, I couldn't have done it without you and your father," she replied. "Goodness knows what would have happened if I hadn't bumped into you on Christmas morning."

"I'm glad you did." The way he looked at her turned up the heat in the pit of her belly. She felt something melt and slide as she held his gaze. Without a word, she took his hand and led him across the room to her bed.

<hr />

"I think it's getting dark outside." Iris leaned across the pillow and pulled back a corner of the curtain.

"I know." He stroked her hair as she settled back into the crook of his arm. "I don't want to go—but I'll have to in a minute. Dad has a Parish Council meeting this evening, and I'm supposed to be making the tea and coffee."

"And I've got life class at half past six."

"Hmm." He traced the shape of her jawbone, sliding his finger down her neck to the slope of her breast. "I wish I could draw you—like this. I don't like to admit how many times I've thought about it."

She turned her face toward his and kissed his nose. "Well, that makes me feel a bit less guilty. I haven't stopped thinking about you. From that first morning we met."

"Really?"

"Really. But I was so scared."

"Why?"

"A hundred reasons."

"Such as?"

"Well, for a start, I didn't know if you felt the same as I did."

"Even after I kissed you at the party?"

"You kissed all the women!"

"Not on the lips!"

"I thought it was the rum punch—and that you'd have forgotten all about it by the morning. And anyway . . ." She hesitated, nuzzling his shoulder, breathing in the warm, musky scent of his skin.

"Anyway what?"

"I had to be careful. I was afraid of what it would do to me—if I fell for you. I felt like one of those crabs—what are they called? The ones who live in a seashell, and when they grow, they need to find a bigger one, but while they're moving, they're exposed."

"A hermit crab?"

"That's the one."

"So, what changed?"

"What do you mean?"

"What made you decide that . . . it . . . this . . . is okay?"

She let out a breath. "I don't know. Something in your eyes." It wasn't a lie. But it had been more than that. Something deeper, darker. The spark of something kindled by the swirling images from the Tarot card called *Lust*, stoked by the thought of Dan's fingers shaping the breasts of the Earth Mother, and set ablaze by the terrifying power of her imagination.

She turned to him, unable, now, to make out his features in the dwindling light. "I hope you don't think I'm in the habit of inviting men into my bed."

"I know you're not, Iris."

"How?"

"It was your first time, wasn't it?" He whispered the words, his lips brushing her ear.

Stupid tears prickled her eyes. Why did it upset her that he knew that? The answer was there, in the back of her mind: there had been other lovers, for him. She'd always told herself that. So why did it hurt so much, to think of it now?

"I'm going to have to get going." He pulled back the sheet and slid his legs over the side of the bed. She lay still, listening to him groping for his clothes, buttoning his trousers, doing up the laces of his shoes.

"I'll see you when I get back." He bent over and kissed her. "I need that letter, don't I? Where is it?"

"On the stool." Her voice sounded croaky. She wondered if he could tell she'd almost been crying.

"Take care of yourself, Iris."

"You too. Say hello to London for me." She tried to make it sound light. But she wished he wasn't catching that train. Wished he was going to be there, waiting for her in the back room of The Castle when she finished life class. Wished he wasn't heading for a place where there would be countless temptations for a good-looking man on his own.

Don't you see? This is what happens when you let them get under your skin.

For some inexplicable reason, it was Nina Grey's voice she heard inside her head.

"Hold tight!" The motorbike keeled dangerously close to the ground as Tony swerved left onto the track to Carreg Cottage. Nina could smell the wet grass inches from her face. In the old days, when they were lovers, she had relished these rides with him. A decade on, she was simply terrified. But she needed to see what he wanted to show her.

"They're round the back," he said when they dismounted. "Hang on a minute—I'll just get the key."

She waited on the path while he went inside. Strange, she thought, that he left the cottage unlocked while being so protective of his studio. When he emerged, she followed him around the side of the building.

"I only bought this yesterday," he said, fumbling with the padlock.

"You're not worried about burglars up here, surely?"

He grunted a laugh. "No. It's Ellen I want to keep out. She was nosing around in here the other day. Didn't close the door properly—that's how I knew."

"And you don't want her seeing your work?"

"It's not that. I've got all my stuff in here." He shrugged. "Private stuff."

Nina didn't need to ask what Tony was hiding from his wife. Clive Snow had told her about the mushrooms. He'd been particularly annoyed that Tony had refused to divulge where he'd found them growing.

"When is Barbara going to London?" It sounded as though he was deliberately changing the subject.

"Next week," Nina replied. "'Did she tell you she's been invited to enter a competition to design a piece for the Westminster Bridge?"

"She did." He turned away as he twisted the key in the lock.

"She's through to the final four, so she has to spend a couple of days on site, getting a feel for the location—and while she's there, she's going to put out feelers for an exhibition at the New Burlington Galleries."

"And you think she might include me?" Tony slipped the padlock into his pocket.

"Well, Ben's very keen on having more painters. I think he's afraid of Barbara dominating the whole scene down here. He doesn't want St Ives to be thought of as Sculpture Central."

"Hmm. Let's hope he'll like this lot, then." He lifted the latch and pushed the door open.

What Nina saw were the backs of five canvasses of varying sizes. "Oh." She smiled as she stepped over the threshold. "You're either worried about Ellen climbing up a ladder to peer in through the window, or you're planning a big reveal . . ."

"The latter." He didn't return her smile. She could tell from the way he pulled at the sleeves of his jacket that he was nervous. She stepped inside, breathing in the familiar, dusty smell. There was still a faint whiff of cow dung clinging to the walls. She remembered sleeping in here, surrounded by bodies. The smell had been much worse in those days—but they'd all been too tipsy to notice. She had a clear memory of Tony's face, his eyes round with wonder, as they arrived at the May Eve party for Frieda's initiation. Entranced by the beauty and wildness of the place, Tony had told her that first night that he would give anything to live in a place like this.

"This is the first one." Tony had turned the first of the canvasses around.

Nina's first impression was of cottage rooftops shrouded in mist, with swirling clouds stretched across a charcoal sky. As she stepped closer, she saw that the clouds were monstrous, ghostly birds, almost prehistoric, with huge wings and beaks like razors. It had an ethereal, menacing allure.

"I love it." She reached out, tracing the outline of a bird's head with her finger, feeling the texture of the paint. "What's it called?"

"*Ghost Birds Invading a Sleeping Town.*" Tony went to the second canvas. "This one's not quite so surrealist—just an abstract landscape."

Nina recognized Zennor Carn. Tony had painted it as a haze of silvery hues streaked with acid yellow and pale turquoise. The rocks looked almost as though they were floating above the hillside. "Ben will love that one," she said. "It's just his kind of thing." She glanced toward the far corner of the studio. "What about the big one over there? What's that?"

"Oh—that's just an experiment. Not something I'd put forward for an exhibition."

"Can I see it?" Nina was there before he could stop her. She turned the canvas around and stepped back, her hands on her hips, jabbing Tony in the stomach with her elbow as he came up behind her.

"Sorry—did I hurt you?" She didn't look around to find out. Her eyes were fixed on the strange image, half human, half animal. A fox with the face of a woman. A very beautiful face—and one that Nina recognized. It was the girl from the School of Painting—the one who had sat beside her in the car on the way to Frieda's party. So, Tony had picked her out. Persuaded her to sit for him. What would his new bride make of that? No wonder he wanted to keep Ellen out of here.

"The face is very flesh-and-blood . . . almost photographic. Not like you, to do something so realistic. Who is she?" Let him squirm a bit. Serve him right, for turning her down.

"Nobody." His voice sounded strained, distant. "A ghost."

"What?" Nina turned to him. He looked as if he was about to throw up. His face was white, and his lips were trembling. "Hey, what's wrong? Sit down a minute." She pulled out a stool from under the table by the wall.

He held on to her arm as he sank down. "It's Stella Bird," he whispered. "The woman who died. I've seen her."

"*Seen* her?"

"Down on the track. She came out of the mist—holding flowers, like she was going to her own funeral. Then I saw her again, after I dropped you off that time you came here. She was walking across Norway Square." He fumbled in his jacket pocket. "Can you pass my pipe? It's on the shelf, over there. And the tin, too."

Nina watched him stuff the dried fragments of mushroom into the bowl of the pipe. His hands shook as he lifted it to his lips. She saw the muscles of his face relax as the drug began to take effect. And behind him, the face of the girl stared out from the canvas. No ghost. Of that she was almost certain. But she wasn't going to tell Tony about the letter in her dressing table drawer back at Rose Lane. The one Lionel Bird had sent the week after Christmas, telling her how devastated he was that his daughter had run away from home.

CHAPTER 22

The smell of stew filled the kitchen when Ellen went downstairs. It was the meal they should have eaten last night. Tony had been so elated when she got home, full of the news that Barbara Hepworth was going to include his paintings in a special exhibition in London. Ellen had opened a bottle of wine to celebrate before asking what they were having to eat.

He'd gazed at her blankly, as if he had no memory of promising to buy food for their evening meal. When she went to the larder, she found a bag of meat on the marble slab. But it was stewing steak, needing several hours cooking time. Somehow, he'd forgotten about preparing the ingredients and getting it in the oven before she came home. They'd ended up having cheese on toast—and she'd spent the rest of the evening making the stew so that there'd be something ready for tonight's meal.

She huffed out a sigh as she filled the kettle, telling herself that things would get easier once the Harrods order was completed. She could ease off a little, keep Iris on the same hours and build up the stock to guard against future emergencies. She'd have more time to shop and cook and fix up the cottage. It would look so much better with new curtains and a lick of paint.

You think that's going to change him? Dream on, my dear.

"Shut up!" She pressed her hands to her ears, hissing the words into the steam rising from the kettle. "This is *my* house! Leave me alone!"

"Who are you talking to?" Tony appeared, bleary-eyed, at the top of the stairs.

"No one," she called back. "Just getting rid of a spider. Would you like a cup of tea?"

Later, when she got to the shop, she found a letter on the doormat with Iris's name on the envelope. She handed it over when Iris arrived for work.

"It's from Dan," Iris said. "He must have pushed it through the door before he caught the train last night. It's the telephone number of the policeman I was telling you about—Ray Crocker."

"Oh—can I see?" Ellen reached for the letter, but Iris held it to her chest.

"I'll write it down for you." Her cheeks were flushed. Apparently, the note contained more than just a telephone number. So much for the denial about Dan being her boyfriend.

"I'll call him this afternoon," Ellen said. "You're sure you don't want to come with me?"

Iris shook her head.

"Okay. If he has anything earth shattering to say, I'll come and find you."

<hr />

Nina Grey made her way across the square, past a cat that was sprawled on the cobbles, basking in the winter sunshine. She could smell the acrid, oily scent of fish being smoked in one of the cellars behind Norway House. She paused for a moment before climbing the steps to the School of Painting, thinking about what she was going to do.

At the top of the steps, she peered through the glass panel in the door. She didn't need to go inside to see the people sitting at the easels. Nor did she want to draw attention to herself by opening the door.

There were fewer people at the portraiture session than the life class. Probably because it was held in the afternoon rather than the evening. The two old biddies were there—the ones who turned up for everything—and looked as though they were joined at the hip. And there was the foreign gentleman—a refugee from Lithuania—who had volunteered to man the desk at the exhibition. But where was the girl?

Nina spotted her over by the sink in the far corner of the room, filling a jar with water. As she turned, the light from the window on the seaward side of the studio caught her face. There was no question. She was the double of the woman Tony had painted. It was not Stella Bird's ghost he'd seen, walking across the square, but her daughter. No doubt the drugs had played a part. His addled brain had told him it was the dead woman, come back to haunt him.

The personal details of the students were kept in the office on the ground floor. It would be easy to find the girl's address. But what if she passed it on to Leo? What would he do? She was going to have to be very stern with him. Tell him not to interfere. Iris wasn't a child, whatever the law might say. She had a right to choose how she lived her life. Leo had to be made to understand that.

There had always been a chemistry between them, a special something that she found irresistible. And he'd always said that her touch reduced him to a quivering heap. But it was years since they'd been together. What if he wouldn't listen? What if he called the police?

Standing there, staring through the glass, Nina felt as though she held the girl's whole future in her hands.

The telephone in Nina's cottage was bright orange, the receiver embellished with a procession of delicately painted crustaceans. It was a nod to Dalí: she'd toyed with the idea of dismantling the receiver and encasing the wires in an actual lobster's carapace, but she'd been afraid of electrocuting herself.

Lionel's telephone number was written in the back of an old diary. It had taken her a while to find it. But as she stood in the narrow hallway, staring at it, she changed her mind and dialed Barbara Hepworth's number instead.

"Hello?"

Nina was surprised to hear Barbara pick up. Usually, one of her assistants answered the phone and it took ages for her to be dragged away from whatever she was working on.

"Barbara—I've got a problem. I need your advice." In a few short sentences she relayed what had happened when she'd gone to see Tony's work.

"And you're certain it's her?" Barbara's gravelly voice came back down the line.

"Honestly, darling, if you'd seen the picture—and then seen her . . . And she calls herself Birch. That's the name she used when she registered at the School of Painting. It's too much of a coincidence, isn't it?"

There was a momentary silence on the other end of the phone. "Well, all I can say is that if one of my kids went missing, I'd be going out of my mind. If I got wind that a friend knew something and hadn't told me, I'd want to kill them."

"What if he calls the police, though? Or jumps on the next train to St Ives?"

"Hmm. If I were you, I wouldn't give him her address."

"But he's bound to ask where she's living."

"Tell him you don't know. Just say she's okay and that he doesn't need to worry."

Nina closed her eyes as she replaced the receiver. Barbara's reaction had stirred up emotions she thought she had locked away. As a young girl, she had been a runaway herself—barely sixteen when a so-called friend of her father's had persuaded her to elope with him. His plan had been to catch a night train from London to Scotland, where marriage was legal for girls of her age. She had lost her virginity in the sleeper carriage of that train. And when they'd arrived at Gretna Green, he had broken the news that there could be no wedding, as he was already married. The memory of her father's face as she'd slunk back into the house would be with her till her dying day.

Opening her eyes, she stared at the phone. What Lionel's daughter had done was very different from her own act of rebellion. But the effect of it on him had been just as devastating. He had no idea that Iris was leading a happy, carefree life as an art student in Cornwall. For all he knew, she could be destitute—hungry and homeless—and possibly driven to earn a crust in the worst possible way.

She took a deep breath. If she was going to do it, she'd better get it over with. Propping the diary open on the hall table, she dialed the number.

"Hello? Lionel?" She tapped the mouthpiece with her fingernails. The line wasn't very good. She could hear a low buzz, like a swarm of bees, in the background. She tried again. "Lionel? It's Nina. In St Ives."

"Nina?" She could hear the surprise in his voice. They never spoke on the telephone. Since she'd moved to Cornwall, the only contact had been by letter.

"Listen, darling, I'm not going to beat around the bush. I think I might know where your daughter is."

For a moment, all she could hear was the bees. Then a gulping sound, as if he were choking. "Winnie? You've found Winnie?"

"She calls herself Iris now."

"Ah . . . of course." She heard him clear his throat. "Is she all right? Where is she?"

"She's here, in St Ives." Before he could react, she said, "Listen, she's fine. You're not to try and drag her back to London. Understand?"

"What? I . . . ," the voice trailed off. She heard a trumpeting sound. Him blowing his nose.

"She's perfectly happy. Just leave her be. I wanted you to know, that's all. Bye, darling."

CHAPTER 23

Ray Crocker lived in one of the new houses on Higher Stennack—the steep hill on the western edge of St Ives. As Ellen walked up the path to the front door, she made a mental checklist of what she was going to say. His telephone manner had been just what she'd expected from an ex-policeman: brusque, almost grudging, when she'd asked if she could speak to him in person. He'd said he wouldn't normally agree to discuss a case he'd been involved in. He was only making an exception because Dan was a family friend.

A woman answered when she rang the bell. Small and neat with a cloud of lilac-tinted hair. Mrs. Crocker, Ellen presumed. The house smelled of furniture polish. She was shown into a living room with a flower-patterned carpet, matching chintz curtains, and a very new-looking three-piece suite. The contrast with Carreg Cottage couldn't have been greater.

Ray Crocker was not as old as she'd imagined. She'd expected a man of a similar age to the Reverend Thomas—but he looked at least ten years younger. He had a shiny bald head and silver-rimmed glasses. He was sitting in an armchair with a black spaniel dog at his feet. The dog didn't stir when he rose to greet Ellen.

"She's very old," he said, glancing down as they shook hands. "Deaf, too. Not much of a guard dog these days, are you, Flossie?" There was a definite Cornish lilt in the voice. He gestured to the chair beside the fireplace. "Please—take a seat." He patted the animal's head as he sat down. "Now, what exactly is it that you think I can tell you?"

When she'd begun to explain on the phone, he'd cut her short, saying that Dan had already given him the details. But she didn't know how much Dan had said. "I read a report in the newspaper about the woman who died after visiting our cottage," she began. "My husband was the one who found her. I think it's preying on his mind, but he can't bear to discuss it. I thought that if I could find out more about what happened, it might help me to talk to him."

"When did you move into the cottage?"

"At Christmas."

"If you don't mind me asking, why did you decide to buy it? If your husband had bad memories, I mean."

"Tony told me he'd always loved the area. He never mentioned what had happened. But I picked up the local gossip about the cottage. That's when I went to the library and found the report of the inquest."

"I interviewed your husband." Crocker nodded. "He was badly shaken up when I told him Mrs. Bird had died. Not a nice thing to happen to someone who'd come here on holiday. I have to say, I'm very surprised that he chose to come back here to live. In the very place where it happened."

"He's an artist. He says there's nothing like the light you get in this part of Cornwall. And he loves the wildness of the landscape."

"Yes, I remember now. That's what he told me, that he was on a painting holiday." The way he said it made it sound as though he didn't believe it. "He said he was studying art in London."

"That's right." She hadn't come here to defend Tony, but that was how it was beginning to feel. "We were both living in London until we came here. We got married the day before we moved into the cottage."

A smile lifted the corners of his mouth. "Well, congratulations. Not much of a wedding present, though, finding out that your new home has an unpleasant history."

"No, it wasn't. But that's the problem—all I have is rumours and a sketchy report in the newspaper. I need to know what really happened—for my own sanity as much as for Tony's." She bit her lip. Had she really said that word? Was she that close to the edge?

"All right." He rubbed his chin with the knuckle of his index finger. "Let me tell you what I saw and heard, in the order it happened. Mrs. Bird was found, by your husband, about a hundred yards down the track from Carreg Cottage. I got there just as they were carrying her down to the ambulance. She was unconscious then, and she didn't regain consciousness before she died later that evening. There were no wounds on her body—no reason to suspect that she'd been attacked by anyone.

"The next morning, I called at the cottage with my sergeant because Mrs. Richards, the housekeeper who gave evidence at the inquest, said she thought Mrs. Bird might have gone there because of some trouble with the people who rented the place. There was a suggestion that the tenant, Mr. Crowley, was about to be given notice to quit. I wanted to talk to him, but he wasn't at home. I was greeted by his lady friend—a Miss Dora Montague. I say 'greeted,' but in actual fact she attacked me. Bit me on the ear. She was like a wild animal. Her clothes were torn, and she'd smashed the place up. She was screaming something about lizards from outer space coming to eat her." He paused, folding his arms across his chest. "I suspected that drugs might be responsible for her behaviour."

"What made you think that?"

He drew in a long breath. "You see that kind of thing in a job like mine—even in a place like Cornwall, unfortunately. And I'd heard rumours about what was going on at Carreg Cottage. Anyway, we searched the place after Miss Montague had been taken away—but found nothing." He paused, his eyes ranging over the flowers on the carpet. "It occurred to me that Mrs. Bird might have been drugged, that she could have been given something to eat or drink that contained a substance strong enough to kill her. But there was no post-mortem—so we'll never know."

"But . . . why not?"

"For the same reason Crowley wasn't brought back from London for the inquest." He looked at her. "I can't spell it out, I'm afraid, Mrs. Wylde. Let's just say the powers that be directed us to drop that line of inquiry."

Ellen stared back at him, bewildered. "Why would they do that? Just because he wasn't at the cottage when Stella Bird went there doesn't mean he wasn't responsible in some way." She was thinking of the mommet, of the intent behind its creation. But she couldn't imagine a policeman taking much notice of a thing like that.

"Quite right," he replied. "As I said, I can't give you the details of why the investigation was brought to a halt. But I will say this . . ." She saw the muscle in his jaw clench as he paused. "You've heard, I'm sure, that Mr. Crowley was involved in certain practices. What people call black magic?"

Ellen nodded.

"Let me paint a picture for you. A picture of something that might or might not have been going on in Germany in the years before Hitler invaded Poland, and we declared war."

"In *Germany*?"

"I said 'might.' You must understand that what I'm about to say is a possibility—nothing more."

"Yes. I'm sorry for interrupting. Please, go on."

"Well, the Nazis had a twisted view of the world—I don't think any right-thinking person would dispute that—but there were rumours circulating before the war that the men closest to Hitler took it a step further. It was said that men like Rudolf Hess were obsessed with the occult—and the possibility of using it against their enemies." He spread his hands, palms up. "I know it sounds far-fetched. I thought that when I heard it. But just imagine if it were true. And then ask yourself how useful a man like Crowley could be in a situation like that."

Ellen shook her head, incredulous. "You're saying he was a spy?"

"I'm not saying anything. Just that Crowley was an expert on the occult—and it doesn't take a genius to see how that would enable . . . well, *connections* to be made."

"And he got away with it because of that?"

"Not entirely. The chief constable banned him from ever entering Cornwall again. So, he was unable to go on living at Carreg Cottage. In that respect at least, Mrs. Bird won the battle." He glanced at his watch. "I'm sorry, Mrs. Wylde, but I have to take Flossie for her afternoon constitutional." He got to his feet. "Come on, old girl." The dog lifted its head. "Walkies!"

After Ellen climbed back into the jeep, she sat for a moment, watching the man and his dog ambling down the hill. She wondered how much of what he had revealed she should tell Iris. How would she react to the suggestion that her mother had been given drugs to bring on the seizure that caused her to collapse on the moor? Probably better to keep quiet about that.

She thought about what the policeman had said about Crowley being banned from Cornwall. That, perhaps, would be some shred of comfort to Iris: justice of a kind. As she turned the key in the engine, something else occurred to her. If Crowley had been prevented from returning to Carreg Cottage during his life, was that why he was haunting the place in death?

⟞⟝

Iris dipped a thin brush into a jar of red paint and began filling in the tracery of flowers around the door of the farmhouse she was finishing. She was alone in the shop. Ellen had gone to the railway station to organize the transport of the first part of the Harrods order.

Iris's hand was steady as she painted the delicate petals, but inside she was seething with fury, playing back what Ellen had told her. It sounded like something from a movie—the sort of thing people would queue up to go and see. But it wasn't make-believe. It was real. The facts about her mother's death had been brushed under the carpet because Crowley's usefulness to the British government was more valuable than the truth.

She wondered how her father fitted into the murky world Crowley had inhabited. Had he known that his friend was a spy? Had he been involved in it, too? She thought of all the foreign business trips her father made: the journeys to Europe and North America—buying and selling old documents and antiquarian books. It was what he did for a living. He'd been doing that before the war. Germany was a place he'd visited often. Could he have used those trips to assist Crowley in his intelligence work?

Ellen had said that Ray Crocker wouldn't go into detail about the government connection—that he'd only hinted at what it was about. So, short of confronting her father, there was no way of finding out.

She stabbed her brush into the paint, cursing under her breath as she almost knocked the jar over. As she wiped the spatters of red off the surface of the table, she went over what Ellen had told her. She had a feeling that there was something else, something Ellen was holding back. If it was some gruesome fact about the state of her mother's body when it was found, Iris was glad she'd kept silent.

There was still the mystery of exactly what had caused her mother's death, and the fact that Crowley had been on the way to London when she'd gone to call at the cottage. If Dora Montague was the only person who knew what had really happened, there was no prospect of ever getting to the truth.

A shadow fell across the table as Iris finished painting the flowers. She glanced up to see a face in the window. A child was looking at the toys on display. A little girl, about eight or nine years old, in a school uniform. She had a wistful look, as if she longed to reach through the glass and touch what she could see. Iris went to the door.

"Hello. You can come inside and have a better look if you like."

The girl looked worried, as if she'd been caught doing something she shouldn't. She had beautiful eyes—dark, like Dan's—and black hair worn in a single long plait. She looked different from anyone Iris had seen in St Ives. Her face was reminiscent of the mountain children at the school run by the nuns in the *Black Narcissus* movie.

"I . . . I can't buy anything. I don't have any money." The child's hand tightened around the battered leather strap of the satchel slung over her shoulder.

"It doesn't matter." Iris smiled. "There's no charge for looking."

Once inside, the girl made a beeline for the Noah's Ark in the center of the display. She picked up one of the elephants and turned it over in her hand, running a finger along the tusks and the trunk. "My mum's promised me something from this shop for my birthday—but it's not until May." She cast a rueful glance at Iris.

"Hmm. That's a way off, isn't it?" Iris felt sorry for her. But she could hardly give one of the toys away. "Would you like to see how we make them? The workshop is just through there."

The girl nodded eagerly. With great care, she replaced the elephant in the procession of animals.

"What's your name?" Iris asked, as she led the way to the back of the shop.

The girl came out with something that sounded like *sea wing*.

"I beg your pardon," Iris said.

The girl repeated the name. "It's Chinese. You spell the first part 'S-z-e,' then 'Wing,' like a bird's wing. My dad was a sailor from Hong Kong, but he died in the war, when I was three."

"Oh." Iris didn't know what to say. The girl seemed unperturbed by the tragic fact she'd imparted. She was looking around at the workshop, running her eyes over the row of chisels hanging on the wall.

"What's *your* name?" The glossy black plait flicked out as Sze Wing turned her head.

"I'm Iris."

"Is this your shop?"

"No—I just work here. The lady who owns it is out. She makes all the toys herself—and I paint them."

"How does she make them?"

Iris explained the process of turning raw planks of wood into shapes that were chiseled and sanded before being painted and varnished. She took a handful of half-finished farm animals from the basket beside the workbench for the child to examine.

"My mum has a shop," the girl said, as she turned a cow upside down to inspect the udders. "But it's not like this one."

"Oh? Which is her shop?"

"It's called The Botanic Store." The girl placed the cow alongside a sheep on the workbench. "It's up Tregenna Hill. We live there— upstairs—with my grandma."

Iris gazed at the small hand moving the wooden figures, bringing them alive. *My grandma.* Could that be Mrs. Richards? Was this little girl the granddaughter of the housekeeper at Rowan Tree House? Was that why Mrs. Richards had been cleaning the window of the shop when Iris had passed by, that first week she was in St Ives?

"What are their names, your mum and your grandma?"

Sze Wing rummaged in the basket and pulled out a horse. "Mum is Mary, and Grandma's name is Elizabeth."'

Aunt Mary. A face swam out of some dark recess of Iris's memory. Smiley blue eyes in a round face framed with golden brown curls. And there were daisies in her hair.

Iris's mother had told stories of long-ago summers, before the First War, when she had spent her days playing with the housekeeper's daughter. They were the same age—born just a month apart, her mother had said. Years later, Mrs. Richards was still the housekeeper— and her grown-up daughter came to visit Rowan Tree House. The image

Iris carried in her head was of Aunt Mary in the garden, showing her how to make daisy chains.

As she watched Sze Wing play with the animals, more memories surfaced. She recollected her mother telling her that Aunt Mary was expecting a baby. Iris had wanted to know if the baby was going to be her cousin—and her mother had explained that the housekeeper's daughter wasn't a real aunt—just a friend. Was it during that last Easter holiday? She wasn't certain. What she did know was that she had never seen the baby. Her mother must have died before it was born. Was Sze Wing that child? She looked the right age.

"I'd probably better go home now." The girl's voice broke into her thoughts. "Mum might be wondering where I am."

"Yes, of course you must."

She followed Sze Wing to the door and stood there, unable to take her eyes off her until she disappeared around the corner of Fore Street. It was like seeing herself at the age she would have been when her mother died. The thought of the girl walking through the door of the shop on Tregenna Hill brought a lump to her throat.

She'd never known that Aunt Mary had married a Chinese man. Her mother hadn't mentioned that. She wondered how close they had been, as adults, her mother and Sze Wing's. Close enough for Aunt Mary to know about the goings-on at Carreg Cottage? Could she know things that weren't revealed at the inquest?

Iris found it difficult to get back to painting. Her mind was buzzing with possibilities. At half past four she locked the shop and left the keys behind the rain barrel in the backyard. As she headed home, she asked herself whether it would matter if she revealed herself to Mrs. Richards and her daughter. Would Mrs. Richards get in touch with Iris's father? There was a good chance she would still remember his telephone number, even after all this time.

She was so lost in thought that she didn't see who was sitting at the top of the steps leading from the fish cellar until she was already halfway up.

Nina Grey was standing in the entrance of the Mariners' Church, watching. It had been a shock when Leo had come banging on the door. She had gone downstairs, bleary-eyed, thinking it was the postman.

She'd tried her best to calm him down. To explain why she couldn't tell him where his daughter was living. But he was having none of it. He said he would knock on every door in St Ives if he had to. He wasn't leaving until he'd had the chance to talk to her, face to face.

In the end, they had made a bargain: she would take him to the place where Iris lived, but she would keep her eye on him. If he attempted to make the girl leave with him against her will, she would be straight on the phone to his wife to tell her just what he got up to on his business trips.

She'd waved away his protests that he wasn't like that anymore, that he and she were ancient history, and there were no other women in his life. He'd been a bad boy—and there were photographs to prove it. She had enough on him to make his life hell.

Iris stopped dead, her brain unable to process what her eyes were telling her.

"Winnie." He stood up, towering over her. She backed down the steps, but he grabbed her by the arm. "Please, Winnie. I haven't come to drag you home. Can't we just talk?"

She looked at his hand on the sleeve of her coat. He released his grip and stepped back. "H . . . how did you know?" Her voice was a hoarse whisper. "Who told you?"

"That is of no consequence. The only thing that matters is for me to say sorry."

"What?" His words blindsided her.

"Can we go inside?"

She stood for a moment, paralyzed, not quite able to believe this was happening. Then, as if some unseen force was controlling her limbs, she pulled the key out of her pocket and moved past him, up the remaining steps to the door.

He couldn't mask his shock at the tiny room with its very basic furnishings. Her eyes narrowed as she watched his face. "You can sit there." She motioned to the one and only chair. She wasn't going to offer him a cup of tea. That would give the wrong signal. Make it seem as though it was all right for him to come barging into her life.

He took off his hat as he sat down. She could see the bald patch beneath his thinning hair. "Why did you run away, Winnie? I've been going frantic."

She kept her distance, standing in the corner by the sink, her arms folded across her chest. "That's not my name. I'm Iris. If you want to talk to me, you should remember that." She felt a surge of power. She had never, ever spoken to him like that.

"I'm sorry. I can't help it. But I'll try to remember." Were those tears in his eyes? She stared in horrified fascination. She had never seen him like this. "Why did you leave home, Iris?"

"Because it didn't *feel* like home—not to me. It was like being in prison. I had no control over my life. You stopped me from doing what I wanted to do—and you were pushing me into things I had no interest in."

His head dropped. "I've made such a hash of things, haven't I? But I only ever had your best interests at heart." She heard him clear his throat, as if he was struggling to get the words out. "I stopped paying for art school because I was worried about you getting in with the wrong crowd."

A flash of pure anger coursed through her body. "The wrong crowd? How can you say that? How can you accuse *me* of keeping bad company when you were friends with a man who put curses on people to make them die?"

He looked up, searching her face.

"You left my mother all alone to face up to that monster. And she *died*. Why did you do that? Did you *want* her to die?"

"Who's told you all this?" His voice was barely audible.

"Nobody." She held his gaze. "I found it out for myself. It's common knowledge around here." She took a breath. She could feel her body trembling. "I saw a photo of him. He was wearing that horrible ring. That's how I knew you were still friends with him—right up until he died. Why was that ring left to me? Did he feel guilty for killing my mother? Did *you* feel guilty?"

In the silence that followed, it felt as though the world had stopped turning. Then she heard the chair creak. He stood up. "It was an accident, Iris. Your mother died because she had a weak heart."

"You expect me to believe that? I *know* what happened. She went to the cottage to confront Crowley—and she saw something that terrified her so much she ran away and collapsed on the hillside."

He took a step toward her. "Would you believe me if I told you that her death was as much of a shock to me as it was to you?" He shook his head. "I'm not going to pretend that it was the perfect marriage. But we had you. Do you really think me so callous as to *want* you to grow up without a mother?"

Iris opened her mouth, but her lower lip quivered so much she couldn't speak.

"It was an accident." He repeated. "A stupid prank that backfired. They only meant to scare her. They didn't know she had a weak heart."

She gazed at him, bewildered. Had Crowley confessed to him? Had he hoodwinked the police with the alibi about catching a train to London? Or had that idea been cooked up by some government official to get him off the hook? The questions zoomed around her head like wasps trapped in a jar.

"I want to know what he told you." She could hear the venom in her voice. A snake's hiss. She saw the muscle in his jaw clench.

"It was the woman, Dora. She did it."

"You said 'they.'"

He shrugged. "There were all kinds of people drifting in and out of the place at the time. I lost track of who was staying there."

"You didn't mean Crowley?"

"He wasn't there. He was on his way to London when it happened."

She frowned. "I read the report of the inquest in the newspaper. Where were these other people? Why weren't they questioned?"

He blew out a breath. "I don't know. The police said Dora was the only person at the cottage, that she'd attacked one of the men who went to investigate."

"I have a friend who knows that policeman," she said. "He said that he was told to stop investigating the case because Crowley was working for the government."

His eyes narrowed. "I don't know anything about that."

"He was useful because of his knowledge of the occult. Hitler and his cronies were obsessed with it, apparently." She searched his face. Waited for him to speak. But he kept silent. "You went to Germany often before the war, didn't you?"

"What are you suggesting?"

She saw a glint of something in his eyes. Another expression she'd never seen before—like a cat about to pounce on an unwary mouse. "I know that you shared his interests," she went on. "I've seen the books in your study—and that Tarot pack you caught me playing with when I was little . . ."

"Stop, Iris." He held up his hand. "You need to know that anyone who was involved in that sort of work is forbidden from talking about it. It would be a breach of the Official Secrets Act."

"So, you *were* involved?"

"I didn't say that."

"Did you know that Crowley was a spy?"

There was another long silence. "Let me just say this. He had his faults—there's no denying that—but he was one of the cleverest men I ever met." He looked away from her, his eyes ranging over the clothes hanging from the hooks on the wall. "I remember him coming into the little bookshop I used to have in Charing Cross Road. He was one of my first customers. I was astonished by the breadth of his knowledge. He'd made a study of every world religion, and he was an expert on Egyptology. He became invaluable to me. And for a while I was drawn to the occult. But for me, it was just a passing phase."

"Why was he living at Carreg Cottage? Did you invite him there?"

"He was down on his luck. He'd had a lot of money and lost it all." He turned his face back to her. "It's something I'll regret for the rest of my days. I know that if I hadn't made that decision, your mother would probably still be alive."

Iris felt her throat swell as tears prickled her eyes. "And yet you remained friends with him?"

"If you'd seen him at the end, you would have felt sorry for him. He was a poor, shambling wreck of a man, living in squalor, too weak to eat what little food he could afford to buy. He would have died all alone if we hadn't been there."

"*We?*"

"Frieda Harris, his artist friend, was with him at the end."

Iris stared at him. "Was she the one who told you I was here?"

"No."

"Who, then?"

"I can't tell you that. All I can say is that the person who told me made me promise not to try to make you go back to London . . . I take it you don't want to come back?"

She shook her head.

"Will you write to me, Iris? Just to let me know that you're all right?"

"Yes, if you want me to."

They stood there awkwardly for a long moment. They had never hugged one another—not that she could remember. In the end, he looked at his watch and mumbled something about catching the evening train.

When he'd gone, she slumped onto the bed and wept into the pillow.

It was hours later, when she'd washed away the tears and made herself a cup of tea, that it occurred to her who had given her away.

CHAPTER 24

Ellen groped behind the rain barrel for the keys to the shop, hoping that Iris had remembered to leave them. In the twilit yard, she couldn't see much, but her fingers found the small heap of metal nestled in the shelter of the wall.

Inside the workshop, she lifted the boxes down from the attic space and carried them out to the jeep. She was pleased that there was space in the goods train for all four. They would be in London by tomorrow morning, ready to be collected. By the weekend, the farm sets and Noah's Arks would be on display in Harrods' toy department.

It took only a matter of minutes to drive to the railway station. She went to find a porter to come and load the boxes onto a trolley to take to the train that was waiting in the sidings. Then she went to the office to sign the dockets for the delivery.

"Going to be a frost tonight, they reckon." The woman behind the desk smiled as she handed Ellen the slips of paper.

"It does feel much colder." Ellen nodded.

"Don't think *they're* feeling it." The woman jerked her head toward the window. On the platform, lit up by the overhead lamps, was a couple necking. The woman had her arms around the man, and, as Ellen watched, she slid one leg up the side of his trousers, her dress riding up to her thigh.

"You'd think they'd know better at their age." The woman grunted a laugh. "Don't look young, do they?"

The man's trilby hat had slipped sideways in the passionate encounter. Ellen could see thinning hair, swept across a bald patch. As they broke free from each other, she saw the woman's face in profile. It was Nina Grey—Tony's friend. The sight of her made Ellen smile inside. How foolish she had been, to fear that Nina and Tony were still an item. Clearly the woman was mad about this older man. She wondered who he was. She didn't remember seeing him at Barbara Hepworth's party.

The screech of the train's whistle filled the air. Ellen saw the man turn away and climb into one of the waiting carriages, blowing a kiss to Nina as he went. He seemed to be the only person boarding. Perhaps that was why they had been so blasé about their behavior, thinking no one was watching.

"Is that the London train?"

"Will be, once it gets to St Erth," the woman behind the desk replied. "They'll put a new engine on there."

So, Nina's lover was probably not a local man. Ellen wondered what the story was. He didn't look like an artist. More a stiff-suited businessman. Did he have a wife and family somewhere? Was Nina his mistress?

As she walked back to the jeep, she felt a lightness, as if a weight had been lifted from her heart. Was it mean-spirited, this relief at the idea of Nina being involved with another woman's husband instead of hers? If it was, she couldn't help it. Now she could banish that horrible image of Nina and Tony making love in the bedroom at Carreg Cottage, lock it away in a dark corner of her mind and forget about it.

As she drove up the hill toward Zennor, she felt the familiar frisson of dread about entering the cottage at night. Would Tony be there, warming up the stew for their evening meal? Or would he be locked in the cowshed?

The new padlock on the studio door hadn't escaped her notice. He intended to keep her out in the future. He didn't know that for her, picking locks was as easy as peeling potatoes, that the penknife she always carried with her had been used many times to break into houses damaged by bombs to check for survivors. Let him hold on to that illusion of privacy if it kept him happy, she thought.

There was no light on in the cottage when she pulled up outside. Nor was there any sign of life in the cowshed. She felt a prickle of apprehension as she walked up the path. Where was he? Why wasn't he at home?

She found a note propped on the kitchen table: *Gone to Pendour Cove. Have eaten already—left some for you!*

Pendour Cove? Why on earth would he go *there* in the dark? She wondered if he was at The Tinners Arms but hadn't wanted to admit it. She glanced at the pot of stew on the stove. There was a slick of dried-on gravy where he'd poured it out. Her appetite had vanished. She turned around and headed out of the cottage, back to the jeep.

Ellen could feel the blood rushing through her fingers as she took the right turn to Zennor village. This was not the kind of wife she wanted to be—a woman who spied on her husband to check that he was behaving himself. She slowed down as she approached the pub. There was no sign of Tony's motorbike. She drove on, to the place where the road ended. She got out of the jeep and looked out into the darkness. As the moon came out from behind a cloud, she could make out the shapes of sheep munching the tussocky grass. Then she caught a glint of metal. The bike was propped against a barbed wire fence, where the field gave way to vertiginous cliffs.

She felt sick. What if he'd fallen? Slipped on the rocks? He could be lying there, injured, unable to call for help. What if the tide was coming in? She scrambled across the grass, almost losing her footing as she misjudged the uneven ground. When she reached the cliffs, she went flat on her belly, edging forward as far as she dared.

"Tony!" Her voice was drowned out by the crash of the sea against the rocks. "Tony! Are you down there?"

In the lull between the waves breaking, she listened. There was no sound but the swish of the restless ocean. Another wave broke. Then she heard him.

"Ellie! Is that you?" His voice sounded very close. Almost as if he were standing beside her.

"Where are you?" She craned her neck, her eyes trained on the white-fringed edge of the water.

"Down here!"

Suddenly she caught sight of his upturned face, lit by the moon as he stepped out of the shadow of the cliffs.

"It's fantastic! The tide's going out—all these creatures in the rock pools . . ." He directed his flashlight up at her. "Come down and see!"

"I can't," she shouted back. "I won't be able to see the path—it's too dangerous!"

"Okay—I . . ." His next words were lost in the roar of a breaking wave. "Stay there," he called when the water receded. "I won't be long."

She hauled herself up into a sitting position to wait for him. Tried not to dwell on the fact that he'd urged her to risk her life on that treacherous path. As she stared out at the moonlit ocean, she heard that other man's voice in her head.

He's slipping away from you. You don't really know him.

"That's not true." She hissed the words into the night air, desperate to convince herself. In the few weeks since the wedding, their relationship had shifted, just as the sea drew back from the cliffs below. She felt raw, exposed, like the creatures in the rock pools. Would he come back, like the tide? Or was he moving farther away?

"Look what I found!" Suddenly he was beside her.

"You made me jump! I didn't hear you coming."

"Sorry." He thrust something toward her—a twisted white shape draped with strands of seaweed.

"Ugh! It stinks! What is it?"

"The remains of a gannet, I think. It's perfect. Just what I was looking for."

"What?" She shuffled back on her bottom, away from the reek of rotting flesh. "Why do you want a thing like that?"

"Barbara likes the idea of *The Ghost Birds*. She thinks a trio of paintings would go down well at the exhibition." He held the dead creature up to the moon, making it move across the sky. "This is going to be my model."

She saw the way his eyes glittered as he spoke. It was wonderful to see him so animated, so enthusiastic. But there was a brittle edge to his voice. A feverish sense of excitement. Again, she asked herself why he had come here in the dark, risking life and limb to find this smelly trophy, when he could have waited until tomorrow.

You don't know him, do you?

The taunting voice echoed around her head as she watched Tony tuck the dead bird into the pannier of his motorbike.

It took a few seconds for Iris to remember what had happened. The image of her father, sitting in the chair at the end of her bed, filled her mind as she lay there, staring at the flaking paint on the ceiling. And then another memory came, crackling through her brain like a bolt of lightning.

Dan. It had to be him. He had been there, in London, with her letter in his pocket. He must have gone to her father and told him where she was.

She got dressed quickly, hating herself for that moment of weakness. It had been her treasure, the memory of their lovemaking. Now she saw what a fool she had been. He had taken what he wanted, then thrown her whole future into jeopardy.

The person who told me made me promise not to try to make you go back to London. Her father's words rang in her ears. She could just imagine Dan striking that bargain as he handed over her letter. But what use was a promise like that? If her father had wanted to, he could have called in the police. And Dan had *known* that.

The figurine he had given her was sitting on the shelf opposite the bed. The naked woman, cupping her breasts, mocked her now. She grabbed it and stuffed it under a sweater in the chest of drawers. Then, with trembling fingers, she unfastened the sea glass pendant she hadn't taken off since the day he'd given it to her.

Her hands were still shaking when she fastened the buttons of her coat. Ellen hadn't asked for her to go into the shop today—but she felt a desperate need to talk to someone: someone she could trust.

Fishy smoke wafted past her as she made her way down the steps. She could see the man in the cellar through the metal grille in the window. He waved to her. She raised her hand to return the gesture, but it was a halfhearted attempt. Her hand went to her stomach. The smell was making her feel nauseous.

Ellen saw her coming. She was in the window, rearranging the display. Her smile made Iris's face crumple. Stupid tears rolled down her cheeks. She hadn't meant to cry. She swiped her face with the sleeve of her coat.

"Hey! What's the matter?" Ellen opened the door and ushered her in.

Iris breathed in the comforting scent of linseed oil as she sank onto the stool by the workbench. This was her safe place. And Ellen was her friend—her only *true* friend. The thought of Dan's treachery was like a knife in her belly.

Ellen made a pot of tea. Iris took a couple of sips, but she felt too churned up to drink the whole cup. It had gone cold by the time she'd related what had happened yesterday afternoon.

"I can understand why you're so upset," Ellen said. "It must have been one hell of a shock. But it's a relief in a way, isn't it? He didn't try to force you to go back with him—so you're free now: you don't have to hide who you are anymore."

"I know. But I keep thinking it might not have turned out like that. He could have brought the police with him. Had me arrested, even.

How could he have done that to me? *He* didn't know how it would turn out."

"You mean Dan?"

Iris nodded. "He must have gone to the house as soon as he arrived in London."

"Did your father tell you that?"

"No. He said he couldn't tell me who'd told him—but they'd made him promise not to make me go back home." She shook her head. "But Dan couldn't have been certain that my father would keep a promise like that, could he?"

"Are you sure it wasn't someone else?"

"No one else knows my real name, or where I live—apart from you."

Ellen blew out a breath. "It's hard when someone you really care about deceives you."

Iris looked at her. It sounded as though she was speaking from experience. Had Ellen been betrayed by a man? Had her husband done something to hurt her? It seemed unlikely, as they'd only just gotten married.

Ellen was staring at a pile of wood shavings on the floor. "I never knew my father," she said. "He left before I was born. Mum said he was German, and he went back there to visit family and never returned."

Iris clicked her tongue against the roof of her mouth. "That must have been awful."

"It was for my mother. Not for me, really, because I never knew him."

"I felt as though *I* never knew my father," Iris said. "Even though I had one. He might as well have been a stranger. I think I saw more of who he really is yesterday than in my whole life before." She paused. "I still don't know how he could have been friends with a man like Crowley. But what was really eating away at me was whether he *wanted* my mother to die. At least I don't believe that anymore."

Ellen got up and moved around the table, wrapping her arms around Iris's shoulders. "You've been so brave. You've been through so much these past few weeks."

"I've been stupid, Ellen." She fought back the sob rising in her throat. "I was a fool to trust Dan. But he seemed so . . ."

"Try not to be too hard on him," Ellen whispered. "I'm sure he only did what he thought was best for you. And it turned out all right, didn't it?"

Iris fumbled in her pocket for her handkerchief and dabbed away fresh tears. "Maybe if he'd talked to me about it—warned me—I could see things differently. But he didn't. He just went storming in."

Ellen straightened up, one hand still on Iris's shoulder. "Where's your father now? Did he book into one of the hotels?"

"No. He went straight back to London on the evening train."

"Oh?"

Iris didn't see the look that passed across Ellen's face.

CHAPTER 25

Tony stared at the body of the gannet. The smell was disgusting—and yet he couldn't tear himself away from it. There was an unearthly beauty in those opaque, sightless eyes, ringed in turquoise and underlined in black. And the beak—a lethal spear of a thing but so elegantly shaped, and such a delicate shade of gray.

What he'd told Ellen—about needing it as a model for the pieces he wanted to create for the exhibition—was not the whole truth. The fox painting hadn't worked. Stella hadn't gone away. He'd seen her when he'd gone to buy meat from the butcher in Wharf Road. She'd been walking toward him, and then it was as if a mist had risen from the sea, hiding her from view. It had rattled him so badly he'd spent the whole afternoon smoking—and he'd forgotten to put the stew on.

Suddenly it had dawned on him that the only way to be rid of Stella was to recreate the mommet. *That* was why she had come back to haunt him—because Ellen had made him destroy the bird-headed doll. He must make a new one. It had worked then, when she was alive—and it would work again to banish her ghost.

What about the hair? Crowley's voice hissed at him, just as it had all those years ago. That had been the riskiest thing, breaking into Rowan Tree House—far more dangerous than climbing down to Pendour Cove in thick fog. He'd had to hide in the bushes and wait until Stella went to church. And even then, he couldn't be sure that the housekeeper wasn't there.

"You can't take hair from a ghost." His own voice sounded strange in the silence of the studio. Like an old man's voice. *Christ,* he thought, *it's his voice.*

⟐

Iris didn't go to the morning service at St Ia's on Sunday. She couldn't bear the thought of seeing Dan. If he wondered where she was, he only had himself to blame. It must have crossed his mind that her father would jump on the first train to St Ives. He would have to be stupid not to realize what the consequences of giving away her secret would be. And while he was clearly deceitful, he was certainly not stupid.

If he came to find her, she would not be at home. Ellen was right about her father's visit having a silver lining: now that there was no need to conceal her identity, she could go and see Mrs. Richards. She would apologize to the housekeeper for running off that time she'd passed the shop instead of stopping to say hello, and she would explain the reason why. And then she would ask Mrs. Richards and Aunt Mary about what they remembered.

The "Closed" sign was hanging in the door of The Botanic Store. Iris hadn't expected it to be open on a Sunday. But Sze Wing had said that they lived above the shop. She peered through the window. Beyond the sprays of dried lavender and the display of teas and tinctures, she could see the silhouette of a woman. She was lifting a heavy-looking jar from a shelf. She took it over to the counter and tipped it into the bowl of a set of scales.

Iris knocked on the window. The woman glanced up. The startled face was familiar. It transported her to another summer afternoon in the garden at Rowan Tree House: not the daisy chain session, but the time she'd found a toad and crept up behind her mother and Aunt Mary with it cupped in her hands.

Mary came to the door. She stood there, blinking in the rays of winter sunlight shining down the street, staring at Iris as if she were something from outer space.

"Aunt Mary . . . can I . . ."

Mary's hand flew to her mouth. "Oh! Winnie! Is it really you?"

"I . . . I'm sorry if I startled you . . ."

"No—it's just that . . ." She pressed her lips together. "You're the image of your mother. I thought . . ." She stepped back, opening the door wider. "Come in. Mum's upstairs—she'll be so thrilled to see you."

"I'm so sorry I didn't stop to talk to her the other day." Iris stood on the threshold. She'd rehearsed what she was going to say, but now that the moment had come, she felt tongue-tied. "I . . . I was hiding, you see."

"Hiding?" The fine lines on Mary's forehead furrowed.

"I'd run away from home. From London. I changed my name. I couldn't tell anyone who I was."

"Come and have a cup of tea." Mary tilted her head toward a curtain that screened off the back of the shop. "You can tell me all about it, and then we'll go upstairs."

The tea was like nothing Iris had ever tasted. Rosehip and linden blossom, Mary said as she poured hot water into the pot. By the time it had brewed, Iris was halfway through the story of her escape to St Ives. Mary listened in silence as it unfolded.

"Your mother would be very proud of you, you know."

"Would she?" Iris tried to swallow some more tea, but her throat felt tight.

Mary nodded. "You've been brave enough to make the kind of life you want. She would have applauded that. And of course, she was a brilliant artist—she would have been delighted that you were following in her footsteps."

"Was she? I didn't know that."

"She went to art school before she married your father. She specialised in flower painting. I think she would have liked to have been a professional illustrator." She lifted the teapot and topped up the cups. "You haven't seen her work?"

"No." Iris frowned. "My father never mentioned it."

A small face appeared around the door behind Mary's chair. "Hello! Have you brought some toys to show Mum?"

Mary glanced over her shoulder, then back at Iris, a bemused expression on her face. "You've met my daughter? How?"

When Iris had explained, Mary sent Sze Wing back upstairs to fetch her grandmother. "I can't tell you what a relief it is to know that Mum really saw you," she said. "She's starting to lose her memory. Sometimes she says things . . . goes back in time, I think. She swore she'd seen your mother's ghost."

"I'm sorry." Iris shook her head. She couldn't bear to think of upsetting the woman who had been so kind, so patient with her when she was growing up. "I just panicked when I saw her. I didn't realise how hard it would be, trying to hide who I was."

Elizabeth Richards came into the room. The gray in her hair was the only thing time had altered. Her heart-shaped face, with its gentle blue eyes, hadn't changed at all. She let out a small sound when she saw Iris—something between a gasp and a cry of alarm, like someone shaken awake from a deep sleep.

"Mrs. Richards!" The face blurred as Iris stood up. She swallowed hard. "It's me—Winnie—but I'm all grown up now."

"Winnie . . ." Elizabeth put her hands on Iris's shoulders, searching her face.

"She's moved to St Ives to live, Ma. Isn't that nice?"

"To Rowan Tree House?" A frown creased the older woman's face.

"No, not there." Iris heard the tremor in her voice as she spoke. "Someone else lives there now. I live in town."

"She's going to be a painter, like her mother," Mary added. "Do you remember those beautiful flower pictures she used to do?"

Elizabeth nodded. "She always used to give me one on my birthday. I've still got them." Her eyes glistened. "Poor lamb." She lifted a hand

and stroked Iris's hair. "Losing your mother so young. Those devils up at the cottage . . . if only she . . ."

"Now, Ma." Mary was on her feet. "She doesn't want to hear about that."

"It's all right—I already know," Iris whispered. "Well, some of it. I was hoping to talk to you both about it. It's been such a shock . . ." She tailed off, glancing from Mary to her mother, and then at Sze Wing, who was listening to everything being said. This wasn't a conversation to be had in front of a child.

"Why don't you come back this evening?" Mary gave her a look that suggested she was thinking the same. "About eight o'clock?"

"Are you sure? I don't want to intrude on your evening."

"You won't be." Mary smiled. "And we'll find those paintings to show you, won't we, Ma?"

Elizabeth nodded. "Won't that be nice? Just the three of us—like the old days."

<hr />

A strange smell invaded Ellen's dream. It triggered a replay of the night she'd taken refuge in the shop. But in this nightmare version of events there was a door in the wall behind the lathe, which opened into the funeral parlor. Walking through it, she was confronted with a row of bodies, bruised and bloodied, some missing arms or legs, like the bomb victims in the Blitz. She stared at them, knowing she should go to them, check for signs of life. But she couldn't bring herself to touch them because of the nauseating stench.

Her eyes snapped open. She hadn't dreamed that smell. It was real. And the space beside her was empty. Tony must be downstairs, in the kitchen. What on earth could be making that awful stink?

She pulled on the clothes draped over the end of the bed. From the top of the stairs, she could see that he was standing over the stove. Steam was rising from her big stew pot. He was prodding the contents with a wooden spoon. Her hand flew to her mouth as a wave of the aroma drifted up to her. She mustn't make a fuss. He'd gotten up before her to prepare Sunday lunch. But the meat smelled like it had gone off.

"You're up bright and early." She came up behind him, trying not to inhale as she touched him on the shoulder.

He whipped round, recoiling from her touch. He stared at her as if she was a stranger, piercing her with cold, glittering eyes. He lifted the spoon above his head as if he planned to hit her with it.

"It's all right." She backed away. "If it's a surprise, I don't want to spoil it."

His lip curled. He looked like a dog about to bite. "What the hell are you talking about, woman?"

She froze. Something had happened to his voice.

"I . . . I just thought you were making something for lunch."

He hissed out a breath between his teeth. "Oh, yes! Why didn't I think of that? What will it be? Rotting seabird rissoles, perhaps? Gamey gannet fricassee?" He lowered the spoon into the pot and dredged up the bird, now almost reduced to a skeleton. "Stupid girl! Did you really think this was something to eat?"

Now she knew whose voice it was. The pitiless, sibilant tone, the cut-glass accent. Her legs trembled as she edged away from him, closer to the door. "I . . ." She tried to swallow. Her tongue stuck to the roof of her mouth. "I . . . I need to pop into town," she mumbled. "Left something in the shop." She grabbed the keys from the hook and pushed her feet into her shoes. As she opened the door, he started to say something else, but she was outside, running down the path, before he'd finished the sentence.

Her first instinct was to drive to the shop and phone her mother. But what would she say? Would she confess to fleeing the cottage because she thought Tony was possessed by the ghost of its former tenant? Her mother would probably think that she, not Tony, had lost her mind. She would be beside herself with worry, would want Ellen to come straight back to London.

And that was not the answer. Whatever was happening to Tony, however disturbing his behavior, he was her husband. She had vowed to stay with him in sickness and health, until parted by death. He was not sick—not in the physical sense—but his mind was unbalanced. He needed help from someone who understood what was going on inside his head. But where could she get that kind of help?

As she drove toward St Ives, she thought about the woman, Dora Montague, who had been taken to Bodmin Asylum after Stella Bird's death. Was that what would happen to Tony if a doctor was brought to the cottage? She couldn't bear the idea of him being locked up in a place like that. But neither could she contemplate returning to the cottage alone. Because she was terrified of what Crowley might make him do to her.

She'd left the house without her coat, and her hands were slippery with perspiration as she turned off the coast road toward the town. Thank God for the shop. Even if she didn't phone her mother, she could lie low there for a while until she worked out what to do.

Before her now was the sea, the palest aquamarine, a glowing jewel beneath a wintry sky. The beauty of this place was heartbreaking. Alluring one moment and threatening the next. Like a mirror of her marriage.

As she headed down Tregenna Hill, the tower of St Ia's church came into view. She remembered the offer the vicar had made, to exorcise the cottage, how she had walked away because she knew what Tony's reaction to such a thing would be. Could the vicar help her now?

She pulled up by the railings of the little garden that separated the church from the vicarage. She sat in the jeep for several minutes, wondering what to say, before getting out and walking across to the house. The bell was an old-fashioned type—you had to pull a metal ring attached to a string to make it work. The sound of it clanging inside the house made her jump. She waited, every nerve in her body strained as she listened for footsteps. But none came. She tried again.

Nothing. Then she remembered. It was Sunday morning. He must be in the church.

Ellen could hear singing as she approached the heavy oak doors of St Ia's. She recognized the hymn: "For Those in Peril on the Sea." They had sung it often at her old church, during the war. The door was ajar. If she went in now, while they were still singing, she shouldn't attract too much attention.

She spotted a vacant pew at the back of the nave and hurried toward it as the final verse of the hymn played out. When everyone sat down, she heard Reverend Thomas's voice. He began the Lord's Prayer, and the rest of the congregation joined in. Ellen murmured the words. *Deliver us from evil.* That line sent a shiver up her spine.

When the prayers ended, the vicar announced the final hymn. Ellen glanced across the pews, looking for Iris. She caught sight of Dan, sitting a couple of rows from the front. But he was on his own. Why wasn't Iris with him? She puzzled over it as she flicked through the pages of the hymn book. Then she recalled what Iris had said about Dan betraying her to her father. No wonder the girl wasn't in church.

As the opening chords of "Bread of Heaven" struck up, the image of Nina Grey and the man at the railway station filled her head. Had that man been Iris's father? She had seen no one else getting on the train that evening. Could it have been Nina, not Dan, who had told Lionel Bird where his daughter was living? Ellen frowned as she joined in the singing. How would Nina have known Iris's real name?

As one part of her brain registered the familiar verses, another grappled with what might have happened. The only way to find out would be to ask Dan outright. She should do that—for Iris's sake. However much she played it down, the girl was clearly in love with him. She must be torturing herself, thinking he'd deceived her. If it wasn't true, Iris needed to know.

When the hymn ended and the blessing had been said, people began to file out of the pews. Ellen saw Dan disappear through a door to the side of the altar. His father was already at the back of the church, standing ready to greet people as they went out. She waited until the last person had left the building. When the vicar was closing the doors, she got up and went over to him.

"Hello." Her voice sounded very loud in the silence that had descended on the place.

"Oh—I'm sorry." The vicar turned to her, a large key in his hand. "I thought everyone had gone."

"I was hoping to speak to you—if you wouldn't mind. It's . . ." She couldn't get the words out. She felt as if a stone had lodged itself in her throat.

"Of course, my dear. Why don't we go into the Lady Chapel? The chairs in there are a bit more comfortable than these pews."

He ushered her through an arch to the right of the nave. The sun lit up the stained-glass window above the altar, casting pools of color onto the stone floor. She glanced up, a feeling of uneasiness overwhelming her. She felt as if God himself were hovering around the gilded beams of the ceiling, shaking his head at her.

Marry in haste, repent at leisure.

How many times had she heard her mother trot that out? *Repent.* It had a hard, archaic sound. It meant you wished you'd never done what you'd done and must beg for forgiveness. Did she wish she hadn't married Tony? At this moment, it was a question she couldn't answer.

"Now, my dear, what's on your mind? How are things up at Carreg Cottage?"

She couldn't meet the vicar's eyes. Couldn't bring herself to tell him that she feared her marriage was disintegrating, that she believed her husband's mind had been taken over by the malevolent ghost of Aleister Crowley.

"The last time we spoke, you said that you thought the cottage might be haunted. Have there been any more . . . ," he trailed off. The question hung in the air.

Ellen nodded. Her eyes were fixed on the stone floor. "Tony. My husband. He's . . ." She bit her lip, searching for a way to put it into words. "He's been acting strangely. I think he's been hearing voices, like I have. But he won't talk about it. And now he's . . ." She didn't finish the sentence. She heard a strange sound—like someone choking on food—and realized it was coming from her. Tears began to stream down her face.

The leg of his chair scraped the floor as he hitched up his robe to retrieve a handkerchief from his trouser pocket. He offered it to her without a word. For a moment he let her cry. And then he said: "Has he hurt you, Ellen?"

"N . . . no . . . he . . . hasn't. B . . . but . . ." Her words were punctuated by sobs.

"Are you afraid that he might hurt you?"

She nodded.

"Would you like me to talk to your husband?"

She shook her head. "He . . . he's an atheist." She mumbled it into the handkerchief. "I . . . d . . . don't think he . . . ," she trailed off, wiping away a tear that had run down to her chin.

"You don't think he'd want to speak to someone like me," the vicar said. "But I could at least try. He might be as frightened by what's happening as you are. It might make him . . ." He paused. "What I'm trying to say is that an experience like this can make people think differently about spiritual things."

Ellen could imagine what would happen if the Reverend Thomas attempted to initiate that kind of conversation. Tony would be furious. In his current state of mind, he might even attack the vicar. "I'm not sure that would work," she murmured. "If you'd seen him this morning—the way he looked at me—it was as if he wanted to kill me."

"You're not thinking of going back there alone, are you? You're welcome to stay at the vicarage—until you decide what to do."

"That's very kind of you." Ellen felt fresh tears well up. "But I can stay at my shop tonight."

"What if he comes looking for you?"

"I don't think he will." She thought about what Tony had been doing in the kitchen, standing over the foul-smelling contents of the stew pot like a storybook witch brewing a magic potion. He would probably be in the cowshed now, arranging the skeleton of the bird, making sketches of it. So totally immersed in the act of creation that he wouldn't even remember that she'd gone.

"Will you come back and see me tomorrow? I can put you in touch with one of the local doctors if you'd like me to. And if you change your mind about me talking to your husband, I'm free to go up to Carreg Cottage anytime during the morning."

Before Ellen left, the Reverend Thomas asked if he could pray for her. He placed his hands on her head as she remained seated. She felt awkward, embarrassed at first, but as he began to speak, those feelings subsided.

"In the name of the Lord Jesus Christ of Nazareth, by the power of his cross, his blood, and his resurrection, I bind you, Satan, the spirits, powers, and forces of darkness. I call upon angels of light to protect Ellen in body and soul. Cover her with the whole armour of God and banish all fear from her heart. Amen."

She felt a shiver run down from her head to her feet as he raised his hands. When she stood up, she felt slightly dizzy. He offered her his arm as they walked out of the Lady Chapel. His limp became more noticeable as they neared the doors of the church. He leaned against the wall when they got there, releasing her arm as he did so.

"You know," he said, "this place is built from the same rocks as the ones on Zennor Carn. They were transported around the coast by boat in the fifteenth century." He patted the smooth honey-colored stone. "So, if the rocks up there have some unknown power, then so does this place." He held her gaze as he opened the door. "Think of that, won't you, if you feel afraid."

CHAPTER 26

Iris didn't go straight home. She took a different route back from The Botanic Store, walking along to the harbor and sitting on a bench for a while, watching the boats. If she'd gone her usual way, she would have run into Dan coming back along Fore Street. So, when she found the note that he'd pushed under the door, she didn't realize that she'd missed him by a matter of minutes.

Her heart thudded when she saw his name on the scrap of paper. It was just a handful of words, saying that he'd gotten back too late last night to come and see her. He'd thought she would come to church and was worried when she didn't arrive. He was hoping they might go to the cinema together this evening.

With trembling fingers, she screwed up the paper and threw it into the bin. Didn't he realize that her father had jumped straight onto the train from London, beating him to St Ives by a good twenty-four hours? If Dan thought she was going to go running into his arms after he'd gone behind her back, he'd got another think coming.

The rest of Sunday seemed interminable. Iris tried working on the drawings she'd made at last week's portraiture class, but she couldn't concentrate. Dan's face kept superimposing itself on the pages of her sketchbook. If she didn't turn up at the cinema, he would probably come knocking on the door. She needed to be out of the way before that happened.

So, even though she wasn't due to return to The Botanic Store until eight o'clock, she set off at half past six. She went to a little café on Wharf Road—one of the few that stayed open during the winter—and ordered beans on toast, which was the cheapest thing on the menu. She felt self-conscious. No one else was dining alone. But she had a magazine in her bag, and even though she'd read it from cover to cover, she flicked through the pages, trying to affect an air of nonchalance. With a cup of tea and an iced bun for dessert, she managed to spin out the meal for more than an hour. Then she made her way through the dark streets to Tregenna Hill.

She felt a pang of guilt as she passed St Ia's church. She could see the lights through the stained-glass windows. Evensong would be just about to come to an end by now. She thought of Reverend Thomas, who had been so good to her, so concerned about her welfare. Had he known that Dan was going to give her away?

It had been the vicar's idea for her to write that letter. It occurred to her that he might have suggested it with the express intention of letting her father know where she was. Had *he* instructed Dan to go and speak to her father?

It was horrible to think that people you thought you could trust had betrayed you. Especially Dan. Why hadn't he stood up for her? Argued against his father—if the idea had come from the vicar. How could Dan have gone straight from her bed to carry out that piece of treachery?

She tried to push him to the back of her mind as she approached the shop. But it was like trying to ignore a broken bone. The pain of loving someone who could treat you with such disdain was unbearable.

Mary put her finger to her lips as she opened the door. "Sze Wing's just gone to bed," she whispered. "And Mum's out for the count." She led Iris through the shop to the back room. "She got a bit worked up, remembering things," she said. "It's exhausted her."

"I'm sorry—I shouldn't have come barging in like that."

"Oh, no—you mustn't feel bad. It means the world to her, knowing that you've come back. And she'll have forgotten all about the lather she got into by tomorrow morning."

Mary reached for a large envelope that was lying on the table. Iris noticed that the name written on the front was Mary Choi. She thought how hard it must have been for Mary, losing her husband in the war and bringing up a child on her own—especially when the child looked so different from all the others in this small town.

"These are the paintings your mother did," Mary said.

There were three images—exquisite watercolors of a wild rose, a foxglove, and a spray of honeysuckle. Iris gazed at them in wonder.

"Mum wants you to have them."

"Oh . . . but I couldn't. They belong to—"

"She insisted," Mary cut in. "It upset her to think you didn't have any of your mother's work."

"Well, I must come back and thank her—when she's ready to see me again."

"I expect there's a lot more you want to know about your mother." Mary reached for a bottle on a shelf above the sink. "This is my elder-flower wine. Would you like some? Or I can make tea if you'd prefer that."

"Wine would be lovely." Iris wondered if it would be as intoxicating as the champagne at Bellair Terrace. The woozy feeling hadn't been entirely unpleasant. If she could have laid her hands on anything alcoholic after that visit from her father, she would probably have ended up very, very drunk.

"I don't know if you knew how close we were, your mother and me," Mary said as she uncorked the wine. "We spent every summer together, from when we were tiny. There were a few years when we didn't see so much of each other, when I moved to Plymouth and met Sze Wing's father, but I came back here in '37, and it was as if we'd never been parted."

"I remember her telling me that you were expecting a baby," Iris said. "She was so excited. She couldn't stop smiling."

"She was like a sister to me." Mary stared at the liquid in the bottle. "I should have been with her that night she went to the cottage."

"Did she ask you to go there?"

"She couldn't. I was in hospital. Sze Wing was about to be born." Mary reached for the elderflower wine. "I knew your mother was angry about what was going on at the cottage. She'd told me she was planning to evict the people living there and put the place up for sale." She poured out the wine and handed a glass to Iris. "You said you knew some of what happened. How did you find out?"

"I went to the library and found the report of the inquest."

Mary nodded. "I was still in hospital when they held it. I went to the police as soon as I could, to tell them what I knew, but they didn't seem very interested. They said the verdict had been delivered, and that was the end of the matter."

"What were you going to tell them?" Iris lifted her glass, struggling to keep her hand steady.

Mary drew in a long breath. "This won't be easy for you to hear. I think your mother was tricked into going to the cottage that night. The tenant—Crowley—lured her there."

"What? How did he do that?"

"He sent one of his cronies down to Rowan Tree House. I was there when she came banging on the door. My mum went to answer it, and she came running through to where we were sitting, saying there was a woman outside who'd ripped her dress and was crying her eyes out." She looked at Iris over the rim of her glass. "Your mother and I went to see what was going on. The woman was standing there with her bosom exposed, and she had a tattoo on her chest—some sort of magical symbol. She said Crowley had done that to her. She told us she was terrified because the cottage was haunted, and she was going to be there all alone that evening. She begged your mother to come and sit with her."

"And my mother said yes?" Iris stared across the table, incredulous.

"I thought she'd only said it to calm the woman down and get rid of her. We talked about calling the doctor to Carreg Cottage. I thought she was going to do that. But she must have changed her mind. I went into labour later that evening, so I didn't have a chance to find out what had happened. Mum was with me at the hospital, so she wasn't there, either. And your father was away, of course."

"I asked him about it. When he came to find me. I . . . ," Iris faltered. It hurt so much to put it into words. "I know he was friendly with Crowley. I couldn't understand why. I still can't. I was afraid he might have . . ."

"I can imagine what went through your mind." Mary clicked her tongue against the roof of her mouth. "They were at loggerheads over Crowley. That was no secret. Your father had been fascinated by the occult long before he met your mother. The problem was, she didn't realise how deep that interest was." She lifted her shoulders and let them fall. "It was what they call a whirlwind romance. Your mother was grieving for her parents after they died within weeks of each other in India. Your father swept her off her feet and took her on honeymoon to Sicily." She drew in a long breath. "Like I said, this is not going to be easy for you to hear. He didn't let on to your mother that they were going to stay with Crowley, who was renting a villa there at the time, full of his so-called disciples. There were all sorts of bizarre goings-on. Your mother told me how a young man died after being made to drink cat's blood in a black magic ceremony."

Iris's hand went to her mouth. "That's abominable."

Mary nodded. "That's when she decided to escape. Her handbag had been taken from her, with her passport in it. All she had was the clothes she stood up in. Somehow, she managed to get to the British consulate in Palermo. She told them what had happened and begged for help—and they got her back to England."

Iris stared at her, struggling to take it in. Her mother had run away. Within days of getting married, she had fled from what sounded like a nightmare situation. "And what about my father? Where was he?"

"He tracked her down, eventually. She'd hidden herself away here in Cornwall because the story got out, about what Crowley had been doing. It was in all the papers. He was booted out of Sicily, and the press were calling him the Wickedest Man in the World."

"I . . . I don't understand. Why did she take my father back after that?"

Mary closed her eyes. "She found out she was expecting you."

<hr>

Dan made his way back along Fore Street, wondering where on earth Iris could be at nine o'clock on a Sunday night. He'd waited for a long time outside the cinema—a good half hour after the movie had started—before going to find her. When she didn't answer the door, he wondered if she might have been out all day and not seen his note. Then something else occurred to him. Could she have decided to catch a train to London to put things right with her father? It seemed unlikely. But he could think of no other explanation.

As he walked past the dark shopfronts, his imagination went into overdrive. What if something bad had happened to her while he'd been away? She could be lying in a ditch somewhere, and no one would realize she was missing. There was Ellen Wylde, of course. But Iris didn't work for her every day. If something had happened to Iris on Friday, it would be Monday before Ellen realized anything was wrong.

He stopped when he reached The Toy Tiger. There was a faint glow coming from the back of the shop. She couldn't be working, could she? Not on a Sunday, surely. And yet . . . He remembered Iris telling him about the order from Harrods, how little time they had to get everything done.

He felt around the door frame for a bell. But there wasn't one. Then he knocked on the glass pane. No response. Perhaps the light was left on all night as a security measure. As he turned away, he remembered that there was a back entrance. His father used it sometimes, if he was going to see bereaved relatives at the funeral parlor next door. It was worth checking, just in case.

He had to go all the way along Fore Street, almost as far as St Ia's, before turning left down Lifeboat Hill and back along Market Strand. The yard that served Ellen's shop and the two buildings on either side was deserted. No vehicles parked there. Nor were there any lights on in the funeral parlor or the florist. Just that yellow glow coming from the window of the workshop. As Dan walked toward it, he caught a movement. Someone *was* in there. He lifted his hand and tapped on the glass.

Nothing happened. He tapped again. Harder this time. To his surprise, the light went off. He stood for a moment, wondering what was going on. Perhaps whoever was in there hadn't heard him. Perhaps they'd just decided to finish up and had gone out through the front of the shop. He was about to turn away when the back door opened. It was the smallest movement—just enough to allow whoever was on the other side to see into the yard.

"Is that you, Tony?"

It was Ellen, not Iris. But her voice sounded different. There was an edginess in the tone. Almost as if she were afraid. It suddenly dawned on him that she'd mistaken his tapping for someone trying to break in.

He took a step forward. "Sorry if I—"

The knife in her hand was a shock. The blade caught the moonlight as her arm jerked upward. Afterward, he saw that it was only a penknife—the one she used for whittling wood, she said, as he followed her inside. But still, she could have done him some damage with it if she'd had a mind to.

"I was working late," she said, as they sat down. "I'm sorry. I thought . . ."

He waved away her apology. "My fault entirely. I shouldn't have come sneaking around the back like that. It's just that I've been trying to get hold of Iris. I was walking back from her place, and I saw a light on in the shop. I thought she might be doing an extra shift."

Ellen shook her head. "I'm glad you're here, though. I think there might have been a misunderstanding." She told him about Lionel Bird turning up in St Ives.

"And she thinks *I* told him where she was?" He put his head in his hands.

"She couldn't work out who else could have done it. I could see she was devastated, believing that you'd betrayed her. Then it occurred to me that it might have been someone else—but I couldn't be certain." She explained what she'd witnessed at the railway station. "I don't know for sure that it was Iris's father—but I didn't see any other man on the platform. And he'd told Iris he was going to catch the evening train back to London."

"They'd have taken her address when she registered at the School of Painting," Dan said. "Nina has the studio next door. She could easily have found out where Iris was living."

"But how would she have known that Iris was Lionel's daughter? That's what I couldn't work out."

"If they're as close as what you saw suggests, he might have shown her photographs of Iris."

Ellen nodded. "That would explain it. Anyway, what matters is it wasn't you—and Iris needs to know that."

"But where can I find her?"

"I can't think where she would be." Ellen frowned. "She's due in tomorrow, though. Shall I tell her I've spoken to you?"

"Yes, please. What time is she coming?"

"Eleven o'clock."

"Would you mind if I dropped by? I wouldn't stay long—I just want to put things right."

"Of course."

Dan stood up. "I'd better be off. I'm sure you'll want to be getting home."

"Er . . . yes." Ellen walked over to the door and held it open. "Just a couple of things to finish off, and I'll be on my way."

Mary Choi reached across the table to top up Iris's wine. "Your father promised to cut Crowley out of his life. Your mother told me so when I went to visit her, just after you were born. I don't want to suggest that he didn't keep that promise. I know that your mother believed he had. But a couple of months after I came back to live in St Ives, I started hearing rumours about the new tenant of Carreg Cottage." She leaned back in her chair, steepling her fingers. "Your mother didn't know it was Crowley. He'd sent that woman—the one I was telling you about—to Cornwall ahead of him and rented the cottage under another name. Mum was the one who told me the gossip about what was going on there. She used to live at Carreg Cottage, you see. She was born there. She still knows everyone who lives in Zennor. People didn't like what Crowley was doing up on the carn. It's always been regarded as a place of natural healing power—and he was desecrating it.

"Anyway, when I told your mother, she confronted your father about it. He said Crowley had written to him, pleading for help because he'd lost all his money. He denied anything bad or strange was going on at the cottage. Rumours were bound to circulate, he said, because of all the stories about him in the newspapers back in the twenties. Your father assured your mother that Crowley was now just a harmless old man down on his luck."

"And she believed him?" Iris shook her head.

"She wanted to. But then she found out that your father was giving him money. She went through bank statements and discovered that Crowley had been made a signatory on their account. She was livid, of course. I remember her showing me a letter she'd written to Crowley at the time. It listed all the extravagant items he'd paid for with her money. She accused him of spending more in a week on cigars and cognac than she spent in two months on herself.

"What really infuriated her was that the money in that account was her inheritance from her parents. As a married woman, she had no control over it. But she went to a solicitor and found out that she *did* have control over Carreg Cottage, because the property was in her name only. That was when she made up her mind to evict Crowley."

"Did she tell my father?" Iris glanced at the flower paintings lying on the table, remembering that last Easter Sunday in the garden at Rowan Tree House. Had her mother already found out about her money being siphoned off by then? Had she been seething with cold fury beneath that serene smile?

"No," Mary replied. "She decided to do it while he was away, in Canada. She delivered the eviction notice the day he was due to sail. Crowley wasn't there when she called. Nor the woman. She gave it to one of the other waifs and strays who were living in the cottage."

Iris looked up, perplexed. "But if there were other people living there, why weren't they questioned by the police?"

"The woman said they'd all gone. Well, that was the story she gave your mother when she was trying to persuade her to spend the night there. But one of them was the man who found your mother the next day, so he can't have gone far." Mary rubbed her fingers on the neck of her wineglass. "Strangely enough, he came into the shop a couple of weeks ago. Mum recognised him. She said she used to see him going past Rowan Tree House on his motorbike."

Iris stared at her. "Tony Wylde?"

Mary frowned. "Mum didn't know his name."

"It was in the report of the inquest. He's my boss's husband. They've *bought* Carreg Cottage." Iris reached for her glass and drained what was left in it.

CHAPTER 27

The smoke from the bonfire snaked up into the night sky. A flurry of flaming sparks scattered onto the sheep-cropped turf as Tony blew on the wood. It was harder, up here on the carn, to get a blaze going. The wind was blowing in from the sea, bringing a salty dampness you could taste when you opened your mouth.

Pockets of mist were beginning to form in the hollows beneath the stones. But the sky was clear. That was the crucial thing. The moon would rise soon. And the mommet was there, waiting. Laid out on the great flat rock that looked like an altar table.

It had taken him all day to prepare the bird's skull and fashion the body, Crowley's voice inside his head, directing him. He'd cut the lining out of one of the living room curtains to make the doll. The wretched things were falling apart, so it wouldn't matter. Ellen had said she was going to make new ones—yet another promise she'd failed to keep. He'd raided her sewing basket for pins and for a needle and cotton to sew the doll's body and attach it to the skull.

Later in the afternoon he'd gone up to the carn to gather fragments of moss to bind around the arms and legs. The moss grew on the stones and held some of their power—he remembered Crowley telling him that when he was making the first doll. Then, for the blood, he'd mixed paint with linseed oil until he achieved the color and consistency he needed.

As he'd dripped the stuff onto the bleached curtain lining, he'd thought about the hair—the only thing this second incarnation of the mommet would lack. He remembered hiding in the garden at Rowan Tree House, watching for Stella to leave. Crowley had described her—but seeing her in the flesh had affected Tony in a way he hadn't expected. She was beautiful. Tall and slim with titian hair and luminous green eyes.

He had crept into her bedroom and lingered longer than he needed to. After tucking strands from the brush on the dressing table into his pocket, he'd opened drawers and run his hands through her silk underwear. Unable to resist, he'd stolen a pair of her knickers, which he'd kept under the pillow of his camp bed in the cowshed. They'd still been there the night Crowley had shaken him awake to provide the alibi he needed when the curse had taken effect.

Did she have to die? Really? Crowley had been furious when he'd asked that question. Said she was a threat to everything he was trying to achieve. The Great Work. The harnessing of demonic forces through the portal of the Zennor stones. The power of these rocks was unique. How could he continue if Stella Bird carried out this threat to evict them all from the cottage?

Crowley hadn't needed to spell out the consequences if Tony hadn't done his bidding. That first night, at the party for Frieda Harris's initiation, the mescaline had been offered. He hadn't known, then, what it was—only that the world had exploded into something more vivid, more enchanting, than he could ever have imagined. Crowley had used it to hook him and reel him in. But knowing that had made no difference. He had tasted the forbidden fruit, and there was no going back.

The fire was giving out some heat now. Tony leaned back against the rock where he'd left his easel and his satchel. He'd brought a blanket, too, so he wouldn't get cold, waiting for night to fade into day. When the dawn came, the mommet would be ready, charged by the magic of moonlight on quartz. And he would stay to paint the sunrise; the ghost birds flying up from the stones in the melting mist.

He reached for his pipe and struck a match, shielding the flame with his fingers as he held it to the bowl. Down below, the cottage was invisible, lost in inky darkness. Ellen would probably be back now. She'd be lying alone in their bed, wondering where he was. She might have tried the studio door, but he'd locked it. Perhaps she'd spot the flickering of the bonfire when she looked out of the bedroom window. Strange that she'd imagined seeing that before—as if she'd caught a glimpse of the past; seen what had unfolded on that warm spring night when his life had blossomed like the hawthorn Nina and Frieda had gathered from the hedgerows to make into garlands for the ritual.

He hadn't believed in it then. The magic. He'd thought it fanciful—the stuff of fairy tales. He'd only gone along with it for the drugs. But it hadn't taken long to discover that life at Carreg Cottage in those days was darker than anything dreamed up by the Brothers Grimm. He'd seen that Crowley's real power lay in an uncanny ability to read people, to spot weakness and vulnerability and milk it for whatever purpose suited him. You could call that magic. Black magic. Because it never ended well.

But you believe in it now, don't you?

He'd thought the voice had gone away. But he could feel it, slithering up from somewhere inside his body, hissing out of his lungs, his throat, his mouth.

Yes. He saw the word float across the space between him and the fire. It bloomed like a rose, turning scarlet as it hovered above the flames. Then it exploded in a cloud of smoke that cast a ghostly veil across the hillside.

※

Iris was up and dressed before it was properly light outside. It had been after midnight when she'd left the shop on Tregenna Hill. Mary had been worried about her walking home alone so late. She'd said Iris was welcome to sleep on the sofa. It had been tempting to stay there, in the warmth, but Iris needed space. Her mind was reeling from what she'd learned from Mary: that Tony Wylde had been involved with Crowley. What he'd told the police—about being on a painting holiday when he'd found her mother—had made it sound as if he was a tourist. But he'd been *living* at Carreg Cottage. If anyone could tell her what had really happened that night, it had to be him.

She'd lain awake all night, planning what to do. She couldn't catch the first bus to Zennor—Ellen would still be at the cottage. She needed to wait until she was certain Ellen was at the shop. Because until she could talk to Tony—get his version of events—there was no point in upsetting Ellen by suggesting that her husband had been keeping things from her.

To pass the time, she went for a walk along the quayside, watching the fishermen unload their catch. The metallic smell of blood drifted on the crisp morning air as guts spilled out onto the cobblestones. People were already gathering around the makeshift stalls, eager to get first pick of the sea's bounty. She spotted Mrs. Dixon, her landlady, picking up a crab and turning it this way and that, its claws flailing helplessly, glistening where the sunlight caught the still-damp shell. Iris quickened her pace, not wanting to be seen. She didn't want to be drawn into a conversation about what she was doing, where she was going. Now was not the time to come clean to yet another of the people she'd deceived.

She reached the bus station a few minutes before nine o'clock. By the time she reached Zennor, it would be nearly half past. Ellen would be safely out of the picture by then. No danger of passing her on the road or the track. She had no idea what Tony Wylde would say when she appeared at the cottage. She hoped he wouldn't be annoyed at being disturbed while he was working. Surely he'd understand, when she explained who she was?

Whatever his association with Crowley, he had done everything humanly possible to help her mother in her hour of need. All she wanted was the missing piece of the puzzle—the truth about Crowley's part in what had happened. Now that the man was dead, there was no need to keep his secrets, was there?

———◆———

Ellen hauled herself up from the floor, leaning back against the work-bench as she rubbed her stiff limbs. She had thought sleep would elude her. She'd stayed up for hours after Dan had gone, rattled by her reaction to his unexpected visit. The knife. Whatever had possessed her? She'd tried to pass it off as fear of a burglar, but she had seen the look on Dan's face. The truth was, she was more afraid of Tony than she dared admit—even to herself.

Lying there in the dark, praying for oblivion, she had decided to go and see Reverend Thomas first thing in the morning. Taking a vicar to the cottage was surely less threatening than summoning a doctor. Perhaps they needn't even say that he was a vicar—not at first. She could make up some story about him being a customer who'd expressed an interest in seeing Tony's work. Then, after putting him at ease, Reverend Thomas could try to draw him out.

She thought it through as she filled the kettle and spooned coffee from the jar. Would Tony challenge her about where she'd spent the night? Would he realize she hadn't been there, in their bed? She thought of the gannet carcass, floating in the scum of boiling water in the stew pot. She had to pin her hopes on that dead creature, pray that the fever-ish obsession it had sparked would distract her husband from working himself up into a rage over her prolonged disappearance.

———◆———

Iris could feel the blood moving faster through her fingers as she gripped the leather strap of her handbag. She couldn't shake the image of her mother making this same journey, no doubt fearful of what awaited her at Carreg Cottage. Whether or not she'd believed Dora Montague's story about the place being haunted, she'd been on her way to visit a woman whose behavior was bizarre, irrational, and alarming. And she'd had no choice but to go there alone.

Iris stopped a few hundred yards from the cottage, wanting to make sure Ellen's jeep wasn't there. No, it wasn't. Just the motorbike, tucked beside the wall. She made her way toward the gate and unlatched it. She stood for a moment outside the front door, scared to knock. She remembered hearing her mother's voice last time she'd passed by the cottage: *No. Don't go there.*

But this time, she had to.

⸻

Ellen felt bad about dragging Reverend Thomas away from his breakfast. He'd answered the door with a napkin tucked into his collar. But he'd waved away her offer to come back later. He'd asked her to wait for a moment in his study and had reappeared wearing an ordinary shirt and tie.

Ellen gave him her arm as he clambered into the passenger seat of the jeep.

"A bit higher than my old jalopy!" He gave her a wry smile as she started the engine.

As they drove out of St Ives, he talked about what he planned to say to Tony. He advised Ellen to let him do the talking at first. To simply introduce him, by name, not by title, then wait to see how Tony reacted.

"I hope you don't mind, but I had to tell my son. He's going to follow in our car. He'll leave it at the bottom of the track and walk up."

Ellen nodded. She didn't trust herself to speak. She wondered if Dan had told his father about the knife. Clearly the vicar thought Tony could be dangerous. Did he think *she* was, too?

⸻

The fire had gone out sometime during the night. Tony had woken to find that his hair was damp with dew. His limbs felt stiff as he reached for his pipe. Luckily there was enough of the mushroom tobacco left for another smoke.

The first hints of dawn had turned the eastern sky the soft gray of a pigeon's wing. As he inhaled, he watched a tiny shoal of clouds on the horizon. The rising sun tinged them coral and amber. Below him, the moorland was blanketed in mist. As the sun climbed higher, the landscape lost its opaque, milky whiteness. He could see the cottage now, but it was like looking through cobwebs.

By the time it was fully light, he was painting. He'd set up the easel next to the flat rock where he'd laid the mommet.

Nothing had disturbed the evil-looking doll during the night. No fox or stoat or bird of prey had tried to take it. He'd done a good job on the gannet skull. Not a trace of any flesh left on it. It was ready now to do its work. He wouldn't be able to hide it inside the chimney, like the last one, because the weather wasn't yet warm enough to stop lighting a fire at night. But he'd found another place. Somewhere Ellen wouldn't find it. He would lay it in the bottom of the box of papers he kept under the bed.

He felt the rush of the drug as he dipped the tip of his brush into the smudge of yellow ochre on his palette. It brought a feeling of warmth to his aching limbs. Made his fingers nimble and his vision more acute. He was mixing the pigments quickly now, catching each fleeting moment as the complexion of the landscape changed beneath the climbing sun.

It made him feel powerful, standing there, on top of the carn. A master of creation. With a stroke of his brush, a dab of damp rag, he was turning rock and earth and grass and sky into something magical, ethereal. China white, burnt sienna, viridian, ultramarine. The names of the pigments swirled from the tubes into the air around him, like a flight of angels singing his praises, urging him on.

Suddenly a new color joined the throng. A shade that was all wrong for this misty winter morning. Titian. A flash of orange-red in the corner of his eye. He whipped his head round. There it was again. Down by the cottage. What was it?

A finger of mist lingered over the roof of the building, blurring his view. But then he saw it again—and his blood froze. It was her hair, streaming out behind her as she skirted the cottage. Stella. She was heading for the cowshed. Coming for him.

He dropped his brush and turned to grab the mommet. What a fool he was. He should have taken it down there at first light. Protected himself before starting on the painting. But he could drive her away. As long as he kept hold of the doll, she couldn't harm him.

He almost stumbled as he wound his way through the jumble of rocks. He could see her standing outside the cowshed. She was pushing at the door, as if the fox painting was drawing her in instead of repelling her, as he'd intended it to. As he reached the garden wall, he raised the mommet to shoulder height.

She heard him coming. Whipped round, her green eyes wide. She looked terrified. Could a ghost be frightened? Was that the power he had conjured from the moon last night?

Kill her.

He heard the voice, loud and clear, as he closed the space between them.

A gannet spears fish. Use the beak.

He heard another voice then. A strange, high-pitched wail, like the monkeys used to make in the lab at Oxford when they were about to be sacrificed.

<hr />

Ellen glanced at the vicar as she pulled off the road onto the track. She was used to the bumps and ruts, but he wasn't. "You might want to hold on to the strap," she said.

He nodded, raising his hand to grasp the loop of canvas dangling from the roof. "I'd forgotten how glorious it is up here. It must be torture for you, surrounded by all this beauty, when you're in such turmoil."

"It was almost dark the day we moved into the cottage—and we'd driven through thick mist on the way here. I didn't appreciate what an incredible spot it is until I woke up that first morning. Just stepping out of the front door, I was bowled over by the views. But then I found that horrible doll up the chimney. That's when everything started to unravel." She pulled down hard on the wheel to avoid a sheep that was crossing the track with its tiny lamb trailing behind. "Do you think the mommet worked? Did it lure Stella Bird up to the cottage, to her death?"

It was a long moment before he replied. "I believe in the power of evil intent, just as I believe in the power of love," he said. "What concerns me is not whether magic works, but the strange and terrifying seeds such concepts plant in the head, and the tragic consequences that may result for those who collude with them."

"Yes," she murmured. "Like Dora Montague, losing her mind and ending up in an asylum. And it's as if those seeds have lain dormant all this time, in the cottage, just waiting to take root in whoever dares to try to make the place a home."

She was about to tell him that she barely recognized the man she'd married just a few short weeks ago. But as she swung around a bend in the track, she caught sight of Tony. He was scrambling down the hillside, his arm raised above his head. What was that in his hand? Something long and pointed.

"Is that your husband?" The vicar let go of the strap, groping for the handle of the door as Ellen slammed on the brakes. Tony was on the flat now, charging toward the back of the cottage. As Ellen ran across to the garden wall, she spotted Iris.

"Oh my God!" She tried to scramble over the rough stones, but her sweater snagged on a bramble. As she struggled to free herself the horror unfolded. He was going to attack Iris, stab her with that thing in his hand.

"Tony!" She screamed out his name, but he took no notice. She caught a fleeting glance of the vicar, who must have gotten in through the front gate and was coming around the side of the cottage. He was trying to run, but he was limping. He wasn't going to get there in time. With an almighty effort, she ripped her sweater free of the thorns and leapt across the wall.

She was aware of hurtling across the garden, but it was as though everything went into slow motion. As Tony closed in, she leapt in front of Iris. He froze. His eyes were terrifying—dark and blank, as if he had no idea who she was. He raised his arm above his head. Now she saw what his fist held: the razor-sharp bill of the dead gannet from Pendour Cove.

"Tony! Stop!" Her hand shot to her pocket, her fingers gripping the penknife. But as she pulled it out, he grabbed her neck. As his arm came down for the strike she thrust out with the blade. But in that terrible moment he fell sideways, dropping the weapon. As he hit the ground, he clutched his chest. The last thing Ellen heard was him calling her name.

CHAPTER 28

Tony was lying in a side ward at St Ives Cottage Hospital, tubes spidering his body. Barely alive when they'd stretchered him down the track. It was impossible to ignore the uncanny parallel with Stella Bird's demise. Like history repeating itself. Like what Eastern religions called karma.

"A heart attack? But he's only thirty years old." Ellen had felt as though it was someone else talking to the surgeon. Her voice sounded so old, so tired. When the man had asked about drug addiction, she'd just stared at him.

Iris had refused to leave her side. And the vicar had been back and forth to the hospital during the blur of days and nights. Dan too. He'd brought them clean clothes, food, and a camp bed so they could take it in turns to snatch some sleep.

On the second day, Tony had opened his eyes. She'd tried to stop him talking, having been told what a strain it would put on his heart. But he wouldn't be stopped. He had to tell her, he murmured, as his eyelids drooped. Half-formed sentences, words barely intelligible. Something about cactus powder in Stella's cocoa, Crowley hiding in the cowshed, a masked face at the window.

He fell back into unconsciousness then. But half an hour later, his eyes snapped open. He looked straight at her, searching her face, and said, "It wasn't all bad, was it? We did have some good times?"

Her eyes blurred as she gazed back at him, part of her desperate to press her face into his chest, to feel him stroke her hair and tell her that everything was going to be okay. How she longed to hear him tell her that.

On the third day, Nina Grey came to the hospital. The nurses wouldn't let her see Tony, but she begged for five minutes with Ellen.

"He's going to be all right, isn't he?" Nina's lips were trembling.

"They can't say.'" Ellen could barely bring herself to look at the woman. "The heart attack was caused by the drugs he'd been taking. Did you know about that?"

Nina shook her head. "I didn't know he'd started that again. He used to take them, before the war. I blame myself for that—for introducing him to Crowley. That man was into anything he could get his hands on. But when Tony came back to London, I thought he'd kicked the habit."

Ellen's eyes narrowed. "Tony was there, wasn't he, when Stella Bird went to the cottage. Iris told me."

"Yes. He stayed on when I returned to London. He'd fallen in love with two things: Zennor Carn and mescaline. If he did what Crowley wanted, he could have both."

"Are you saying that Crowley used Tony to kill Stella?"

Nina looked away. "He didn't kill her. Crowley wanted her to leave him alone. To scare her away. He got Tony to break into her house, to steal her hair, to make a cursing doll."

"*Tony* made that thing?" Ellen sank back against the wall of the corridor. She felt as if her legs were about to give way.

Nina whipped her head around. "You saw it? It was still there?"

Ellen closed her eyes. The image of the mommet lying in the fireplace, that malevolent skull staring up at her, was branded on her brain.

"Crowley thought it wasn't working," Nina went on. "He grew impatient. He made Dora Montague go to Rowan Tree House. Tony knew about the plan to lure Stella to the cottage and drug her, but he wasn't involved. He was asleep when it happened. He told me Crowley dropped him right in it. He had to lie to the police."

"Lie to them?" Ellen shook her head. "Why?"

"He had to pretend to find Stella. Crowley was very clever. He'd created an alibi for himself by buying two train tickets—one to London and one to Lelant. He caught the London train on the Saturday afternoon, to make it look as though he'd left Cornwall before Stella's visit. He put on a disguise in the train toilet, got off at Lelant and caught the bus back to Zennor. Then, wearing the same disguise, he caught the milk train to London before Tony raised the alarm."

Ellen stared into the pale green eyes, struggling to process what the woman was telling her.

"Tony couldn't go back to the cottage." Nina lifted her shoulders and let them fall. "He had to keep up the pretence of having been on a painting holiday in Cornwall. He came back to London. He was a different person, though: he pined for Zennor. He told me he couldn't go back to working in a studio after painting outside on the moors. But he was haunted by what had happened. It was as though he was tied to the place by an invisible thread. Sooner or later, he had to come back."

Ellen felt as if the wall she was leaning against was giving way. As if the ground beneath her feet was crumbling. What a fool she'd been. The whirlwind romance. The promise of a new life in a chocolate-box cottage in the country. All those years, Tony had been waiting for a girl like her; someone naive enough to finance his twisted fantasy. And now he was lying there, on the other side of the wall, covered in tubes, fighting for his life.

Till death us do part.

That was the vow she'd made.

After Nina had gone, Reverend Thomas came to sit with her. Iris was lying asleep on the camp bed and didn't stir when the vicar came into the room. He didn't need to ask how Tony was doing. The pallor and the labored breathing told him the end was near.

It was a shock when Tony opened his eyes. He looked at her, then at the vicar. A perplexed look crossed his face. And then he fixed his gaze on her, murmuring something she couldn't make out. Bending closer, she angled her ear to his mouth.

"Forgive me," he whispered.

—◈—

Ellen left the hospital in a daze. Dan took charge, driving everyone back to the vicarage and sorting out a room for her to share with Iris, so she wouldn't have to spend the night alone. Then he prepared supper before taking Iris to collect what she needed from home.

Ellen couldn't face eating anything, but she accepted the brandy the vicar offered her as they sat together in the parlor.

"I can't believe he's gone." Her lips trembled as she lifted the glass. "I should have done something. I should have realised that stuff he was smoking wasn't for his asthma. Why was I so blind?"

"Tony lied to you, Ellen, and you believed him. There's no blame in that."

The brandy burned as she swallowed it down. "There were so many lies," she murmured. "I spent so long believing—to keep the dream alive."

"And it was a beautiful dream," he replied. "You married the man you loved and gave up your life in London to allow him to fulfil a long-held ambition. You took a leap of faith for his sake. That was very brave."

"Or very stupid." She shook her head. "I remember that voice in my head—Crowley's voice—saying to me that I was stupid to believe love could conquer anything. *Sometimes it carries you into the abyss.* That's what he said." She pressed her lips together, turning them white. "He was right about that, wasn't he? But I *did* believe it—that if I just tried hard enough, I could make the marriage work."

The vicar stared at the liquid in his glass. "There are many kinds of love, Ellen. Your love for Tony was of the highest order—you put your heart and soul into the commitment you'd made to him. But when you tie yourself to someone who is destructive to themselves, it can destroy you, too."

"I keep thinking that if only we'd gone back sooner, if only I'd taken you there when you first offered to talk to him, things might have turned out differently . . . He might still be . . ."

"Try not to torture yourself with those thoughts. We can't know how that might have turned out. Try to hold on to what he said to you in those last few minutes at the hospital."

Ellen closed her eyes. Tony's face was there, in front of her. There was no trace of the person he had been in those last days at the cottage, nothing but gentleness in those beautiful blue eyes. And . . . dare she say it . . . love. It had been barely a whisper, but she had heard those words.

Forgive me.

Tears seeped out, trickling down her face. "Yes," she murmured, "I'll try."

CHAPTER 29

Dan reached for Iris's hand as they crossed the square outside the church. It was the first time they'd had the chance to talk without being overheard.

"It's so sad for Ellen," he said. "But I can't bear to think what might have happened to you if she and Dad hadn't arrived when they did."

"It was all my fault." Her eyes were fixed on the ground beneath her feet. "If I hadn't gone looking for him, Tony might still be alive."

"You mustn't think that." Dan squeezed her hand tighter. "He was a drug addict. The stuff he was taking weakened his heart. The doctor said it could have happened at any moment."

"Why was he taking drugs? Ellen never explained that."

"Probably because she didn't know." He shrugged. "Barbara has a theory about it. She came to the hospital the day after he was admitted, but they wouldn't let her in. She told me she'd known for ages that he'd been smoking something illicit—and that Ellen thought it was herbal tobacco to help his asthma."

Iris shook her head. "Poor Ellen."

"Barbara said she wondered if he was taking the wrong antidote for something he was trying to cure in himself."

"Do you think he felt guilty about my mother? Nina Grey told Ellen that he was asleep that night she went to the cottage—but he made the cursing doll to lure her there."

"I don't suppose we'll ever know how he felt about that," Dan said. "But Barbara reckons that, as an artist, he was very insecure. He lacked belief in his ability. Apparently, Ben was in St Ives when Tony first came here. He was part of the crowd that went to the parties Crowley held at Carreg Cottage. He thinks Crowley spotted that insecurity in Tony—and used it. He made him into a kind of slave, to carry out all that occult stuff."

Iris found it hard to reconcile the two images she carried in her head: the pale, wasted man in the hospital bed and the wild-eyed attacker who'd tried to kill her. "I was desperate to talk to him," she said. "He was the only one who knew what really happened to my mother. It didn't occur to me how dangerous that might be. I should have told Ellen I was going up there. But I didn't want her to know what Mary Choi had told me—that he'd been keeping things from her."

"Seems there was plenty Ellen didn't know about him." Dan huffed out a breath. "I wonder what she'll do now?"

They were about to walk past The Toy Tiger. Iris had to look the other way. She couldn't bear the sight of the wooden animals in the window. Ellen had given everything to the new life she'd embarked on with Tony—and now it was in ruins.

When they got back to her room, she closed the door and stood for a moment, overwhelmed at being back in her own private space. She reached for Dan and wrapped her arms around him. "I'm sorry," she murmured.

"What for?" His mouth was on her ear.

"I shouldn't have jumped to conclusions. About how my father found me . . . I . . ."

"Shush," he whispered. "You don't need to apologise. I can see how it must have looked." His hands cupped her face. "I'd never do anything to hurt you. I want you to know that."

She took him by the hand and led him to the bed. Hard to believe they'd made love here just last week. It felt like a hundred years ago.

"Could we just lie here for a while?" She stroked his hair. "I don't think I can . . . not yet."

He nodded. "When I was in London, I was desperate to talk to you. I shouldn't have done that, Iris. I took advantage of you."

"You didn't do anything I didn't want you to do."

"But I'm twenty-four and you're nineteen." He closed his eyes. "I should've realised it was your first time. It's just that . . ."

"What?"

"Oh, nothing really. It's no excuse, what happened during the war. I lost so many friends, and I got used to living for each day because I never knew if it would be my last. I just sort of reverted to that way of thinking, I suppose. I'm sorry."

"You don't have to be." Her fingers traced the outline of his jaw. She could feel the stubble on his chin. "I felt it that first moment I laid eyes on you, outside the church on Christmas Day. I didn't think you'd be interested—and then, when I thought you might be, I told myself I had to keep you at arm's length."

"Why?" As her fingers brushed his lips, he lifted his hand and held them there.

"I was afraid."

"Of what?"

"Of . . ." She took her hand away, unable to meet his eyes. "Of having my heart broken. I'd burnt my bridges, coming here. There was nowhere to go back to if the new life I was trying to make went wrong."

He made a soft sound, a mixture of a sigh and a laugh. "You probably don't realise, Iris, how strong you are. It's one of the things that makes you so irresistible."

She looked up at him, perplexed.

"I'd never try to change you," he said. "But I'd love to be part of your life, if you'll let me."

CHAPTER 30

Spring came early to Cornwall. It was only the middle of February, but primroses and violets were already pushing through the grass in the shelter of the great stones on Zennor Carn. Shoots of new bracken, curled up like snail shells, were beginning to unfurl. In the garden at Carreg Cottage dozens of daffodils had come up, and the forsythia bush that grew against the wall of the cowshed was a blaze of golden blossom. Everywhere there was birdsong. Robins, blackbirds, and skylarks. There was a sense of everything coming alive, throwing off the mantle of winter.

It was a strange thing to be doing on such a glorious sunny day. There were six of them there for the ritual. Reverend Thomas led the way into the cottage. Dan followed, holding a silver bowl into which the holy water would be poured. Ellen kept a tight hold of Iris's arm as they went in, glancing over her shoulder at Mary Choi, who was bringing her mother up the garden path.

It had been the vicar's idea to invite Elizabeth Richards. Not only had she been born at Carreg Cottage, but she'd lived there for nearly a quarter of a century. The presence of someone who had good memories of the place would foster a positive atmosphere, he felt.

Ellen clung to that thought as she crossed the threshold. But she was trembling. She so wanted this to work. But could the malevolent spirit that had cost Tony his life really be banished with a few prayers and a sprinkling of water?

The unquiet dead. That was the term Reverend Thomas had used when he had explained the procedure the church recommended in such circumstances. Crowley had died just three weeks before she and Tony had moved into the cottage. Not surprising, the vicar said, that a man who had blighted so many lives should remain earthbound in death and haunt the place he had chosen for its fabled power.

They formed a circle in the living room. Ellen glanced at Iris, thinking how hard this must be for her. Impossible for her to stand in this room without picturing her mother here on that May evening in 1938.

The vicar held up his hand and made the sign of the cross. "Almighty God, we acknowledge our own powerlessness, yet we rejoice that in Christ we can do all things by his strength. Come, Creator Spirit: protect and surround us with your power, through Jesus Christ our Lord."

Dan poured the holy water into the bowl and handed it to his father, along with a sprig of dried hyssop, provided by Mary from her shop. The use of this herb for banishing rituals dated back to biblical times, the vicar had explained. He dipped the hyssop in the bowl and sprinkled it in each of the four corners of the room. As he went, he said: "Deliver this room from all evil spirits, all vain imaginations, projections, and phantasms and all deceits of the evil one. Bid them harm no one, but depart to the place appointed to them, there to remain forever."

Ellen held her breath. She wasn't sure what she expected to happen. What she was most afraid of was hearing that voice in her head. But all she could hear was the distant trill of a blackbird in the thorn bush outside the front door.

"The blessing of God Almighty, the Father, the Son, and the Holy Ghost, be upon this place and upon all here present now and always." Reverend Thomas made the sign of the cross again as he returned to the circle. Then he led them upstairs, to repeat the ritual there.

The final part of the exorcism was the blessing of each person taking part. The vicar laid his hands on them, one by one, and said a prayer he called St Patrick's Lorica. It was the same prayer he'd used when Ellen had gone to find him in the church: a prayer for protection, imagining God's power wrapping itself around you like a suit of armor.

As she stood there, watching Reverend Thomas repeat the prayer over the others, Ellen felt a warmth flood her body. It dawned on her that whether this ritual held any real power or not, it was the support of these good people that would carry her through the days to come.

When it was over, they went out into the garden. Mary had brought a picnic lunch for them all, and they sat in a circle on blankets, eating salmon and cucumber sandwiches and drinking elderflower wine.

The vicar raised his glass. "To a new chapter in the life of Carreg Cottage," he said. "It was a happy place once—Mrs. Richards can testify to that. Because of what happened before the war, it's been cast as sinister—but inside, at its heart, this Cornish home has seen more birth than death, more creativity than destruction, more light than dark, more love than fear."

On the other side of the circle, Elizabeth Richards lifted her glass, a wistful smile lighting her eyes. "Long life and happiness to those within its walls."

The vicar leaned forward to clink his glass against hers, and everyone else joined in.

Iris searched Ellen's face as they settled back onto the blanket. "How do you feel now, about staying on?"

"All right, I think. I'm glad you're going to keep me company, though."

Iris lifted her shoulders and let them fall. "It'd be a bit much to expect you to be here on your own tonight. I'll stay for as long as you want me to."

"I can only imagine how . . . ," Ellen trailed off, unable to put into words what she was thinking: that for Iris, spending the night here would be an ordeal most people would avoid at all costs.

"It's all right," Iris said. "I've thought about it a lot. It's something I need to do. I'm not scared. I really believe she wanted me to come here, to Cornwall—almost like she drew me back. And look what's happened: I'm living in a beautiful place, studying art, earning my own money, and . . ." She smiled as she glanced at Dan, who was chatting with Mary Choi.

"I'm so glad things are working out for the two of you," Ellen said. She felt Iris's hand touch hers. The gentle squeeze said it all. "Don't feel guilty about being happy," Ellen murmured. "And don't worry about me when you need to go back to town. I'm not going to be on my own for much longer."

Iris cocked her head to one side. "Is your mother coming to stay?"

"No." Ellen pursed her lips. "She tried to persuade me to go back to my old life. *This was Tony's dream, not yours,* she said. I don't think she can understand why I want to stay."

"A friend from London, then?"

Ellen shook her head. She leaned closer, lowering her voice to a whisper. "I'm expecting a baby."

Iris clapped her hand to her mouth. She stood up, motioning to Ellen to follow her over to the garden wall. "That's wonderful," she gasped when they were out of earshot. "I . . . I mean it *is* wonderful, isn't it?"

"It feels that way to me—although it's taken a while to accept that it's . . . ," Ellen trailed off, leaning against the wall. "I couldn't believe it at first. I thought it was the shock of losing Tony. But I've seen a doctor." She ran her fingers over the moss-covered stones. "I know what you must be thinking: how am I going to manage, on my own, with a baby. It won't be easy—I realise that. But when it's born, I can bring him or her into the shop with me. And eventually—as long as the orders keep coming in—I'll be able to afford to pay a nanny." She looked up with a wry smile. "I always thought it would be impossible to be successful *and* have a baby—until Tony told me about Barbara Hepworth carrying on working after having triplets. I was jealous of the woman when I first met her—but I should probably thank her for proving me wrong."

She turned her face toward the hillside, where the granite rocks glinted in the sunlight. This afternoon, when everyone else had gone, she and Iris would walk up there. As the sun set over the sea, she would scatter Tony's ashes, let the wind carry them across the wild landscape he'd loved so much.

And tomorrow, the new chapter would begin. It wouldn't be the life she'd imagined. But it would be a good life.

CODA

The inspiration for *Through the Mist* came from a true event that took place at Carn Cottage—an isolated house situated just below the crest of Zennor Carn in Cornwall.

In May 1938 Katherine Arnold-Forster—a friend of Virginia Woolf—died after visiting Carn Cottage. According to local rumor, the notorious occultist Aleister Crowley had been staying there at the time and had performed a black magic ritual in which he attempted to raise the Devil.

Katherine Arnold-Forster collapsed on the moor a short distance from her home, Eagle's Nest, located on the road below Carn Cottage. She died in the hospital the following day, never having regained consciousness.

People living in the nearby village of Zennor said that she had gone to the aid of the couple who rented the cottage—associates of Crowley who had become frightened of what he planned to do there. What happened that night was never established by the subsequent police investigation, but the mental state of one of the tenants resulted in his permanent incarceration in Bodmin Lunatic Asylum.

Carn Cottage lay empty until the end of World War Two, when it was bought by an artist, Bryan Wynter, and became a gathering place for prominent members of the St Ives arts scene. Wynter took drugs such as Benzedrine and mescaline to ramp up his perception of the natural world. He died of a heart attack in 1975.

More than eight decades after Katherine Arnold-Forster's death, local people continue to refer to Carn Cottage as "the Crowley House."

A GLIMPSE OF THE HISTORICAL

CHARACTERS IN *Through the Mist*

Aleister Crowley: The man who liked to be known as "the Beast" died on December 1, 1947, aged seventy-two, in a boarding house in Hastings, England. He was penniless and a heroin addict. According to Deirdre MacAlpine—one of his "scarlet women" and the mother of his son—his last words were "Sometimes I hate myself."

In the hours following his death, as his corpse lay unattended, someone entered his room and stole one of the few precious objects he still possessed: his gold watch.

The following day Crowley's London doctor was found dead in the bath. The doctor had been attempting to wean Crowley off heroin by reducing his prescriptions—and it was said that Crowley had cursed him for this. Rumors circulated that the doctor's death was Crowley's revenge. It was the start of the posthumous legend attached to his name that persists to this day.

Lady Frieda Harris: The artist who created Crowley's Tarot pack appears to be one of the few people who was not harmed by an acquaintance with him.

After the death of her husband in 1952, she moved to Srinagar, India, where she lived and worked until her death at the age of eighty-five.

The Thoth Tarot pack, which had been five years in the making, was not published until 1969—seven years after she died. It has been in print ever since, and according to Crowley's biographer, Martin Booth, the Thoth pack is now the most sought-after design of Tarot cards in the world.

Barbara Hepworth: One of the most important artists of the twentieth century, Barbara Hepworth was made a Dame of the British Empire in 1965.

An early feminist, she always maintained—even after giving birth to triplets—that a woman needn't be hampered as an artist by having children, provided she always did some work each day, even a single half hour.

She and Ben Nicholson divorced in 1951, and she moved to Trewyn Studio in the center of St Ives, a short distance from St Ia's church. When her eldest son, Paul, was killed in a plane crash while serving with the RAF in Thailand in 1953, Barbara sculpted a memorial to him, *Madonna and Child*, which stands in the Lady Chapel at St Ia's.

Barbara died, aged seventy-two, in an accidental fire at her home in 1975. Following her death, the house and studio in St Ives became the Barbara Hepworth Museum.

Ben Nicholson: After his divorce from Barbara Hepworth, Ben continued to live in St Ives. He won the prestigious Carnegie Prize in 1952 and the first Guggenheim International painting prize in 1956. He died in 1982, aged eighty-seven.

Denis Mitchell: After working for Barbara Hepworth for many years, Denis was creating sculptures himself by the 1950s, based in a studio off Fore Street in St Ives. He became known in the 1960s for his polished bronzes, achieving international recognition with exhibitions in New York and London.

His brother, **Endell**, ran The Castle Inn, in St Ives, from 1938. The pub was known for its bohemian atmosphere and was a venue for exhibitions of the work of local artists. The poet Dylan Thomas—a friend of Endell's—was an occasional visitor. The Castle Inn still stands on Fore Street.

Leonard Fuller: A noted portrait and still life painter, he started the St Ives School of Painting in 1938 with his wife, Marjorie Mostyn. The couple was responsible for encouraging and nurturing many men and women who became leading figures in the post-war British art scene.

The Inspiration for Fictional Characters

Tony Wylde: The origin of his character is the artist Bryan Wynter, who bought Carn Cottage in 1945.

He was a student of art at the Slade in London, but his studies were interrupted by World War Two. A conscientious objector, he was sent to assist in Solly Zuckerman's work at the Department of Primates, Oxford University. His involvement with Zuckerman's vivisection experiments affected him psychologically, and he found solace in trips to St Ives. He was introduced to Cornwall by Zuckerman, who was a friend of some of the artists who had moved there during the war—including Barbara Hepworth and Ben Nicholson.

At first, Bryan lived alone at Carn Cottage, but soon after buying the place he married a St Ives woman, Susie Lethbridge, who joined him there.

A leading figure among the artists of St Ives, Bryan was a cofounder of the Crypt Group of painters and sculptors who met and exhibited in the basement of the deconsecrated Mariners' Church.

Bryan was in love with the landscape of Zennor Carn and drew the inspiration for his abstract paintings from the natural world. But his use of mind-expanding drugs is likely to have contributed to heart failure. He suffered his first heart attack in 1961 and was subsequently afflicted with angina. He died from a coronary seizure at the age of fifty-nine.

One of his paintings, *In the Stream's Path*, was acquired by David Bowie. In 2016 it sold at auction for more than £130,000.

Ellen Wylde: Her background is an imagined glimpse of the early life of Susie Lethbridge, who ran a successful toy-making business in St Ives from the age of twenty-three, supplying major London stores such as Harrods and Fortnum & Mason. Her work was so highly regarded that critics called her "the magical toymaker."

Susie developed a love of woodworking as a child in London, using offcuts from Thurston's, who made billiard tables in a factory next door to her home. Later she moved to Cornwall with her mother. A photo exists of her putting the finishing touches to a collection of miniature horse-drawn caravans at her workshop in St Ives.

After marrying Bryan Wynter, she gave birth to three children while living at Carn Cottage. However, the couple subsequently divorced.

Susie lived to be ninety years old.

Iris Bird: The depiction of Iris owes something to the life of Wilhelmina Barns-Graham, who was one of the foremost British abstract artists of the twentieth century. She went to live in St Ives at the age of twenty-two and was befriended by Barbara Hepworth.

Her long journey to Cornwall by train, in pouring rain and high winds, is mirrored in *Through the Mist*, including her memory of the station porter's poetic observation that "the stars were too close to the moon last night."

Nina Grey: Her persona is loosely based on Eileen Agar, the surrealist artist and photographer, who had a deep interest in the symbolism of the sea.

She is best known for *Angel of Anarchy*, a head embellished with osprey feathers, diamante, cowrie shells, and black satin. She also experimented with surrealist fashion: a Pathé newsreel shows her parading around London in a hat made from an upturned cork basket stuck with crustacean shells—to the bemusement of passers-by. She called it *Ceremonial Hat for Eating Bouillabaisse*.

Sexually liberated, she was photographed bare breasted at fancy dress parties and enjoyed polyamorous relationships. Her enduring spirit of rebellion and vitality was celebrated at a major retrospective of her work at London's Whitechapel Gallery in 2021.

She died in 1991 at the age of ninety-one.

ACKNOWLEDGMENTS

Paul Newman's book *The Tregerthen Horror*, was an invaluable source of information about Aleister Crowley and the haunting legacy of Carn Cottage.

I am indebted to Ray Crocker, a member of the congregation of St Ia's church, St Ives, for taking the time to show me around the building and tell me about its history. This happened at the beginning of my research for the novel, and what he revealed proved truly inspirational. I named the retired policeman in *Through the Mist* in his honor.

I would also like to thank Helen Jenkins, whose collection of memories of growing up at St Ia's vicarage in the 1930s and 1940s—entitled *Short Tall Stories*—helped me to create the character of Reverend Idris Thomas.

I'm grateful to Phil Dalton, a woodturner based in my village in Wales, who kindly took the time to show me his workshop and explain what tools and materials Ellen would have used in her toy-making enterprise.

Thank you to Danielle Marshall, Chantelle Aimée Osman, and everyone at Lake Union Publishing for the great job they do. I'm also grateful to Jon Reyes for his perceptive suggestions during the editing process.

My friend Janet Thomas also provided invaluable service, acting as a sounding board for my ideas, as she has throughout my writing career.

Many thanks, as always, to my family for their unwavering love and support—particularly to the newest member, my granddaughter, Ivy, who cleverly timed her arrival to coincide with me finishing the book—and to Steve, my husband, for the fun we had exploring Cornwall together.

ABOUT THE AUTHOR

Photo © 2017 Isabella Ashford

Lindsay Jayne Ashford is the bestselling author of the historical mysteries *A Feather on the Water*, *The House at Mermaid's Cove*, *The Snow Gypsy*, *Whisper of the Moon Moth*, *The Woman on the Orient Express*, and *The Color of Secrets*, as well as the Megan Rhys contemporary crime series. The first woman to graduate from Queens' College, Cambridge, Lindsay earned a degree in criminology and was a reporter for the BBC before becoming a freelance journalist, writing for a number of national magazines and newspapers. She was raised in Wolverhampton in the United Kingdom, has four children, and now divides her time between a seaside home on the west coast of Wales and a farmhouse in Spain's Sierra de Los Filabres. Lindsay enjoys kayaking, bodyboarding, and walking her dogs, Milly and Pablo. For more information, visit lindsayashford.com.